NEWFANGLED MADNESS

E.M. CHAFFIN

BEARDED RAT MYSTERIES, LLC

ISBN 978-1-7365327-1-3 (paperback) ISBN 978-1-7365327-2-0 (ebook)

Published by Bearded Rat Mysteries, LLC
901 S. Main St.
Stillwater, OK 74074
www.beardedrat.com

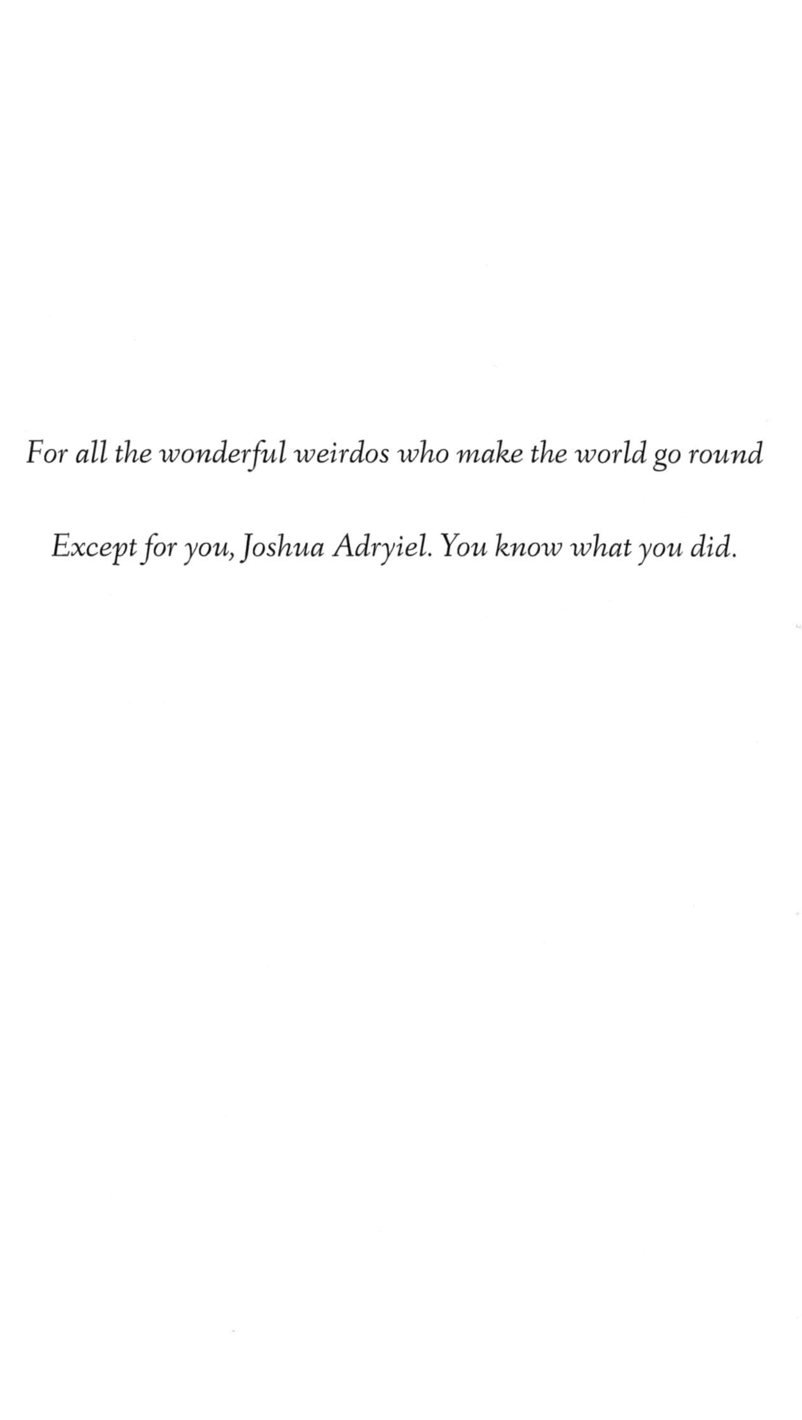

For all the wonderful weirdos who make the world go round

Except for you, Joshua Adryiel. You know what you did.

CHAPTER ONE

I wore green the day I saw a dead body on my bed.

It was the same day Grandma escaped from the old folks' home to chase gnomes in the woods, the same day I found her in a small garden, tucked in the trees and out of sight. Mom and Dad looked for her down the main road, but I knew better. I always know better. It's our special bond – I may only be fourteen, but I'm always the one who knows where to find Grandma. That's why Mom sends me out like the cavalry every time ninety-year-old Beatrice Morrissey sets out on an adventure.

"There are no gnomes here, Grandma," I said, swatting at a small thicket of ground cover with a long stick. I stabbed the middle and pushed the stems to the side – no gnomes. "Maybe they ran away."

"They're here, I saw them." Grandma sat on a bench with her walker in front of her, her purple braid slung over one shoulder, and her feet swinging back and forth. Resolve flexed in her clenched jaw. "Look behind that pine tree, the one with the bent trunk." She waved vaguely to my left, and I marched to the tree with a sigh. It waved its needles at me and I lurched behind it, stick extended like a sword, and stabbed the air.

"No gnomes," I announced, arms above my head.

Grandma frowned, pulling on her braid. "That can't be right. Try farther down."

I followed the border of the pond, swatting at trees and bushes, stopping here and there to look underneath a rock. Grandma sat on the other side of the water, watching me. A fountain bubbled in the pond's center, and several Japanese maples dipped their branches into the water as birds chirped and sang and fluffed their feathers. I adjusted my tunic, retying the sides with the stick balanced on my leg.

"Why are you wearing green, Marion?" Grandma asked, leaning forward, eager for my answer. She peered at me with bright, alert eyes, eyes I had not seen so clearly in a long time.

"I always wear green when I am faced with trials," I answered, taking up the stick again and swatting at a fern.

"Yes, I know that." She leaned back, her voice scratchy and offended. "But don't you want to see me?"

She was so tiny, sitting on a bench at the edge of the water. She was tiny before the hip replacement, but since then she'd lost what little weight she had — and now, as she watched me expectantly, a sad smile pulling at her lips, I felt that weight sit on my chest like an anvil. What a wonder-full old woman, tiny and fierce, and she thought I didn't want to see her.

"We're moving you out today," I said, making my voice light, "which means there will be physical labor. I do not enjoy physical labor. That's all." I smiled with my whole body, throwing back my shoulders and standing with my hands on my hips.

"Oh, I see." She tapped her fingers to the rhythm of a song in her head until an idea sparkled in her eyes. She let it sparkle down to her toes, which she pointed as she asked, "Do you ever wonder what the water remembers?"

I bowed my head. Agreeing with Grandma is a cardinal rule I live by; it makes my mundane life interesting. "Every day."

"Me too," Grandma sighed. She pointed behind me. "How about in there? In the woods?"

I nodded and wandered farther into the trees, where twisted live oaks grew up between long leaf pines, and I poked and prodded my way through the brush. Something moved in the wax myrtle to my right – I reeled around and dashed toward it, but it was only a squirrel, crashing through the bush before scurrying up a lone maple.

"What was that?" Grandma's voice reached me through the trees, high, quiet, and almost breathless.

"Just a squirrel," I answered. "No gnomes."

When Grandma runs away it's to do one (or both) of two things: eat waffles or look for gnomes. There were no waffle restaurants close by, so I knew she would be looking for gnomes, and gnomes like the woods. Mom said Grandma liked to look for gnomes because she had some sort of childhood picture book about them that had recently come to the forefront of her mind, but I wondered if maybe Grandma knew something we didn't.

"Did you know," Grandma called from her bench, her voice strained and cracking from the effort, "that when my brother died and left your dad the house, your mother didn't want to move in?"

I twisted to face her, startled by her words, and wounded, like they'd been sharpened with betrayal. I couldn't see Grandma for the line of trees between us, but I could see the hint of purple between pine needles and branches. I did not know my mom didn't want to move in; Mom never breathed a negative word about our house. Our house was old, and big, and beautiful. It was everything wonderful, everything worth loving. A person would have to be crazy not to love it.

"Why not?" I called back, using all the force of my lungs to make sure she heard me.

"She said 'the crazy runs deep.' Like they'd move into the family home and go mad. Mad like your Great Aunt Tilda."

A breeze pushed at my back and I stepped forward, making my way to the pond. "The aunt that started that club?"

"Cult," Grandma corrected, with vigor. "She thought that squirrels were taking over the world." She cackled, and a flock of birds burst through the trees. "Squirrels."

I exhaled a laugh. That wasn't our only slice of crazy. Mom had a point, there were a number of eccentrics in Dad's family tree. My great-great-grandfather published seven volumes dedicated to the migration patterns of the coastal Red-Breasted Stook – there is no such creature. But then again, maybe there is.

Grandma came into view again, sitting patiently on her bench. "But it's not so bad, living in a house with water and space to spare, is it?"

"No," I said. "It's not so bad." She was right – it's a special privilege to live right smack dab at the waterfront, though I never go swimming. The water is too wild and hungry; too many people drown. I left behind the thick of the woods, stick dragging behind me, and Grandma waved me to her.

"Come sit by me, Marion. Take a break." She patted the space beside her and scooched over – or at least *tried* to scooch over. She did the best she could, in her condition. "The gnomes can wait."

Maybe some people think her antics are born of an old and confused mind, remnants of a childhood forgotten then pieced together, but it's not lost on me that she always, without fail, remembers my name. I sat next to her, throwing my stick on the ground by our feet.

"What color would you wear if you *wanted* to see me?" she asked, squinting her old, cheerful eyes.

It was a good day. She was her old self, like a cloud had lifted; she must not have slept the night before. That's the way it worked, sometimes. She stayed up all night, and then her brain flipped a switch.

"But I do want to see you, I just – "

"None of that," she held up one finger. "What color would you wear?"

I took a deep breath, buying time to form my answer. I *always* wanted to see Grandma. It's not like I wore a certain color when I didn't want to see her, and another color when I did. It made for an impossible question, with an impossible answer.

"I woke up today and wore gray – "

She stopped me. "And what is gray for?"

I shrugged. "It's the most whimsical color, obviously."

"Ah," she smiled, and each of her wrinkles smiled too, and so she smiled one hundred smiles. "Whimsy."

"What color would you wear, to see me?" I prodded her with my shoulder, eyeing the purple in her hair. Purple is the color of exuberance, the color of boldness and drive. I dyed her hair myself. "What color would you wear to see me, if you could wear any color?"

She bounced up and down on the bench, clapping softly under her chin. "Lime green!"

"Lime green?" I repeated, recoiling. "Why on earth *lime green?*"

"Why not lime green? It's happy."

I gathered my knowledge from the pit of my stomach and said, "Yes, but lime green is too bright. It's a chemically-fake color and is, therefore, a half-truth." I shuddered. "But you can wear whatever you like, of course."

I cannot abide half-truths. Feed me lies or feed me the truth, but don't smoosh them all together, all willy-nilly, and expect me not to roll my eyes and sigh. And I always dress according to what I'll be facing, or how I'm feeling. I make my own tunics that I pull over a t-shirt and jeans, tied at the sides with ribbons like the back of a wedding dress. I wear nice, earthy tones, and I sew one tunic for every color I need to wear. I dye the fabrics myself, besides. No half-truths for me. I smoothed my tunic and shook out my hair.

"Anyway, Grandma, they're looking for you – "

"You know what's unique about us, Marion?" Grandma ignored my turn of conversation, swiping at my knees. "The gnomes talk to us." She leaned in close and whispered in my ear, "I followed the gnomes to the water. Where are they?"

The air stilled, a bird sang, and I shook my head. "I don't know. I couldn't find them."

"I don't want the gnomes to leave," she pleaded, her wrinkles hugging her frown. She sighed and clicked her tongue, her lips pale and trembling. "What if they don't come back?"

"But they always come back." I squeezed her hand, smiling at her eyes until it caught her lips and she smiled, too. "Remember?"

"Yes." Her eyes twinkled. "They always come back. Does the water remember, do you think?"

"Of course. The water always remembers."

"Yes it does. Of course it does." She squeezed my hand in turn, her shoulders relaxing as the birds rushed over us, racing to their next perch. "Wise girl."

"Grandma." I placed one hand gently on her arm, leaning in to speak softly. "We should go back. Everyone's looking for you. They're worried."

"Worried?" Her brow knitted together in a confused lump, full of wrinkles and second guesses.

I nodded. "Yes, because you ran away. Again."

She pulled away from me. "Oh. But there were gnomes."

"Yes, and now they're gone." With one hand under each of her elbows, I boosted her up, and she gripped the walker in front of her. I lifted my voice to speak like sunshine. "But they'll be back. Let's go."

Grandma chuckled, and it was like a million diamonds trickling down a river.

"If you say so." She stopped, turning to me with a smile. "Today, everything changes."

Chapter Two

We inched back to the facility, Grandma gripping her walker with the careful deliberateness of a woman with a brand-new hip, and me with one hand under her armpit for balance. She was right; it was a day of change, a day when she would move out of the old folks' home and back into our house. She would take up her old room next to Dad's office, and she'd run away to her usual places, scaring Mom instead of the nurses.

We followed the path out of the woods and onto the outskirts of the property, which was dotted with old, twisted live oak trees and sturdy wooden benches. The grass was sparse and choked out by sand, and Peaceful Shores Assisted Living Center jumped out at us beyond the live oaks. It was a two-story structure made of bricks, white pillars, and money, surrounded by bird baths and cement walkways with chalked-on encouragements shouting things like, "Every storm has a rainbow!" and, "Faith, Family, Friends!" The back door crashed open and a nurse ran to meet us, a band of blue jays scattering in her wake. She was a haze of blue and sunshine, and her chin quivered on a face made of powdered eggshells.

"I'm so sorry – I don't know how she escaped – all the doors are alarmed – it's really unacceptable – "

But these were all half-truths, of course. I cannot abide half-truths. At least with a lie I can tell what someone wants me to believe, which is almost better than knowing a black and white fact. Not better, exactly, but almost better. My mom says I did nothing but lie when I was a kid, but that's a half-truth. I had an overactive imagination, and it's not like I lied, I just really, truly believed there were gnomes under my bed. Which is why I'm so good at spotting a liar; not because I can spot the twitches and the sweat, but because I am familiar with the most powerful lie of all: the lie one believes.

The nurse waddled behind, apologizing, while I walked Grandma to her room. She insisted that she didn't know how Grandma escaped, as if she didn't know Grandma figured out the alarm code. Punching in the code was the only way out of Peaceful Shores Assisted Living Center. Now, *how* Grandma figured out the code, well, that's a good question. But she didn't ask this question, she only claimed ignorance. Half-truths, again.

We turned left at the next hallway. The halls were a maze, festooned with paintings of gardens and beaches, and each room held a sign that bragged, "Pearl's Room," or "Reginald's Room," because without the signs, no one would know where they're going or why they're trapped in a labyrinth of carpet and ammonia.

A voice called from the room across from me and I jumped, turning to face a bald man with a broad smile, his cellphone clipped to his belt, and his penny loafers bright and shiny.

"Well! You must be the granddaughter!" He beamed at me. "I've heard so much about you I feel like family, ha! You are the granddaughter, yes?"

He was short and squat. I don't trust short men. Short men are just tall men weighed down by their indiscretions. More so with the squat ones; in the little fat pockets behind their arms and in the folds of their stomach, that's where they keep their secrets. Like a chipmunk preparing for winter, the short, squat man stores his secrets in his flesh so to feed on his follies while no one is looking.

"I am indeed," I said, as the nurse led Grandma through the open door of her room. Grandma eyed me, stroking her braid with one free hand.

"Where are the gnomes?" she asked.

"In the garden," the nurse cooed, helping Grandma into her chair. "I'll make sure they come to say goodbye."

The bald man grinned at me. "Do you like this place, then? I did, when Dad was here. He recently passed, you see. I'm still cleaning out his room. It's hard to find time, because my wife is sick, too. We just got back from a clinic in Switzerland. The things they do in Switzerland! I shouldn't be surprised, times change, medicine advances. No, no, don't be sorry, it's not your fault. It's hard to get all this cleaning done when I have no one to help me. It's ironic, too, because my family's been here for generations, we just all split up. Now we're all over the world. Really, we are. I have a cousin in Australia. Are you ready for this hurricane? Better to be safe than sorry, I always say. It's not supposed to be too bad, though. It'll get us good and flooded – "

Mom and Dad turned a corner and sighed with relief when they saw Grandma in her chair, and the man swallowed his words, a smile nailed to his face.

"Where'd you find her, Marion?" Mom asked, her head scarf unraveling around her head. She retied it, making sure its red edges showed just a tad of her graying hairline. Dad tucked in his shirt and buttoned his collar, then absentmindedly patted Mom on the back as he smoothed his belly. Both my parents are a nice, average height, and a nice, average build. Nothing sinister or secretive about them. No secrets fester in their love handles.

Max trailed behind, shooting me a pair of finger guns as his little legs worked hard to catch up.

"What's up, woman."

It wasn't a question. But little brothers are like that, prone to spouting statements that might be questions to the untrained ear but are in fact vaguely concealed insults borrowed from the uncouth older brother. I wrinkled my nose at him and turned to Mom. "In the woods, looking for gnomes."

"Oh, of course." Mom nodded and veered into Grandma's room, Max frolicking at her heels, shooting the walls and demanding to know when we would go home. Dad stopped next to me.

"Hey, Doug," he said. "I was sorry to hear about your dad."

Doug bent his head and looped his fingers around his leather belt. "Thank you, thank you. I was just telling your daughter about this hurricane, I – "

He talked for another ten minutes, until Dad told him we were in a hurry and we scurried out the front door, arms filled with the last hauls of the room as the nurse held open the door. It was a clear, early fall day (perfect for gnome hunting), and I breathed in deeply as we made our way to the minivan.

It's good for my lungs to get a big dose of fresh air after the questionable intake of old person air. Otherwise, the smell sticks to my lungs and my nostrils and the insides of my tunic. And there's no telling what the smell will do; maybe it will turn me old before I know it. Maybe it will twist my tongue until I speak nothing but half-truths.

We piled in the van and went home.

***

Our house was large, and white, and pillar-y, with black shutters and a sign out front that read,

FINNEGAN'S GALLEY
Bed, Breakfast, & Restaurant

Truth be told, we hadn't hosted a single lodger for at least a week, so maybe the sign should have said,

FINNEGAN'S GALLEY
Restaurant

The house had no basement, the earth in Lady's Madness, North Carolina is too wet, but there was an attic, though it held nothing but old furniture and a few bags of black curtains my parents bought for one fateful evening of candlelight and vomit. A portion of the house jutted out the back and to the side, and that was where we lived. It was the servant's quarters; the main house was for the guests.

Delia sat on our porch wearing black, wide legged jeans, a studded belt with a large Union Jack belt buckle and a gray t-shirt that read SAVE NESSIE in big, bold letters in front of a shadowy Loch Ness Monster. She stood when I got out of the minivan, and addressed me formally, as all best friends should.

"I've come for my bedtime reading, Marion Morrissey."

"I'm at your service, Delia Fortescue."

I draped my arm around her and checked the mail while Mom and Dad helped Grandma out of the van. It was the usual delivery, lots of junk mail, a few bills, and one large, thick envelope addressed to Mr. & Mrs. George Morrissey on Old Port Road. I didn't think much of it, just tucked it under my arm and led Delia through the back door and into the kitchen, then to the living room, dropping off the mail on a small table outside Dad's office door.

Everything in the house was rather grand and colonial. Our living room was small, just an open room and a front door we almost never used, but the ceiling was high, and the floors were wood. Even going up to my room was an act of Georgian dramatics. A straight, white staircase in the living room turned sharply to the right and lead to three bedrooms. A thin, red carpet draped the stairs, some areas worn so thin the wood showed underneath.

The moment I stepped through the door, roots grew from my feet, through the floorboards, and into the earth. My house was the fortress that stood between me and the ocean, the wild, unpredictable thing that devours and conceals. It was solid, it knew me, and I knew it so well it was like my name was written on the walls. It grounded me, kept me solid, anchored me in reality.

That's not to say Finnegan's Galley had no secrets. I'd looked for secret passageways and hidden rooms and magical wardrobes to no success, but every step I took made the corners giggle and the windows wink.

So I greeted my house like I always do, "May you be blessed, Finney," then I patted her on the arm (otherwise known as the staircase railing) and nodded to my little sister, who sat on the couch doing homework. It was Saturday, but as Mom put it, Posey had been indolent.

She greeted us with an uninspired, "Hey, dorks." Wisps of her hair clung to her temples – it was humid and she sweats when she does math, so her sweat mixed with the swamp brown of her hair and the swamp green of her eyes on her flat, open face made her whole face look like a marsh.

"Keep to your work, peasant."

Posey sighed. When she sighs her bangs fly upward, because she sighs out of her bottom lip, like she's trying to be a fairytale evil stepsister (but she is my whole sister, my parents swear to it, I did perform an inquisition). I like this about her; at the very least, it shows she has aspirations.

Mom gasped so loud that Finney shivered – Max must have frolicked one too many times and almost tripped up Grandma, but I didn't stick around to find out. I led Delia up the stairs to my bedroom, closed my door, and tossed *Harry Potter and the Half-Blood Prince* into her hands. It was 2005 and the most anticipated read of the year, but Delia's mom drew the line at witchcraft.

"Thanks," she said. "Grandma's back, then?"

"Yeah. But she ran away again, took us longer than we thought."

"Did she find waffles?"

"Gnomes, this time."

"Oh, of course."

I plopped on my bed and stared at my wall (I say "my wall," because this was Posey's room too, and her bed was against the opposite wall) and looked over all my quotes. I painted my favorite quotes on my wall, because if I did not, they swirl around in my head and I can't think about anything else. I am plagued by them, the way they toss around, nag at me, punch at my ear drums. I wear words like a cape; they wear me down and keep me warm. I paint them so I forget.

In the biggest, swirliest letters in the center I'd painted THESE ARE BUT WILD AND WHIRLING WORDS (Shakespeare) and around it, up, down, and sideways, every nook and cranny was filled with some word or another: WHAT A WICKED WEB WE WEAVE WHEN FIRST WE PRACTICE TO DECEIVE (Sir Walter Scott), THOUGH THIS BE MADNESS, YET THERE IS METHOD IN IT (Shakespeare), BY NATURE, MEN LOVE NEWFANGLEDNESS (Chaucer), NOTHING FEAR BASED IS TRUTH BASED (Ms. Caroline said this one day at play practice), FLEE FROM THE CROWD AND DWELL WITH TRUTHFULNESS (Chaucer), HERE'S NOT YOUR HOME, HERE IS BUT WILDER-NESS (Chaucer), SHE WALKS IN BEAUTY (Byron. I first saw this on a gravestone in Olde Towne Cemetery, next to Captain Finnegan's grave. Sometimes I read Chaucer in the graveyard) and others that went on and on, in small, large, and medium sizes, and many colors, of course, to match their mood.

Delia sank into Posey's bed and shook the book at me. "I can't bring it in my house like this. Wizards have been outlawed."

"Right," I said. "I can fix that."

She flopped on her back with a groan, holding the book above her eyes. "Someday Mom's rules will have no hold on me."

"Do they have a hold on you now?" I flung open my bedroom door and backed out, watching her face.

"More than I'd like," she answered, flipping through pages. Her face was dispassionate, a classic sign of deep thoughts and churning undercurrents. Delia was like the sea in that way: sometimes her surface did not match the deep. She's lived too long at the sea's edges – I told her that once. She said I have too, and fair enough.

I passed Max's room and slowed to a crawl, something in the air shushing me, something unusual, a sound I couldn't place. I leaned toward his door, but his room was silent, so I tiptoed to my parents' bedroom and – whimpers. Someone inhaled, the long, deep inhale of weeping. I stopped, every part of me tingling, and inched closer. It was Mom, and Mom never cries. For all her color and vibrancy, she keeps her tears for the real things, the things that would make her head explode if she doesn't let something out.

"We can go to the bank," Mom said, through sniffles. "Ask for a loan."

"I don't think any bank is going to loan to us presently, Helena Lynn. That's why we're in this position in the first place."

I pressed my ear to the door.

"We have to eat." She blew her nose. "How will we eat? How can he just call in the loan, all of a sudden?"

"He can do whatever he wants. We're behind, and he has the law to fall back on."

"Well, what do *we* have to fall back on?" There was a soft plop of feathers and air. Mom was fluffing the pillows, a thing she does when she's discombobulated.

"Finnegan's Galley. We might have to sell the house."

Mom stopped her fluffing. "But it's your dream!"

"The contract specifically states that he can call in the loan, complete with interest, should we default" – I couldn't see through the door, but I'd bet the house and my older brother that Dad was rubbing the bridge of his nose – "and we haven't made a payment in six months."

"I don't like this. Everything's happening at once. First your mom's hips, now this. It was so expensive. That assisted living center was so expensive. Don't get me wrong, I'm glad she could be there, but thank God she's out. It bled us dry. And I'm a little worried about Marion, by the way."

"What about her?"

"She identifies with your mom so well..." Mom paused, Dad sighed, and I fought the urge to run away.

"So? Isn't that a good thing?" Dad's words were low and careful, like a dare.

"Yes, of course. And no. With your mom, it's just dementia. But that side of your family – "

"Oh, for crying out loud, Helena – "

"Just listen. Yesterday Marion told me the house winked at her."

Dad laughed. "The windows wink, not the house."

"Not you too." A distressed edge scraped at Mom's voice, the same edge that often nipped the air when she talked to me. It surfaced a lot, ever since Grandma started talking about gnomes, at the beginning of her downhill slope after Grandpa died, like Mom expected me to follow suit.

"So what, if me too? Just because of that, you think she's...what, delusional? If she's crazy, call me King George the Third."

My chest seized and my lungs swelled. I closed my eyes; Finney held my hand.

"I'm not trying to be harsh. Really." Mom's speech slowed to a gentle sing-song style, the style she adopted when reading to me, back when letters were nothing but scratches on paper and every book was a thousand different colors. "But it's not normal, it doesn't feel normal, right? She's not — she's not like I was when I was fourteen. Something's wrong in my gut, George. Trust me."

Their voices faded and Dad did something that made the walls *thud* (he must have been throwing his shoes in the closet) and I left for the living room, a heaviness in my stomach that I couldn't shake. Reality tore at me, words snatched at me, assumptions pulled at me — we were broke. And I was crazy.

Very well; if the crazy runs deep there's no running from it, best not to dwell on it. Onward and upward, to quote my wall. I had a book to find.

I grabbed the first hard cover I saw (*How to Run a Business and Stay Sane* by H. Ronald Clemmons) and stood for a minute by the bookshelf, feeling the house close in. Not a claustrophobic close in, but like a hug. It was kind of Finney to be sympathetic. I breathed deeply and shook my head. No, no, I wasn't crazy. So what if I understood Grandma? So what if I loved this house? But then – Finney squeezed me tighter – what about the house? What if we had to – but no. I wouldn't think about that. There was no reason to worry about selling the house, not yet, not while Delia was waiting.

I took the book back to my room, where I switched its sleeve with *Harry Potter and the Half-Blood Prince* and handed the latter back to Delia. She accepted it without looking, her attention on Posey's camera, which sat openly on the bedside table. I sat on my bed and spied my face in the mirror beside it, a long, antique mirror Mom found in the attic not long after she and Dad moved in. It reflected my whole person, but it was only my face that concerned me. I was pale, especially while framed by the mirror's gilded edges.

"What's wrong?" Delia asked, snapping a picture of me. "You look weird."

"Nothing," I lied. A least it wasn't a half-truth. I didn't feel like talking about it, so instead I asked her about the one thing that would switch her focus. "How are party plans coming?"

She sighed and smoothed her pin straight, inky black hair, then straightened her shirt and tucked the front behind her belt buckle. "No one will agree to be the herald. I can't even bribe any of the guys, they're all dingbats."

"Conrad would do it, if he weren't at college. It's the least he could do to recommend his existence."

All our birthday parties had heralds, usually played by older boys like my brother. Big brothers like Conrad Morrissey can afford to do one or two nice things. But big brothers don't do nice things, not unless the nice things include dirty socks or farts, and nice things never include dirty socks or farts.

"Well, he's not here." She threw her head against the wall, pulling her feet underneath her. The dimple in her chin pointed to the ceiling. "Maybe I can advertise."

"Just place a bet with Sebastian. We'll see him tonight. He'll lose and have to do it."

We both knew Sebastian was susceptible to a friendly wager. We'd grown up with him, after all. Delia stretched out her arm and pointed at my head.

"That's bloody brilliant, Marion."

"Yes, I know." But Delia's face was still impassive and empty, hiding the churning underneath. I raised my eyebrow to ask her what else was on her mind, and she frowned at the ceiling.

"I'm dreading this play practice. It's going to go all night."

"Just like it always does."

"It's not like we're needed the whole time." She inspected her fingernails, painted black. She narrowed her eyes in the way she does when she's annoyed by something only happening in her head, and then tossed the thought aside with a flick of her wrist. "At least it's almost over. Founder's Day is in, like, ten days."

"Ten days will seem like years, or my name isn't Marion Morrissey."

"The play's the thing," Delia answered, nodding to my wall, where the quote sat staring at us. And the play was, indeed, the thing.

It was everything, really.

CHAPTER THREE

We left for our Saturday Dose of Trials and Tribulations after dinner. Rehearsal was in Olde Towne Park, where we'd perform on the big day, and it was only a few blocks from my house. There were no swing sets or picnic tables at Olde Towne Park, only shrubberies and trees and one single stage in the middle, used by the Lady's Madness locals for all sorts of local jamborees and performances. The birds enjoyed their own little jamborees on the stage too, as was obvious from the spattering of poop on every inch of the platform. Birds never clean up after themselves. They're rude like that.

Our homeschool co-op had reserved the stage at Olde Towne Park to perform the annual Founder's Day play. We wrote an original script as a group project, with Ms. Caroline as our director, because she had a background in theater and the backbone to boss us around. Delia and I were homeschooled, and our siblings were homeschooled, and our friends were homeschooled, and the Founder's Day play rehearsals were a weekly staple among the Lady's Madness homeschool co-op. We knew the history of our town like our own family history, which for some of us was one and the same.

Delia and I sat behind a row of curated bushes as the others rehearsed a dance number we were not asked to join (Delia falls for no reason when she dances; I add my own verbal commentary with each move, it cannot be helped, so I am usually asked to distance myself) and tasted the snacks Delia brought on the sly.

"If I had to eat only one thing for the rest of my life, I think I would choose cheese puffs." I popped three in my mouth.

"I'd choose anything chocolate," Delia said, as James Mobley plopped down in front of us.

"Hey, Maid Marion!" He crossed his arms, nodding at the snacks with his chin. "What you got there?"

I pointed to Delia, and she waved her hands over the pile of refreshments. "Nourishment for growing boys, courtesy of yours truly."

"Oh good." James grabbed a handful of cheese puffs and tipped them to Delia. Even at sixteen he was still growing and constantly hungry, and his little brother was too, but Sebastian was fourteen and still waiting for his growth spurt.

Sebastian sat a few feet away from us and nodded to me.

"Your Grace, Empress of Land and Sea." He did a little twirl-bow with his hands.

"Sebastian."

"Please, call me Bash."

James tossed the bag of cheese puffs to him as I dipped my head in a condescending manner, one hand up to monitor my (imaginary) crown. James was a steady sort of fellow, with a face like a shiny potato, and dark hair and gray eyes, and Sebastian had those colors too, but he was tricky, his mind always leaping from one thing to another, his body built to wiggle and writhe and squeeze through small spaces. James had the beefy kind of body that earned him the title of "attractive" from giggly teenage girls but would certainly make him fat in ten years' time. Mark my words.

"James has got it bad." Sebastian picked up a cluster of pine needles and braided them together, grinning as he avoided his brother's glare.

"Dude," James warned.

"Got what bad?" I asked. Hopefully nothing that involved vomiting; I hated vomiting.

"He's in love."

It undoubtedly involved vomiting. Sebastian snickered and James, expressionless, shook his head as Delia and I waited for an answer.

"I'm not in love."

"Not again, you mean." Sebastian waited for his brother to argue, his feet dancing from side to side. James only bit into a cheese puff, pointedly, like a message.

"What's different about this one, James?" Delia leaned back into the bushes and smiled, the gleam in her eyes saying *yet again we play love's cruel game*. She tucked a blade of grass between her thumbs and blew into it, calling for his answer with the squeal, like a handheld grass-trumpet. James not only liked girls, but he liked to like girls. He liked to like girls almost as much as I like similes.

"It's all in his head." Sebastian's voice dropped to a low, serious tone. "He's talked to her less than we've talked to Dad all week."

James nodded. "Dad's been super busy. The work of a small-town detective is never done. Lots of weird stuff happening, right? Dogs are going missing. And lots of over-doses, so Dad thinks there's been a recent drug shipment or something."

"Organized by Sebastian, no doubt," I said.

"Naturally." James shrugged. "Although he'd probably start some sort of underground casino."

"Who's to say I haven't already?" Sebastian held out his hands and Delia threw him a piece of candy.

"If you eat a cheese puff with the rope candy, it makes an explosion of flavor that tingles." Delia smiled widely, the corners of her mouth orange.

"Gross," James mumbled.

"Let's make a bet." Sebastian, excited by the thought of everyday gambling, stood up and held out his palms to make us pay attention. He once bet me that James would never agree to be in the Founder's Day play, and I said he'd relent to being an extra; loser had to remain ten paces behind the other and greet them with whichever title the winner chose, for a whole month. He was three weeks in. "If I win, I don't have to stay ten paces behind you anymore, Marion, but if I lose, I'll...I'll..." He looked around. "I'll lick any surface in this park, your choosing."

I clicked my tongue. "Not enough."

"Okay, I'll lick *two* things."

"Hmmm."

"And I won't stop after one thing, no matter how many times Mom tells me to" – he held up a finger – "I won't lick a person."

Delia sat up straight and threw out her arms so enthusiastically that she punched the shrubbery behind her. "How about this: you lose, and you agree to be the herald for my birthday?"

"I like it," I said.

Sebastian snapped at her face and pointed at me. "Deal."

"And what's the bet?" I asked.

"I bet James can throw a cheese puff from there to here" – he backed up, keeping a good six feet between them – "and I can catch it in my mouth."

"Let's see it," I said.

"I'm afraid you're wrong." James lowered his eyes and picked at the lint on his t-shirt. "I can't throw a cheese puff that far."

"Don't be stupid, James."

James shrugged. "I really can't."

"Try, then."

James threw a puff and it fell sadly on the crabgrass between them, awaiting its doom as dinner for the fire ants. He grinned. Sebastian glared. "It doesn't count if you don't try."

"You keep making up rules."

The interaction turned into a fight, which eventually led to Sebastian reciting "The Gettysburg Address" while James threw cheese puffs (one almost made it into Sebastian's open mouth) and Delia and I belly laughed, well aware that the terms of the bet were meaningless within the confines of brotherly conflict. Delia wouldn't get her herald, and Sebastian still had his ten paces, unless they stopped fighting and got on with the bet in earnest – which didn't happen. Sebastian's recital got so loud that Ms. Caroline shot him dagger eyes and even yelled a few times, but it didn't stop him.

By the time Sebastian had finished, his mind was on something else completely, as per usual.

"By the way, we're having a hurricane party." He sat down, out of breath. "Feel like some games and snacks while Ophelia rages? Looks like she'll only be a category one, if that, so there's no reason to go too big. But Mom said we can invite friends so that's what we're doing. You in?"

I gave two thumbs up. "Yeah sure."

Delia nodded. "Bloody brilliant."

Sebastian collapsed onto the grass, the crook of his elbow

over his eyes. "Can't wait 'till Founder's Day is over. Mom's a wreck. She's losing her mind."

"Keep her away from the pier," Delia said drily, referring to the play, which was about a woman who jumped off the pier to her death. We laughed, and Ms. Caroline called for us, and we spent the night yelling insults and brandishing pitchforks (our roles as angry villagers) before we walked home. James and Sebastian walked with us until we got to Old Port Street, where Sebastian said goodbye with two fingers saluting from his temple.

I entered my house through the kitchen whispering, "hello, Finney," a big smile on my face. The trials and tribulations were over, at last.

My parents were still cleaning after the restaurant's dinner rush, so I hurried by them on my way to the living room, where Posey and Max were home early from play practice and sitting on the couch. Posey twisted to face me, her brow pinched, like she was a strict governess and not my little sister, fourteen months younger than me and subject to my rule.

"Where have you been?" Posey asked as I strode by. "We got home, like, twenty minutes ago."

I held my arms open wide. "Why? Did you miss me? Need a hug?"

"Touch me and I'll kill you," she growled.

I ignored her and ran up the stairs, squeezing Finney's arm and planning the pajamas I would wear to bed (yellow, the color of suffering, to protest Posey's attitude) when the air shifted. Finney shivered. I switched on my bedroom light and saw reflected in my mirror a woman, white dress wet and clinging to her skin as she lay on my bed, her eyes wide and vacant, with one arm outstretched and dripping water onto the hardwood floor.

Good thing I was wearing green.

Chapter Four

I didn't scream, not at first. I stood paralyzed, and then I remembered I had legs, and I ran out of my room and out the back door, and it wasn't until the night air hit me that I screamed. I screamed so hard that I couldn't see, and I ran straight into a body that wrapped its arms around me and held tight so I couldn't get out.

"Marion! What happened?"

Mom held onto me and looked at me like I crawled out of the sea covered in tentacles. I must have been running circles, running around in a chaotic madness until Mom ran after me and I crashed into her arms. Dad stood in the doorway with a rag in his hands and a cloud of worry above his head. I stopped screaming.

"She's dead," I panted, wiping hair from my cheeks, where my tears had plastered stray wisps to my skin.

"Who's dead?"

I squeezed my eyes shut, tossing my head to shake the memory. "I don't know. But she's dead, and she's in my bed."

"A dead body is in your bed?"

I nodded. Mom squeezed my arms so hard I could feel the heartbeat in her fingertips, and Dad disappeared into the house, the thumping of his footsteps up the stairs reaching out into the night. Mom searched my eyes.

"Do you want to go in?" she asked, leaning close to my face. "Or stay here?"

I swallowed hard. My stomach fluttered and my hands shook, and I could see nothing but that dead woman's eyes. Maybe, if I went back to her, prepared and ready, I could remember something else instead of her wide, vacant eyes.

"I'll show you," I whispered, nodding, and shuffled to my room, Mom beside me. Dad was already there, and Posey and Max were standing by my bed too, eyebrows crinkled together and arms crossed. I peered over Dad's shoulder – there was nothing. No dead body, no woman, no sign of anything except my own blanket and pillow. Heat rose to my cheeks – certainly I did not imagine it. I saw her, plain as day, dead on my bed. Didn't I?

"I think you were just seeing things, honey." Mom rubbed my back and glanced at Dad in a secret, knowing way.

Static shouted in my brain. I couldn't understand it, nothing made sense except the twisting in my stomach. This was no figment of my imagination. Nothing fake could make my stomach drop and my throat raw. But where had she gone? My lips trembled and I held up one finger, pointing at the bed as I slowly, quietly, stated what I knew.

"She, umm, was in a white dress. She was dripping wet. And her arm was outstretched, like this" – I stretched out my arm, letting my wrist dangle loosely – "and she dripped water on the floor." I pointed – no water. I stepped up to the bed and felt the covers – bone dry. "I don't understand." I glanced at the mirror. It had been, probably, only a reflection – but how can it reflect something out of nothing?

"Is this the water troll all over again?" Dad asked, a wry smile on his lips, and Mom swatted him on the arm.

I shifted uncomfortably, not meeting his gaze. Even Detective Mobley (I remember this vividly) had laughed at me after The Water Troll Incident and said, *"Take your crazy pills today?"* like he was a stupid teenage boy with a primal need to humiliate. I ate far too many deviled eggs that Memorial Day, and they floated up my stomach and to my eyes and sneered at me like a large pig-like creature with scales that dove into the water and left me shivering in the grass. For some reason I thought it was real.

"This isn't like the water troll," I said. Then I added, "And I was seven. I'm fourteen now."

Dad donned one of those classic dad-looks, like an exasperated general, and he tossed the dirty rag onto his shoulder as he headed to the door, one hand on the back of Max's neck. "Well, anyway, there's no dead body. Maybe you should go to bed."

I backed away. "I don't want to sleep in my bed." There was no way I was going to sleep on the same surface as a dying woman, reflection or not.

"You can sleep on the pull-out couch," Mom suggested. "I'll get the sheets."

The couch – typical. Finnegan's Galley boasted twelve empty rooms, but Mom put me on the couch. She wanted to keep an eye on me, probably. But then again, I wanted someone to keep an eye on me, too.

"I'll check the rest of the house, see if anyone's here," Max declared, advancing down the stairs, holding his plastic rifle aloft. He hurled back his shoulders and marched with heavy heels, a child weathered and weary by too many (imaginary) responsibilities.

"You do that," Dad said under his breath. His lips tipped into a smile as Max sauntered toward the kitchen, but Mom tightened her head scarf.

"Tell him to take the trash out while he's at it. I've asked him ten times. The boy doesn't want to do anything unless he's being watched."

Dad grunted and followed Max (I shut my bedroom door for good measure), and Mom and I made the couch bed. Posey crawled in beside me (with care not to touch me), and we watched home movies while my mind drifted back to my childhood days, before I kept my daydreams to myself, when they were real and urgent and captivating. They had felt similar; like all my senses were exploding at once.

"Did you really see it?" Posey asked quietly.

"Yes."

"Do you think it was a ghost?"

We'd never seen a ghost in the house before. As far as I knew, no one had seen a ghost in Finnegan's Galley, ever. So why would a ghost meander through our house, invisible, only to let herself be seen once every generation, at most? That would be boring and pointless. "I don't know if I believe in ghosts."

Posey turned her back to me, and my mind wandered to the water troll, and then to Grandma's gnomes, and then to Grandpa, and then to azalea bushes. Sometimes when my mind wanders, it goes back to one particular day under the azaleas.

Posey and I sat with Grandpa while he read to us, his voice low and wavering, while I watched the flutter of the blossoms in the breeze. There was something musical about his voice. It was soothing, like a blanket of notes that were weighted and warm. But something was wrong. The story dropped into silence, and he sort of paused, and breathed, then collapsed onto the ground, bringing Posey with him. I had to drag her out from under him, fighting against the dead weight of his body. Everyone else was out running errands, and when they came back, the house was full of EMTs and two little girls curled up in a corner, telling stories. Or rather, I was telling Posey a story. The story about how Grandpa died.

"He held his favorite granddaughter in his arms," I whispered (Posey was a sucker for flattery), "when The Grand Fairy of the Special Intelligence Fairy Congress tapped him on the shoulder and informed him that he had been selected for secret service work, effective immediately."

"What's that?" Posey asked, sucking her thumb.

"That's doing secret spy stuff for fairies." I wrapped us both in a throw blanket and squeezed. I wanted her to feel safe, closed in at all corners, like a fortress, impermeable to attacks. "But anyway, just listen. Grandpa was so surprised he fell off his chair and brought you with him."

"Will he be back?"

"No." I bit my lip, fighting back tears. "Those spies disappear forever. And when they complete their mission, they go to heaven."

Posey buried her face in my neck. Mom and Grandma burst through the door and cried, and Posey elbowed me and ran to hide in the hallway closet. She stopped hugging after that. She claimed it was a touching thing, that she didn't like to feel crushed, but I suspected it was a comfort thing, that her comfort and grief got all mixed up until she couldn't tell one from the other.

I held so hard onto my story of how Grandpa died, that fanciful elements seeped into my memories and my perception and colored them fantastic. But it is, I will always argue, what keeps me grounded in reality. I think more goes on than we give credit for; I think Grandma knows something we do not; I think crazy is reality told without a filter.

I rolled toward Posey, the moonlight filtering through the window and landing on her marshy face. She looked peaceful, but yet, somehow, like cold marble, like she would be cold and hard to the touch.

When sleep came, it was dark and dreamless.

Chapter Five

A knock on the door woke me up. Light streamed in through the windows, so it was morning, but early morning, because not even my dad was up – no one shuffled in the kitchen or pitter-pattered in the hallway.

Someone knocked again.

It came from the front door, the one we never use, that leads straight into our living room, where I was sleeping on the couch bed. Posey slept at the foot of the mattress, curled up with her head next to my feet, like the uncivilized animal she was. I blinked.

Another knock.

Stumbling out of bed, I flipped the blanket over Posey to cover her drool and flung open the door without a thought to who it could be (besides the devil himself, the only being awake at that hour), a scowl plastered on my face. It was

Doug, the short man from the old folks' home, grinning widely, cell phone strapped to his belt.

"Morning! I'm sorry to wake you so early on a Sunday morning, but I got this idea in the night – best time for ideas, right? They say all geniuses are night owls – and when I get an idea I can't rest until I've jumped on it. Finnegan's Galley! The family business! Your dad told me it's a bed and breakfast *and* the family home. Isn't that wonderful! I can't think of a better way to grow up! You must love it! You go to church, yes? I thought I remembered your grandmother saying so. So you were already up, right? Nothing like the morning, really, when the world is sleeping and you're awake. I came right over. Are your parents here? It's funny, really –"

Dad came out then, his hair sticking up straight and glasses crooked on his nose, and Doug brightened. "Hello, George! I hope you don't mind me coming over, it's just I had an idea and I couldn't rest –"

"Hi, Doug," Dad said, with lack luster. "How can I help you?"

Doug grinned stupidly for a second, scratching the back of his calf with his opposite foot; he wore sandals and knee length white socks. He looked more like a dad than my dad, who was still in a robe, albeit a rather short robe, which showcased his leg hair with a tad too much enthusiasm.

"Well, my wife's family has been in Lady's Madness for generations. Long time. Since its founding, really. And my wife has always fancied this house – she's not well, you see, the doctors only give her a year, maybe two, it's awful, she's my life, I don't know what I'd do without her, I'd do anything for her, I'd take her cancer if I could, but the doctors can't do that, can they? No, not yet, not for any amount of money – and we were talking about it yesterday and I just thought 'Hey! What if we bought the house?' and I couldn't sleep, and I just had to come over and say, you know, if there's any chance you'd be willing to sell, you'd make a dying woman's wish come true – "

He stopped abruptly with a smile on his face, and Dad cleared his throat, straightening his glasses as he took his time to answer.

"I hope I never have to sell this house."

"Right. Of course." Doug stuffed his hands in his pockets and stepped back.

I smiled at Dad, somehow relieved to hear him say that, even if he did say it with a kind of flimsiness, like words steeped in regret. Doug took a deep breath, but Mom ran around the corner, opening every door and waving at Dad, the panic in her movements louder than her voice. "Your mom. Have you seen her?"

Dad turned around. "What? No. Is she gone?"

"I can't find her." Mom threw off Posey's blanket and motioned for me to – well, I don't know what, she was gesturing wildly and I was confused. "She's not in her room, or in any of the bathrooms. I looked in all the guest rooms. We have to find her. Up, up! Get up! Posey! Up! Who knows how long she's been gone. She could be halfway to Raleigh by now. Marion, look awake. You help too."

Max ran out of his room, wearing no shirt and a pair of jeans that stopped mid-calf. He brandished a spatula (why he had a spatula in the first place remains to be seen, but my guess is he grabbed it during one of his sleepwalking episodes) and screamed, "I'll search Market Street!"

"No, you will not." Mom pointed to her side. "Stay with me." She clenched her jaw and seared him with a fiery gaze and tilted chin, and Max froze, slowly lowering his spatula. His shoulders slumped and he filed beside her with downcast eyes.

"Oh, dear. Do you need my help?" Doug's hands shot over his heart and his voice got high and breathy. Dad shook his head and slowly began to shut the door.

"No, no, we've got it. Sorry, Doug, but we've got to go."

"Of course." He bowed a little (weird) and stumbled back into his truck (never trust a man with a truck) and drove away.

This was a call to action. I grabbed a few dollars from my sock drawer (I work sometimes at the restaurant and tips almost always are wads of ones, which makes me uncomfortable, but I like to have ice cream money, and anyway I digress), then bolted out the door without my shoes or a thought to my wild morning hair.

"I'll follow the waterfront!" I shouted, just as Mom grabbed her car keys and Dad put on his last loafer.

If Grandma went to eat waffles, the bill would need to be

paid. I didn't want her to dine and dash, as that would be a blight on the family name — it was in a precarious position after Conrad backed the van into a park bench — so I set out in nothing but my pajamas and a handful of dollar bills. I wore pink pajamas, which was entirely inappropriate, as pink is the color of celebration and I was certainly not celebrating. I was too shaken up the night before to dress appropriately; I should have gone to bed in yellow. Running after Grandma is a "state of emergency" situation, and that naturally calls for orange (and not red, as some would have you believe).

I ran up and down the pier on the way to the Waffle Madness, but she was not there. I even searched under the pier (a prime make out spot among the public schoolers, apparently, but I'm sure Grandma had no such intention) and found nothing but a discarded penny, which I picked up and placed in the little front pocket of my shirt. The wind whipped around me, and it smelled like salt and rotten fish, the calling card of low tide. It made sense that she would want waffles. Waffles smelled better.

I reached Waffle Madness out of breath and sweaty, and I threw open the doors and ran inside, barefoot and in celebratory pink, hair salty and wild from the morning air. Everything stopped. All chatter, clinking, shuffling, laughing, dropped to the floor like a weighted balloon. The patrons looked up at me and the owner, recognizing me, smiled and asked how he could help. I scanned the room; no Grandma.

"Have you seen my grandmother?" I asked him, knowing

the answer in my bones. Every other time this had happened he would nod to me and point to where she sat, contentedly eating her waffles. We had a ritual, and it worked. But this time he just looked at me and smiled.

"No, I can't say that I have."

I cleared my throat and pulled up my pajama bottoms, trying not to make eye contact with the early waffle crowd. "Okay. Thanks."

Slowly, I slinked back into the street and shut the door behind me. I retraced my steps back to the waterfront, taking the safe, level sidewalks because sidewalks are ideal pathways for unstable grandmas. I combed the area, eyes peeled for any signs of a pajama'd and outlandish old woman, cursing her wandering feet and their influence on my early morning social interactions. I found a cardigan I recognized (baby blue with an embroidered dove) on the retaining wall, and a hat (one of those veiled ones that Grandma wore to weddings), and farther down I saw a scarf, pink paisley, that Mom had given her for Christmas. So that was it, then. Grandma was stripping.

I had to find Grandma before things got breezy. Wasn't she cold from the angry ocean wind? The water beat against the shore, the waves sharp and small – surely she didn't jump in. I would have to believe she didn't jump in. The water was hungry, all restless and choppy, hoping for a stray Grandma for Sunday breakfast. Hopefully Grandma stayed within the barriers, safe from the water, safe from the waves.

I gathered her abandoned ensemble and ran along the

grass, keeping watch for signs of life. Seagulls screeched and scattered, landing on nearby benches and congregating on the retaining walls to watch me run.

Retaining walls guard the edges of the waterfront, so that at high tide the waves rise above the rocks and boulders and hit the walls instead of houses. Sometimes I wonder what would happen if the walls crumbled and the waves swallowed the town. Devastation, of course. But maybe we have it coming.

I jumped the wall and scanned the shore, when something blue caught my eye. It was an old piece of pottery, white with blue flowers (maybe in its prime it had been a vase), and I slipped it into my front pocket with the penny. These things wash up from time to time. Old shipwrecks close to shore keep lots of secrets, and occasionally treasures like old pottery bits are spit out of the sea, like little whispers from the wreckage. Anything I find lying about I keep. I assume I see things because I'll need them in the future — lost things find themselves thrown into our lives for a reason, after all.

I found one more ruffled sock before I decided to try Waffle Madness again (surely Grandma was after waffles). It worked like that sometimes — I'd check someplace several times before I finally found her there, all grandma-like and content. Once I asked her if she was hiding from me, and she simply said, "The gnomes are feisty today." I agreed and took her home. Sometimes the gnomes *are* feisty.

Cardigan, scarf, sock, hat, and money clutched in my

hands, I made my way to the restaurant and nodded to a woman with hair piled like straw and dressed in orange (appropriate) as she held the door open for me and tossed her hair (it hardly moved).

Grandma.

She sat at a table near the door, a stack of waffles before her, her purple hair piled on top of her head as Doug chatted with a smile and a cup of coffee. He looked up at me and beamed.

"Oh, Marion, good. Marion! That's what they call you, right? I was going to get your parents. Your grandma knows how to string a story! Been telling this whole place that you had a dead body in your bed. Ha! What a story!"

The patrons stared, sizing me up, whispering *dead body?* to each other, and I marched straight to the owner behind the register without giving a reply. He leaned on the counter, his bald head glimmering in the florescent lights. The morning rush brought a flush to his cheeks. He looked like an Easter egg fresh out of the dye bath.

"What's her bill?" I asked.

"Nothing. That gentleman's paid it." He nodded to Doug, and Doug smiled and finger waved at me. I tried to smile back, but my smile was nothing but knives and thorns and sharp edges of rocks.

"My pleasure," he said.

"Thank you."

We did it entirely wrong and out of order, so I nodded at him for good measure and he waved me away like he was embarrassed about his good deed (doubtful). A woman sat beside him, smiling at me. Doug put his arm around her.

"My wife, Penelope. Penelope, this is Marion, Beatrice's granddaughter."

Penelope held out her hand and I shook it, a smile on my face that I couldn't hide. She wore a headwrap of sparkly gold, a loose, ruffled dress covered in sunflowers, and gold bands on her wrists and arms. Her face was perfectly round (probably swollen, but I couldn't be sure) and her eyes were a perfect Kansas sky, blue and wide. When she smiled Doug leaned into her, like her sunbeam was magnetic.

"Pleased to meet you, Marion."

"Mutual, I'm sure." It was a stupid thing to say but it came out of my mouth, regardless. "You look like sunshine."

She laughed and it was high and empty, filled with glass. I took my hand away, lest her laugh cut my skin. She was a dying woman – for a moment I had forgotten. Death has a way of squeezing into laughter, turning it brittle. Dad had laughed like that for a while, after Grandpa died. But it didn't last forever. That's the good news.

Grandma pushed her plate away and motioned for me to sit down, but I shook my head. "We need to get ready for church, Grandma. We should go."

I grabbed her elbow and hoisted her up, then put my arm through hers (how did she make it so far without her walker?) and turned to the door.

That's when I saw him. A teenager, not much older than me, giving us one last glance before he slipped away. He stopped briefly when I caught his eye, then ducked out and disappeared down an alley, the gleam of the trident-shaped pin on the flap of his backpack the last thing I saw before the door snapped shut.

"Do you need a ride?" Doug asked, but Grandma, suddenly lucid, yelled to the restaurant,

"I want to take a walk!" and traipsed out the door, her summer nightgown fluttering above the ears of her bunny slippers.

I thanked Doug again and chased after Grandma with her clothes in my arms, threading one arm through hers to guide her back home (no more escapades for her, by gosh and by golly). I squeezed her close to me.

"Did you find any gnomes, Grandma?"

She sighed, leaning into me. "I hobble too much, I think."

Her slippers made a scratching, shuffling sound against the sidewalk, and every few steps she stopped, breathed deeply, and clutched me tighter. I bit my lip. "You should have taken your walker."

"I can make it," she said eagerly, picking up her pace.

I held back a smile. "You can do anything, Grandma."

We settled into silence, heading toward the waterfront. Downtown Lady's Madness was lined with businesses made of brick, that wielded signs over their front doors like medieval shops. Every few blocks an old house stood proudly overlooking the town, with flower boxes in the windows and an American flag leaning out from the porch. Cobblestone streets connected everything. Grandma commented on every shop we passed.

"That used to be a pharmacy," she said, pointing to an antique store. "That's where we'd get our drinks. Every Sunday afternoon papa would give me a nickel and say, 'Go to the soda fountain before I change my mind.'" She chuckled to herself and squeezed me tighter. "Oh, papa."

"I bet they tasted better back then."

"Oh, they did. Sweeter, I think." She paused. "I think I need to rest."

She slowed down and clung to me a little tighter, so I steered her to the nearest bench, where we sat down next to three old men in front of the Lady's Madness Maritime Museum. All three men wore the same green canvas utility jackets and U.S. ARMY VETERAN hats, and they mirrored each other as they waved, cleared their throats, and crossed their legs. I'd only met the gentlemen once before, but they greeted us heartily. Their reception gave me no surprise. They found me delightful.

"You ladies out for a stroll?"

Grandma didn't miss a beat. "Marion saw a dead body."

Their great, bushy eyebrows raised in unison and the one in the middle said, "Oh really?"

"It was nothing." I shuffled my feet and tried not to make eye contact. I didn't know how I felt about it yet, and the last thing I wanted to do was discuss it with three old men on a bench. I slumped, trying to make myself small, and their eyes pressed into me like a heated lamp, warm and fervent.

"It was probably the ghost of Lady's Madness," The Middle One said. "What'd she look like?"

I shrugged. "White dress, dripping water."

His eyes lit up. "That's it then, I told ya. Definitely the ghost of Lady's Madness, poor thing. She was wearing a white dress when she drowned. Her wedding dress, maybe. I don't remember. Clyde, you remember?" Clyde slowly shook his head and grumbled to himself. The Middle One elbowed his friend on the other side, but he only huffed and wiped his nose. All three were remarkably similar, all eyebrows and leather skin and knobby hands. I blinked to make sure I wasn't seeing triple. The Middle One turned back to me. "Anyway, definitely The Lady. See?"

"Yeah, maybe," I said, my stomach in knots and my fingers trembling. I searched my mind for something else to talk about, anything other than my late-night visions of death. The old men fell silent, and I watched the water, the waves crashing and churning and begging for food.

The Lady's name was Máire Finnegan. She drowned too, sure enough. Everyone in Lady's Madness knew the story. The villagers said she was crazy (she talked to birds and claimed she saw the future), and when she found out her lover was unfaithful, she went to the waterfront, flung herself from the pier, and drowned. The whole event came to be referred to as "Lady's Madness." They tried to drag her back to shore but couldn't find her body; it washed up a day later, after a storm. Naturally, they named the port after her moment of doom.

The Founder's Day play was based on the tragedy, and one would think they would have asked me to play the lead role. Máire grew up in Finnegan's Inn – Captain Finnegan was her father, and it is now called Finnegan's Galley, named so by my father – but I'm rather too chatty onstage and not "Máire material." Delia's mom wanted her to play the lead role, but Delia generally does the opposite of what her mom wants her to do, so that didn't work out.

"I'm Buckminster Hall." The Middle One winked at me. "But you can call me Buck. This is Buzz." He shot a thumb to his immediate left, at the huffy man who resembled a shriveled mushroom on a midsummer's sidewalk in Arizona (Delia went there once and told me she saw someone fry an egg on the sidewalk, I often wonder what else one could fry in Phoenix). He was, if I wasn't mistaken, asleep. Buck pointed to Clyde, the grumbly man on his other side, but spit something brown into a can before he introduced him (gross). "And this is Clyde. We used to have one more, but he went and got old and died on us. We'll never forgive him. We're The Gatekeepers."

"The gatekeepers of what?"

His eyes twinkled. "That's the question, isn't it?"

I chuckled politely and nodded. I didn't know what he meant by "The Gatekeepers," and I wasn't about to ask him to explain. Something in me was wearing thin, fraying at the corners. I'd gone to bed stressed and woken up stressed, and I was tired of playing games. I was tired of chasing after old people. The waves crashed against the retaining wall, the wind sprayed saltwater in my face, and the seagulls screamed for their breakfast. High tide was coming in, and it was high time to leave.

Buck smiled. "And what's your name?"

"Marion," I said, tersely. They'd met me before, they just didn't remember. I studied my feet, but Grandma clucked at me, scolding me and my tone with one glance. I sat up straight and smiled at Buck.

"Oh, I knew a Marion once," Buck murmured. "I'd rather forget it."

The men coasted into a long tirade of their past loves and lives, and Grandma nodded with every sentence while my mind drifted to other things. I set Grandma's clothes beside me and took a deep breath.

My parents were losing the house.

The past two summers Dad said things were going to pick up, and for the past two summers he was wrong.

The ground under my feet moved, so I gripped the bench and closed my eyes.

I saw a dead body. I could see her still, on my bed, dripping wet, eyes wide and lifeless. The more I thought about her, the more her face became alive and crying, her tears dripping with the ocean water, down her arm, and onto the floor.

But the body wasn't there. No one else saw her. The floor, the bed, were both dry, and there could only be one explanation: I was crazy. Of course, now that I was completely out of my mind, it opened up a whole new world of possibilities — I could fling myself into the ocean in search of water trolls, and everyone would just have to put up with it. They'd have to frown and shake their heads and leave me to it, because who wants to argue with a crazy person?

A young woman passed us, her head down and in a hurry. Something gleamed on her crossbody bag. It was a trident-shaped pin, exactly the same as the one I saw on the backpack of the teenage boy in Waffle Madness. I watched her disappear into Waffle Madness and I stood up to follow, but was jolted from my reverie when Buck addressed me.

"Are you one to visit the museum on Sundays, Marion?" he asked, his eyebrow hairs quivering in the wind.

"No." I scrunched my forehead. "I thought it was closed on Sundays?"

He shrugged. "Well, I just thought I'd ask."

I grunted and turned to the water, watching the birds fly over the sea. I'm a fan of questions, can't fault a man for asking any, but I had things to think about, my own sense of self to evaluate. I folded my arms and stood, feet apart, letting the old men roll back into their conversation about the women of their past.

On the other hand, maybe I wasn't crazy. Everyone else seemed to turn a blind eye to reality, to accept the world in a manner that is, to me, outrageous. There's so much more that is obvious to me, that others refuse to see: that the sea is hiding something, that pink is the color of celebration, that things show up in your life that are meant to be taken and saved for a future time. Without this reality the world is just a half-truth. I cannot abide half-truths. Half-truths are fuzzy. They're manipulative. They're slippery. I cannot stand a world that is not seen in all its rough and raw edges. Some people may claim I have no foot hold in reality, but I'm not the one feeding myself half-truths and going through life with eyes closed, hoping to bump into something real every now and again.

But then those words came back to me, words said so casually that one summer day, *"Take your crazy pills today?"* that remind me why I should keep my mouth shut to guard the fear in my heart that whispers *the crazy runs deep.*

I wasn't the crazy one. Was I?

I was confused by the time I got ready for church, so I wore brown. I didn't say much to Delia, except that I'd see her later, and after the service I got in the van to wait in silence. There's a lot to be said of silence, but I couldn't say it at the time, for obvious reasons.

"I don't understand why we can't go out to eat for lunch," Posey complained, buckling her seatbelt as Dad turned on the ignition.

"It's expensive," Mom answered.

"But we gotta eat." Posey loosened her seatbelt and leaned forward, sticking her head between the captain's chairs where Mom and I sat. "Plus, it's the day of rest. You don't want to cook on the day of rest, right, Mom?"

Dad snickered and Mom laughed in such a way that the apples of her cheeks reached up her heart-shaped face and squeezed her eyes. "Who says *I'm* cooking?" She raised an eyebrow and Posey groaned, flopping back in place just as Max belted out the first line of an impromptu ditty, "Max-imus is Awesome-us."

"– I am my parents' favorite child, oooooooh ohhh, both my sisters are adopted!" He spread out his arms, singing at the top of his lungs, and swung his feet with the beat. "Max-imus! Is Awesome-us!"

But it wasn't cute – he kicked the back of my seat, and he kept kicking, and he wouldn't stop. I grumbled. He kicked harder. I growled.

"I am my parents' favorite child!"

Grandma sang along from the front, her Sunday hat cocked just right, and I snatched at Max's ankles, yelling, "STOP KICKING MY SEAT IT'S ANNOYING," while Mom sighed. Posey grabbed his shoes, but Max sang louder –

"I AM MY PARENTS' FAVORITE CHILD!" and he kicked her in the face.

Posey shrieked and pointed at Max, covering her cheek with one hand. Words would not escape her mouth. She gawked, clutching the beige upholstery of the seat in front of her, picking at a torn corner - until, after a deep breath, she screamed, "MOM, MAX KICKED ME IN THE FACE!"

"I DIDN'T MEAN TO, IT WAS AN ACCIDENT!" Max sat up straight, scooching forward, straining at his seat-belt. His eyes were wide and desperate.

"HOW COULD IT BE AN ACCIDENT WHEN YOU WERE TRYING TO KICK ME?"

Mom held up one finger to Posey and addressed Max, her voice calm and steady. "Don't kick your sister in the face." She reached for her headscarf out of habit, but she wasn't wearing one, so she smoothed her hair instead.

"I DIDN'T MEAN TO KICK HER!"

"I don't care. Say you're sorry."

"But Mom – "

"MAXIMUS MORRISSEY!" Mom screeched, turning sharply to face him.

Max slumped, throwing out his lower lip and crossing his arms as he glared out the window. "It was an accident," he insisted, faintly, to the passing trees.

Dad twisted to look at him, his glasses pressed up against his forehead. "Max, you will not talk back to your mother. I do not allow it. Apologize right now."

"Sorry," Max mumbled.

"Watch the road, George," Mom said.

Max kicked the back of my seat with one hard anger-kick, and I slapped my arm rest.

"Would you PLEASE stop kicking me?" I howled, shooting him a look of death and daggers. Max flinched, his face pale, like he knew he was digging his own grave with each impulsive blow.

"He still hasn't apologized to ME." Posey waved at Mom, one hand still covering her face, and Mom raised her hands to silence us all, but she didn't have to. Dad pulled into our driveway and we froze, eyes on our lawn, shouts falling from our lips. All around the house, from the front yard to the back, were many deep holes, spotting the ground like pockmarks on an inflamed adolescent.

"The gnomes!" Grandma wailed.

I leaned my forehead against the cool window glass. "Stupid gnomes," I breathed, and Mom sighed.

CHAPTER SIX

The holes weren't even round. Everyone knows a proper hole in the ground should be round, but these were square and crude. Dad stopped in the middle of the driveway and Mom mumbled, "what in the world?" and the rest of us stared with our mouths agape.

"I'll call Kyle," Dad said, and he took out his cell phone and called Detective Mobley. But Detective Mobley couldn't help, and by the time a report had been made and the officer left, we had nothing to do but fill in the holes ourselves. It was not how I wanted to spend my afternoon. It didn't help that Max dropped a handful of dirt down the back of my shirt and called me ugly or that Posey complained so much that I almost agreed to do her part (almost, but not quite). She couldn't trick me *that* easily.

Conrad, however, was the master of trickeries. He once tricked me into digging a hole *on my birthday*. He gave me a treasure map and told me X marks the spot, and I skipped away singing, my braids bouncing off my back. It turned out he did not bury any treasure, he had simply found a dead squirrel and wanted to have a funeral, but he didn't want to dig a grave. I started crying, Posey heard *"dead squirrel"* and started crying, and Mom got mad and made Conrad take us both out for ice cream. Thus began our birthday tradition, where Conrad takes us out to ice cream and sometime during the trip one of us cries.

Another tradition is my Sunday night patrol. Every Sunday night, Delia and I sneak out and patrol the waterfront in our capes (made with enthusiasm after we saw *The Fellowship of the Ring*) for no reason whatsoever. It's a sacred custom, and we could not, would not, should not break it, not for any reason other than death or gross dismemberment. So once the holes were filled and night bloomed over Lady's Madness, it was time. I wrapped my cape under my arm (black, the color of mystery) and opened my window to climb out, but Posey cleared her throat.

"Going again, are you?" Wisps of her hair floated around her head, and the edges of her lips were tipped in a smile, like she knew something I didn't.

I bowed, apprehension and impatience mingling in my stomach. She was up to something; I could smell it.

"As I do."

We stared at each other, neither of us blinking, until Posey looked at her fingernails. It was an act. There was nothing interesting about her fingernails.

"I sure could use ten bucks."

"That's too bad for you."

She shrugged. "I'll tell mom."

I didn't think Mom actually cared, but it would ruin the magic of patrol night if the parents knew my whereabouts; I pressed my forehead onto the window frame and spoke through clenched teeth. "Two."

"Five."

"Three."

She raised her eyebrows. "Five"

"Okay, fine. Five." I marched to my dresser and grabbed a handful of dollar bills, threw them at her, and watched as they floated to my feet. "Don't spend it all at once."

Posey snorted and fell to her knees, gathering the bills as I rearranged the cape under my arm. "Where are you going this time?" she asked, not looking at me.

"As if we ever know." I turned back to the window and straddled the ledge, keeping an eye on Posey. Her face was muddy, her thoughts stirring up the dirt inside her. I groaned. "What is it?"

She counted and recounted each dollar. "Is it just you two?" she asked, still on her knees.

"Delia and I, yes. Just us."

"Will you do anything interesting?"

"It is the nature of our friendship to do interesting things."

"You know what I mean." She waved the bills at me, as if it would compel me to speak up. I turned my head to read the words on my wall, but it was an act. I wanted her to wait.

"Interesting things hardly ever happen. We walk and then go home." I drummed my fingers on my thigh and shrugged. "That's it."

She fanned the money over her toes, chin in between her knees, and coughed. "Cool." But she didn't look at me, and the silence stretched between us like a question, pointed and cumbersome.

"Is that all?" I tapped my foot against the wall, stealing a glance at the darkness outside, where Delia was waiting for me, somewhere by the water. A seagull cried. Its friend answered. I sighed. "Posey? Is that all?"

She pocketed her cash and narrowed her eyes, rising to her feet like a challenge. "Do you have my camera?" she asked, quickly, the words strong and demanding but running together, nonetheless.

"What?" I threw back my head and knocked my skull into the window frame with a dull *thump*. I rubbed at it, squinting. "No. Why would I have your camera?"

She eyed me doubtfully, so I spread out my arms, free of cameras and secrets, and she pressed her lips together and wrinkled her nose. "I can't find it. Thought you might have stolen it."

"Sorry to disappoint," I said, and turned back to the darkness outside my window. "I didn't take your camera."

She sighed and nodded, and I watched as she crawled into bed and opened a book without another word.

"If that's all..." I began, and she turned a page. I nodded to no one in particular, dropped my cape out the window and to the ground, and took a deep breath, rubbing my head. It was time to go.

I climbed out, shimmied down the magnolia tree close to the house, and hurried to the water. Delia would be waiting. She lived just a block from me – her dad was a doctor and her mom a former beauty pageant queen slash news anchor, and together they bought a nice house on the waterfront with all the ease and consideration of buying a basket of oranges. Her mom named her Cordelia Rose Fortescue because she wanted her to be a Victorian socialite with a penchant for tea and crumpets, but Delia wanted to be a sea fairy, so we called her Delia. I was called Marion Morrissey because I was named by someone with a mouthful of marsh-mallows. Mom still has not owned up to it.

Delia waited under the pier, her cape wrapped around her shoulders (green, the color of trials, and by extension, courage). "So why are you being weird?" she asked, as soon as I came into view. "You didn't talk much at church."

"For varied and sundry reasons," I answered, then I took a deep breath and told her about losing the house, and the vandalism, and seeing a dead woman on my bed, who actually wasn't there.

"It's just the play," Delia surmised, after I'd finished. "It's stressing you out. And it's put the idea of a drowned woman in your head. That's all. You saw the body reflected in the mirror, after all. Who hasn't thought they saw something weird reflected in a mirror?" She pulled her cape up to her knees as the water bit at her ankles. The lighthouse lit up her shirt. This one said, KRAKEN JUST NEEDS A HUG around a Kraken rising above a churning ocean, crushing a ship in its tentacles. "The holes, though, are another thing. Who would do that? And why?"

I considered the question for a moment, watching the moonlight on the water. Then I stumbled over a small rock and coughed up an answer. "I mean, Grandma told all of Waffle Madness that I saw a dead body on my bed. Maybe someone's trying to mess with me." I paused. "Could be the same person did both things, I guess. The body and the holes."

"Oh, that's bollocks." Delia tut-tutted and flipped her hair, confidently throwing her words to the ocean. She loved to use "edgy" British jargon that actually didn't offend anyone she knew in Lady's Madness, North Carolina, USA. "Honestly, what would they be trying to prove? I bet it's a stray dog or something. Now, if you want to talk drama, when I left home, Mom was talking on the phone to one of her crazy friends. All she does is call Mom and cry. It's exhausting."

"Your mom has the weirdest friends," I said, and it was true. The previous year she introduced us to one of her college buddies, a year-round sandal-wearer who might have been a cult leader. She gave us candy, but we were too worried about it to do anything else but drop it in a park trash can when no one was looking.

Delia pulled out a tattered old piece of paper from her back pocket. It was actually quite new – it only looked old because she carried it everywhere and never learned how to properly refold things. She opened it and pointed to a small dot on the map of Lady's Madness. "Fairy sighting. Olde Towne Cemetery."

I followed her finger on the map, even though I knew Olde Towne Cemetery like the back of my hand; that's where I read Chaucer. "When?"

"Last Tuesday." She folded up the paper again. Delia was a frequent visitor to a website that documented various fantastical sightings, and she regularly printed the updated map of Lady's Madness, and even more regularly checked the locations of each sighting. Her dream was to one day contribute.

This is why we're friends: we both dabble in whimsy.

"We should check it out."

"It's a plan," I said. Fairies *and* cemeteries? Count me in.

Delia usually spent her Saturday evenings watching documentaries (not practicing plays) on stuff other people might consider fairytales, AKA the Loch Ness Monster, Dragons, Bigfoot, that sort of thing. I watch them with her, but she used to watch them with her sister (now in college) until her mom put Millie in pageants and cotillion and speech class, and Millie decided it was beneath her. "That's stupid stuff," Millie had stated, and Delia threw her sister's high heels into the ocean. Then she vowed she would never follow in Millie's footsteps or do anything her mom wanted her to do, like starring in the Founder's Day play. Delia flunked the audition on purpose.

"Mom wants me to take this stupid speech class at the extension," Delia said.

"Blech," I replied.

"I said over my dead body."

"What'd she say?" I danced away from the fingers of a wave that snatched at my feet. Delia continued on, unperturbed, and the water kissed her shoes.

"That I lost my TV privileges."

"Well."

"But she's not making me."

"That's good, right?"

"It's only a matter of time, Marion. My fate has been sealed. My name has been drawn." Delia drew the hood of her cape over her face and stepped in front of me, pursuing the darkness of her thoughts in solitude.

The waterfront stretched out before us, and every movement caught my eye, every sound was noted, my every step calculated. We never watched for anything specific on our patrols, we just liked walking on the shore in our capes. But it was nice to pretend we were on high alert, like our lives had a mission and a little danger.

The air was thick and dead. The waves crashed and fizzled. The birds screamed and flapped their wings. I took a deep breath, and almost drowned – humidity drenched the air. Was this how the air had felt almost three hundred years ago? Did the water toss and turn like this before the storm that washed Máire Finnegan ashore? It must have been that way, because as far as the ocean and the air were concerned, that day was only yesterday. I looked out to the sea and followed the waves to where they met the pier. She had jumped from that pier, jumped into the waves and drowned. And then the sea raged, and threw her back, and rejected the evidence of its own crime.

Sometimes, if I listened hard enough, I could hear something conspiratorial. Something whispered and muttered in the deep. The waterfront is a meeting of two waters: the intracoastal waterway and the local river. Beyond that meeting, the ocean. In the middle, Grackle Island. I liked that about this spot; it's a collision, a dance, a sharing of secrets.

But it dropped ice in my veins, too. The water was hungry and restless, full of secrets in its bed. When I saw the churning of the waves, I remembered the water troll, slipping into its depths, and I could not step in; I could look all I wanted, but I did not touch. The water, so help me, would never feed on me. I looked out over the dark waves as a lighthouse flashed and the secrets dove for cover.

"No wonder so many people drown," I said. Delia, used to my sudden topics, nodded.

"Mom says it's the strong current."

"That blasted current."

But blaming the current is a half-truth, really. People drown on the waterfront all the time; from toppling out of boats unprepared, or hitting their head on the way in, or taking ill-advised swims in bad weather, or jumping on purpose. The current could not be the only thing to blame. The dead woman I saw was dripping wet. Her end, for sure, was met in the water. But what kind of end was it, exactly?

I saw her.

Clear as day, without a doubt, she was there, in her white dress, talking to The Gatekeepers on their bench. It was the dead woman, walking and talking, the woman I saw on my bed. I grabbed Delia's arm.

"It's her," I whispered, my heart beating against my chest and thrashing in my ears.

"Who?"

"The dead woman." I nodded to the woman, just as she disappeared into the backstreets behind the maritime museum. I squeezed Delia's arm harder, my knees shaking, my lungs freezing in place.

"Are you serious?" Delia asked.

"It's her. I'm sure of it." I swallowed and stomped my feet, resolve consuming me like fire. I'd know that white dress anywhere – white. White, the color of mourning. I shivered, but something awakened in me, like the light that squeezes through my doorframe at night when the hall light is on. It was small and bright like hope, but also mysterious, a sign that something was different on the other side. "She might be in trouble," I said, knowing it sounded strange.

"Don't poke the beast, Marion." Delia went rigid, her breathing quick and shallow. "It's fine, probably."

"Of course it's not fine." I turned to Delia and drew back my hood. Her hesitation only made me stronger, made my feet itch to move and my gut whisper *you need to follow her now*. Delia stared back at me, anxiously biting her lip, and I took a deep breath. "That's the woman I saw dead on my bed, a woman I've never seen before in my life, and she's walking the streets. It has to mean something. We have to follow."

"But it's..." Delia laughed awkwardly, holding her hand out to the darkness. "She was dead, and now...are you sure it's, like, safe?"

"Oh, I have no idea." I clapped her on the back, like a comrade, and smiled. "But I think she needs help."

"And its...it's really her?"

"Yes, it's really her." I waited for her to respond, clinging to the silence like it could help me persuade Delia, like the silence had a voice of its own. Following the woman was something we needed to do. The urge practically burst out of my stomach and onto the shoreline. I took one step toward town and paused, letting the wind whip my hair over my eyes. Delia swallowed, one hand on her throat, and in the moment I knew, if she brought up that blasted water troll, I was going to scream. But she closed her eyes, let out one long breath, and hiked up the ends of her cape.

"Okay, but if things go south, I'm running home."

"Naturally."

With one nod, we pulled our capes closer and hopped up the retaining wall and crept down a narrow street, away from the waterfront.

We found her. The woman hurried through the shadows

of an alleyway, and as we drew closer, I could see she held something in her hand, dark and flat – a file folder. Delia held me back.

"We're getting too close," she whispered.

We followed her as she slipped through alleys and scurried up streets, taking the long way to the cemetery – we clung to the shadows, hoods up, willing ourselves to breathe low and slow, so as to not make a sound –

A hand pressed over my mouth, pulling my whole body into a circle of boney arms. I screamed and stomped the foot behind me, elbowing into the stomach –

"UGH!"

I turned around. I knew the voice, and the face matched.

"Posey!" I gasped, and Delia looked up from where she had collapsed on the ground.

"Sweet Mary and Joseph!" Delia hissed to herself.

"You idiot," Posey panted, holding her stomach and foot simultaneously. "Why on earth –"

"You're the idiot, sneaking up on us from behind." I adjusted my cape. "How'd you know where we were?" Irritation bubbled up my throat and I glared, but Posey wouldn't look at me.

"I followed you, genius." She shook her foot, her arms wrapped around her stomach. "I think you broke my toes."

"Small price to pay for your sins." I raised my hood and scanned the street; the woman was nowhere to be seen. The alleyway was empty. The night was silent. "We lost her," I groaned. I finger-stabbed Posey in the chest. "Why'd you pick this time and place for a nice cuddle?"

"Lost who?" Posey asked, swatting me away and following my gaze.

"The dead lady," I answered. "She's alive, and we were following her." I turned in circles, my cape flowing around me, and I growled. Posey ruined everything. Panic slammed my heart. "She was here, and we lost her."

Posey stood up straight, dropping her arms and her foot. "Really?"

I breathed in my mouth and out my nose twice over, trying to focus. Trying to form a plan. But thoughts of Posey pushed into my mind, and I spent my effort breathing her out. Delia brushed off the backside of her cape.

"We're losing her," she reminded us, and we ran to the end of the alley and looked both ways. No woman. Nothing but the dark eeriness of Olde Towne Cemetery. I hung my head.

"I think we lost her," Delia said.

I motioned for silence, and we listened for a footstep or a voice; nothing. I looked both ways again. Where had she gone? Left, right, or straight across into the graveyard? I shook out my cape, forcing the disappointment to fall to the ground. Whatever she did, wherever she went, Posey's scream blew our cover, and she was lost to us. I stepped toward the graveyard, breathing a sigh of resignation. The chase was over. Our opportunity, gone. There was nothing to do, best not to dwell on it. Onward and upward, to quote my wall.

I kicked away my disappointment and said slowly, "Well, I guess this is as good a time as any to check out that fairy sighting, Delia."

"You don't have to tell me twice," Delia chirped, leading the way, her gait bright and easy.

We crossed the street and entered the old graveyard, a dark and quiet place thick with crumbling tombstones and wayward trees. Shadows moved in every corner. An owl hooted from somewhere overhead, and the creaks of the trees muted the sea, concealing the pulse of the waves. Delia took out her map and we poked around the gravestones, each going our separate ways.

I started with Captain Finnegan's grave, kicking my feet before and behind his headstone to check for magical creatures, and then I circled his family plot in general, but nothing scurried or flew or spit in the shadows. No fairies, and no gnomes. But gnomes may not hang out in graveyards. Gardens and forests may be more their thing, I would have to ask Grandma – few questions are truly worth asking, but the common whereabouts of the North American Gnome seemed like a worthwhile query. I kicked at a geocache box chained to a tree behind Colleen Finnegan's gravestone, but nothing magical jumped out at me or challenged me to a duel. Disappointing, but not surprising.

Delia checked the opposite side of the cemetery and Posey paced the perimeter, watching for any signs of fairy activity (or Fae, Delia noted, we couldn't be sure which one without a documented interaction), until Posey complained.

"There's nothing here," she said, holding out her arms in the darkness. She tried to sound frustrated but there was a note of glee in her voice, a hint that she was just glad to be included.

Delia was the frustrated one, her head down as she combed the graveyard for clues but finding only trees and vines and moonlight. She kicked a tree. A few leaves fell to the ground, and she sighed. Live oaks dripped Spanish moss over the tombstones and in the night, the moon kissed the names of the bodies buried underneath the soil. But there were no fairies.

Posey and Delia wandered back to me, hands on their hips and grumbling. Posey's face was covered in shadow, but I could see Delia's map under a sliver of moonlight, and we were standing exactly where the last sighting had been. Posey was right, there was nothing to see.

"And it's your fault," I answered, turning to my sister. "Your antics caused us to lose the woman and scare the fairies."

"Thanks, Posey," Delia muttered.

Posey crossed her arms. "If Marion had only told me what you were doing this wouldn't have happened."

"We never know what we're doing." I swished the wing of my cape dramatically and stepped forward to take the lead back to Old Port Street. I wanted to go home. The night air was still and filled with something weighty and lined with teeth; I closed my eyes and imagined the woman ahead of us, running, her dress dripping wet.

Screaming.

People really were screaming.

Except, it wasn't the screaming of humans. It was the screaming of birds. Hundreds of loud, frantic birds – seagulls. I opened my eyes as a great cloud dove toward us and around us, but it was not a cloud, it was a flock of seagulls, spinning and screaming and flapping around us, and we covered our ears and cowered together for a thousand years, or perhaps only a minute. Then they left.

A car drove by, only one headlight, and in the flash, I saw Delia's face as she grabbed my arm. She was pale, and her nostrils flared above her wide-open mouth.

"I want to go home," she said, and I did, too.

We sprinted toward Old Port Street, arm in arm in arm, out of breath and shaking – a shadow moved. Delia squealed and Posey ducked behind a tree, but there was something familiar about the silhouette. The top pointed to the sky like a long skinny finger, and as I studied it, the ocean and sunshine and freshly dyed Easter eggs flashed in my mind – but that was silly. I blinked. The shadow inched closer and the finger became a feather, and under the feather, a veiled hat. Under the hat, one long braid.

"Grandma!"

I threw back my hood and ran to her, but she jumped, squinting ahead as she balled her fists into her chest. She couldn't see me in the darkness. Her eyes were too old.

"It's me. Marion." I backed up, unwilling to scare her, and her shoulders relaxed. She knew my voice. "See, in my cape? And Posey. What are you doing out here?" I took her arm and she smiled, but I did a double take as the shadows behind her moved – but it must have been Delia, who caught up with us, cape flying in the breeze.

"Marion!" Grandma patted my knuckles and eyed the camera around her neck. "I can't remember." She leaned into me, her old bones weary and unsteady.

Posey caught my eye and nodded to the camera. "That's where it went," she said, taking Grandma's other arm. Wisps of hair stood on end around Posey's head, and the streetlights above her gave her an otherworldly glow, like swamp gas in a peat bog. "I wondered."

"Does the water remember?" Grandma asked, hobbling between us. "Do you know?"

"It remembers everything," I answered, just to please her, and we walked home.

Chapter Seven

Delia and I went to the Mobley's for a hurricane party (I wore pink, the color of celebration) and as the winds of Hurricane Ophelia began to howl, we brought out *Weapons of War: Plague Edition*. A fan favorite, it was a boardgame of armies, weapons, and disease, played on a map of Europe with two pairs of dice. It was a typical war game, but we played it with flair. Each player got a journal, a pen, and a custom figurine (mine was the Rat King from their mom's nutcracker collection) and was assigned to hand make at least one special element for their costume. I made a simple crown out of toilet paper (in addition to wearing my cape), Delia made a sash and medals out of aluminum foil (in addition to wearing her cape), and the guys made various elements out of unrelated articles of clothing they found in my old dress-up box. Sebastian wore my tutu on his head like a wig.

Each of us made our own character (Generals), wrote in our journals our intentions and moves for the next round, and were granted only so many extra moves, the nature of which depended on the special abilities we chose for our Generals. We could choose a combination of points, chosen from Strength, Cunning, Healing, Deception, and Endurance, all adding up to twenty. It was, in essence, a kind of one-time role-playing boardgame experience. It made the game last even longer, if that can be done.

While we were putting together our costumes, I informed the guys about the dead lady and the vandalism, but they already knew about the vandalism.

"Dad said those things are impossible to solve, unless someone saw something or caught something on tape." James pinned a throw blanket around his shoulders to act as a cape (it looked more like a toga). He shrugged. "Sorry."

We sat at the kitchen table, the game before us and note-books at our sides, the heart of the house. The Mobley kitchen was the kind of kitchen one sees on TV: clean, deco-rated, and aggressively middle class. The hand towels matched the curtains, the refrigerator dripped with family pictures and wedding invitations, and the walls were freshly painted something Ms. Caroline called, "Ivory Blush." She was somewhere else doing whatever it was moms do before a hurricane, and Detective Mobley was off in his solitude, working in whatever way he could, because the man never stopped working.

We called him Detective Mobley instead of Mr. Kyle or

Mr. Mobley, even though we called his wife Ms. Caroline (miss, never missus), because he had an unmistakable authoritative aura, and therefore we had no choice but to call him something reverential.

"Foul deeds will rise," Delia said.

"What's that from?" I asked.

"Your wall," she replied.

"Oh. Right."

"Nothing fear based is truth based." Ms. Caroline breezed past us, a blur of color and hair. She thought we were exchanging sayings; Delia chuckled.

"It's just someone being stupid," James added, duct taping his t-shirt to make a symbol on his chest that must have been his intended coat of arms. His next task was to tape a stuffed frog to his shoulder like a mascot counselor (his character kept council with amphibians). "Don't take it personally."

"Yeah, who cares?" Sebastian asked, swiping the tutu away from his eyes.

"It's just a whole lot of coincidences," I said.

I'd spent that last couple days thinking about the coincidences while waitressing at Finnegan's Galley and doing schoolwork in between shifts. Mom and Dad try to keep my hours low since I am in the spring of youth, so I only work a dinner shift every once in a while. Usually I am a busboy, but it was busy enough on Monday that I was assigned to waitressing for both the lunch and dinner shift. It was difficult to keep my mind settled on one thing (what else is new?) and I spilled spaghetti in the lap of a woman with hair like baled hay. She did not tip me, and I gained very little to add to my money sock in my top drawer. So the days moved on in mental chaos, until the hurricane party.

Detective Mobley walked by, his eyebrows furrowed, his shoulders slumped.

"Wanna play, Dad?" Sebastian asked.

"Next time." He didn't glance our way, just passed us like we were billboards on the highway to his office. His heels clicked on the kitchen tiles, his work shoes still on his feet, laces tied in a double knot. Perhaps he would have slowed down if it were poker night, the Mobley's Friday night ritual, but it was not poker night.

"Dad's obsessed with his new case," James whispered, watching him walk away. "There's been a lot of overdoses lately. He's trying to find the source."

"The kingpin," Sebastian added.

"The last death was a guy my age." James adjusted his cape. "So he's taking it kind of personally."

"That's depressing. Moving on." Delia rolled her dice and pushed back her cape so that the words on her t-shirt were visible: BIGFOOT HAS FEELINGS TOO over a sad Sasquatch standing alone in a forest. Sometimes her t-shirts influence her mood.

A guy James' age. Like the guy I saw with the trident pin, the day Grandma ran away. I put down my notebook. "Do you guys know what a trident-shaped pin means?"

The others looked up from their journals, irritation fluttering from their eyelashes. We were supposed to be writing our intentions for the first skirmish.

"What are you talking about?" Sebastian asked, from the far end of the table. He sat far away to remain ten paces behind me. I coughed.

"How did you address me?"

"What are you talking about, Your Majesty, Empress of the Coastlands?" He rolled his eyes.

"A pin. Like, a pin that you put on a backpack or something. You know what I mean? I think it was a pitchfork or a trident or something, I'm not sure."

"This is a very vague question," James said.

"Honestly, Marion, how would we know?" Sebastian went back to writing his journal entry, and I shifted in my seat while my question fell flat on the floor. I needed to explain myself.

"Just thought I'd ask. I saw two people with the same pin, like they were part of a secret order. One of them was definitely suspicious. He looked at me strange, then ran away. He had a backpack."

James raised his head. "That's interesting."

"But what does it mean, exactly?" I picked up my pen. "Never mind, it doesn't make sense."

"Nothing makes sense." Delia waved the topic away with her open notebook. "It is our lot in life to be constantly confused."

We forgot about everything as the wind punched at the windows and the lights flickered. We played two rounds of

Weapons of War: Plague Edition before anything relevant to our lives came up again. Sebastian, surprisingly, was the one to mention it – James decimated one of Delia's armies and flexed his biceps at her, leading her to vomit (in pretend) on the board. Sebastian whistled low under his breath.

"Save it for the waffles, hot stuff." He folded his hands together to make a heart over his chest. James froze.

"Shut up."

"Waffles?" Delia repeated. "What's that mean?"

"It means he wants waffles," James answered, not meeting our eyes.

"It means, it's too bad his lady friend wasn't here to see him bring out the guns, or she'd melt on the spot." Sebastian wiggled his eyebrows, a mischievous smile on his lips. James stared at him, one elbow on the table.

"Lady friend?" We all said at once.

"Sebastian's being stupid," James mumbled, turning away from this brother.

"She works at Waffle Madness." Sebastian leaned over his end of the table and spoke softly. "She's older, so, you know, he's smitten."

"It's nothing." James' voice was so matter of fact and passionless that I almost believed him. I slid down my chair, hands behind my head.

"Well, it's nothing new. Who was the last one, again? The skater chic at the mall?"

"The check-out girl at Cheap Mart," Sebastian answered.

"And that one blonde across the street," Delia said.

"Can't seem to reel them in, though, poor thing." There had been six in the last year by my reckoning, yet none had stuck. "He needs bait. You just need a plan, James." I surveyed the board for my next move. I was the next to die unless Sebastian distracted James with his own skirmish long enough for me to regroup. "We can organize some chivalrous tasks, sweep her off her feet."

"No thanks." A sea of red crept up James' neck and splashed on his cheeks.

A pang of sympathy hit me in the ribs, so I made my voice gentle. "It really would be no trouble. I see flowers. And a triumphant entry; Nay!" I threw my hands into the air. "A rescue! We can kidnap her. You can save her. Near death experiences have a tremendous effect on the female psyche."

James sat before us, stewing in his anger, and he sighed. "There are about a million things wrong with that idea."

"Ah, but – " I held up one finger, tilting my head to the side, daring him to disagree, "only the small minded say things like that."

"I think it's brilliant!" Sebastian bellowed, rubbing his hands together.

"Courtly love is a big deal. You have to follow the rules." I beat the table with every word for emphasis, then took out my journal to jot down a few ideas. "Trust me."

"We'll just go to Waffle Madness to check her out," Delia said.

"Waffle Madness," I repeated, writing it down.

"Maybe put in a good word," Delia tapped my notebook.

"Give good references," I muttered, writing it down.

James stood up, pushing his chair back, and leaned across the table. "Don't you dare."

"What else are we supposed to do?" I looked up from my writing and waited for James to answer. He only shook his head, his cheeks heavy with the words he wouldn't spit out. I rolled my eyes. "Seriously, James. You have so many rules."

He pointed a finger at my nose and addressed me like a bad dog. The hair on the back of my neck bristled. "You will not go to Waffle Madness."

I crossed my arms and grumbled but knew better than to provoke him. James was bigger than me, after all, being a good two years older, not to mention that those extra years came with two years' worth of life experience and repressed anger. I dropped the topic with an eye roll and a shrug, and we coasted back into our game.

Sebastian made an unprecedented victory on his next turn, and James moaned. "What a stroke of luck," he said, throwing down his journal like *it* was the thing that cost him ten armies.

"There's no luck in it," Sebastian corrected, leaning back. "I'm just that good. In fact, I'll bet you that I win this game. You make the stakes. That's how confident I am."

"I make the stakes?" James echoed, grinning.

"You make the stakes."

"Well." James ripped out a page from his journal and

began to write. "You win, you and the others can come with me to eat at Waffle Madness. You lose, you have to run around the house screaming, 'My lady is a fair queen, Empress of Land and Sea.'"

"No." Sebastian wagged a finger in disapproval, mimicking how James had addressed me just moments before. "No. The stakes have to do with me. We're coming to the restaurant regardless of the bet. It's a free country."

I jumped in, an idea pushing at my lips. "You win, I will absolve you of your pacing and verbal duties and accolades."

Sebastian raised an eyebrow. "Really?"

I nodded, pleased that I held such power. "Those are my terms." I sat up straight and smoothed my cape.

James wrote down the terms and handed the paper to Sebastian. His smile was confident, and somehow, all-knowing. "Sign your name; so it shall be done."

But Sebastian didn't stand a chance. Armed with the insatiable desire to see him running around outside during a hurricane, we teamed up to destroy Sebastian and his troublesome armies. He was dead and gone shortly after he signed his name. He scowled.

"I don't think this is fair."

We didn't care. In unison, we pounded our fists on the table and chanted, "Run! Run! Run! Run!" as Sebastian threw off his tutu with a groan.

"Tutu stays on," James said. "It's your General's signature piece."

Sebastian sighed and pushed it back on his head. We

followed him to the back door, where he paused, took a deep breath, and opened it wide.

"LONG LIVE THE QUEEN!" He screamed, and he sprinted into the tears and shrieks of hurricane Ophelia. We gathered around the windows to watch.

"MY LADY IS A FAIR QUEEN, EMPRESS OF LAND AND SEA!" He waved his arms above his head, shouting each word, and the storm swallowed each one like an open drain. We darted to the next window and he ran by, tutu falling off, still screaming my adoration (as it should be).

"MY LADY IS A FAIR QUEEN, EMPRESS OF LAND AND SEA!"

He ran out of view as the wind blew hard, the windows rattled, and a boom shook the house, as if the heavens came down and landed on the Mobleys' roof. Delia screamed – the shouting was funny, but Sebastian dying was decidedly *not* funny.

We ran out the door – I threw off my toilet paper crown – and raced through the lawn, eyes peeled for Sebastian (through the curtain of rain before our eyes) as we stumbled to the front yard, where a large branch of a sycamore tree had fallen through the porch roof, and Sebastian lay on the other side of it, eyes wide and mouth in a large smile. He sat up.

"I almost died!" He yelled over the rain, tutu flowing like a waterfall onto his shoulders. "Bet you didn't see that coming!"

A gust of wind blew hard against us, the trees around us bent to its push, and a sheet of rain pelted us from the side.

I saw a flash of color behind Sebastian – blue, like sapphire – I darted forward, pointing –

"There! What was that?" My voice was scratchy, eager, tearing through the rain.

Sebastian looked behind him, then back at me, confused. "What was what?"

I cupped my hand over my eyes, trying to see through the rain. I didn't know what it was, and I couldn't see it anymore, and for some reason it made my stomach twist and turn. "I don't know, something blue, and fast!"

"Marion." He cleared his throat to speak louder – the wind had picked up. "There's a hurricane happening, nothing's out running around!"

"But, I could have sworn – " I turned to the others, who shrugged. I scanned the forest behind Sebastian again – nothing. But I could have sworn I saw something fast and colorful, running into the trees at the edge of the yard.

"I can't see anything," Delia yelled over the rain.

"You're just seeing things," James assured me, his voice as gentle as it could be while shouting over the wind. "It's all the wind and rain, and stuff."

"WHAT ARE YOU IDIOTS DOING?"

We jumped.

Detective Mobley stood in the open front door, shouting at us, hands over his eyes. He stepped forward and cringed – rain showered him, hard, from all directions, soaking him all at once. The branch had torn a hole in the porch roof, and water poured over him like he was a statue in a water fountain. He really did look like a statue. He was even all gray and stone like, from his eyes to the clothes on his back. He yelled again.

"GET BACK INSIDE!"

But we froze on the spot, feeling at once powerless and stupid by the ire in his eyes. He pointed to the foyer. "NOW!"

As if on command, an angry gale sent sheets of rain every which way, pushing us toward the door and chiding us with howls. We scurried inside to shiver in the hallway, dripping wet. James and Sebastian left to change, Detective Mobley following, while Ms. Caroline brought Delia and me towels. She shook her head, her lips pursed and pale.

"Don't you dare go out again." She shoved one towel in my arms, and another in Delia's. "I expect this of stupid teenage boys, but not you two."

Delia sighed. "Sometimes we're stupid too."

"Well, that's true," Ms. Caroline agreed, breaking into a grin. She covered my head in a towel and rubbed my hair, playfully digging her knuckles into my scalp.

Ms. Caroline was a modern-day Morgana Pendragon — stately, to quote my mom. Dark hair (graying at the part), creamy skin, arms that could change tires and hold babies. Not to mention impeccable posture, with the kind of dreamy swagger theater majors perfect. But her face, of course, was the kicker; she had the kind of cheekbones that could cut glass (and ears like wings, though I don't think she could fly).

She dropped a towel to soak up the trail of water the boys left from the front door to their bedroom. I watched her drag the towel with her foot, shaking her head, keeping one hand on the hallway wall for balance. Beside her hung a family photo, taken on the beach at sunset. I stepped slightly to my left, so her head covered the part that revealed Detective Mobley's bare feet; something about his toe hair made me uncomfortable.

"We're sorry, Ms. Caroline." Delia's jet-black hair was stringy and dripping wet, and it clung to her temples like a frame for her big, sunken eyes. Her eyes were not actually sunken, they just looked that way, because her hair was so dark and wet that her eyeballs retreated to stay dry. She wrapped her hair in a towel and the dimple in her chin was, once again, the center of attention. "Please don't stay mad. I'd hate it if my favorite play director was mad at me." Her voice was playful and syrupy, and it worked. Ms. Caroline giggled.

"We can't afford for you to die, is all. You're not our kids." She winked, a smile pulling at her lips. "Sebastian got lucky. I'm afraid he won't always be lucky, is the thing. He's always betting on something. I told Kyle to stop playing poker with him, but – " she was cut short when a voice thundered over hers.

"I'm sorry about the vandalism, Marion," Detective Mobley boomed, turning the corner into the hall wearing fresh, dry clothes. I draped my dripping cape over a chair by the door as he talked at me. "But I have to tell you, there's no way we can find the guy. We have all those overdoses, you know. I think there's been a new shipment. But I don't know how or where. It takes up most of my time. Plus, all these dogs keep getting stolen, and those cases are hopeless too. Do you remember anything else about it? Any ideas?" He leaned against the wall, waiting for the answer he already knew by heart. Ms. Caroline passed him, arms full of wet towels, and she reached out to rub his tummy. Sebastian returned just in time to see it and lamented loudly, but Detective Mobley made no movement to suggest he noticed anything but my face. He waited for my answer, scrutiny in his gaze, and something like a challenge in his shoulders.

I swallowed hard to buy myself a second. The more I thought about it, the more he stared at me, the more my memory faded. Were there even holes in the ground? Did it even happen? After all, I tend to see things that aren't there, like colors in a storm.

He kept his stare. His eyes were like James', and his shoulders had the same personality, kind of; straight and ready for combat (the kind of shoulders that would have deep, gravelly voices, if shoulders had voices) – which made sense, seeing as he was James' father. And Sebastian's too, but Sebastian was spindly like his mom.

"I don't know anything, Detective Mobley. I'm sorry."

He nodded. "That's to be expected."

"Told ya," Sebastian said, and slapped me on the shoulder. "It's a lost cause. Best to let it go." He was too close, far too close, for his commanded ten paces. I raised an eyebrow and he backed up. "Sorry." He counted back ten paces and bowed, flourishing his (imaginary) hat before him. "Empress of Land and Sea."

His act turned our minds to other things, and the air lifted. Detective Mobley shook his head, his shoulders holding in a chuckle instead of a challenge, and I shook out my arms; they no longer held the weight of expectations and inspections.

"Peasants," I sighed, and nodded at Detective Mobley as I passed him, making my way to the kitchen. "They never learn."

Chapter Eight

We played sardines in the dark after the power went out, until we lit the lamps and the candles and started another game of *Weapons of War: Plague Edition*, this time playing characters the others had to pick (I was a Water Troll General. Suffice it to say, I was not amused, my revenge will be swift and cold).

James won (again) after playing master campaigner and seductress Lady Scarlett (he did not wear a dress, though we asked him to), and he fell hard into a pit of hubris.

"I am indestructible!" he cried, fists above his head, eyes ablaze with avarice. The red tablecloth he had wrapped around his shoulders slid off onto the floor. "Bow before me and weep!"

"You are indecent," Sebastian corrected, "your dress fell off."

James looked at the floor, the grandeur slipping from him in waves. "It was a tunic, not a dress."

Sebastian shrugged. "Whatever."

"You'll lose eventually, James, like the rest of us poor mortals." Delia stretched and yawned as the wind snapped at the windows. The candles flickered, and in their glow James' eyes became deep pools of defiance. He puffed out his chest.

"Impossible."

"Alright, I'll bite." Sebastian smacked the table and leaned forward. "You and me, one game, we'll see if you're indestructible."

"What are the stakes?" James stroked his chin, head angled, knees bouncing up and down.

"You lose, you have to drive me wherever I want to go, for two weeks."

James crossed his arms and drummed his fingers, eyeing Sebastian as he leaned back onto his chair. "And if I win?"

Delia lurched over the table, palm outstretched to keep Sebastian silent. "Sebastian has to be the herald for my party!" She leapt back and clapped her hands, smiling. I clapped too, agreeing to the term with every ounce of my body.

"I like it!" I shouted, high-fiving Delia, going for the around-the-world type. I missed her hand up top and slapped it as she came down.

"That doesn't benefit me," James said.

"Frankly, Delia, he doesn't care if I'm your herald or

not." Sebastian waved Delia away and she scowled, but he continued, "Let me think. If you win, I'll do your chores for two weeks."

"I prefer the herald thing," I said. The guys ignored me.

"Fine. Chores it is." James reached out his hand and they shook on it. "Good luck doing a man's work with those skinny little arms."

The game began in full force, with lots of name calling and Your Mom Jokes (which was weird, coming from brothers) while Delia and I watched, and lo and behold, of all things, Sebastian won. Just when all seemed lost, Lady Luck smiled upon him and he rolled a handful of sixes, decimating his brother in one fell swoop. There was a moment of thick silence as James stared in disbelief, and then Sebastian flipped over the gameboard and game pieces filled the air, showering us in knickknacks and figurines, spilling to the floor and spreading far and wide.

Sebastian stood on his chair and roared at the ceiling, the veins in his neck and arms straining at his skin.

"I HAVE VANQUISHED THE ENEMY!"

James ran his fingers through his hair, staring into space, oblivious to the words coming out of his brother's mouth. He swallowed, then laughed, then sat in silence.

"To the victor the spoils!" Sebastian cried, hands cupped around his mouth. Delia and I slow clapped, stomping our feet in time. Sebastian had never won a game against his brother, not a game of anything and much less a game of *Weapons of War*, and we didn't begrudge him basking in the splendor. It was good for James to lose, anyway. Older brothers win far too often for their own good.

"I can't believe I have to drive you everywhere," James said, barely above a whisper. "This is not good. This is not good at all."

"It is a long time coming," Sebastian answered, out of breath. "So it is good, indeed."

James slid onto his back until he was flat against the seat of his chair, his head and hips hanging off. The silence emanating from him was slow and solid, until a small, cracking voice rose above it –

"What have I done?"

As if to answer, the wind beat at the windows and howled into the night, and the candlelight danced on the ceiling, and I stifled a giggle while James mumbled into the dead space underneath the table, "I'm an idiot. I can't believe it. I can't believe I lost."

Rain slapped the house like a nun slaps a sailor home on leave, and we froze until it settled back into an angry torrent. The storm had an opinion or two as well.

James moaned. "Even Ophelia knows I deserve a good beating."

"That little fact nugget has nothing to do with this game," Sebastian said. "You always deserve a good beating. Ophelia's just weepin' and wailin for no good reason, like a woman." Delia and I glared at him while he punched the air and James set up another game (Sebastian would not agree to any more bets, he knew to quit while he was ahead), and we fell asleep in the living room after playing all night and most of the morning.

When I woke up, the storm had died, and Sebastian was eating beef jerky with his feet propped on James' sleeping frame.

"I've been thinking," he said, ripping off a bite with his teeth, "about your predicament. Let's assume ghosts exist."

I blinked at him. The air was stale and hot, the power still had not come on, and I felt sticky and dry, simultaneously. My mind was not in the right state to consider supernatural phenomenon.

"Okay," I croaked.

"If ghosts exist, then there is a simple explanation for both strange occurrences."

I stared at him. "You mean Máire Finnegan."

"Yes, Máire Finnegan. She's haunting you. But if ghosts don't exist..." He hesitated. I tried to make my face blank and open so he would hurry up and spit out his accusation (I'd rather rip it off like a nose strip), but he still took a long gander at his beef jerky instead of looking me in the eyes. "Then either you are a little, umm, crazy, or someone's playing a rather intricate trick on you."

"These things have all occurred to me," I said. "But I'm not crazy." Not sure I believed it, though.

"Well of course not." Sebastian waved the beef jerky in the air as James groaned and rolled over, leading Sebastian to kick him in the derriere. James yelled and called him an idiot, but never opened his eyes. Sebastian was unmoved.

"Do you think someone's trying to make you think you're crazy? Setting up the circumstances, digging holes to China around your house?"

"Who would want to do that?"

He shrugged. "Your sworn enemies?"

I pulled the hair out of my face, doubt climbing up my insides. "My only sworn enemy is the woman at that one cafeteria who wouldn't give me seconds on corn pudding" – the cafeteria ladies at youth conferences are always the worst – "and that one guy who made pig noises at Amelia."

"Well, maybe there's someone else out there."

"Yes, Marion," James slurred, half asleep and completely oblivious to the topic of conversation. "Someday you will find love."

Sebastian knocked him in the face with a piece of jerky and I kicked him in the shin. He yelled, swatted at the air, and sighed. Sebastian turned to me again, his face serious and a question hanging over him, but Ms. Caroline appeared and he brushed it away. Something in me breathed a sigh of relief.

"Oh, good! You're waking up." She held up a handful of granola bars, wearing a smile that was a little too stressed to be genuine. Her hair was a tangled poof of darkness around her head (humidity), and her face glistened with sweat even though she kept a sweat-wiping hand towel around her shoulders. "It's like three o'clock, you know. Storm's gone. Hungry?" She threw one at Sebastian, who caught it in the air.

He grinned. "Oh, good. Breakfast."

She threw another at me, but I was too distracted by Detective Mobley to catch it. He burst into the room, urgency in his steps, his face a stormy night.

"I have to go," he said to Ms. Caroline, "a body washed up on shore."

Chapter Nine

The body washed up close to Delia's house, so Detective Mobley took us home on his way to the scene. I told him about seeing the dead body while he drove us, and he nodded along, all polite and gentle-like, even when I insisted we saw her resurrected form a few nights before the hurricane, wandering the alleyways with her file folder.

"What'd she look like?" he asked, not meeting my eyes, his tone dull and bored. I got the feeling that he just wanted to keep me happy until I was out of his car.

"White dress, soaking wet," I said. "When she was dead. Alive, she had a white dress and was dry."

"But what did she *look* like?"

I closed one eye and stuck out my tongue, willing the memory back to my frontal lobes. "White. Umm, thin. Dark hair." Then I saw her eyes, wide and vacant, and my stomach dropped. "Green eyes. Yes, green. Like emeralds." I paused. "Or seaweed."

"You know, Marion..." He had that voice adults have, when they think they're giving me life-changing advice and I have to restrain myself from handing them a lit pipe before I lie down on a couch. "When I was a child my dad told me I was getting lots of presents for Christmas, and I believed him, so I told anyone who would listen that my dad had a closet full of toys just waiting to go under the Christmas tree. And you know what happened?"

"What?"

"He was late to work one too many times and lost his job. I got nothing for Christmas. When the other kids asked me about it, I lied and said I got a bike. When the truth got out, well, I never lived it down. But I learned two things: one, work hard and keep your job, and two, tell nothing but cold, hard facts, and accept nothing else in return. Just because you believe something is the truth, doesn't make it the truth."

I met Delia's eyes and we smirked at each other, then wiped the smiles from our faces as we coughed in our hands. He didn't believe us and he was talking down to us, but it was so true-to-form that we couldn't help but giggle.

"Yes, sir," I said. I couldn't agree more. In fact, one could say those words were my life motto; I thought about telling him that half-truths are worse than lies, and that most people gobble up a half-truth like Sunday dinner, but I refrained. Better to keep things simple, to let him think he taught us a lesson, and enjoy the ride.

The rest of the car ride oozed heavy silences and sly glances. Detective Mobley drove slowly through the battered roads (they really weren't bad) and took detours along the way, and I counted seconds like sand on the seashore. But they ended, and Delia went home to shower (utilities were working again) and I went to my house, but I only dropped my stuff by the door and followed Detective Mobley as soon as he turned his back. I wanted to see the body, even if he told me to stay away.

The water rose over the retaining wall and almost into our backyard. Doug was right: the hurricane got us good and flooded. I plodded through the very edge of the water, the soggy earth squashing underneath my shoes, past the Fortescue house toward a group of men in important looking uniforms standing in a circle, their attention on the ground and their (cute) little notebooks. The water was dark and filthy; the air smelled dank and stale, and sometimes, with the turn of the wind, a rotten kind of sweet. The waves were still angry, they leapt at my legs and yelled at the sky. I expected nothing less. Hurricanes must be very distressful for the ocean; they make everything so topsy turvy.

Two men moved and I saw her through the gap – exactly as she had been on my bed, white dress clinging to her skin and her arm outstretched. Her lips were blue, and her hair fell over her face just enough to hide her swollen cheeks. She lay at the edge of the water, and the waves lapped at her, pulling and pushing her dress, trickling gently up to her lips. I stared at her, a hand over my mouth, while I told myself it wasn't my fault, I didn't kill her, I couldn't save her, and I wasn't crazy. A uniformed man turned and saw me, and his face flashed a warning.

"You don't need to be here," he said.

"Sorry," I stammered, shriveling under his gaze. I made to leave but thought better of it, the memory of her face, of following her through the streets popping up before my eyes. "It's just...I saw her the other night, here, at the waterfront."

He raised an eyebrow and took out his notebook, stepping toward me. I told him everything, including my name and address, and he snapped his notebook shut and thrust out his chin.

"I have to ask you to leave. It's not a pretty sight." He stepped forward, forcing me to step back.

I wanted to protest, but the seagulls, free from their hideouts, screamed. My words could not compete with their chants, so I nodded and turned away, disappointment seeping into my pores.

What was this, then? A premonition? Did I have some sort of power? Did I have a gift? A curse? I might have imagined everything – but what were the chances? I followed the waterline, head pointed to the sky.

I didn't want to go home. Something about it all made me restless, and I wanted to take a walk. The seagulls flew above me, wings flapping, slapping at the sky, crying to the wind and the waves and their friends – *we're here, we're here, we're here!* And no one, not even Detective Mobley, could tell them to stop talking.

Because seagulls, by nature, cannot be silenced. Not like me; I gave my statement and left, questions and revelations still burning in my chest. But the gulls screamed until others heard them, and it was admirable, and perhaps I should have imitated them, but I am rather opposed to screaming. They are birds, and I am human, and that's the way the world works.

I watched my feet as I walked, half wanting to find some old bits of pottery washed ashore from one of those old ship-wrecks. Or perhaps an object of some intrigue, like an old medicine bottle or a coin. The seagulls' voices hit me, sharp and jarring. Bits of glass glittered in the morning light – and something else. I stopped and leaned closer. It was a ring, a black, oval stone set in a gold band, half buried in the mud. I picked it up and rubbed off the sand and salt, and the ring glistened (like a smile) so I couldn't help but put it on, and it fit perfectly.

"He's a liar! A drifter! A down-right cad!"

My ears burned; I was alone by the water, but her voice was loud and clear, a whining rant.

"He tells me he loves me then, bam! He's after some new pretty thing, chasing her tail feathers like she's the Grand Master, giving me not a thought in the world –"

"He doesn't deserve you," said another voice, this one not quite so loud. She spoke methodically, trying to calm the other, pacing her words in a practiced kind of way, like she'd said all of it before. "You were the best thing in his life, and he's an idiot."

The voices were close, but I could see no one. I turned in circles – nothing. My heart slammed my ribs – was I...was I *hearing voices?*

"I gave him everything, and he threw it away."

No. That voice came from without, not within, I was sure of it. I relaxed, scanning the shore for someone I might have missed. There was no one, I was alone – except for the houses, the water, the police, and the birds.

"Don't say I didn't warn you. He was too pretty. Never trust the pretty ones."

It came from nearby, that calm, quiet voice. I jogged toward it, gaining on it steadily, but I only saw two seagulls, congregating on a nearby bench.

"IT WAS THE PRIME OF MY LIFE!"

I stopped in my tracks. "No," I said, under my breath. "Surely not."

"As I said before, do you want me to dive-bomb him? Because I'll dive-bomb him, just give me the word."

I stood in front of the two seagulls, mouth open, a tingling in my fingers and toes.

Maybe I *was* crazy.

A gust of wind blew my hair into my mouth and I pulled it away, grabbing it at the base of my neck. Strands escaped at the crown of my head and poked my eyes, and I cupped my other hand at my brow, facing the birds and ignoring the wind that poked me, wild and ranting, like a madman. The seagulls turned to me.

"Human," said one.

"Human," said the other, like a greeting.

"They always look so stupid," said the first one. "Not much going on, eh?"

"They have a language, you know," said the other. "They can't be all that stupid."

Then they stared at me, and I stared back.

"Do you think she has food?" asked the first.

They eyed my hands, so I showed them my empty palms, and they sighed.

"Oh, well," said the second. "That would have been nice."

A thick silence enveloped us as the ocean lapped and my lungs strained at my ribs. I watched the talking birds as I told my body to keep functioning, to keep breathing, to calm down.

"Maybe you should dive-bomb him," said the first, changing the subject. "But if anyone asks, it was your idea. I don't want him thinking I don't do my own dirty work."

I couldn't keep silent anymore. I cleared my throat. "Are you two...talking?"

They both considered me, stretching their wings.

"That sounded very much like words, didn't it?" asked one to the other.

"Like words exactly," it replied.

"I should hope I speak words," I said, suddenly annoyed. There I was, standing before two talking birds, and *they* were confused about *me*? "Why wouldn't I?"

"It speaks!" said one. "Do you have food, then?"

I shook my head. "No." Every word they'd spoken raced through my head, again and again, on repeat. A boy had lied to her. He stole the prime of her life. I studied them, trying to imagine what a bird would consider the prime of her life. They were both white, of course, with gray wings fading to black at the tips, and small, yellow beaks. Their webbed feet were clean and a pale, fleshy color. They were young, as far as I could tell, and plump. But what was I to know about a seagull's prime? "What are you talking about?"

"Oh!" the first bird screeched, shaking her head. "My lover left me for another. Right before the storm. Typical, eh? Always flying when they should be staying."

Had I finally snapped? The seagull was complaining, and I was listening. And not only was this seagull complaining, but she was complaining about boys – like a human. I scratched my head, scanning the area around me for any sign of a well-executed prank – benches, retaining wall, horizon, dead body, police. No cameras or speakers or giggling onlookers. No prank. "Yes," I said. "Typical."

"He pledged his love to me, you know. To the Honorable Seagull Council. Not that it matters."

"She doesn't want to hear about this," said the other bird.

"Well I'm telling her," said the first.

"It's good to get it out," I encouraged, timidly. They both hopped closer, bending toward me with their curved little beaks spread open like hungry chicks. The sounds that came out were words, not screeches – I couldn't believe it. Except that I did believe it, in the deep, hidden parts of me. Something in the back of my mind was expecting it, like it was destiny, like I'd been waiting for it.

"Right." The first bird bounced on the bench, agitated. "But they do love something new and shiny, right? Always new and shiny."

"Right," I said.

"Of course, before this, he flew with me every day."

"Every day." The other bird rocked back and forth, wings out.

"Always bringing me things; food, bits of string, shiny things..."

"Always," the other bird agreed.

"Then, poof! Off with another gull!" Her voice was a screech. "Who had shinier, straighter feathers!"

Her screech graduated to a sharp kind of wail, and I rocked uncomfortably. "Your feathers are shiny and straight, too," I said, trying to comfort her.

"Not! Straight! Enough!"

I surveyed the soggy earth. I had never been taught how to comfort a wild bird. I didn't even know how to comfort a heartbroken human; Delia had never been heartbroken, and neither had I. The sad seagull wailed, and I was lost in my indecision, trying to decide between offering her a hug and declaring the boy seagull a rogue, when I had an idea.

"If you don't mind me asking..." They turned to me expectantly, their eyes blank slates. "Do you know anything about that dead woman?" I pointed toward the body.

"Oh, that," said the first bird, through her sobs, "that happened ages ago."

"What happened?" I asked. "Did you see something?"

"Of course we saw something," said the second bird. "We have eyes, don't we?"

"Sorry," I said. "Do tell."

"Well, Squawky was flying with me." Her voice trembled. "And we saw him hit her."

"I was there too," said the second bird. "Most of us were, actually."

"There was blood." The first bird shuddered, burying her head beneath her wing.

"And?"

"Well, he hit her, and there was blood, and then he threw her over his shoulder and went to the Big Wooden Thing and threw her over the edge."

"The pier," I said. "Go on."

"That's all," she said.

So it was murder. It was murder, and the birds saw it, and they told me. Something sharp and hot frothed in my stomach. "Do you know why he hit her?"

"Does anyone know why humans do what they do?" She bent her head toward the sky. "All I know is they made these awful loud noises, and then he hit her."

"And we screamed and flew away," said the second bird. "It was uncomfortable."

I opened my mouth to ask them what he looked like, but just as I did, the second bird jumped and yelled, "FOOD!"

and they flew away toward a uniformed officer who had pulled out a sandwich.

I slid onto the bench, the waves washing up against my ankles (wet ankles are the worst) and tried to recover my senses.

If ever there was a time to believe I was crazy, this was it. I closed my eyes.

Humans don't talk to animals.

Nice girls don't talk to animals.

I don't talk to animals.

I opened my eyes. I talk to animals.

Well, like I had surmised before: this could open up a whole host of opportunities. No one could call me crazy if I'm actually crazy, that would be rude. I could embrace all my eccentricities, and who knows, conversing with the stray bird or alley rat could prove a very enlightening and productive enterprise. I had always wanted to debate dolphins.

The ocean was still restless and angry, but I could hardly blame it. Things were brewing, I could feel it, like things were bubbling up and I was the only person to listen. It didn't help, honestly, when I looked out over the waves; I had to burrow my toes in the sand to convince my brain I was on land, and safe, and breathing. "I noticed," I said to the sea, "I'll help her, I promise."

My mind buzzed. I could talk to animals. The woman was murdered. I'd seen the future in my mirror, and that changed everything. I stretched out my hand, and the ring sparkled.

"This is very strange," I said to myself, and brushed my thumb over the black gemstone.

The waves crashed, and I watched them, keeping my thoughts in tune with the shouts of the waves, agreeing with everything expressed on the horizon.

The world, indeed, was strange and harsh.

As I watched, something crawled up my spine; a feeling, really, that I couldn't ignore. I caught movement – it was the same suspicious boy, watching me, on the far side of the road beyond my neighbor's house.

He ran.

I sprang up from the bench and followed, my heart punching at my chest – this was it. This was my chance to get an answer for something, one simple, stupid thing in my life that needed answering.

He cut through an alleyway and I followed, my feet trying to escape my middle while my knees threatened to buckle, but I was the wind, and I pursued. The wet ends of my jeans smacked at the pavement (my jeans are always too long for my legs) and the soles of my shoes squirted water with every step.

"Stop! Ruffian!" I yelled. "I want to talk to you!"

He was clever, dodging this way and that, but little did he know that I spent years running in woods and beaches and I could chase with the best of them. I trailed him down Market Street, through an alley, and across Main Street, the cobblestones rolling underneath me (they have it out for ankles). He took a sharp turn and sprinted back the way we came, and I stumbled, gasping for air. But I pursued. He cut through the old graveyard and I ran faster, past the gravestone for Colleen Finnegan (it said "the sea is only filled with sorrows but mine are now gone," which cannot be true, the sea is filled with so many things, I wonder about people sometimes) but his legs were longer and he crossed the graveyard in a few strides and disappeared into the bordering neighborhood.

"Stop, vagrant!" I yelled, but he didn't listen.

I stopped to catch my breath and looked both ways. He was nowhere to be seen. I turned in circles. Still nothing. He'd disappeared, lost to me in the maze of houses, and I didn't even know his name. It was over.

Panting, I trudged through the graveyard toward Old Port Street, back to where we started. I had failed in my pursuit, and thus had no way of answering the questions that pervaded my mind: what *is* that pin? What does it mean? Why did he run? Was he following me? Who was he? Where did he go? What was he up to? But I couldn't make any sense of it, and anyway, I could talk to animals.

There was only one thing to do. It was time to test out my new powers.

A cat sat grooming himself in the alleyway perpendicular to the graveyard, where Posey had surprised us and scared the fairies. I would start there first.

"Greetings," I said, standing before him. He licked his paw. "My name is Marion."

The cat said nothing.

"Lovely day, isn't it?" The cat flopped his tail, in the floppy, graceful, furry way that cats move their tails. "Don't you understand me?" I asked, and he meowed. I hmmm'd, shoulders sagging. "Maybe not."

He swished his tail, turned up his nose, and pranced away. Point taken; I would have to look elsewhere. I spotted something dark dart behind a dumpster as it watched the cat from a distance, planning its next move.

"Hello," I said, and the rat faced me. "How are you?" She scurried behind the dumpster (it must have been a she, she held a chocolate wrapped in her mouth that said *devilishly dark*), and I tapped my foot. "No one will talk to me, it seems." An uneasiness clouded my thoughts, like I was coming out of an episode, like my brain had burped and I wasn't meant to mistake the burp for words. But then –

"Rats don't talk."

I scanned the alley; no one was there.

"Humans don't, either. But you do. Are you human?" I looked up. A crow sat perched on a gutter, observing me, tilting his head.

"I'm human," I answered. "You can understand me?"

"It helps that you speak words," he said.

"It helps that *you* speak words," I countered, "and sentences." Giddiness filled my body, and it dried out my tongue. It stuck to the roof of my mouth with my last word and scrambled it, but the crow got the gist, anyway.

"Yes, well, that's what we're made to do, right?"

I cocked my head. He looked straight at me, comprehension in his eyes. He was talking to me. I was talking back.

My day had taken many sharp turns.

"You're much more intelligent than I thought."

He huffed. "Is that so? You thought I was stupid?"

"Yes, kind of." I'd always assumed birds thought about food and flying and pooping, and not much else. I never considered that a crow could hold a conversation. Of course, I'd never considered a lot of things – I'd never considered a seagull could have her heart broken, or accuse a human of murder, or rant and rave to other birds about her loves and losses. "But I see I was –"

"Stupid human." He fluffed his feathers and danced side to side on the gutter. The sun glittered on his feathers, sparking shades of blue and deep purple. "Who tried to talk to a cat! And a rat! Ha!" And without another word, he flew away.

"But – " but he was gone, and there were no more animals, no more birds in the alley. It was just me, standing alone, talking to the silence. I scratched my head. Perhaps that was it: I could only talk to birds.

I could talk to birds, just like I could talk to humans.

Or just like a crazy woman talks to herself.

Chapter Ten

I ran to Delia's house and rapped on her door, mumbling *I can talk to birds* under my breath, trying out the sound before I told her, and bouncing side to side on the balls of my feet. It would be an interesting conversation, for sure, but Delia spent her days looking for fairies. It wouldn't take much to convince her I could chat and gossip with the fowl of the earth.

Delia opened the door freshly cleansed. "You look rough," she said.

"I've had a number of life changing experiences whilst you were fondling soap," I answered.

She shrugged. "What else is new?"

She let me in while I stammered about bodies and talking birds, the whole day washing over me in sudden, spastic moments.

"Biscuit?" she asked, throwing several different packages of brand-name cookies onto her kitchen table.

Her words tumbled through my brain and fell out my ears. I trembled from head to toe, my breath coming fast and shallow, as I geared up to explain the craziest, most exciting thing I'd ever experienced. I couldn't be bothered with vittles.

"The dead body is the lady we saw the night before the hurricane, Delia. And the lady I saw dead on my bed. But they wouldn't let me get close. And then, I heard someone talking, and I looked around, and there were only seagulls, no humans." I raised my hands in the air. "I'm all of a dither!"

I froze, waiting for her reaction. Delia opened the refrigerator and pulled out the milk, then grabbed two cups. "Milk?"

I waved the question away. "I'm too discombobulated to ingest."

"Well." She considered the milk and the cups, shrugged, and put it all away again.

"I think I'm crazy," I said, leaning my head on the kitchen island. My heart thump, thump, thumped my fear right back to me.

"You're not crazy."

"I can talk to birds," I continued, speaking into the granite countertop. Delia bit into a cookie. I tried again, a little louder this time. "I said, I can talk to birds."

"Like Lady's Madness?"

Pausing, I looked up. "Yes, in fact. Very much like the lady."

Delia nodded sagely. "The play's gotten to your head again, Marion." She patted my head like an old maid pats a child. "Don't let it worry you."

I groaned, crumpled over the kitchen island, and drummed a death march on the counter. "I don't think it's in my head, this time. Not really, not deep down."

Delia ignored me as she surveyed her cookies, picking out the next with one finger high above her head. She bit into her lower lip.

Cordelia Rose Fortescue did not match her own kitchen. The refrigerator was twice her size and stainless steel, the white cabinets lined the walls from top to bottom in perfect uniform order, and the counters shined from a fresh coat of polish. Yet Delia stood before me, black hair and wrinkled t-shirt, eating a cookie and dropping crumbs.

I spoke slowly, dragging her attention back to me. "I saw the guy again, with the pin. I chased him."

She took another bite. "You chased him?"

"I didn't catch him. And then I talked to another bird."

She raised an eyebrow, squinting at me as crumbs sprayed out of her mouth. "I'm not sure I understand."

"What's to understand? I can talk to birds." I waited for her to face the issue at hand, to fully accept the things I was saying, but she closed her eyes.

"How on earth can you talk to birds?"

Now, that was an excellent question. I had no idea. I

looked down at my hand; the ring sparkled. It sparkled like a wink, or a smile, or a secret. I held it up to the light. "Maybe it's the ring," I said.

"Oh!" Delia snatched my hand and rocked it back and forth. "Where'd you get that?"

I wiggled my fingers and the stone caught the light. It was the night sky, dark and velvety and sprinkled with glitter. "The waterfront. It must have washed up after the hurricane."

"Same time as the body?" She tapped her dimple. "That's interesting."

"Not as interesting as the fact that I can talk to birds."

She sighed, dropping my hand. "You can't talk to birds, Marion."

"Are you my friend or not?"

Her face hardened like an icy river, her entire body still and silent, cracking at the edges. Then slowly she began to melt, and she held out her hand, waving her fingers. "Fine. If you're so sure this gives special powers, let me try."

"Gladly." I slipped it off and dropped it in her palm, just as her mom paraded into the kitchen, her hair perfectly coiffed and smelling fresh even though we had just been through a hurricane, and all that that entails. Ms. Gretchen was blond, but not really blond, if you know what I mean. Not that she was a straight-up natural brunette, or redhead, or raven-locked. She was something in between dirty creek water and freshly barreled hay. I know this because once, I caught a glimpse of her over-grown roots before she left for her hair appointment, and her roots matched the color palette of a wet hamster (Delia told me to never speak of it. Apparently she mentioned her roots once and it did not go well).

"Isn't it just awful?" Ms. Gretchen cried, hand over her heart. "The storm cleared up and I looked outside and I saw her..." her voice caught in her throat as she peered into nothingness, shaking her head. "I just knew. I knew it was a dead body. I don't think I'll ever be able to sleep again."

"You said the same thing after I dyed my hair." Delia stuffed a cookie into her mouth and smiled, tossing her head so her hair flew over her eyes.

"You did that without my permission, sweetheart," Ms. Gretchen grumbled, her southern accent slithering out thick and sticky, "I would have taken you to a professional if you'd just asked."

Delia huffed and held up the ring. The black stone gleamed and glimmered, and the gold band winked at her as it sat tucked between her fingertips, so dainty and bright. Something about it didn't look real; it was too pristine, too chatty. Ms. Gretchen shuffled behind her, fluffing Delia's hair and flipping it from side to side.

"Pretty," she said, eyeing the ring.

"It's Marion's. She found it at the waterfront."

"No kidding."

She pulled Delia's hair into a ponytail. Delia twitched, trying to shrug off her mom's hands, but Ms. Gretchen took it as a challenge. She finger-combed it fiercely, examining the split ends.

"It's time for a trim, Cordelia Rose." She smoothed the split ends across her palm. Delia scowled.

"Did you get a good look at the body?" I asked, drawing Ms. Gretchen's attention away from her inspection. Delia smiled gratefully.

She shuddered. "No, I didn't want to look. Poor thing."

"She's the dead woman Marion saw on her bed." Delia pointed her chin at me and grabbed another cookie. Her mom let her go, turning to me with her hands on her hips.

"Is that right?"

I nodded. "I only saw her once, then she disappeared."

Delia held up a finger and spoke through a mouthful of cookie. "Until we saw her on the waterfront, before the hurricane, alive."

"Right, until the waterfront."

Ms. Gretchen stared at us, looking from one to the other, her mouth hanging open just enough to see her tongue behind the bright white spears of her teeth. She cleared her throat and asked gingerly, "You girls aren't...you aren't *experimenting,* are you? Because I've heard –"

"Oh my gosh Mom, no, we aren't on drugs." Delia rolled her eyes so hard I thought they'd pop out of her head, and I stifled a giggle.

"I'm glad to hear it," Ms. Gretchen said. "It's just that Kyle Mobley said there's been more overdoses, and in some cases they're young kids..." her voice trailed off and she sighed, taking an extra gander at me.

"I have no interest in such extracurricular activities," I assured her, shooing the thought away with a shake of my head.

She smiled, waving her hands to change the subject. "Marion, dear" – she opened the refrigerator and addressed me like I was going to save the world – "don't you think Cordelia should take a speech class?" After a beat, she threw her arms into the air and shrilled, "you could take it with her!"

"Oh, Ms. Gretchen." I backed away, palms out to shield my vital organs from her destructive ideas. "I'm afraid I could not stick to my prescribed assignment. I would be kicked out faster than you can say, 'speech on gnomes and the political state of The Honorable Seagull Council.'"

She nodded, leaning into the open refrigerator with a sigh. "I expect nothing less."

"We have other things to do anyway, Marion." Delia slipped the ring onto her left pointer finger and led me out the back door, clearly overcome with a desire to end the conversation. I waved goodbye to her mom as I followed at her heels.

"BIRDS!" she called. "Calling all birds!"

The back door opened to the waterfront, so we could see the police to our right, and a few locals walking the water-line, heads bent toward the ground, searching for washed up treasures. Except when Delia called for the birds the locals looked up, confused.

"You there!" Delia pointed to a seagull sitting on a bench ahead. A middle-aged man behind the bird put a hand to his chest. Delia didn't notice. "Bird! Can you understand me?"

The bird made no reply.

"Be polite." I lowered her arm, my hand on her wrist, and nodded to the man who watched us with his mouth open. "We're not hooligans."

"Maybe it's the same seagull," she said. "Did she have a name?"

"I didn't ask. Sally, probably."

She turned toward me, head tipped, and smacked her lips. "Probably?"

"Seagull Sally has a nice ring to it." Delia frowned. I continued, "It doesn't matter, just say something."

She took a deep breath and addressed Seagull Sally with outstretched arms and flamboyant fingers. "Hark! I hear the dulcet tones of a songbird; nay! A seagull! Pardon me, ye fowl of noble birth, doth thou comprehend my words upon the wind?" All the locals were watching now. The seagull made no sound.

I leaned into her, speaking from the corner of my mouth. "I don't think they speak Shakespeare."

Delia sighed, dropped her arms, and pinched the ridge of her nose. "Pardon me, but can you understand me?" she asked, finally serious, but the seagull flew away.

It wasn't working. "Let me try." I put on the ring and

looked around. A crow sat on a live oak tree to our left, and I nodded to him. "Good day," I said.

"Is it?" he replied, not looking at me.

"Well, you've got a point."

"What?" Delia examined the trees, hands on her hips. I pointed to the crow.

"He's not so sure it's a good day."

"Oh. Right."

"Can you speak Crow, then?" he asked. "The language of the unintelligent?"

"Apparently so," I answered, stepping toward him. His beak pointed at me, and his dark eyes stared at me, like I was a target. "Did you understand my friend a moment ago? She was speaking to you."

The crow cawed, picking at his feathers, his wings shining like they were made of shadows and stars. "She can't speak Crow." The disdain in his voice was palpable. "So of course not."

I turned to Delia, furrowing my brow, and twisted the ring on my finger. The black stone sparkled in the sunlight. "Apparently he couldn't understand you. I wonder why?"

"This still doesn't prove anything to me." Delia crossed her arms and pointed her chin to the ring. "We need some sort of test."

"Ah, right." She was right. Fire tests gold, and all that. "Can't deny it, 'tis the best way. All things claimed true should be tested."

"How about you leave, I'll say something to the bird, and you can come back and ask him?"

I shook my head. "He doesn't understand you."

"Alright. How about I'll do something, and you can come back and ask him what I did?"

It was a solid idea. I turned to the crow (he was cleaning his wings) and cleared my throat, ready to prove the miracle. "Will you help us? I'm going to leave. Keep an eye on this human, and when I come back, tell me what she did."

"No," the crow answered.

I stepped back. "Why not?"

"Because you offended me once, and crows don't forget." He lifted his beak ever so slightly and flew away, making sure to turn his butt toward our faces before he took off. My heart sank. I'd botched it.

"Stupid birds," I mumbled.

"What happened?" Delia asked, watching him fly away with vague interest.

I closed my eyes, rubbing my forehead as I cursed my own tactlessness. "He's a wild cantankerous animal. And I may have insulted his intelligence a few minutes ago, in an alley, on the way here."

"Well." Delia turned to go back inside. "This was fun."

The sun was setting, and the sky was pinkish (it's appropriate to celebrate the end of a storm) and I couldn't help but feel like every minute was a waste. I wanted to put the whole bird thing to rest, to not experience the plot twist alone, but Delia didn't believe me. I hated that she didn't believe me. It went against everything she stood for. And if she didn't believe me, did she stand with me, at all?

I would have to be more sensitive to crows in the future if I wanted any sort of cooperation, and until then I would have to believe myself, at least. There was no proving it now, and other questions pressed against me. I brushed off Delia's doubts and started again.

"Anyhow," I said, "what really matters is the dead woman. Obviously, she was murdered. I say we test that theory. If something is true, it will stand the test."

Delia paused in the doorway, one foot in her kitchen. "How do you propose we test it?" She shook out her hair and rubbed her scalp. She was all frizz. The air was exceptionally humid, as ruffled and upset as the sea. Not that it made a difference in her mother's hair (she was Miss North Carolina for a reason), but then again there wasn't much of Ms. Gretchen in Delia.

"We can start by asking Detective Mobley what he thinks," I turned back toward the waterfront. "Let's ask him now."

Delia followed me as I hopped off her porch, making a beeline for the policemen. They stood around the body, looking at their notebooks. We spotted Detective Mobley instantly. He had the most talkative shoulders.

"Detective Mobley!"

He glowered at us. His eyes matched the color of the water behind him, and I preferred the water, as hungry and unpredictable as it was. I took a deep breath, balling my hands into fists to summon my resolve.

"A word, if you please?"

He snapped shut his notebook and stepped toward us. "You don't need to be here."

"So I've been told."

"It won't take a second," Delia lied. It had, after all, already taken a second. She nudged me with her elbow and I stood up straight, pretending to be mature.

"How do you think she died?" I spoke directly to his eyes with no preamble because it is always best to get straight to the point.

"Ah." He glanced over his shoulder. "We're not sure yet, but there's really no proof of foul play. She was probably out watching the hurricane when she should have been inside. Or maybe she..." His words leapt back into his mouth and scampered down to his stomach, and he cleared his throat. "Could be she jumped."

"You really believe that?" I asked, throwing my hip to the side, trying to ignore the grumpy side-eyes of the other officers.

"I have no reason not to."

"But her head – it's all swollen, I saw it."

"That can happen if you're in the water for a few days. When a person drowns, they sink first, and as their body decays and the gasses release, they bloat up, and float to the surface." He removed his fedora and wiped his forehead. James loved to make fun of that fedora; it was his dad's only means of expressing emotion, a terrific tell during poker. "You really don't need to be around here."

"It's practically my property." Delia was unnecessarily loud as she took a step forward and motioned to her house. Detective Mobley gave her a sharp stare and she swallowed. "Sir."

"I have an inquiry, anyway," I said.

He looked down at me in silence. For a second I thought I should explain some major misdoing in my past, but that wasn't what I needed to talk about. And I couldn't think of a major misdoing, anyway. Then, words began to tumble out of my mouth (as they often do), and I found myself saying a little too much, being a little too blunt. But what else was there to say? If I didn't reveal what I'd seen and heard, I'd be nothing but a half-truth, hiding my raw edges like a fool. If I was going to find the truth, I would have to speak whole-truths: I would have to tell him everything.

"What do you know about magic rings?"

He rolled his eyes and his stony face flushed until it resembled rosehip soup (I've never had it, but I saw a picture once). "Marion, this is not the time for a joke. A woman died – "

"No, no, I'm not joking." I leaned forward. "I can talk to birds. And they told me they saw someone hit her – "

"Enough." His voice hit us like the crash of a wave and a few of the men behind him turned to watch. Their eyes settled on me, and they looked at me like I caused the crash of the sea. I resented that; I am not a hurricane, filled with groans and gales. I am the wings of a hummingbird, soft and strong and beyond all comprehension. "You're wasting my time."

I flinched, but I couldn't let him stop me, not just yet. "One more thing!" I rose to my tippy toes and clasped my hands in front of my chest. "Remember what I said about seeing a dead body? That's her. And we saw her Sunday night, running around with a folder. Did you find her folder?"

He sighed, drawing out his answer in careful measures. "No, we didn't. I remember what you said. I thought of it as soon as I saw her, I really did. White dress. And she's certainly wet." He took my arm in one hand and Delia's in another and slowly guided us back toward Delia's house. "And I'll keep it in mind. But it's not hard evidence, is it? Trust me. Nothing you've told me is conclusive. Don't worry, I wrote it down. I've heard you, and that's enough. Now it's time for you to go."

He left us at the Fortescue porch and turned back to the crime scene (it was a crime scene, even if they wouldn't admit it). Delia looked at me and shrugged. I looked at her and asked, "My house?"

She nodded.

The new turn of events laid out a few options for me that could not be denied: I had to solve the murder if I did not want to resign myself to madness. It was too late now, the world knew I had seen the dead body before it was a dead body, and I had declared – quite honestly – that a bird had told me she was murdered. There was nothing to do but lean into it, to talk to birds and solve a murder, to prove I was right. I was committed, and if I could not do it, there was a good chance I would *be* committed. I needed to know if I could prove it. I needed to know the state of my own mind, because if my theory was wrong, if she wasn't murdered and birds don't speak, but I *had* seen the future in my mirror, then am I anything but a half-truth? I cannot abide half-truths. I needed to know.

I raced through the threshold of my house and roots grew out of my feet, and the walls closed in, and my thoughts anchored in my mind. "Blessings, Finney," I breathed, and I patted her on the arm.

She sighed. She'd been through an ordeal lately; she'd been beaten and rammed by a storm and stood her ground. She would help me do the same.

It was either that, or madness.

CHAPTER ELEVEN

Once I too had fondled soap, Delia and I stood in front of my bedroom wall, brainstorming.

"We'll need index cards," I said, draping my towel over the full-length gilded mirror (best to keep it covered, I didn't want to see another body) and left for the craft supply closet (all homeschool moms have this).

Soon we were sitting on my bed, writing what we knew on index cards.

The body of a dead woman washed ashore after the hurricane

I saw her dead body on Saturday night, September 10th, 2005 before her death

She was wearing a white dress

We saw her alive on Sunday night, running through the streets

She was holding a file folder

She was found dead Thursday, September 15th, 2005

I have a magic ring that helps me talk to birds

The birds saw someone hit her and throw her over the pier

Guy and girl seen with mysterious pins

Someone's digging holes in my yard

And:

I chased the guy w/mysterious pin through the graveyard

We thumbtacked the cards onto the wall, with *The body of a dead woman washed ashore after the hurricane* in the middle. THESE ARE BUT WILD AND WHIRLING WORDS stood out above it.

"I've always wanted to make a mind map," Delia said. She smiled at me.

"I suppose it will have to do." The thing about a mind map is they always miss so much. I only knew what I knew, and I knew so little. "It will be better once we have a news-paper article or something."

"Think you're a detective now, Marion?"

I turned to see Posey, reclining on her bed, flipping through the pages of a book. She had showered too, and her face was especially marshy when moist.

"What's it to you?" I turned back to my wall, writing her off as a nosey busy body.

"You have enough hobbies, is all. Talking to birds, chasing water trolls."

I faced her again and asked sharply, "How do you know I talk to birds?" as I twirled the ring on my finger, examining her face. She kept her eyes on her book.

"I saw you on Delia's back porch."

"Oh." My shoulders dropped.

"And you were just talking about it." She licked her fingers and turned another page. "In front of me."

"Right."

"You're not exactly the world's greatest mystery, Marion."

"Right." I turned away from her and Delia coughed, inching toward the door.

"My mom said I could only stay until dark." She glanced at the window between our beds, where the shadow of the magnolia tree swayed back and forth. "It's dark."

"So it is," I conceded, offering my hand. "Don't forget me."

Delia bowed, lightly holding my fingers. "Impossible,

darling." And she left the room, waving like a queen as she shut the door.

Posey snorted. "About time."

"For what?"

She eyed me over the spine of her book. "For peace and quiet."

"Ah." I sat on my bed and pulled up my feet, resting my chin on my knees. "We might not get that for a while. Things are getting kind of crazy."

Her marshy eyes bored into mine. "And whose fault is that?"

"Mine, I guess," I said. "Or the birds.'"

They mentioned the body on the nightly news. I liked watching the news, mostly because of the anchor, Pat Blakeman. He had trouble keeping a straight face when the news stories were funny. I can always tell when he's on the verge of laughing because his ears turn red, but this news story was not funny. My ears rang, my ear drums overwhelmed by my million different thoughts that were loud and furious in my head, but his ears were normal, and probably not ringing at all.

"A body washed ashore in Lady's Madness after hurricane Ophelia. Authorities say she took her own life by jumping off the pier during the storm – "

"Lies," I hissed, webbing my fingers over my mouth. I sat on the couch next to Mom, who scrunched the front of her robe.

"How sad," she said, shaking her head.

I huffed. "It's not sad, it's infuriating. They're lying."

Mom pressed her lips together, watching me warily. "You don't know that, Marion." She let the words sink into me, and I began to sway, unanchored in my own house, until Finney closed me in and grounded me. The colors of the TV screen reflected off the living room window, bright and forceful, like Mom's headscarves. "This is a serious tragedy. Don't make accusations so easily. You don't know what happened."

"But I do, Seagull Sally – "

Max appeared in front of me and held out his hand, and I shut my mouth. His eyes were glassy and nimble, dancing around the room but never once meeting my gaze. I poked his palm and he stepped closer, his hand in my face. I pushed it away. He was sleep walking again.

"Mom. That's the woman I saw on my bed. She was dead. Murdered. It's a little more than sad."

Mom stuffed a dirty tissue into Max's palm and turned him to face the stairs. "There you go, sweetie. Go back to bed."

He trudged up the staircase, hand out and holding the tissue like a treasure. We watched him silently, and once we heard his bedroom door shut, I stretched out my legs, determined to plead my case. No half-truths for me, not in my own house. I'd speak those wild and whirling truths and face the consequences. "She was murdered. The birds told me."

Mom muted the TV. Her features were hazy in the dim light. She had one of those small, heart-shaped faces that made her look twelve until she was thirty, and at fifty she looked like a retelling of a renaissance portrait, or like a shadow of something – like a dream or a forgotten poem. She wouldn't meet my eyes. "While you're here, I want to talk to you about something." She patted my knee, just like Grandma. I didn't like it. It was too nice, like a half-truth. "Your father's in his office talking to Leo. We will probably have to sell the house." Her words hit me like a ton of bricks, and my face betrayed me; she winced. "We don't want to, and we may not have to, but I just want to pick your brain about...what would you think if we did?"

I slouched, my stomach sinking into the couch, where the cushions smothered it and pressed it flat. "Why?"

Her lips trembled. "Things aren't...there aren't many options."

"Not many options," I repeated, following the course of her eyes to just above my left shoulder. She wouldn't meet mine. "Surely that can't be right."

"I wish there was another option, Marion."

I bit my lip, counting the cuts on her fingers, the dangers of food prep. Food prep for my dad's dream. I didn't even know if it was her dream, too. "What would you do, if you didn't have the business?"

"Well, your dad –"

"Not him. You." I prodded her with my toes, tapping her ankles. Selling the house wasn't just a move – it was an upheaval of purpose, of mission, of dreams. She had dreams too, right?

"Haven't a clue." She blinked. "I always wanted to be an artist. Did you know that?"

"Really?" Colors and mediums and artistic mood swings – these things were not my mother. Not on the inside, anyway. Her scarves were wild, but her decisions were always calculated, cautious, logical. Every change made to Finnegan's Galley was deliberated over a detailed spreadsheet. One time, Dad wanted to add free breadsticks and cheese for each table at the restaurant, and she spent a week double and triple checking the numbers. She spent months researching and sampling cheeses before settling on a soft brie. I couldn't picture her covered in paint and following her heart – I'd never even seen her doodle. I'd never seen her go with the flow. She looked like a painting, but I didn't think she'd *do* the painting. I tilted my head. "I've never seen you paint anything. Why don't you paint?"

She scratched the nape of her neck, shrugging off the question. "Your grandfather told me it was silly. I guess it's not who I am anymore."

My heart sank, the picture of my young mother before my eyes, dreams crushed and bruised – and here another dream, smashed to pieces. "Do you *want* to sell the house?"

She hesitated, mouth open, like it was a question she had never been asked. I leaned forward, intrigued, but the phone rang, and Mom left to answer it without a word. A second later it was pressed against my ear. A gruff voice met me on the other line.

"Marion. I heard you were harboring a dead body."

It was Conrad, calling from college. He always did that, said my name before saying something else, usually a false accusation. He was a freshman at NC State, and it would undoubtedly be good for him. He needed someone to tell him he's wrong every now and then. The whole *I-am-constantly-wrong* experience is woefully lacking in the upbringing of an oldest child.

"I had a dead body in my bed, yes, but I didn't put it there."

"Then who put it there?"

"Wish I knew."

"Well, what'd you do with it?"

What did I do with it? What, did he think I buried a strange body in my backyard and kept it to myself? Did he think this was a hobby? Did he think I stumbled across a body and thought, *haha, what an anecdote, perhaps the gnomes would enjoy a friend?* Men come up with the strangest ideas. "It didn't stay, Conrad. It was gone by the time the parental units checked."

"A dead body got up and walked away?"

I suppressed a sigh, forcing my answer to be calm and logical. "Well, she washed ashore. So in theory, yes, and then she came back."

He made a high-pitched noise before he bothered to use his words. "What on earth is going on?"

"I saw a dead body. Then the same dead body washed up on shore after the hurricane."

Silence. I tapped my foot.

"Did you murder a woman, Marion?"

"If I were to murder anyone, buttface, it would be you." I'd told him this many times, in fact. He knew better than to ask.

"Oh," he sighed. "Well, that's all I had to say then."

I hung up after a brief goodbye. No time to waste chatting away with brothers; I had thinking to do, and Conrad always disturbs my thoughts. Sometimes, when I forget what he's like, I imagine standing in a back alley at night, holding a wad of cash, and calling out, *"Conrad!"* in a hissing voice like I'm summoning a demon from the depths of the earth. I get a funny feeling in my guts, just behind my rib cage – and that's what my brother is like. He's made of that feeling.

I put the phone on the coffee table and Mom took a deep breath, releasing it slowly as she adjusted her head scarf. "I'm glad he's calling you from college. It's good to keep in touch."

I shrugged. "I guess."

"Maybe he's a good one to talk to about...well, you know...the things going on. With you. And the house, too." Something about her face looked pained, so I frowned.

"What do you mean?"

The air in the room constricted, making my lungs heavy

and shrunken. Mom inched closer. "He could be a good person to listen, don't you think? About that poor woman, and the birds. Because, Marion, if you think birds are talking to you, maybe – "

"I'm not sure Conrad is the best listener."

Mom leaned back, affronted. "He's your big brother! And you should talk to someone, because –" she caught herself, something startled in her eyes, like vocalizing her thoughts scared her. She swallowed. "I think you should be talking about this, with someone you're comfortable with. If it's Conrad instead of me, that's okay. And if you wanted, I could call –"

"I'm okay, Mom. Promise." I said it loudly so Finney could hear too, determined to prove that I was, really, okay. I didn't want Mom or Finney to worry, especially seeing as I depended on them both to prop me up and keep me sane. The walls moved in and hugged me, and the roots grew from my feet and burrowed in the earth.

Mom paused, enveloped in a wave of gentleness. Then she smiled. "Okay, then." She squeezed my arm and sat up straight, her voice growing stronger with each word. "Selling the house might be our only option. So just try to be okay with it, alright?"

I didn't want to be okay with it. Even thinking about it made my bottom lip shake, and I swallowed the rasp in my throat that threatened tears. "But" – I clenched my fists to gather myself – "how did things even get this way?"

Mom's face dropped. She tied and untied the belt of her

robe, fumbling through words, trying to start the answer many times before she finally said, "Things have been slow. The bank wouldn't lend to us. Your father met a man looking for an investment opportunity. Then things got even slower." She scratched at the hair poking out from beneath her head-scarf. "And that, as they say, was that."

And that was that.

At one time, business was good for Finnegan's Galley. We used to be famous for our organic barley salad (which was a rather anticlimactic thing to be famous for, especially in a tourist town dripping with ice cream), but eventually it went out of fashion, and nothing would bring back business. Mom and Dad even tried adding theme nights, the first being a dark, romantic aesthetic – but then chaos ensued, the blackout curtains almost caught fire, the live pianist got sick and cancelled, and Mom asked to borrow my boombox because the sound system wasn't working. Two different women spent the night in tears. It wasn't exactly a classic, successful evening, if you count the man who choked and subsequently projectile vomited onto three consecutive tables. They stuffed the curtains in the attic and vowed not to try for the dark, romantic aesthetic again until they forgot about the whole thing. Disaster had been chasing us, and now this – a private loan, and a man demanding it be paid in full.

"It's legal, what he's doing?"

"Oh, honey." Mom tilted her head the way she used to when I scraped my knee, or when a kid on the playground called me ugly. "It's all very legal."

"I don't understand it." I buried my head between my knees, like they tell you to do in a plane crash. Nothing was making sense, absolutely nothing in my life, and there was nothing to do but brace for impact.

"What don't you understand?"

But Dad walked in, forgotten pencil behind his ear, grumbling. "I don't know about this, Helena Lynn." It was always a bad sign when he said Mom's full name. He pushed his glasses up his nose, shaking his head.

"What'd he say?" she asked, smoothing the sleeves of her robe.

"He won't budge." He sat down on the couch. "And there's nothing I can do about it."

"The lout." Mom readjusted the scarf around her hair. Dad took off his glasses and rubbed his eyes. His hair was on end again, and he was slouching so hard that his nice, average height was reduced to a solid shortness. We fell into a thick silence, and I folded into it, sinking into its soft belly.

"Time for church!" Grandma sang, prancing into the living room with her pocketbook in the bent of her elbow, her nice hat on her head, and her pajamas dangerously see-through. The mood lifted, and Mom even chuckled, watching Grandma stand before us, proud and ready to go.

"Mom, there's no church today," Dad said, cleaning his glasses on the hem of his shirt. He got up with a groan to guide her to her chair, but she slapped him away.

"There's not? Did I miss it?" Her voice was scratchy as

she hobbled forward, cheerful but slow, every step a mission. Dad kept watch with his arms out to catch her until she made it around the coffee table.

"Nope, you didn't miss it," he answered.

She waved at me, her pocketbook swinging at her elbow. "How are you, dear?"

"I can talk to birds, Grandma," I said.

"Oh, good, good." She sat down and Dad gave her a magazine, which she ignored, choosing instead to open the romance novel tucked away in the chair's crevice. She snubbed the bookmark and started at the beginning, my bird announcement slipping from her mind and burrowing beneath the cushions.

Dad slapped his knee, sighing. "Should we sell the house?"

We stared at him, each of us unwilling to be the first to agree, until Grandma reached over me to pat him on the arm. "Always a sweet little boy. Always wanted to open a restaurant." Her wrinkles smiled at him. "Take what you can get. Let go of what you can't."

Dad nodded and swung his arm around me and squeezed, and I was seven again, seeking refuge from the water troll. I could feel his heartbeat, a steady and reassuring sound, and that made tears sting my eyes. He takes everything in stride, even when his dreams die.

"Is that really the only option?" I asked.

He thumped the part of his stomach that hung over his belt. "Well, we used the house as collateral. Which means if we don't make our payments, eventually he could have the legal right to take the house." He thumped again, probably to the beat of a song in his head. He used to do that, sing and thump his belly, whenever we were sick or sad or scared. "And the house is worth more than we owe – admittedly not much more, but a little more. So it'd be better for us to think ahead and sell now, unless we want to sit around and hope business picks up." His arm tensed, and he balled his hands into fists. "Tourist season is over. I don't expect business to pick up until next summer."

I closed my eyes and Finney closed in around me, but this time it was a little too hard, like she was getting scared, too.

"I don't like the idea of anyone else taking care of Finney," I said. Mom glanced at Dad in a *see what I mean* kind of way, her lips tight and eyes beating at him with a magnetic force. I began to sway, like a drifter in my own body, unbound and lightheaded. I pushed my feet against the floor, letting my roots grow, feeling them seep into the earth.

"I don't either," Dad said.

I left to go to my room and closed the door behind me. Posey was nose deep in a book and the mind map jumped out at me from my wall, a swirling jumble of words, words, words, that meant nothing to me except that someday, maybe soon, all this would be gone.

Chapter Twelve

The next day I did my schoolwork as quickly as I could (not quick enough) and called the others. We agreed to meet at Waffle Madness to surreptitiously inspect James' new lady love, and I wore gold, the color of love.

"What's with the love get up?" Posey asked from her bed. She watched me as I got ready, silently judging me with the current behind her eyes. Never mind the quote on my wall that said EVIL EYES TURN IN ON THEM-SELVES. She never listens to my wall.

"There will be great feats of courtly passions today," I said, tying the sides of my tunic together. "I want to be prepared."

Posey dropped her book on her lap, interest glowing in her skin. "Who is the object of your passion?" The afternoon light made our room hot and sunny, and a mist formed around her temples. Her schoolbooks sat scattered around her, assignments half finished. I glared at her.

"It's not me, dingbat." I threw my pillow at her face, careful to avoid the folded stack of laundry by her side. She caught the pillow and hugged it close, throwing back her head to address the ceiling.

"Oh, thank goodness! The men of the world just let out a collective sigh of relief."

"I'll hug you," I threatened, blood dripping from my voice. She ignored me.

"Well, if it's not you, who is it?"

"James." I stuffed a few dollar bills into my pocket. "He's sweet on some girl at Waffle Madness."

Posey straightened up and brushed at her bangs. "Oh. James?"

"Yes." I opened the door. "You heard correctly. James."

I shut the door behind me before she could reply. I was late, and the others would be waiting for me if I didn't get a move on. I rushed through the house, saying a silent goodbye to Finney (she hugged me) but as I stepped outside, I knew things had changed. I mean, things had changed in a basic, practical way: most of the flooding had already receded and the streets were relatively clean, but things were different in an intangible way, too. Mostly I could tell in the air. The air was buzzing, bouncing off my skin, feeding off the energy of the living things out and about. I wasn't used to that. I was used to the thick, dead air of hurricanes and humidity. And then I saw the posters in every shop window:

SUICIDE PREVENTION, YOU ARE NOT ALONE!

I stopped in front of the closest one. The letters were big and shiny. A phone number sat under the words, along with the promise:

THIS IS A SAFE SPACE

Odd, really. Someone certainly made the posters exceptionally fast. I hurried past the other shops and stopped in front of an antique store, where a vendor sat behind a table full of t-shirts that read:

CHOOSE LIFE

And in smaller letters underneath:

YOU ARE WORTH IT

"Did you make these?" I asked the lady behind the table. She was portly and gray, full of folds and lines earned from a hard life spent making poor decisions. She shook her head.

"They're all over the place, sweetheart." She re-folded the shirt I had unfolded and ruffled in my irritation, and eyed me in a pinched, sour kind of way.

"Sorry," I muttered, backing away before I jogged across the street to Waffle Madness.

The whole town had embraced the reported narrative,

the half-truth of the woman's suicide. Every business, it seemed, was eager to scream virtues and encouragement, while turning away from the truth and justice of it all – if everyone spread the theory of suicide, the woman's murderer would never be caught. It was genius. But who had control of an entire town?

I stepped inside Waffle Madness, and my eyes landed on a sign above the counter that read:

WE TAKE DONATIONS FOR SUICIDE PREVENTION

"It continues," I said to myself, pausing to wrap my mind around the collective mission of my little town. Lady's Madness had gobbled up the suicide rumor and spat it out.

"Marion!" Delia waved at me from where she sat across from James, in a booth with an uninterrupted view of the front counter. She wore a shirt that said LEPRECHAUNS ARE PEOPLE TOO in gold letters over a green background, with two smiling leprechauns beside a pot of gold. I sat beside her.

"Are you done with school?" she asked, scooching over. The vinyl upholstery made a nice scratching noise – it was covered in cuts and wayward edges.

"Barely," I answered. "By the skin of my teeth."

"I got up early and finished." Delia elevated her nose ever so slightly. "So I'd be ready."

I rolled my eyes and sighed for dramatic effect. "I had much to do."

Delia could be a trifle more disciplined than me, so usually she finished stuff before me and had more free time. I get distracted; too many things happen around me, and I want to be there to see them. Especially seeing as others usually cannot see them, "them" being things from my own mind, which makes them that much more exciting. And if I don't look, who will?

"Well either way, that means we can take our time." She leaned around me to catch a glimpse of the counter. "Unless you have to work?"

"Not today," I said. "Things are slow."

"We should eat." James picked up a menu and smiled with too much zeal, his teeth clenched together, both his legs bouncing up and down. "And stop looking at the counter."

Delia crossed her arms. "I can't help it if I'm curious."

"We're all curious." Sebastian peered over the back of the booth; he sat in the booth behind James to respect the ten paces between us. The restaurant was empty, except for a few men at a table in a corner and the employees behind the front counter. Sebastian had the whole booth to himself. He nodded to me. "Good day, Royal Empress of the Coastlands."

"Greetings, peasant."

"We need to eat something," James said, again. His voice dropped to a whisper. "You guys are being loud."

"We're not loud, you're paranoid," Delia whispered

back. She stacked a menu at the edge of the table so that it hid our faces. "We've yet to declare your undying love for her, you know."

The waitress greeted us, pen and paper in hand, and James jumped. "What can I get ya?"

Her name tag said FERN and she wore one of those t-shirts form the corner that said CHOOSE LIFE. As soon as I saw her, I recognized her – she was the girl with the pin, the one I almost followed at the waterfront. James shifted uncomfortably in his seat.

"Waffles," he said. Sebastian snickered from the other booth.

"Yeah, what kind?"

"Umm..." James looked down at his menu. "Plain."

She nodded and turned to me. All day I had been eager to see the kind of girl James fancied (this time), but I was disappointed. The only thing special about her was her mouth. It was huge, so huge that when she smiled, it stretched across her face, almost to her ears. Everything else was annoyingly ordinary. Her nose was standard, her chin normal, her eyes placed perfectly on her head, so that every-thing was symmetrical on her face. No birth marks or scars or broken jawlines. Nothing that told a story or spoke of char-acter strengths like courage or perseverance or gumption; just ordinary.

I would have to take a closer look.

"The same, I guess. With, umm, water." I leaned forward

and whispered, "What are your thoughts and feelings on forest gnomes?"

She coughed a cough-laugh and clutched her pen a little tighter. A flash of youth sprung in her cheeks, but she still looked older than James – old enough, at least, to buy cigarettes, or vote, or order something from TV. "Uh, I don't know."

"Oh," I said, deflating. "That's too bad." James buried his head in his hands and I kicked his shin. *Look lively,* I mouthed.

"Are you with them?" Fern asked Sebastian, who watched from his booth.

"Yep," he said.

"You're staying in that booth?"

"Yep."

"That's fine, but if we get busy you'll have to join them."

"Sure thing." Sebastian saluted her.

Fern turned to Delia and Delia ordered waffles with chocolate and Sebastian ordered something I didn't quite get, but that made Fern laugh and James scowl. When she left, James covered his eyes with the palms of his hands.

"You guys can't be cool for one second."

"I'm cool for every second. You're the one hiding your face when she's around." I smoothed my tunic.

"That's because you're ridiculous." He sighed. "Promise me you won't try to talk to her again."

"I can make no such promise." I prickled, stared him down. "Such pacts are foolhardy and useless. They lead to pain and destruction. How can you think you can dictate what I do or do not say with my own mouth –"

"Okay, okay, fine." James dropped his hand on the table and it made a *thump*. Fern looked up from behind the counter. "Just don't embarrass me, okay? Also, Dad told us about the dead lady."

"She was murdered."

He pulled at the collar of his Sunday-best shirt, blue and gray striped, and nodded. "He said you were under that impression."

"It's more than an impression, it's a premonition."

"Are you going to look into it?" He said this so matter-of-factly that I was caught off guard. Usually the others tried to talk me out of my escapades, but maybe he was just trying to distract me.

"Of course." I stole a side glance at Delia, who looked back at me with pursed lips.

"Well you should. Don't be offended if Dad doesn't believe you." James looked up at the ceiling in a not-so-subtle attempt to catch a glimpse of Fern on the way up; Delia smothered a laugh. "It's how he operates. Like, there was this one time I went to work with him on a Bring Your Kid to Work Day. Just so happened to be a dead body kind of day. I saw the dead guy's wife. It was kind of awful. So I asked him how he deals with it. And he said – " James sat up straight and pretended to take off a fedora and turn it in his hands. "Mentally, I lay out the facts on a table, and I focus on the facts. That's my job." James slouched again and shrugged.

"He's got a point. You have to protect your head somehow. Plus, for that kind of job, if something can't be proven as fact, it won't hold up in court and so it's not worth the brain space. So that's how Dad works. All facts. It's how he keeps sane. Don't be offended."

"And that's the story of how James lost his childlike whimsy." Sebastian leaned over his booth, his palm over James' head like a prize model. "He took up Dad's banner and married facts."

James shrugged and fixed his hair, scuffing it at the top and smoothing the back. "It works for him."

Sebastian snorted. "Yeah, okay. Also, Dad told us they've ordered an autopsy done, they want to check for illicit substances, you know, 'cause of all the overdoses. But the official report will take a while, 'cause the lab is so backed up."

"So even if they do find that it's a murder, it won't officially be declared one for a while," James added. "Just FYI, if you're gonna look into it."

"That's good to know," I said.

"Well, we can't let two unaccompanied ladies investigate a murder by themselves," Sebastian declared gallantly. James huffed logically (only James can do this; even his breaths are logical, somehow) and Sebastian swiped his shoulder. "Hey!" James recoiled but Sebastian ignored it. "How cool would it be if we solved the murder before Dad?"

James thrust his fist in the air, and Sebastian fell back to avoid a punch in the nose. "I guess that'd be fine."

"We'll help!" Sebastian promised from the safety of his

booth, one hand in the air so I could see the exuberance of his fingers.

I bowed my head. "That's very kind of you."

But I wasn't thinking about it anymore. I was watching Fern, who was taking the order of some guy who looked at her like she was free meat in a meat packing factory. Her smile was strained, and she stood an arm's length away from him, avoiding his eyes. Across from him sat a tall, sunburned man, who leaned his elbows on a pile of papers filled with numbers typed in little boxes.

"And anyhow, they know who she was!" Sebastian still cowered in his seat. "It took a bit 'cause no one reported her missing. But Dad can't tell us, there hasn't been an official release yet. But he says it's no one we know. I guess you knew that, though."

"I didn't know that." The booth upholstery was patterned with brown and red polka dots, and I pictured Sebastian's face through them, all dotted and colorful.

Fern turned away from the man, her fake smile gone, and he laughed as she walked away.

"How chivalrous are you feeling today, James?"

"Huh?"

But then Fern placed my food in front of me and smiled one of her gargantuan smiles. A smile like that said she didn't want to talk about the man at the table in the corner, so I didn't mention it.

"Waffles!" she chimed.

I thought of her pin, and the guy I chased, and I couldn't help myself. "I have another imperative question."

"What's that?" She didn't look as excited as I felt, even with the vast smile on her face.

"I saw you the other day. You had a pin on your purse. And I saw the same pin on another guy's backpack."

"Ah."

"What kind of pin is it?"

"Latin Club." But she didn't look at me.

"Do you know who the guy was, then?" I stabbed my waffle with my fork. "Dark hair, fast runner, strange priorities?"

"There's a lot of kids in Latin Club." She shrugged. "Could be this kid Nick. Or Chad. Was he tall? Short? Fat? Skinny?"

"Kind of short, I guess." I paused. "The face of a gourd lost at sea."

She hesitated, the ends of her mouth twitching, like she didn't know if she should laugh. Then she smiled, and it stretched beyond her ears. Okay, not really. But it seemed like it.

"Might be Chad, then." She pulled a piece of paper from the pocket of her apron (this always amazes me; waitress aprons are magical, probably. Maybe she kept gnomes in the pockets, but it wasn't kosher to ask). "You guys hear about that body?" We nodded and she tapped at the paper – a flyer. "I know her sister. She thinks it wasn't suicide. Asked me to hand out these."

Across the flyer in big, red letters, were the words:

REWARD! For anyone with information leading to the arrest of Lily Anderson's MURDERER $30,000

And under it, a phone number. I met James' eyes from across the table as both his eyebrows reached for his hairline.

"That's a lot of money," I said, and I saw the letter on my dad's desk, the one that demanded the loan to be paid in full, with interest, and no exceptions; but would thirty thousand be enough?

"She's pretty convinced." Fern brushed the hair out of her eyes – normal, average eyes. "Even though the police aren't."

Excitement bubbled up from my stomach and left my mouth as words. "I saw the murdered woman running around the night before the hurricane." I threw a thumb at Delia. "Delia saw her, too."

Fern froze. "Did you tell the police?"

"Yeah. They don't care."

She shook her head, one hand on her hip. "Crazy world, huh?" she crooned, and left the table, taking a pen from her magic apron.

"That's something," Sebastian added from behind the booth.

But I didn't notice, because Mr. Creepy was leaning against the front counter, talking to Fern as she grimaced and inched away. He grabbed her arm, smiling like a fox in a henhouse.

"Are you ready for your act of courtly love?" I asked James. He furrowed his eyebrows at me.

"What?"

I nodded to the spectacle. "She needs saving."

James' face became the color of the Cape Fear River on a rainy day, a stirring storm of anger and resolve. He looked like his dad, honestly, and I was relieved that I was not the recipient of those colors, for once in my life. "What do I do?"

"Stand between them," Delia suggested. "And ask for water or something."

"I have water."

"Then ask for something else."

James jumped from his seat and slipped gracefully between them, forcing McCreepy to drop his arm. He said something that we couldn't hear; Fern nodded excitedly, her smile wrapping around her whole head and touching the opposite edges of her own lips (okay, not really, but almost). She disappeared into the kitchen. Creepy McCreeperson said something to James and walked away, and James sauntered back to his seat, wearing a kind of bashful, slightly terrified smile.

"What'd he say?" I asked.

"I don't want to repeat it," he answered.

"What'd you say?" Delia asked.

"I asked for more waffles." He looked down at his plate.

He still hadn't touched his waffles. "This could be a problem."

"I'll eat them," Sebastian offered, bending over the top of the booth, reaching for his plate. James pushed him away and breathed out one long sigh. He swayed slightly to the left, so Delia pushed his water glass closer.

"Drink something," she ordered, and he did. We sat in silence for a moment, Sebastian sniggering from his hovel, as James guzzled the entire glass.

"I think it was a success," I said. "But you would have been better off to ask for more water."

We called the number on the flyer, and the woman who answered gave us her name and address and a no-buts instruction to meet her at her house as soon as possible to talk about it. Her name was Violet Anderson, and I was giddy. She was the first clue in our new investigation, the first step in my quest for sanity. I had trouble finishing my own waffles, but still we split James' extras. We were going to Violet Anderson's house after, and James had no desire to bring a box of waffles with us in his car. He's precious about his car. Personally, I didn't know what he was worried about, it already smelled of dirty socks, so waffles seemed like an improvement, but whatever.

"So, what you guys think?" James asked, in a kind of lets-get-it-over-with way, as soon as we stepped out of the restaurant. I already had a fully formed opinion and jumped at the chance to share it as we walked to his 1999 Mazda Protege (Mable, he called her, because she was slow and a little shaky).

"Honestly, I was hoping she'd be more interesting."

"Interesting? How?"

I waved at the air, to point out the myriad of different ways I could answer. "You know, like had a lazy eye or something."

He looked down at me, weariness in his voice. "You wish she had a lazy eye?"

"Or dimples, maybe."

"Right."

"I think she was pretty," Delia said. "And nice."

But I wasn't done. I tried the car door but it was still locked, so I twirled around and held one hand out to my side like I was serving a tray of edible wisdom. "Also, Fern? Really? You couldn't have gone for an Ivy, or a Heather, or a Laurel?"

"I wasn't thinking much about the name, Marion." James unlocked his car and sighed.

"Well, then." I turned around. "There's nothing we can do about it now. Let's go." I slid into my seat, spinning the ring around my finger, wondering if I should bring up the whole talking-birds thing now, or after I was double sure I wasn't crazy. I stole a glance at James' face and decided I would make triple sure I wasn't crazy – at the very least.

Chapter Thirteen

James drove us straight to Violet Anderson's house, even though he grumbled and groaned about stranger danger the whole way, like a powerless dad.

"This is how people get murdered," he said, turning on his blinker to take a right turn onto a dirt road. Pines trees towered beside us, and Mable bounced with every lump and dip of the earth. Violet lived on the edge of Lady's Madness, a good ten minutes away, but the roads were clear enough. James only had to maneuver around a few puddles and stray branches.

"The murder already happened, James. There are bigger things to worry about than homicidal grieving women." I caught Delia's eye and she gave me one of her classic looks that said *we might die there* and I reminded her that it was worth the risk with one of my classic looks that said *we're doing this anyway.*

James rolled down his window to let his hand ride the wind. "If I die saving you guys from getting killed, I'm going to come back as a ghost and spend my days clogging your plumbing."

"As if you would die heroically," Sebastian scoffed, "instead of meeting your end by falling on the wrong end of a garden rake."

The sky above us was a crisp blue, the kind of clean, brilliant sky that only appears after a storm. The air, though warm and humid, was clean too, and even the trees looked clean, ready for me to eat off their bark without a second thought. We pulled up to Violet's house and sat for a moment, staring, unsure of what to do.

If I had been told to sit down and decide what I expected, I probably would have said she lived in a blue house (the color of severity) with a wide front porch (trimmed white) and collected plastic floral arrangements with the pointed eccentricity only the rich seem to muster; what I saw was much different. This woman lived in a steep A-frame house painted a rather rude shade of yellow (this is its own form of severity, so perhaps I was almost correct) lined with flower boxes filled with dead plants. The deadness struck me as poetic. I mentioned as much to James, but he only shook his head.

The driveway was dirt (I would have expected asphalt) and as we stared, a woman crossed the yard to greet us. She looked like a groundhog that had taken up hobby gardening, but I kept this observation to myself.

"Thank you for coming," she said, reaching out to take our hands in both of hers. "I was so grateful for your call." Her voice was low and scratchy, her eyes had no lines, and her neck had that springy look that said *look how naturally hydrated I am!* (no one likes a bragger) and it made me think that she might have been young enough to be my sister, too. She turned and motioned for us to follow, leading us up the front porch. "Come inside, come inside. But close your eyes, it's a mess." We stepped into her house and she gestured to the pictures that lined the walls, framed and laid out like a museum. "We'll sit outside. It's too hard for me, right now, to, you know, look at Lily's face."

Almost every picture was Lily. Smiling, dramatic, silly, unawares, her face was everywhere. She was striking, with her green eyes and dark hair and wild, genuine smile. I twirled in place to catch a glimpse of every picture, but Violet didn't pause for us to gawk. She powered by the pictures, and we followed the walls of Lilies through the house and out the back door, onto a large, sprawling deck that looked out to a wall of long leaf pines.

Violet sat on a wicker chair and started crying. James cleared his throat. Sebastian looked at the sky. Delia sat beside her and patted her back.

"We're umm, very sorry for your loss." Delia caught my eye and shrank; perhaps we were not ready for this.

"Thank you." She sniffed, and her hand fiddled with something in her pocket. She was a different person than the one on the phone – guarded, almost, like she'd changed her mind about our visit in the short ten minutes we took to get there.

"So, like we said on the phone, we saw your sister walking the waterfront Sunday night," I ventured, and Violet nodded, head down, and I wrung my hands, suddenly aware of the awkwardness of the situation. "And we, uh, we want to look into it, too…"

"The reward money," Violet said, eyes on her lap.

"Well, yes, but, we're curious too. So, yeah, we want to ask you questions – "

"I applaud your pursuit of the truth." Violet rubbed her thighs, taking a deep breath. "I'll tell you whatever you want to know, but I should say…" but her words drifted off, and as I waited for her to continue, I clambered up the deck railing and sat facing her, feet swinging.

The house had a shroud feeling, like it was a secret spot, or like it was made from elements not found in Lady's Madness. This brought with it a sense of otherness, or, more accurately, a secret goal heretofore unknown to my sensibilities. I twisted to check behind my back, just in case.

"What's the house's secret?" I asked.

"Marion," Delia groaned. *Stay on track* was written on her forehead.

"Oh, no." Violet soothed Delia's concerns with a shake of her head. "She's right. This house has a lot of secrets, I'm sure, but I don't know them. I've only lived here a few months."

The deck had not been painted, but it had been stained

(is that a half-truth?) and the black tiles of the A-frame roof came starkly down on each side like the house was trying to hold itself together. Above us there was a small second floor balcony; more dead plants sat in pots on the railing.

"I'm Lily's only family. We lived here, together." Violet stared into the line of trees. "Any of you have a sister?"

"Kind of," I answered. "Mine is rather marsh-like. All browns and greens with putrid slime hidden underneath the surface."

"I disowned mine." Delia pointed to me. "Marion is my sister now."

Violet wiped her eyes. "I love my sister." Her fingers trembled, and we studied our feet as the wind blew through us. The breeze whispered comfort to Violet; she gathered herself, taking a deep breath. "She was everything to me."

"Why didn't you report it?" James asked. "Her disappearance, I mean?"

Her head sprang up. "I did indeed report her missing," she barked, her voice burning, and the sparks almost caught her skin on fire. "But the officer said they wouldn't do anything about it until she'd been missing forty-eight hours." She tugged at her hair. "I'm not sure if that's the truth, but that's what they told me."

I lounged on my back along the deck railing and stared at the dead plants. "Why didn't the plants fall off during the storm?"

Violet followed my gaze. "They were inside."

"Oh, right." I was wearing gold, an incredibly inappropriate color to wear while investigating a murder; I sat up quickly. Sudden realizations require sudden movements. "So what can you tell us about Lily?"

She stood up, one hand on the railing. "I need a drink. Do you want anything?"

We all said no, and she disappeared into the house. Delia whistled slowly, while James and Sebastian exchanged uncomfortable squints. I didn't say anything. No one said anything. Our tongues were glued to our mouths, and Violet pranced back onto a quiet porch without warning, holding something that resembled sweet tea in a tall glass. She sat down and pulled a letter from her pocket, shifting in her seat, checking over her shoulder. She picked at the corners absent-mindedly as she peered into the pine canopies, silent until Delia cleared her throat.

"Violet?"

She jumped. "Oh, sorry." Her eyes landed on the envelope in her hand. "I just got this." Setting down her glass, she handed the letter to Delia, who scanned it, then looked at me, her eyeballs just visible over the top edge of the paper.

"Suicide note," she said. I took it from her. Sure enough, a few hasty lines typed up in Times New Roman twelve-point font sat on the page, expressing some vague malaise and heartbreak. I held it up, pinching one corner between two fingertips.

"Did she write this?"

"It would seem so." Violet pressed her fingers over her mouth. "It has her name."

It did, indeed, have her name; but it was typed, not signed, as if it was a hum-drum letter to an editor about the appropriate use of pesticides on the suburban lawn. "She didn't even sign it," I observed, making note of her reaction.

Violet sat motionless. Delia fiddled with her belt buckle.

"Before you saw this, why didn't you think she killed herself?"

"Because she wasn't sick, you know?" The words were sharp needles in her mouth. She stroked the hem of her shirt, her focus on one stray thread. She pulled, it snapped. "They found her car downtown, by the shops. Why would she park downtown, then walk to the pier? Why not park by the pier? 'Course, they say maybe the hurricane washed it backwards. It didn't look washed backwards. It looked parked. And then they suggested that maybe she was distraught that some lowlife broke up with her. Bunch of bull – sorry – bologna. I didn't know anything about a boyfriend." She took the letter back from Sebastian, who was the last to read it. She caressed the words with her fingertips. "This does mention heartbreak."

"What did she do?" I asked. "For a job?"

"Receptionist. For the newspaper. Dreams – I mean, dreamt of being a reporter." Then she added, "That detective was worthless," completely unprompted, for no apparent reason. I exchanged wary glances with James and Sebastian. "Hardly talked to me. If there's a boyfriend, he should have been found. Lazy detective work. Worthless dump of a man." She took a sip of her tea.

"He's my dad," James said.

She froze, her cup midair, and slowly lowered the glass onto the railing (I think the stain was a half- truth, for sure). "Oh. I'm so sorry. I didn't mean to –"

"It's no problem," James said, in a gruff and hurried kind of way from deep within his throat, like he wanted to forget it.

"Is that why you called me? Is your dad...?"

"No." I let my heels hit the railing as I swung my feet back and forth, nervously. "It was my idea. Because of what we told you on the phone."

The trees captivated her again. They must have been pretty interesting. I, for one, found them common.

"What do you do, Violet?" Delia asked, trying to draw her back from her reverie. Violet startled and ran her hand through her hair, combing out a thought.

"I work for the city. Pruning and planting trees and flowers and stuff by the sidewalks. I just started, though." She took a drink. "It's new."

"Who else would know something?" I asked. "Who else knew Lily well?"

Violet studied each one of us, then her hands, then the door. She tapped her glass anxiously, and with one confident leg cross she answered, "Francesca Lovely. Reporter."

"At the newspaper?"

She nodded, held up a pointer finger, and disappeared inside, returning with a pad of paper and a pencil. "I don't know her house number or anything." She wrote out a detailed description, drawing a simple map with directions to her house. "Her house is here. Her office is the newspaper, of course. But she's hardly ever there." She placed it in my hand and squeezed my fingers. "I wish I had more to tell you."

"It's worth checking out," I assured her, but more to the others than to Violet. She studied the trees again, letting silence envelope her. Then it happened – her thoughts burst out of her, one after the other, and we sat and listened as they barreled at us.

"It makes me so angry that the town is preaching that suicide message. They do it with flair, like they're such good people, even though they're profiting, making themselves feel good by using the reality of my sister's death. They're stuck up in their self-righteous, self-happy mission. It's sickening, honestly. Because of it, I can't go into town. But I can't stand to be in this house, either. It's just – there are too many pictures. Too many memories.

"We put up those pictures when we first moved in, vowed we'd make better memories here in Lady's Madness. I chose those pictures, you know. Because Lily was always happy, she always made everything sunny. My first memory" – Violet's eyes glazed over, her words slurring together like snakes – "is Lily clutching her teddy to her chest as we hid underneath the kitchen table. I watched that man's feet as he walked out the door. Lily was too young to remember, that's for the best.

"She always took care of me, you know. I had this stupid

boyfriend in high school. Mom was useless, always high on delusions and dreams. She didn't see the warning signs. But Lily held my hand as I left him."

The wind hissed through the pine trees and through her hair – she dragged it out of her face to take a long drink.

"Blimey," Delia said, in accordance with her adopted British vernacular. Violet wiped her mouth with the back of her hand.

"She always had my back since then, even though I'm the older one. Always looking out for me. Vetting my boyfriends. She was my only family. Part of me is relieved she was the one that needed help, for once." She picked at the corners of the envelope and licked her lips, inhaling sharply before spitting out her words, each one chasing the next with urgency. "But the one time she needed me, and I didn't help." We were silent, unsure how to leave the conversation gracefully, counting the seconds between sad revelations. Something in Violet was slipping. "Mom died of an overdose five years ago."

"Hey! Hello there!" A strange voice cut through Violet, calling at us from above in sharp, ragged tones.

"And now I have to plan Lily's funeral – "

"What's happened? What's going on?" the voice asked, again. I looked up to see a crow sitting on the lowest branch of a live oak tree, positively bouncing with impatience. "Hey! Hello! Tell me! Hi!"

Violet was oblivious. " – hits me like a truck every time I think about it, and then there are moments I – "

"Hey! What happened? What's going on?"

I couldn't keep track of either talkers; and the crow, it seemed, was simply nosey.

"Could you please wait your turn?" I snapped, irritation sparking out of my mouth. The others looked at me. Delia held her face in her hands. Violet giggled uncomfortably and took a drink as the bird huffed and flew away. "Sorry about that," I said to Violet, "please, go on."

She glanced at Delia and back at me, unsure what to do. Delia nodded for her to continue, and Violet cleared her throat. "Yes. Well. Anyway, it's – " She leaned onto the arm of her chair but her elbow slipped; half her body fell over, and her tea spilled onto her lap. "Oh shoot, how on earth – umm, right, anyway, it's been difficult. And that reward – it was my life savings, and now that I know – now that I have this letter – well, it'd be better off going toward the funeral." She stood up, dripping tea, brushing it off her lap. "So I'm sorry, I know you were interested in the money – anyway, I'm meeting with the funeral director soon, so, I hate to make you leave, but I appreciate you coming by – "

"We'll be going," I said. "Thank you for the map."

We walked back through the house, past the Lilies, and to the car, where the crow was waiting, pacing back and forth on Mable's hood. I greeted him as Violet locked her front door, trying each key separately.

"I've seen you around," the bird said, "rumor has it you can talk." He was a brilliant black, so shiny his feathers had an iridescent sheen. He stepped forward, his feet black as his feathers, and cocked his head.

I shrugged. "This appears to be true."

He looked away, his beak pointed to the tops of the pine trees, and sighed. "I was trying to tell you that she's been crying all day."

"Yes," I said. "I can imagine."

He fluffed his feathers. "Why?"

I crossed my arms, eyeing the gentle curve of his beak (black, like his feathers). He must have had some sort of empathy for humans, to notice she was crying and to want to know why. That made him different from the seagulls, who seemed rather indifferent to Lily's murder. "Her sister was murdered. Did you know?"

"Murdered!" he screeched, his tone horrified, all urgent and guttural. He jumped up and down and spread out his wings, like he would punch someone. But birds don't have fists, and anyway I don't think they get urges to punch humans (I could be wrong). "It was the man, wasn't it?"

I stepped closer. "Did you see something?"

He lifted his beak. "I see very little. I don't poke around in other people's business."

"Well you must have seen something," I said, "or you wouldn't have guessed who murdered her."

The sunlight glinted off his feathers, and he puffed his chest. He was beautiful. Completely beautiful, in a mysterious, unexpected kind of way. Like other crows I'd seen, he was both one color and many colors, as black as the night but shiny and carrying hints of blue and purple. His tail was short and curved, and when he talked, he stretched his neck and spoke to the sky. So many times, I had passed a crow and assumed it was common and uninteresting, when all along, there were a thousand things to notice, and a thousand questions to ask.

"Well, if you must know, I've seen a man here sometimes. They always fight. He always makes me uncomfortable. So I go other places, and other places is where I've seen this one." He turned to Sebastian, who stared at me, his nose scrunched up and his upper lip following it, like that would help him understand birds. "He's always doing something, eh? Passing shinies. I've seen lots of shinies in his hand."

I nodded, motioning to Sebastian. "Yes, he makes a lot of bets."

"Perhaps it's a problem."

"Could be," I conceded.

"What?" Sebastian asked.

Delia rolled her eyes. "You don't want to know."

"I have places to be," the crow declared, flapping his wings. "I just wanted to warn you about her mourning." And then he flew off, briskly, and without ceremony. That's the thing with birds. There's never any sort of goodbye ritual.

James turned to me, his face a mountain pass filled with static. "Were you talking to a bird?"

I took a deep breath to gather my courage. There was something about James that made me nervous, something about the way his eyes search a person to weigh and measure their character with his scales of logic and proof. What I had to say contained neither logic nor proof, only bold and colorful whole truths. But I was going to say it, nonetheless. "Yes. I can talk to birds now, if you haven't heard." I opened the car door and sat down, waiting for him to respond. The others followed me in, one by one, and Delia nodded at James, merging her nod with a shoulder shrug and a chin tilt (whatever that meant), and James started the car.

Fine. If they were going to be that way, I would not explain.

"It's always something with you, isn't it, Marion?"

"It's the nature of being human, James," I said, and turned my attention out the window.

Chapter Fourteen

Francesca Lovely lived in an old pillar house with a plaque on the front that read *Lovely House, circa 1722.* She was home when we knocked on her door, and she smiled at us and told us to sit down, all southern charm and hospitality. There was something familiar about her that I couldn't quite place. I was sure I'd seen her before – but equally sure I hadn't. I studied her, trying to summon up a memory, but no memory resurfaced, no chance encounter reemerged.

She had an annoyingly open face, with all her thoughts and emotions written on the surface and nothing underneath. She was a warm yellow blond (with dark blond roots, so the whole debacle was a half-truth, and I cannot abide half-truths) and short and pudgy, and as she looked at us, she opened her mouth wide and pushed out her lips, so that it looked like all her hopes and dreams dangled from her mouth and hung on, for dear life, to our words. It really was too much pressure; I didn't like it.

"Oh!" Francesca gasped. "You must be the detective friends! Violet called me."

It was one thing to mention that we were keen on finding the truth behind a murder, but it was quite another to give us a condescending title like we were six-year-olds playing doctor. I stared at her. She stared back, mouth all smiley and dripping her innermost thoughts, and I shrugged.

James jumped in. "We think there is a possibility that Lily Anderson was murdered."

"And are you the one – " Francesca grabbed my hand in hers, her eyes bright with zeal. "The one that lives nearby? In that beautiful house?"

"That is true," I said, trying not to think about the fake nails touching my skin, and if their undersides were clean. "My dad inherited it. It's a bed and breakfast." The eager way in which she stared at me and ignored the others made me squeeze my toes.

"Oh, how wonderful!" She dropped my hand and put both her hands over her heart, and I chuckled awkwardly. People always have strange ideas about what it must be like to run a bed and breakfast. It's really quite tedious, I think, but no one wants to hear that. "What a life! I'd love to live in a house like that!" Then her eyes sparkled, and she leaned in close to me, her voice low like she was sharing a conspiracy, and like a fool, I leaned close to her to hear it all the better. "Have you found any secret passageways?"

"Not unless you count the crawl space under the house."

She laughed at that. It wasn't all that funny, but whatever.

"What about any treasures? Anything from the original owners?" She leaned her chin on her knuckles and dug her elbows into her knees. I was just about to mumble something about my mirror when Delia coughed, and Francesca took the hint.

"Anyway." She smiled at us. "I'm so pleased you are doing an investigation!" She said the last word like "super-secret spy club!" but I suppose that didn't matter.

"Did you know anything about Lily Anderson?" Delia asked.

Francesca pressed her lips together. "I know she died."

"When did you find out?" I asked, leaning closer. Francesca sat up straight.

"Just now, when Violet called me. The police wouldn't give me a name when I asked yesterday. It wasn't ready to be released, I guess. I'm floored. Absolutely floored." All the smiles left her face, her spirit dried up and gone at the mention of Lily.

"Do you think it was suicide?" I asked.

"I have no idea." She tipped her head. "Is there evidence otherwise?"

"There's not a whole lot to suggest suicide." My mind was still on that letter, and that pathetically typed name. "Will you report on it?"

She consulted her watch. "I already did. Listen, I have to

go. And Lily was new to town, just started at the front desk –
it's tragic, but I don't know much. Maybe – maybe talk to
Marv, at the museum." She hesitated, mouth open, and
nodded, like she was convincing herself. "He knows
everybody."

Francesca opened the door and we filed out, stepping out
onto the sidewalk. We watched as she hopped in her car and
backed out of the driveway.

"I'm sorry!" she called from the open window, waving at
us as she passed. She really was in a hurry.

"If you're looking for the shiny, she always keeps it with
her."

I stopped and spun in circles; the others didn't even
flinch, just walked to Mable. I spotted a crow on a nearby
live oak and stepped toward him, re-tying the sides of my
tunic together to look like I was doing something other than
talking to a bird. "The shiny?" I asked.

"On her bag."

Oh, right. The pin. She must have the pin, too. I forced
myself to stop tying and re-tying the knot – maybe it would
be best to own the whole talking-to-birds thing, anyway. I
looked up at him, my hand over my eyes. "Do you know
what it is?"

"It's treasure. Priceless."

Probably not, but it wasn't worth debating. "Right.
Treasure."

The others stood at the car, doors open, watching me.
Well, James and Delia, that is; Sebastian stood ten paces

behind me, as per the terms of the bet. I bowed to the crow, my hands clasped below my chin – I had to be polite this time. There was no sense in offending another bird. "Have I talked to you before?"

"What?" He froze and cawed a laugh. "I think I'd remember talking to a human. No. No, we haven't talked before. I always remember a face."

My heart raced. "You always remember a face?"

"That's correct."

Lily Anderson's bright green eyes flashed before me, and the unknown face, the one traced with darkness, smothered her. I stepped closer. "Even human faces?"

He snorted. "Naturally."

My stomach fluttered. Could it – could it be he saw something? Maybe, just maybe, he was at the waterfront that night, when Lily was killed and tossed in the sea. I gathered my thoughts and asked calmly, "Did you see the murder? Did you see a man kill a woman, before the storm? Did you see the man that killed her?"

"No, no." He shook his head, flying to a lower branch, just inches from my face. "I didn't see anything of the sort. Sorry to disappoint."

I lightly kicked at a tree root curving up from the ground and slid my hands into the front pockets of my jeans. "Oh, well. It was worth a try. Thank you...what's your name?"

"Albert," he said. "Thank you for asking." He wouldn't keep still, his head lurching this way and that, catching every moment and following every sound.

"You're welcome."

"Why did you think you've talked to me before?" A few crows gathered around him, watching me. They lined the branch, and as he cocked his head, they did too, curious for my answer. I gestured to them, my explanation hesitant and bashful.

"Well, I've talked to a few other crows recently. I'm not sure how to tell you apart, yet."

He laughed again, and his friends joined in – their laughs were short and loud, aimed at the sky. "Humans," he cackled, and he flew away without a goodbye, his friends following behind. The live oak swayed, moved by their weight and wings, and waves of laughter trickled back to me as they flew out of sight. I walked to the car, making sure to look James in the eyes like I had all the confidence in the world.

"Guys." I adjusted my tunic. "I think we need to talk about this."

"You think you can talk to birds," James said, his voice monotone, like he was repeating a joke that had long ago turned unfunny.

"What would you say if I told you it's really true?"

"Cool trick." James nodded to the back seat. "Get in, we're going to the waterfront."

I obeyed, one hand on the head rest of the driver's seat, determined to have the conversation now, rather than later, seeing as the secret was out. "But, like, for real."

Sebastian rubbed his forehead as he climbed in the car

after me, his face a swirling pool of questions. "How on earth can you talk to birds?"

It was the ultimate question, the one I'd asked myself time and time again, and the only possible answer I could give involved found jewelry and a very specific form of magic. "I found this ring at the waterfront," I said, holding up my hand. "And ever since I put it on, I can hear what birds are saying."

James stared at me blankly from the rearview mirror, but Delia nodded. "Like the legend."

"Exactly." I clapped once, for emphasis.

"Let's just deal with one wild theory at a time okay, guys?" James started up the car.

"No, I'm serious. I could understand what that crow was saying. See? He just told me Francesca has one of those pins. And his name is Albert."

"What kind of name is Albert for a bird?" Sebastian asked, but James had other objections.

"Is this the water troll all over again?"

Again with the water troll. "No, it's not. Try the ring on. See?"

James opened his door to hear the birds properly, then put the ring on his pinky (the only finger it would fit) and glared at me. "How about that. Nothing." He turned back to the steering wheel and put Mable in reverse. Sebastian grabbed the ring and leaned out his window.

"Talk to me, birds!" he screamed, waving his ring hand at the sky like a flapping wing. He strained his ear toward the birds flying above him and waited, but after a few seconds he gave up. "Me neither, Marion." He slumped back in his seat and tossed the ring back to me without looking, and I cursed him under my breath (British style) for his carelessness. "Why does it work for you?"

"Well, it only makes sense." Delia twisted around to face me, hand out to showcase my chin. "She looks like a bird, right?'

Everyone turned to me, eyes squinted, and I shifted in my seat. "What's that supposed to mean, Delia?"

"Just that you look like you could have been a falcon or something in another life. See it? Pointed chin, high cheek bones, amber eyes, amber hair. She's a bird of prey." Delia smiled. "Actually, the more I think of it, the more it makes sense."

A warm blanket of feathers squeezed my heart and I mouthed *thank you*. She was supporting me. Participating in the conversation was something close to believing me, too.

"Yeah, I can see it," Sebastian relented, one eye closed.

"I don't think someone learns to talk to animals just because they happen to look like one." James, ever practical, was the voice of reason – even if it was, in my opinion, rooted in folly.

"The crow at Violet's house knew you place a lot of bets, Sebastian."

"Call me Bash," he said.

"You must make a lot of bets, *Sebastian*, if even the birds know." I emphasized *Sebastian* because he was still serving time as my servant and walking ten paces behind me, and I would call him what I wished.

He shrugged. "I do okay."

"You don't think you have a problem?"

"Of course not." He crossed his arms. "I thought we were talking about you?"

"Not anymore. I said what I wanted to say, and now it's time to change the subject. How long have you been into gambling, anyway? Do you even remember your first bet? Or have there been too many?"

"Of course I remember. My mind's a steel trap. The best in the family. It was a gray fall day – "

"Oh, spare me." James slammed on his breaks, but Sebastian didn't flinch.

" – and James had a soccer game. And of course it was James' fancy soccer league, so Dad actually comes to watch. Anyway, it's boring 'cause it's James so I make Dad a bet: James will get kicked in the face by the other team's full back who will do a bicycle kick. Dad thought it was outrageous, but he took me up on it. And it actually happened. He was so impressed he took us out for ice cream."

"I had a bruised jaw for an eternity," James mumbled, turning a corner to the waterfront, where he parked and sighed like an old man. "It was not a good time."

"It was glorious." Sebastian opened his door and whispered, "he cried."

The museum was underwhelming, really. It was one story, made of brick, and connected to a string of old shops that lined Market Street, looking toward the water. We walked through the doors (no gatekeepers) and greeted the man called Marv behind the counter. He was reading the newspaper, but his eyes flicked up at us and he set it down. "One dollar for students."

"We have a few questions, if you don't mind," I said. James dropped a few bills into the collection box on the counter and I snuck a peek at the article Marv was reading.

BODY WASHED ASHORE AFTER HURRICANE
By Francesca Lovely

The body of a young woman was discovered in Lady's Madness in the aftermath of Hurricane Ophelia, police said. They suspect she had been in the water for "a few days" before washing ashore.

"I saw [the body], and I just knew. I knew something was wrong," said Gretchen Fortescue, a longtime resident of Lady's Madness, who found the body Thursday afternoon. "It's a sad, sad thing for our town."

Police investigators believe the cause of death to be suicide. The identity of the body has not been released.

Marv waited for me to continue, and when I didn't, he barked, "Shoot." I looked up from the article and met his eyes. He was tall (I don't trust tall men, they're always up to something), somewhat narrow, and looked like a candy cane lost underneath a couch cushion: sunburn striped his body, and he was rather hairy.

I nodded to the paper. "Do you know anything about the woman who washed up on shore?"

He scratched his nose, sniffing like he smelled something foul. "No. Why do you ask?" Slowly, he slid the paper toward himself and leaned on it, his elbow blocking the headline. The skin on his face was a layer of instant mashed potatoes, just one brush and it would flake off. I moved my gaze to just over his left shoulder, so I didn't have to look.

"We were told you have your thumb on the heartbeat of the town. That you know everything." It was a slight exaggeration, but I hoped to massage his ego, to get him talking.

He laughed. "I don't know anything. It was a suicide, right?"

"I have my doubts," I said.

"Did you know her?" Sebastian asked, leaning on the counter until he was oddly close to Marv.

"Don't know." Marv pointed to the last sentence of the article. "No name, yet."

"Her name's Lily Anderson." I searched his face for any sign of recognition and found nothing. "It hasn't been officially released, but we just talked to her sister. Know her?"

"Nope. You kids detectives?" His words were smooth, almost too smooth, with a certain flash on the uptick of *detectives?* that made me tip my head.

"No, but my dad is." Sebastian squared his shoulders and James, I'm almost certain, rolled his eyes.

"No way! Does he tell you stuff?" Marv smiled broadly, too interested in Sebastian's revelation. The fillings in his molars glistened in the beam of the overhead lights.

Sebastian shook his head. "Never."

Marv chuckled, wiping his hand over his face, like he was wiping away his thoughts. "Seems about right. No, I know nothing about the girl. Sorry to disappoint you. It's a bit crazy to go looking for crimes when the police found none, isn't it?"

I bristled. "We're not crazy."

He gave me a double look, rubbing his chin. "Sorry, sunshine, I didn't mean it." Then his eyes found my ring, and he lit up. "Can I see it?" he asked, holding out his hand. Slowly, I slipped it off and dropped it in his open palm. He held it up to the light, turning it back and forth to catch the sparkles. "It's a beauty," he said, bringing it close to his eyes. He held it under a magnifying glass. "Quite a beauty. Pretty old piece, I'd say." His lips turned up in a smile. "Black sapphire and gold. Beautiful." And then, with a touch of reluctance, he gave it back. "Family heirloom?"

"I found it, actually," I answered, sliding it back onto my finger.

"Ah, some people have all the luck."

"Yes." I hid my hands behind my back to keep his eyes off my ring. "I'm very lucky."

He noticed my discomfort, something like amusement passing in his eyes, and then he pushed forward a scrap piece of paper and pointed to the pen beside it. "Here, leave a number, and if I hear something about the girl, I'll call, alright?" I hesitated, so James wrote down his number and Marv pinned it to the corkboard behind his head. His eyes settled on Delia, who stood in a corner, so quiet she was loud.

"Bit late for St. Patty's Day, ain't it? Or maybe a bit early?" Delia pulled at her t-shirt and crossed her arms. She looked away, melting into herself. Marv chuckled again, and this time the skin on his face turned to scales. "I'll call if I think of something, alright?"

"Great." James opened the door, waving us out. "Thanks." We hurried past him, keen for the fresh air.

"And I'll take that ring off your hands, if you ever wanna sell," Marv called after us. "I always set a good price, scout's honor."

We mumbled our thanks as we filed out into the open air, breathing a sigh of relief when the door shut behind us. Delia shuddered.

"I don't like him," she said.

James crossed his arms and took a deep breath as a salty breeze rushed through us. "Do you think 'I'll take that ring off your hands,' is a threat or an offer?"

I wiped away the lingering unease from my shoulders. "Either way, it's suspicious." Marv sure was determined to change the subject, like he was looking for something to distract us.

"Everyone seems suspicious to me." Sebastian looked back at the sign that said, *Lady's Madness Maritime*

Museum. Under it, a large poster was taped to the window:

WE SUPPORT THE SUICIDE PREVENTION LIFELINE

And under that, a phone number. TEN PERCENT OF ALL PROFITS ARE DONATED TO THE SUICIDE PREVENTION LIFELINE filled the bottom.

Sebastian wrinkled his nose. "That place smelled like guilt. Maybe Marion's right. Maybe Lily was murdered."

"You mean maybe the birds are right," I said. He only grunted.

***

We continued to the waterfront (Sebastian ten paces behind me), where we scanned the ground for any discarded clues. It was no longer flooded, so the grass and sand were there before us, clear as day, and yet it was fruitless. There was nothing to find. I tried to talk to the seagulls, but none of them would stop to chat or even give me the time of day; they were too busy screaming at each other.

"She was here," I said, pointing to the spot where she washed up. I indicated how she was found, but it was no use. There were no clues to be uncovered, no revelations, nothing. "This is a waste of time."

This was partly because James was useless. He kept

looking over in the direction of Waffle Madness, and finally I gave up and suggested the inevitable. "You should just bring her some coffee, James."

"What?" he mumbled, hardly innocent, although he wanted to be.

"Buy her some fancy coffee. But leave it at that. No expectations. Don't be creepy."

James looked as if he would argue, but then his shoulders slumped and his face flushed a soft pink. "But uh, I don't know what she likes."

"Get at least three things," I said.

"Three things?"

"You can tell her to pick from three, and it's more likely you'll get something she likes."

Delia added, "Better yet, get five things, and what she doesn't pick, we can drink."

James scratched his ear, taking an unsubtle survey of the downtown shops. "This doesn't seem practical."

I placed a hand on his shoulder. "Practicality has no place in courtly love." He groaned, and I sighed. "Do you have a better idea?"

"Fine. I'll get three things." He started toward Lady's Coffee and Cakes, on the same street as Waffle Madness, his hands in his pockets.

On the window of Lady's Coffee and Cakes sat the poster CHOOSE LIFE, the words YOU ARE WORTH IT scrawled on the bottom. People had signed it, adding their own personal phone numbers beside their names. Little notes like, *call if you need to talk!* and *I'll ALWAYS listen* <3 filled the spaces in between. We followed James into the shop and stood behind him as he made his coffee orders. Sebastian, a big grin on his face, took the opportunity to make a bet.

"Five bucks Fern throws the coffee at him."

"Why would she throw it at him?" I asked. "That's a waste of good coffee."

"Okay, fine. Five bucks she turns him down."

"I'm not going to ask her anything," James said.

"He's just wooing her, Sebastian. Making his prey comfortable before he pounces." I shined my fingernails on my tunic and raised one eyebrow. "Anyway, why aren't you ten paces behind me?"

Delia stepped between us, her face drawn out and weary. "Mom won't stop with the speech class," she said, the words spewing out of her like they'd been pushing at her tongue all day.

I hmmm'd. The turn of conversation distracted me and saved Sebastian from his seven lashings, and he backed away, careful not to make a big deal about it.

"Maybe you should just take it, get it over with."

"Maybe," she said. "But I think I'd rather die."

I put my hands on her shoulders, speaking into her soul with the lure of my irises. "I'll be sure to plan a tasteful funeral. Bigfoot will be invited."

She nodded, closing her eyes. "That's a comfort."

"I'm busy," Sebastian said, calling loudly through the ten

paces between us. "Can't make it, sorry." He grinned, but we ignored him.

James paid for the drinks, and he wrote his instant messenger username on each cup with an old marker we found in his car, and then he delivered them, shaking, to Waffle Madness. We watched through the window. This proved a rather disappointing form of entertainment; very little could be seen, and nothing could be heard, or touched, or tasted, obviously, so the only thing left was to smell, and the only thing I could smell was waffles. I leaned against the wall, disappointed.

"Beautiful day."

"Yes, it is," I agreed.

Delia looked at me. "What?"

"I said yes, it is." She arched an eyebrow, so I explained. "It's a beautiful day."

"Oh."

"What's that?" Sebastian yelled, ten paces away. "I can't hear you guys."

"I agreed with Delia." I motioned to the sky. "It's a beautiful day."

"I didn't say anything," Delia protested.

"Beautiful day."

There it was again.

A bluebird sat on a bench against the face of the restaurant, eyes pointed to the sky. "Beautiful day," she repeated. She was a soft gray blue on her back, her chest a faded kind of apricot.

I twirled the ring around my finger and kept an eye on the bird. "Oh, well, I could have sworn it was your voice, Delia."

The bluebird turned to face me, toes pointed straight ahead. "Beautiful day, then, human?"

I swallowed. "Yes, beautiful day." I was drawn to her, like there was an invisible chain connecting us and it was shrinking, link by link. Inching forward, I stared at her, the bird that was talking to me and asking me questions. Talking birds were hard to ignore – especially ones that sounded like another human, so happy and carefree, like a friend. She flew away, and Delia glowered.

"I think we need to do something about this."

I shook my body, forcing myself out of my thoughts. "Do something about what?"

"Your sudden ability to communicate with birds."

I narrowed my eyes. "You want it to stop."

"No. I..." She crossed her arms. I could only see the feet of the leprechauns on her shirt, below her elbows. Such cute shoe buckles. "Either you're crazy, you're lying, or you're telling the truth. So we need to try to prove it, and see which one it is."

"Well, I'm not lying."

"No, I didn't think you were." And then she smiled, and I crossed my arms too.

"I thought you believed me now. Back in the car, you said I looked like a bird."

Delia pressed her lips together and tucked her hair

behind her ears. "It's not that I don't believe you. I don't *not* believe you, you know? It's just that, well, I don't completely believe you either, right? Like, you say it's a magic ring, but it doesn't work for anyone else. And you just what, all of a sudden can talk to birds? Right after you saw a dead body? Are you sure it's not...it's not like a coping mechanism, or something?" She winced, like the idea hurt her, too.

"No," I said, as a command, but my stomach fluttered. "No, I don't think so. And anyway, you believe in Bigfoot and the Loch Ness Monster. Why don't you believe in me?"

She opened her mouth, but her words were lost in her throat as James waltzed through the door, all smiles and carrying two coffees. He held the drink carrier aloft in his left hand, too high and too casually, just begging for a latte face bath.

"Alright, let's go." The door slammed shut behind him.

"Well? How'd it go?" Delia asked, our conversation dropping from her mind as she waited for his answer. James motioned for us to follow him, smiling bashfully.

"Fine, I guess," he said. "She took the iced mocha." And he made a beeline for the water, a pep in his step, twirling his keys around his finger.

Chapter Fifteen

The first thing I did when I got home (we piddled around at the waterfront for a while, then James wanted to see if Fern hit him up on instant messenger, and Delia's mom screamed for her) was stare at my mind map. Everything had stayed in the same place, so that was good; no cards had grown feet or wings and escaped – and I had more to add. I got out my index cards and listed the few things we'd learned that day:

The victim's name was Lily Anderson

Under that I pinned Francesca Lovely's article (stolen from my dad's paper, he didn't notice) about the body, the headline BODY WASHED ASHORE AFTER HURRI-CANE staring back at me. I continued:

Lily moved to town recently, with her sister

Her sister Violet received a (fake) suicide letter

Violet seemed suddenly secretive

Francesca has a pin too

And then I wrote *MARV* in big letters on copy paper and pinned it next to Lily Anderson. And then, after a thought, I wrote one more thing on an index card:

Violet's plants all dead

"Curiouser and curiouser," I said to myself, and to my wall. But I didn't say it to Posey, although she answered anyway.

"Find more clues, Marion?"

I tapped Marv's name, his smile creeping up my memories. "More like answers to a question I didn't know I asked."

"Right." Posey flopped on the bed. "Play practice is tomorrow."

Finney groaned, and I did too, rubbing my eyes with a sigh. "Ugh. Don't remind me."

"I still haven't memorized my lines."

Posey's bed was a mess of pillows and sheets, and she sat on top of it all, leaning against a pile of (hopefully) clean laundry as she opened a book and began to read. I gaped at her.

"You have one line, woman."

"And I haven't memorized it."

I passed her on the way to the door and flipped my hair. "It's your funeral, darling. I wash my hands of it."

I, for one, had memorized my lines weeks before; although my lines were all standard lines said in a crowd, and it didn't matter if I said them so much as acted them, with a fist to the air and a pitchfork at my side, but I conjured supremacy and left the room anyway. Posey called me back in, so I poked my head around the doorway and flashed her a look that said *make this quick.*

"Where have you been all day?"

"Looking into the murder, obviously." I pointed to my mind map.

"No, I mean, where exactly did you go? After waffles?"

I shrugged. "We met the dead woman's sister, Violet. And Violet sent us to talk to a few people. Why?"

Posey turned a page. "Sounds interesting, is all."

"Right." I waited for her to continue, but her focus was on her book. Her eyes never moved – just sat lifeless before the page, like the words would move themselves. The title *A History of Lady's Madness* stared back at me. School reading, no doubt, although Mom never made me read it. "Exciting stuff?"

She didn't look up. "Not really."

"Ah, well –"

"Actually." She raised her eyes. "There is this one thing I never knew. I mean, we all know about Máire Finnegan and how she was crazy and everything, but did you know her uncle and sister died too, like all in the same week? And her uncle was crazy too, claimed to have a miracle tincture." She cocked her head. "I wonder why no one talks about that?"

"Crazy men are just not as interesting as crazy women, tincture or not."

"Well" – she turned another page – "guess it couldn't heal a broken heart."

"Right. Suppose not." I drummed my fingers on the doorframe and excused myself from her presence, shutting the door behind me.

I found Grandma sitting on the couch watching the news. She wore a hat again, although this time it was a straw gardening hat that she secured to her head with a scarf, tied under her chin. Wisps of her purple hair floated out from underneath it, but her pajamas, at least, were a matching set, even if they did say *Have a Holly Jolly Christmas!* and it was only September.

"Whatcha watchin,' Grandma?"

"Oh!" She jumped, and then smiled her one hundred smiles. "A sermon."

Pat Blakeman sat behind his desk, reciting the nightly news. "Looks like the news to me," I said.

She paused, like she was seeing the TV for the first time. "Why, so it is."

I turned up the volume.

"The body found on the shore of Lady's Madness has been identified as local resident Lily Anderson,"

Pat looked back at his audience with sad eyes. But then he spewed half-truths:

"Our sources believe Lily Anderson killed herself after a lethal combination of depression and heartbreak – "

She may have been depressed, of that I had no idea; and she may have been heartbroken, that's possible too; but she most certainly had not committed suicide. Not when every-thing around me was changing, doing weird, unexplainable things, and it had all started with her body on my bed.

It most definitely was not a suicide.

Max wandered into the room, spatula in hand, and sat down next to me. "Good evening, sister," he said. His pajama top rode up, exposing his belly button, and he patted it with his free hand as he swung his feet – his pajama bottoms were too small for him, ending midcalf. The outfit was mismatched, the top of him a salute to superheroes, the bottom the red and green stripes of Christmas. He inherited his sense of style form Grandma.

"Good evening, peasant," I replied.

He shook his spatula at my nose. "One, I am not a peas-ant. Two, I'm armed, and you're not."

I snorted and he crossed his arms, his "weapon" resting on his shoulder, and I ruffled his nut brown, curly hair. One ringlet fit perfectly around my pointer finger; he swatted at my hand, and I surrendered.

"Why aren't you in bed?"

"Can't sleep." He slumped and leaned back, eyelids half closed. I poked his knee and he kicked the air. "Can you *please* stop touching me?"

"Why do you have a spatula?"

"Dunno. I keep waking up with it." He held it up to my eyes and twirled it, apparently hoping I would admire it, but I only studied his little face. He wasn't so little anymore, but still kind of little, and just little enough to sometimes resemble something that could someday, maybe, if the weather is just right and the stars align, be called cute. He furrowed his brow and stuck out his tongue, so I wiped my palm on it and he gagged.

"MARION!"

I dried off my palm on my pant leg, holding back a smile. "You're a weird little man, Max."

"Yeah, you're weird, too. And I'm not a man, I'm a kid." He scrubbed his tongue on the inside of his shirt.

"You just wake up with spatulas? What's next, the toaster?"

"I can't help it." His pitch heightened to a whine-y, baby tone, and I glared at him. He glared back. "I sleepwalk. And Conrad isn't here to stop me."

He had a point. Conrad and Max shared a room, but when Mr. Know-It-All left for college, he left Max to fend for himself; usually Conrad would hear him pitter-pattering around and guide him back to bed. I offered to move into the room so that Max could stay with Posey (out of the kindness of my heart) but Mom said Conrad will still need his bed during breaks. It's just as well, I'd miss my wall.

"I wish I had a part in the play," Max said, sighing so deeply that his head snapped back into the couch cushion and his chest all but collapsed into his stomach.

"I thought you did have a part in the play?"

"I'm a villager. There's no glory in being a villager."

"I'm a villager, Max."

"But you *want* to be a villager. I want to be an actual person. With a name. And lines."

"Well, maybe next time." I patted the top of his head, my other hand pinching his cheek.

He pushed me away, spatting the words, "But it's always next time. I hate being the youngest. I'm never old enough for anything, and everyone always says, 'next time,' and next time never comes." He threw the spatula on the floor and Grandma, sitting sweetly in her chair, clicked her tongue at him. He crossed his arms and scowled at his feet. "Stupid."

"Oh, sweet Maxy-boy," I cooed, squeezing him like a human strait jacket. "Poor, sweet baby." I smacked loudly in his ears and he thrashed from side to side.

"Let me go!" he screeched, through giggles, so I squeezed harder and pushed him into the couch, pressing my knees into his back while demanding of the living room,

"WHY IS THE COUCH SO LUMPY?"

And he kicked me once, hard, in the shin. The phone rang, and I relaxed my grip just enough to let him leap off the couch and run to his room. I limped to the kitchen and picked up the receiver, my shin throbbing.

"Marion."

Conrad. I should have known. I leaned against the kitchen wall and pressed my forehead into the nearby corkboard, where my parents pinned all their reminders and hard-to-remember recipes. The back of a thumbtack pushed into my skin. "Keep your word weapons to yourself."

"What?"

I sighed. "Never mind. What do you want?"

He chewed on something, the crunch of it smacking in my ear, and then he swallowed, coughing a little. "I called to talk to you about something. Mom said you think the woman was murdered. I'm watching the news. They say it's suicide."

"They're lying."

He crunched again. Sour cream and onion potato chips, I'd bet my life on it. He cleared his throat. "Why would they lie about that?"

"I don't know."

"Then why do you think they're lying?"

"Because she was murdered." I collected all the free thumbtacks, arranging them into a smiley face on an empty corner of the corkboard. The conversation was going nowhere, but at least the corkboard was happy.

Conrad was losing patience. "And what makes you think that?"

I paused, weighing my options. Conrad was tiresome and undoubtedly wouldn't understand, but for me it's all or nothing – no half-truths. I would have to tell him the raw truth, no sugar coating, no pretty words, if I wanted to be consistent. "Well, if you must know, the birds told me."

Silence. Then, "The birds."

"That's correct."

"You talk to birds now?"

"That's correct."

Silence. He was probably waiting for an explanation, so I gave him one, as succinctly and clearly as I could manage. "I found a magic ring that washed up on shore."

"A magic ring."

"That's correct."

His voice garbled in the back of his throat, and the sound muffled, like he was switching hands and changing position. "Marion, you can't talk to birds."

"You wouldn't know."

"Yes I would. I know everything."

I sighed again. Apparently, college had taught him nothing. "Well she was murdered, the birds told me, and I think her sister, deep down, agrees. So I'm going to figure it out. I think the sea wants me to."

"The sea wants you to."

"That's correct. You don't have to keep repeating me." I moved a few thumbtacks down, to make a sad face.

"This doesn't sound good."

"You're right, it sounds great."

"No, it sounds weird. Be careful."

I rested a hand on my hip and glared at the wall. "Don't

tell me to be careful, Mr. Jumped-Off-A-Roof-On-To-A-Trampoline." If he'd said that to my face, I would have punched him in the gut with Max's spatula. I half expected him to tell me to bring my smelling salts in case I suffered a fainting spell.

"Marion, I am your older brother. I am indestructible. And it is my job to protect you."

Weariness flooded my bones, so I said, "I have to go, Conrad. Farewell, pleasant partings," and I heard a muddled,

"Fine, bye –" before I hung up.

It is always best to take control of a conversation when the other party is being wearisome.

I rolled my eyes – it's his job to protect me, indeed.

I left the corkboard and its sad face and plopped on the couch next to Grandma, ready to forget the world and my troubles, but a picture of Lily Anderson flashed on TV. She was young and smiley; it was one of the pictures in Violet's house.

"How horrible," Grandma said, shaking her head. "She was such a nice girl." She retied the scarf underneath her chin, adjusting her straw hat as she tucked her purple hair behind her ears. It took me a moment to capture her words, but then they hit me like a tidal wave. I sat up straight.

"You knew her, Grandma?"

She nodded. "Oh yes. She was scared, poor thing." Her face dropped and she closed her eyes, balling her hands into fists in her lap. My heart jumped.

"Scared? What do you mean?"

"Scared for someone. I can't remember who. Do you remember?" She searched me up and down, worry stretching her wrinkles. I shook my head slowly.

"No, I don't remember." I looked to the TV, then to Grandma, then to the TV; Pat was going on about suicide prevention ("*Make your donation at any participating business!*") and my stomach sloshed and twisted, so I focused on Grandma. "When did she tell you she was scared?"

"Oh, not too long ago." She leaned into me, to whisper in my ear. "While we chased garden gnomes." Her eyes sparkled and she pressed a finger to her lips.

Something in me believed her, and that's when I knew I was crazy, too.

Chapter Sixteen

More holes appeared in the yard the next morning. I found Mom on the porch, sipping coffee while she stared at the holes, like her stares would fill them in.

"Someone did this while we were sleeping," she said, her back to me as I opened the door and stepped outside. It was a beautiful day, and the birds sang like it wasn't Saturday, and there was no all-day play practice looming ahead of me.

"Perhaps this is a good time to remind you that I suggested we get a dog, but you turned me down." I leaned over the railing. The holes were incredible, really. They doubled over night. And they were deeper this time, deep enough to swallow my legs. Max kneeled over one, his army men poised over the edge, and he shot them into their earthen graves, one by one.

"Someone's stealing dogs," Mom mumbled, and checked her watch. "You have to leave soon, Marion. Get dressed."

I took one last look at the holes (they were unsettling) and donned my tunic, not in the least surprised when Delia marched into my room, completely ready to go.

"Ready for this?" she asked. She wore a sea-blue shirt that said FREE THE MERMAIDS with a splash (that's the collective term for them, I asked) of mermaids looking, quite frankly, imprisoned. Delia held up her backpack and shook it in front of me, sunshine spilling out of her. "I brought snacks."

I smiled gratefully. "We will need nourishment for our weary bodies."

She tossed her backpack on my bed and stood at my side, looking at the mind map. Her head dipped to the side and she stuck out her hip. This was her curious pose.

"You think the dead plants are something?"

"It feels like it, doesn't it? Violet works with plants. She brings her flowers inside during the storm. And she lets them die? It doesn't fit. I don't know what it means, but it's something." I poked the card and stood back, head tilted. "But what is it?"

We pondered the map until we had to leave for our Saturday Dose of Trials and Tribulations, and I wore green. We took our usual seats by the shrubbery, and I sat next to Delia eating cheese puffs (orange is the color of emergency, which means they must be eaten with vengeance) while James and Sebastian munched on popcorn and talked incessantly about something related to paintball. I had no interest, and Delia had a mild interest that I knew she was faking. Neither of the boys noticed.

Talking about paintball was okay with me, as disinterest is better than distaste. Sebastian once tried to talk to me about trucks and I had to tell him in no uncertain terms that it was a conversation topic in which I would not partake. When he continued, I offered him facts about childbirth and he left the room.

Anyway, they were talking about paintball, and I was thinking about gnomes, as I am wont to do.

"I'm saving up for a better gun," Sebastian said. He sat two shrubs away from us, and his voice was just a little too loud to make up for the distance, and Ms. Caroline shot him a frown from her place at the foot of the outdoor stage, one villager costume slung over her arm and a pencil behind her ear. Sebastian saluted her an apology. She turned away.

Sebastian had never been in the military, of course, and neither had his mom. But he did have a habit of saluting people – do gnomes salute? Do they have a military? That would depend on whether or not they have boundaries to protect and jobs to tax; but of course, I had no idea what gnomes do for a living. Guard cabbages, maybe?

"How can you save up when you're constantly losing your money in bets?" Delia asked. James snickered.

"I don't always lose my money in bets." Sebastian quieted, his voice weak and bleeding from the wound of injustice. "I have money."

"If you say so."

He scowled, taking a deep breath as he crossed his arms. "Mostly my bets are not money related."

"Here he goes." James stuffed his mouth with popcorn and smiled. "We Wonth hear the enf of ith now."

"No, listen." Sebastian slapped the ground. "I'm not an idiot. I'm responsible. I bet *experiences*, mostly –"

"I didn't say you were an idiot." Delia pulled up a handful of crabgrass and let it fall through her fingers and onto her lap, her expression cold and peeved. "Don't put words in my mouth."

"It's called reading between the lines. You insinuated it." He sat up straight and took a deep breath. Delia rested her chin on her knees, waiting for his speech. James sighed.

If Sebastian felt wronged, he fought his case until all present tore their clothes and sat in a pile of sackcloth and ashes. Which would be good for gardens, as wood ash can add nutrients to soil, which in turn would make garden gnomes happy – I assumed. Did garden gnomes care about their gardens?

"I'll make a bet right now," Sebastian continued, "that I can tell you exactly what Marion is thinking about. How about it?" He looked at me expectantly, and I had to shake my head to receive the moment.

"What?"

"I bet I know exactly what you were thinking about. If I get it right, I don't have to walk ten paces behind you. If I get it wrong, my fate is extended another week." He smiled. "Simple. Straight forward."

"Easy," Delia agreed, nudging me. But James had a warning.

"Never delve into the deep recesses of a woman's mind." He popped another oversized handful of popcorn into his mouth. He said something else, but it was muffled and unintelligible.

Sebastian crossed his arms at me, a sparkle in his eye.

"Hmmm," I examined my cheese puffs, "you're taking a big risk there, Mobley."

"It's not a risk when I know you as well as I do, Morrissey."

I laughed, heat creeping up my neck, but then I remembered it was Sebastian speaking, and I balked.

It felt like a challenge. I stuffed my mouth with my remaining cheese puffs, chewed, swallowed, and clapped my hands together. "Fine, I agree to your terms. How do we proceed?"

He wiped his hands off on his jeans and hopped to his feet, running to his mom and returning with a script and a pencil. "Write down the topic of your thoughts. Not a specific sentence or anything – " I shot him a look of deep distrust and he rolled his eyes. "I said I know what you were thinking *about*. Not what you were thinking word for word."

"Fine." I took the script and pencil and hurriedly scribbled *gnomes* along the edge. Then I turned it face down. "Ready."

"Ladies and gentlemen." Sebastian stood on top of a nearby cooler, this time getting a frown from Ms. Caroline for both speaking loudly and standing on coolers. "I do hereby pronounce that Marion Morrissey of Lady's Madness, North Carolina, while we were having a perfectly stimulating conversation about paintball, was thinking about gnomes!"

Eyes wide, I turned the script over and showed the others that, indeed, I had written *gnomes*. Sebastian bowed so low that his head touched his knees. Delia clapped like a lunatic and James mumbled something about a lucky break.

"Well done," I praised, bowing in turn, racking my brain for the common signs of a mind reader, trying to understand how on earth Sebastian knew I was thinking about gnomes. I sat on my ankles, inching farther away from him, something unsettling in the space between us. The innermost parts of me were too exposed, too readily understood, by a teenage boy. I had absolutely no idea how he had read my mind. The cheese puffs in the pit of my stomach shifted and rumbled.

"Thank you, thank you!" he shouted, still bowing. Then, arms widespread and humming "Pomp and Circumstance" under his breath, Sebastian hopped off the cooler and sat down next to me, unencumbered by the usual ten paces. "It's nice to be free."

"Congratulations," I said, scribbling *gnomes* on the script again and again, over and over, until it covered all the edges.

"How'd you know that?" Delia asked, hands still clasped together. Her hair fell over her eyes, and her smile was so wide I could count her teeth. I dropped the script and pencil, my fingers picking at the crabgrass instead.

"Easy." Sebastian stretched out his legs and laced his fingers together behind his head, grinning at me. "You always squint your eyes while you think about gnomes. Last week when we talked about your Grandma's gnome hunting hobby, your eyes were so squinted I thought you went permanently blind."

I had no words. I laughed a little, an open mouth, breathy laugh, and leaned back on my elbows. I didn't know I had a habit of squinting. Then again, how could I, when there are more interesting topics to think about, more interesting things to notice? Sebastian tapped a finger on his temple, and I shook my head. Maybe he knew me better than I knew myself.

"Do you realize..." James swallowed his popcorn and lay on his back on the grass, staring at the clouds. "That you were under such a punishment because you did not know your brother well enough, but won the second bet because you know Marion far too well?"

"No one wants to know you well, James," Sebastian deadpanned.

Delia grinned, drumming her fingers together. "I beg to differ."

The edges of James' lips turned up (or over, as it looked from my angle, but I could also see up his nose, so I wasn't looking) and he smacked a nervous beat on his stomach.

"Ah, yes," Sebastian groaned. "The girl."

Delia threw a cheese puff at James. "Spill!"

"If you must know," James said, and Sebastian looked at me and mouthed *we mustn't*. "We've been instant messaging."

"He was hogging the computer all night," Sebastian added. "Dingbat."

"And who would you talk to?" James asked, and Sebastian shot back,

"Anyone but you."

"Idiot," James said.

"Dingbat."

"So what'd you talk about?" Delia ended the spat before it could begin. Her voice was casual, but she was desperate – her nostrils flared and her ear lobes were red, and both those things were her classic tell of desperation. She wanted to know everything. She was hiding it rather well, considering. Junk food usually makes her less subtle.

"Stuff," James muttered, scratching his nose.

"We're meeting up on Sunday," Sebastian said.

"What are you doing?"

Sebastian shrugged. "Stuff."

We waited for more. Sebastian studied his left pant leg. James studied the clouds. The wind rustled through the dead pine needles on the ground. A car honked; waves crashed against the retaining wall; seagulls begged for food. Delia and I sighed.

"Okay, weirdos." Delia rolled her eyes and opened a chocolate bar. I glared at Sebastian, one eyebrow raised.

He didn't break, and Ms. Caroline called to me from the stage.

"Marion!"

I stood up, arms at my sides, ready for orders. "Yes, ma'am."

"Go to my car." She threw her keys at me but I missed them, and they flew past me and hit Sebastian in the face; he was engrossed by his left pant leg and wasn't looking, and subsequently he made a noise that was not unlike a cat in heat. "And look to see if I have any more black fabric in the back. We need more for the stage backdrop. I could have sworn I measured everything, but it appears there's not enough." She hung her head and pinched the bridge of her nose. "It's always something."

"Right," I said, sure I had been given this assignment because she didn't trust her sons, and because I was closest to her and doing nothing. I should always look like I'm doing something.

Ms. Caroline, as it turned out, had parked as far away as she could manage. It was a point of pride for her, I supposed, to walk the length of Lady's Madness needlessly. Perhaps it was some sort of workout regimen. Middle aged women are always trying new diets and regimens; their hobbies tend to be fairly limited.

This wouldn't have been a problem normally, but as soon as I left the park and stepped onto the sidewalk, I became a fancy fish at a dentist's office. There I was, minding my own business (or Ms. Caroline's business, technically, but that's neither here nor there), when I suddenly knew, deep down, that I was not alone. The hairs on my arms stood on end and a growing unease crawled up my spine. I was being watched. I didn't see anyone; not a person, not a movement, nothing out of place. But the image of a colorful fish wouldn't leave my mind and I knew, from that minute on, that I would always politely look the other way when aquariums are forced into my line of vision.

I picked up my pace and power-walked to her car. It would have been faster, maybe, if Ms. Caroline actually did have fabric in her car, but she did not. This realization caused me to search again and again, in the trunk and under the seats until it could not be denied, in any way shape or form, that the car was devoid of fabric.

My skin crawled, like eyeballs caressed my back, traveling up and down my spine. Those eyes never looked away, always watching from somewhere unseen. The hairs on the nape of my neck prickled and poked – I was not alone. I was sure of it.

I scanned the street, but I saw no one. There was nothing new or unusual either, except for the posters stapled to each light pole that read:

NATIONAL SUICIDE PREVENTION LIFELINE
Suicide is a Permanent Solution to a Temporary Problem

I locked her car and ran back to the park, where I stumbled over a root and screamed (I was on edge, after all) and everyone turned, mouths open.

"Sorry." I stood up and folded my arms around my ribs, like appearing smaller would make the past-me quieter and graceful. "I tripped."

Everyone went back to what they were doing except Ms. Caroline, who stepped toward me, eyeing my empty hands. "No fabric?" she asked, disappointed.

"No fabric. I looked everywhere." I tossed the car keys back to her, and she caught them.

"That's too bad."

"Marion!" Delia leaned around the bushes. "Don't you have a bunch of black curtains in your attic? From that one theme night your parents did?"

Finnegan's Galley with blackout curtains and burning candles – of course! I turned to Ms. Caroline.

"Yes, we do. We have lots of curtains. I just have to find them."

She brightened, the gray roots of her part glowing in the sunlight. "That'd be wonderful. You're a lifesaver. A play-saver, I mean." She pointed at me in a rock star kind of way, and I straightened up. "Ask your parents if we can borrow them, and if we can, bring them to me tomorrow, okay?" She squeezed my arm.

"Sure thing," I said. She jogged back to the stage, and I sat down next to Delia, who changed the subject.

"I've been thinking about this museum owner, Marion."

"Who?" Sebastian asked.

"Mr. Sunshine." Delia glared in the general direction of the museum.

"Marv," James said.

"Mr. Sunshine," Delia corrected. "He's hiding something."

"You think he did it, then?" I agreed with her, deep down, though I couldn't pinpoint why, *exactly*. There was a harshness to his face, a weightiness to his gaze, which wasn't proof, but it was a gut feeling. He knew something, but he lied and said he knew nothing.

"I'm certain of it." She crossed her arms and tossed her hair with a shake of her head. "He was creepy."

James pfff'd with his lips, rolling his eyes at the sky. "Plenty of guys are creepy." He pointed at his brother. "Sebastian, for instance." He smiled, self-satisfied, and Sebastian snorted, reaching into Delia's backpack for more snacks.

"Fair enough," I said, as Delia giggled.

"Funny." Sebastian bit off the head of a gummy bear. "Real clever."

I studied Delia's face, hoping for a clue I'd missed. "What makes you so sure he did it?"

"Well, he wasn't exactly open to the homicide theory, was he?" She ate a cheese puff angrily, which was very appropriate. "And he kinda rushed us out. Evidence of a guilty conscience, if you ask me."

"Everyone rushed us out," James said. "Francesca especially. Did you even read her article today? Bizarre."

I groaned. I had seen her article. It was one paragraph devoted to Lily Anderson and her tragic suicide, and five paragraphs devoted to the current self-harm epidemic and our duty as citizens to combat it; she ended the monstrosity with a list of phone numbers for the suicide prevention lifeline, mental health hospitals, local therapists, and local clergy. It was not an article about Lily Anderson. It was an article about an issue. Even if Lily had thrown herself into the ocean, such a rant would be considered impertinent. It was using her like a mascot instead of paying tribute to a woman, or, you know, doing what a newspaper is supposed to do: report the news. The whole thing was disrespectful and pandering to the wrong audience. If I were Violet, I'd be livid.

"Do you think someone is paying Francesca to talk about suicide?" I picked up an oak leaf and split it in half, slowly, like the speed of my thoughts. "I can't think of any other reason for her to write all that stuff." I ripped the leaf into tiny pieces and made it rain over Sebastian's head; he swatted the pieces away.

"That's a good question." James pointed to the sky and snapped his head left and right; his neck popped. "Maybe she's a puppet."

"Maybe she's Marv's puppet. Lily *was* killed by a man," I said. "According to Seagull Sally."

"Right," Delia agreed. "According to the bird."

"We'll prove I can talk to birds one of these days. And then you'll spend your days in grand wonder."

James laughed through a handful of popcorn and Ms. Caroline filled the park with her loud, screechy voice, and we all turned to listen. The village scene was next, and all participants were to participate, and it was time to leave our comfortable hovel filled with snacks to yell insults at Máire Finnegan, the (crazy) woman who could talk to birds.

Chapter Seventeen

After our Saturday Dose of Trials and Tribulations I went to Delia's house. It had been one full week since I saw Lily Anderson's dead body on my bed, and I still had not moved from my makeshift bed on the couch. My normal bed was all fine and dandy in the daytime, but at night, I could still see her outstretched arm and dripping fingers – and so I chose to sleep in the living room. Posey called me a wimp. I called Posey a dingbat and filled her underwear drawer with wet toilet paper. We're even.

All this to say, with it being the one-week anniversary, I didn't exactly want to go home right away. I didn't want to think about Saturday nights and dead bodies. Delia asked me to go over to her house for a quick cuppa (her British vocabulary was expanding) and I agreed. We ran through her front door and headed straight for her bedroom, where she collapsed on her bed, and I perched on the empty space at the edge of her desk.

Delia didn't have any words painted on her bedroom walls. She did, however, have a giant map of North America above her headboard, where she scrupulously kept track of all known Bigfoot sightings. A few areas she circled, as places – this is what she told me, anyway – called "Sasquatch Hotspots." She had a Sasquatch hunting license, given to her by her uncle in Oregon, but she buried it in her desk drawer because "Bigfoot hunting is gross and inhumane," as she once told me, and when I explained to her that it can't possibly be inhumane, because Bigfoot is, by his nature, not human, she kicked me out of her house and I had to write up a formal apology (complete with the definition of inhumane) to Bigfoot and mail it to some place in Colorado. Later we found out the license was homemade, and it's actually illegal to kill Bigfoot in Oregon. "As it should be," Delia had said, and then she wrote a letter to the governor of Texas (where it is legal to hunt and kill Sasquatch).

Delia also had a full-length mirror, and she taped a life-size picture of Blackbeard's face right in the middle, where her head reached when she stood in front of it. She had clothes hanging off the edges of her chest of drawers, and off the bed, and in piles around her laundry hamper. The feeble scent of wet rags wafted from her closet. She was not what I would call a well-kept girl; Ms. Gretchen said she was wild and made of weeds.

Delia sighed unexpectedly (her face was impassive, a

classic sign of churning waters) and got up off the bed and turned off her lights. All the golden twinkles of her glow-in-the-dark stars popped awake and we both sat in silence for a moment, watching them.

Apparently, there would be no tea.

Then Delia sighed again. "My birthday party is going to be the pits, Marion."

Ah, right. The party. "Why?"

"Yet still, no one agrees to be the herald. I am scorned and hated. Put that on my tombstone."

"If all else fails, we can get Max to do it. Just buy him a bag of gummy worms."

"It's not the same. His voice hasn't changed yet."

"Well," I said. "That's true."

As per usual for most kids in our home school group, she was planning a big formal birthday bash, herald and all. Initially she wanted an "only mythical creature dance," but I told her if she did that there'd be fifty million fairies and all the boys would wear shirts that said, "Good Man," and call it a costume. She opted for a masquerade instead.

Delia's door opened and a light streamed across the bed and smothered the beams of the stars.

"How was practice?" Ms. Gretchen leaned against the doorframe and smiled. She waited for an answer, her head framed by her platinum tresses, tapping her fingers (red manicure, red is the color of violence, and her nails were certainly weapons, so I approved) while her eyes traced the piles of dirty clothes that adorned the room.

"It was fine," Delia said.

"It's coming along alright?"

"Yeah." Delia stared at her ceiling, her mouth closed tight, feet twitching impatiently.

"Don't be such a chatterbox."

A painful silence. I usually enjoy a good awkward silence, but this was not good; there was way too much being spoken in the silence, and it was getting loud, so I cleared my throat and ploughed on.

"We are not convinced Lily Anderson killed herself."

Ms. Gretchen turned my way and flicked on the light. "Why, hello, Marion."

"Good evening, Ms. Gretchen."

She opened the door wider. "Tell me more."

"It's a little convenient, right? Jumped in the sea during a hurricane. No one's asking questions. Now the whole town is prevention-crazed."

"It is suspicious." She tapped her chin and closed her eyes. Ms. Gretchen was once co-anchor of our local news channel (with Pat Blakeman, I remember he came to a Christmas party at Delia's house once, I spent the night eating cranberry sauce and counting the number of times he said "sure, sure," which was a rather solid seventy-eight) and her inner journalist was showing. "I was just thinking about that today, actually. I read that article. Feels like propaganda, doesn't it?"

"Yes!" I raised my hands and stretched my fingers, reaching for the world. "Someone gets it."

Delia just rolled her eyes.

"You know what?" Ms. Gretchen strolled over to the bed and sat at the foot of it. She grabbed Delia's ankles and rolled her feet back and forth. "I still have a friend at the news station. I bet she might have a few things to share if I called her. Maybe she'd be willing to look into things if I batted my eyes."

"She won't be able to see your eyes, if you're calling her."

"You know what I mean, Cordelia Rose."

"I think it's grand," I said. The concept of professional help, to know concretely if I was crazy or sane, was a wonderful thing – but it also sent fear into the tips of my toes. But nothing fear based is truth based, as Ms. Caroline would say, so I gritted my teeth and smiled.

"Positively brilliant," Delia agreed, and I knew she wasn't as sarcastic as she was trying to sound.

"I'll make you a deal!" Ms. Gretchen held out her palms, so giddy that she didn't know what to do with herself. "You take the speech class, Cordelia Rose, and I will help you to the best of my ability. I'll pull strings, call connections, the works. I'll even help you with your fairytale hunts."

"They're not fairytales, they're documented creature sightings."

"Right. I'll help you with your creature sightings."

Delia groaned. "But you don't believe in it. It's a passion project, Mom."

"It's a one-time offer. The best you'll get."

Delia groaned again, but this time she said, "Fine," the

words landing on her tongue and squeezing through her teeth like lemon juice.

"It's a deal!" Ms. Gretchen checked her watch. "I'll call her in a little while. She's always busy this time of night. I need to call her anyway, she had some boyfriend that turned out to be a loser." She looked from me to her daughter and grinned with her teeth. "But maybe you're too young for this."

"Not too young," Delia corrected. "But too uncomfortable, yes."

Ms. Gretchen swatted playfully at Delia's shins and strolled out of the room.

I left for my house soon after by way of the waterfront, pausing briefly to gaze out over the water. The sea was restless. It must have been very distressing to spit out a murdered body, and then have that murdered body be ignored. Perhaps that is the real reason for tidal waves.

"Oh. It's you again."

A woman's voice, addressing me in the darkness. I followed the sound and there she was, Seagull Sally, perched on the retaining wall, regarding me with what appeared to be mild amusement. Her head was tipped to the side, and her beak was wide open.

I stopped, hands on my hips. "It is me. And it's you."

"I hear you're still asking about that human." Seagull Sally (or her friend, perhaps) was a sight for sore eyes, my first clue, my first confidante. I sat next to her on the wall, feet dangling above the waves, and I smiled.

"I am, indeed. Have you remembered anything else?"

"Not a thing," she answered. "I really didn't get a good look." Her feathers were clean and bright in the flash of the lighthouse. She hopped closer and stretched her wings, and the tips brushed against my forearm. My heart warmed, knowing she felt comfortable enough to be so close.

"Do you remember what he looked like?"

"Of course not. He was a human. Completely nondescript." She scanned my body from head to toe, nodding to herself like she proved her point. I coughed, drawing her attention away from my figure, and offered a different idea.

"What if I brought you pictures? Like, pictures of several different men? Could you identify him?"

She cocked her head. "What's a picture?"

It was a fair question, but part of me wanted to roll my eyes. Working with birds was not the fairytale dream I wanted it to be – princesses must have had a harder time of it than movies suggest. I held out my hand to shape an example, but Sally pepped up, excited for food, so I put my hand away and tried again.

"It's a flat, small copy of a face." I had to raise my voice to be heard over the wind and waves. "Maybe you'll recognize him in a picture."

"Oh. Honestly, I'm not the best at recognizing human faces. And I didn't see him clearly, anyway. I can't tell you what he looked like. I can only tell it's you because I've talked to you before. And because of that shiny on your finger." I looked at my black sapphire, gleaming in the flash of the lighthouse. "And because you're distinctly female. I heard you give tokens?"

"I'm all out of tokens," I said, "but I may have food." I searched my pockets (nothing) the cuffs of my jeans (nothing), and finally found one stray popped corn tangled in the ribbons on the side of my tunic (green). "Here." I held it up between my fingers. "But you can only get it if you tell me something useful."

"I don't know anything else." Seagull Sally puffed her chest and squawked, offended that I would require something of her. "I've told you all I know, but –" She stopped herself and turned around. "Never mind."

"What?"

She gazed at the horizon, her words getting faster and louder as she spoke into the night sky. "I might know someone else who saw something. He was closer. But he is a cad, he was untrue to me – "

"Yes, he left you for another bird."

She nodded. "Precisely."

"Maybe you can ask him to talk to me, though?" I leaned down to catch her at eye level, and she faced me, bouncing from side to side.

"Maybe." She eyed my hand. "If you give me food, I'll think about it."

I held out my palm and she took the popcorn and flew away without a *goodbye*, or a *thank you*, or a *nice to see you again* (just like a bird). So I sat on the retaining wall alone, staring out into the darkness, half expecting to see her return by the light of the lighthouse. I waited until it was clear she wasn't coming back, and then I went home, following the edge of the water so I could listen to the waves clash and pulse.

I entered through the kitchen (Dad had filled in the holes in the yard, customers are generally stupid and fall into holes, so it needed to be done) and was struck by a yellow gleam, a smile, and various sensations of slime and grime – it was the creepy man from Waffle Madness.

I stopped in my tracks. He smiled at me, all innocent like, and I pressed my lips together to keep from spitting in his face. He sat with my parents at the big kitchen island, a stainless-steel wonder reserved for cutting vegetables and sorting table wear. It would need to be disinfected later.

"Hi, there," he said, raising his fingertips as a greeting. His fingers were beefy and freckled, and he'd bitten his nails to the quick. His fingerprints fogged the stainless steel. He couldn't even be bothered to raise his whole hand. Lazy coward.

"Hello...there." I didn't take my eyes off him until Mom cleared her throat.

"Marion, this is Leo. He gave us the loan on the house."

Her face revealed a mingling of worry and hope; they must have been discussing the terms, hoping for a change of heart, but that man had a heart of darkness that even Conrad couldn't comprehend. By the way he smiled at Fern – hungrily, like a fox spotting an abandoned egg – he would be capable of demanding (with delight) the title of the house at a moment's whim. His smile was selfish, and gleeful, and how could he be anything else with my own home? Finney shivered. I pressed my feet firmly on the floor to help her steady herself, and my roots grew deep. He wouldn't take her. He couldn't.

Mom's head scarf slipped a little, and she caught it before it slipped past her ears. Her fingers trembling, she dragged it back in place, smoothing the stray hairs underneath. She sat unnervingly close to Dad, who leaned over the table, all slumped and powerless looking. The paperwork sat between them. Leo wore a suit and tie, and his red hair was slicked back, like he wanted to look like he had money. The stench of trying too hard filled my nostrils and I sneezed.

"Bless you," he said, smiling. The yellow tint of his teeth winked at me and I sniffed.

"I didn't know you loaned the money."

His smile broadened, and he raised an eyebrow. "I was happy to help." He searched me up and down, trying to figure out if he knew me – but he did not. I knew him, though, and I faced him like we were old enemies.

Happy, indeed. No one doubted he was happy – happy to make demands, happy to take the house, happy to upend our lives forever. Finney hugged me and it gave me a burst of courage. "Had any waffles lately?"

His eyes narrowed and his forehead furrowed as he tried to make sense of my question and Mom hissed, "Marion." She didn't know why I had asked, but her motherly instincts told her it was a question born in rudeness, and I couldn't deny it.

I faked a smile. "If you were happy to help, why are you so desperate to call in this loan?"

"Marion," Dad warned, sitting up straight.

"No, no, it's okay, George." Leo lifted his whole hand in the air this time, to reassure my dad. "It always comes down to family, doesn't it? It's a typical story, actually. A loved one is faced with a problem, and I can help if I, you know, shuffle my resources." He grabbed the papers as his eyes stayed on me, suspicious. "You would do the same, I think."

I dipped my head as a sort of bow. Mom's pointed silence told me to leave, and if I were in a castle, I would have curtsied and tossed my skirts as I retreated down the corridor. But I was not in a castle, only my childhood home, which urged me on, so I simply turned and left for my room to stare at my mind map, turning over the vision of Leo in my mind.

Suit. Tie. Smile. Money.

He was trouble, but there was nothing I could do about it. If there's one thing I've learned in life, it's that depending on the mercy of a scoundrel will get you stuck in an oubliette, and fast.

My mind map told me nothing, and I spent more time staring at BY NATURE, MEN LOVE NEWFANGLED-NESS than at the actual clues. Chaucer always seemed to know what to say. I always seemed to live in limbo, living between questions and revelations, between the changing of tides. No wonder I couldn't make sense of anything – all the clues kept getting washed out to sea.

When I finally descended the stairs to go to bed, Posey was sitting on the couch arm, knees to her chin, looking pensive.

"Did you meet Creepy Leo?" I asked.

"No. Who?"

I gestured to Dad's office, where the door was shut tight, the light squeezing through the gaps. "The guy who's forcing us to sell the house."

She hugged her knees tighter, wiggling her bare toes. "Oh. No, I was upstairs reading, which you would have noticed, if you weren't so in love with that map." She arched an eyebrow. "Staying here tonight?"

"Yup."

"Coward."

"Takes one to know one."

She stuck out her tongue and left for our room, but turned around at the foot of the stairs, one hand on the railing.

"Did James say anything about me?" she asked, playing with the collar of her nightshirt.

"No. Why would he say anything about you?"

She shrugged. "I made the popcorn."

I watched her back as she climbed the stairs, bent over and dragging her feet. There was a lot about Posey I had yet to learn, and if I ever got the chance, I would start with her bizarre need to microwave snack foods and surreptitiously ask about their reception twelve hours later.

I unfolded the blankets for my couch bed and Mom grabbed the opposite sides, helping me to drape the mattress in silence. I watched her as she tucked one corner and paused.

"Marion," she said, not unlike my brother, which made me wary. "You should know, we're entertaining Doug's offer to buy the house."

"Oh," I said, quite brilliantly (to quote Delia). Mom's face was detached. Not literally, of course; it was very much attached to her body, but her expressions were void, and standard. Usually her expressions are vibrant, like her head scarf, sometimes too loud and alarming. I sucked in a breath. She fluffed my pillow.

"Leo is seizing the house unless we make a plan to get the money to him."

"So you're selling the house. Just like that, then?"

She massaged her temples, readjusting her scarf behind her ears. Then she challenged me head on, hands on her hips. "The loan is for less than the house is worth. If we sell, we will have some money to start over. If he takes the house, what then? Do you have any other ideas?"

I hugged my pillow to my chest, speaking into the feathers. "I can't imagine not living next to Delia."

"That's hard," Mom agreed. "But you have Posey."

"Posey is hardly a consolation."

"Marion." She spoke like my brother again.

"Yes?"

"Be civil."

"I will certainly try."

But a very uncivil knock bellowed from the front door. It was frantic and angry, and if I was not mistaken, sounded very much the sharp wallops of the Grim Reaper. I jumped and Mom ran to the door, first peeking out and then opening it wide to let in Delia, who was red-faced and out of breath.

"Marion," she said, her frizz sticking up straight and tall above her head – these people kept attacking me with my own name. I crossed my arms over my heart as a shield. Delia didn't miss a beat. "Mom called her friend."

"And?"

"And, and, AND everything is censored. CENSORED, Marion! They can only refer to it as a suicide! Someone is hushing them up! We were right!" She spread out her arms and gasped the last words. "Someone is silencing the truth!"

Chapter Eighteen

I woke up early on Sunday and couldn't fall back asleep. The living room was dark, and my dreams still danced before my eyes. I dreamt of Pat Blakeman, and he followed me around saying "sure, sure," constantly, even when I declared Lily Anderson was murdered by a pod of dolphins and a plate of spaghetti. But then I truly woke up, and reality came at me like a truck, and I was left flattened on my bed, wondering about the ramifications of corrupt media. Not that it was surprising, really, just disappointing, like when my parents say, "We're not angry, we're just disappointed," and something in their eyes makes me wonder if maybe they expected nothing else in the first place. In this case, I expected nothing less than public manipulation from the local media, as that's exactly what the WNYT News You Trust was doing. I knew it all along. They were hiding a crime.

Definitely not news I trusted.

It wasn't even news I could watch anymore. It was too infuriating.

Anyway, I couldn't go back to sleep. Maybe I should have dropped it, resigned myself to madness. Maybe I should have realized it was too big for me to handle, but something gnawed at the pit of my stomach, and I couldn't let it go.

Then my mind wandered to Violet, and her heartbroken tears on the back porch of that A-framed house.

I got out of bed and tiptoed to my room, where I slowly opened the door, peeking through the crack to make sure I wasn't waking up Posey. Silly worry. Posey is the world's deepest sleeper. She lay on her stomach, one leg fully off the bed, mouth wide open. I closed the door and beheld my mind map.

I hadn't done anything to it yet. I was waiting for a genius revelation that I could pin along with everything else, but nothing came.

I wrote *WNYT News Cover Up* on an index card and pinned it to the side of Lily Anderson. Then, I wrote *Talk to Ms. Gretchen's friend* on another index card and pinned it to the side. I stood back to admire it; it was growing. Soon I could add string and sticky notes, like in the detective shows, but that would mean I'd have to order takeout and drink stale coffee, and I didn't want to do either of those things. I dropped that idea.

In a stroke of genius (it happens sometimes) I wrote, *Who Owns WNYT News?* and pinned it under *Talk to Ms. Gretchen's friend.*

"Now we're getting somewhere," I said to myself.

It is imperative, after conceiving a great idea, to eat a hearty meal. So, I gamboled to the kitchen, where I heard something pattering around in miserable silence. It was Dad, but when I entered the room, he was no longer pattering but standing at the kitchen sink, eyes locked on a page of the newspaper he had clearly been scanning a moment before – only to see something that caused everything to stop. Except for Max, who fought circles around him, spatula out like a sword, humming something that sounded like cannons and bees and earthquakes.

"What is it?" I asked. Dad looked up, his eyes filled with frowns and melting gelatin (figuratively, of course). They were the same eyes he had back when Posey's pet rabbit died, and he was the first to notice. "Dad?"

He looked down at the paper again, and with one slow, smooth motion, handed it to me. I scanned the page, and my eyes landed on one particular headline:

FUMBLING FURY AT FINNEGAN'S GALLEY
By Francesca Lovely

I went on to read:

Take my advice and steer clear of this dumpster fire of an establishment, and disaster of a waitress, who has yet to learn how to function as a human being.

Then she called the food *a semblance of civil war rations*, and the waitress *a waif of a girl with wildness in her eyes*, who was, naturally, me. She said she visited on Monday. I just happened to be working that day, and I do recall that I had been struck by a brilliant theory connecting trident-shaped pins to visions of the future-predicting variety, and the idea spangled in my eyes, as I am often told ideas do. I think I might have spilled spaghetti on her lap. That's why I had recognized her when we talked to her: I had seen her before. Dad stared at me. I handed the paper back to him.

"Brilliant," I said, like the British (Delia would be proud).

"This won't help things." He dropped the paper on the counter, rubbing at his morning stubble.

A dull pain sprouted in the pit of my stomach, the kind that burrows deep and says *I'm here until the day you die.* I tried to ignore it, but one glance at the paper made my insides ache like the day after eating discounted gas station sushi. Dad was right: that article certainly would not help things. In fact, it propelled Finnegan's Galley to its demise, lighting a fire over the pit of Things To Do To Save The House. The ache in my stomach traveled to my fingertips, which trembled so much I buried them in my armpits.

"I'm sorry, Dad."

He shook his head and rubbed his messy hair, but he didn't meet my eyes, only turned toward the door as he mumbled, "You didn't do anything wrong," and left the kitchen, Max at his heels. I sat on the kitchen floor and fought back tears.

I was, single handedly, ruining the reputation of the business, eliminating options to do anything besides sell the house. I laid my hands flat on the tiles and pressed my bare feet onto the floor, feeling my roots grow deeper, through the foundation and into the earth. I leaned onto the wall and Finney leaned back into me, and I took a deep breath, trying to expel the words of the article that ran circles in my brain.

All morning the paper passed from person to person. I read the article three times. Mom read it at least seven times while Max reenacted everything, from my sudden space-out to The Great Spilling of Spaghetti. Grandma read the article upside down and expressed outrage with every breath. Posey called me "Waif" repeatedly, until I hit her over the head with the newspaper and gave her a paper cut above her left eyebrow.

Before we left for church, I ripped out the article and stuffed it in the pockets of my skirt (I highly recommend pocketed skirts), determined to carry it with me everywhere, to remind myself that I had a mortal enemy. That one cafeteria lady and those guys who made pig noises at Amelia were now second place.

Delia sat down next to me in church and skipped the pleasantries. "I read that article."

I rolled my eyes and fell forward onto my knees. "The woman breathes fire and titters with the goblins of hell."

"I wouldn't go that far. It was bad, though."

I groaned into the space between us, my left cheek

pressed against my knee. "It doesn't help anything. They were already talking about selling the place. Now this."

Delia's eyes exploded in my face. Not literally. They just grew really wide and bright, so bright they were almost sharp, and I couldn't look at them.

"Do you think – "

"We're doomed," I answered. Then I breathed, "And it's all my fault."

We found The Gatekeepers after church. The more I could learn about Francesca, the better. I had an enemy. It was time to get to know her, and The Gatekeepers knew everyone in Lady's Madness – if they could remember. They saw me coming and their faces lit up and they waved in unison, like three old, leathery sirens.

"How goes it, little ladies?" Buck asked, hand in the air as a greeting.

We stopped in front of them, our backs to the water (a dangerous thing to do, really, as the water cannot be trusted) and greeted them loudly, so as to be heard over the wind and waves. "Just fine, thank you. And you?"

"Grand, just grand. My name is Buck." He gestured to the others. "They are Buzz and Clyde."

I really tried not to sigh. I really did. But something escaped anyway.

"Do I know you?" Clyde asked.

"We've talked before." I held out my hand. "My name is Marion."

Buck accepted my handshake, his gaze clouded with memories. "Marion. I knew a Marion once."

"I have a question for you." Call me impatient, but I wanted to spend exactly zero minutes having a conversation I've had twice before. "Do you know Francesca Lovely?"

"Frannie!" Buck yelled, far more excited about the question than seemed necessary. "Of course I know Frannie. One of the oldest families in town."

Something out of the corner of my eye stirred and I turned – and saw nothing but the lazy Sunday afternoon streets. The clouds parted and the sun blazed directly into my eyes. I blinked and gave my attention to Buck, who smiled at me.

"Do you know her deepest fears, then?" I asked.

"Well." Buck rubbed his chin like he was thinking about it, when clearly he either knew or he didn't, and I was impatient for the answer. "I saw her scream at a snake once."

He went on for some time about the history of the Lovelys and how his family knew them back in the day, and how his great granddaddy was a fisherman and the Lovelys had some sort of merchant business and I don't remember much else, because I was busy thinking about how to leave the conversation. Then he said something interesting.

"Then one day, the town ran the business into the ground. Out of spite, it seemed. Not sure who was behind it, but the poor Lovelys – they never made a cent again. Closed up shop. Only Francesca remains. Poor girl. Only one left of her family. Her grandpa died of heartbreak, I'll bet my life on it. Her dad left town, died somewhere in the city from who knows what. Sad thing. But they kept the house."

"You don't know why the business went under?" The words *dumpster fire of an establishment* danced around me, and I kicked them away to hear him the better.

Buck shook his head. "I only know that one day, the whole town up and decided they hated them. Don't know why. It's like someone bribed every person who had a voice 'round here."

"Or blackmailed 'em," Clyde added, his face unchanging.

"When did this happen?"

"Oh, been a few years now. Not too long."

I hadn't heard about any of this before, but then again I glaze over when others talk about town affairs, my mind usually slipping to gnomes and where Grandma would chase one next. Francesca's family business had been bullied and beaten down – that had to mean something. But how dare she! How dare she turn around and bully *me*, and *my* family! How dare she attack our family business, when she knew so very well the devastating consequences of small-town harassment.

I thanked The Gatekeepers, then Delia and I walked up Big Oak Street until we found the house with pillars and shutters and a porch swing, and a plaque by the front door which read, *Lovely House, circa 1722.*

The windows were closed and dark. Caution replaced my rage, and Delia, wanting to get it over with and leave, asked, "What do we do?"

It was a fair question, really, but I didn't have an answer.

"Leave a note?" she suggested, but the front door opened, and Francesca Lovely frowned at us, darkness in her gaze. Outlined by the sun, she was a force of shadow and dazzle and my eyes hurt to look at her, but I still glared: Francesca Lovely, my arch enemy, in the flesh.

My stomach burned and my fingers shook as I slowly walked to her porch, Delia whispering "What are you doing?" behind me. Francesca's hair, the color of wet straw, was a curly poof around her head and her dark, beady eyes caught me staring and stared right back.

"The waif of a girl with wildness in her eyes has come to speak to you," I said.

She squinted. It was the kind of squint that had nothing to do with her eyesight, and everything to do with the physical act of trying to look like she was making an effort, like she was pulling her thoughts together. She looked both ways, then waved us in. "Come in."

We stepped into her house (it smelled like cedar and sun-soaked cotton) and we passed her purse sitting by the front door, on which a trident-shaped pin gleamed and glimmered. I elbowed Delia and nodded toward it. *Like the bird said*, I mouthed.

"Look." Francesca disappeared down a narrow hallway,

expecting us to follow. "I didn't want to write that about your restaurant. I really didn't."

She turned into the living room and sat down, waving for us to do the same. The room was sparse. There was a couch, two chairs, and a coffee table. A few family portraits hung on the walls, and it was so clean that the furniture looked cold.

Francesca was dressed to leave her house; she wore heels, and her keys were in her hands. She jingled them nervously, scanning the room like we might be overheard. Beads of sweat covered her forehead, and her breath was shallow and labored. I considered reminding her that we were in her house, and she should therefore feel safe, but she finished her thought.

"You should stop snooping. I'm worried about you."

I had no interest in her concern, and no time for her mind games. "Why'd you write such a bad review?"

Her mouthed twitched, and her eyes darted all over the place, barely landing on mine before they skipped to the other side of the room. "I'm sorry about all this. You're a sweet kid."

"Indeed." I chuckled to myself. Yes, I am all sunshine and rainbows and the soft underbelly of a chinchilla. "That's one way to put it."

"Just tell us what's going on, before we sick the birds on you." Delia extended her legs to sit like a trucker, her patience slipping out of her with every second lost. That's the thing about Delia: first, she's hesitant, then she's committed. I'm the opposite. I tend to dive into things headfirst, then lose my steam when it's too late. Together, we make a good team.

Delia challenged Francesca with a tilt of her chin, and Francesca scrunched her forehead, *what birds* written on her face. But she cleared her throat and went on.

"I need to leave, I'm sorry. I, uh, forgot I had an appointment. And I'm sorry about the review, but I can't control everything, can I?" There was something so straightforward, so honest about her eyes, that I (unfortunately) believed her. My righteous indignation, the pent-up fire behind my ribs, sizzled and shrank. There was someone else, then. Someone else deserved my wrath. She watched the door, worrying about something she wouldn't name.

"Right," I said, my resolve slipping away.

Her eyes focused on me again. "What?"

"Right," I repeated, then I nodded toward the door. "What kind of pin is on your purse, anyway?"

She hesitated. "Sorority," she lied, and she showed us out.

A lie is better than a half-truth, and almost as good as the truth. We knew the pin definitely *was* a secret, and we knew what she wanted us to think, even if we didn't know the truth.

I turned to Delia as Francesca drove away. "That pin is the crux of everything."

Delia and I went to my house to brainstorm. Dad was busy filling in holes (more appeared while we were at church) while Max jumped in them, declaring how deep they were in relation to his anatomy ("This one goes up to my chin! Marion! It goes up to my chin!"). Delia and I went to my room, where we were until I got a phone call from Sebastian.

"I'm in trouble, Marion, and Dad can't know. Got it?"

"Sure, Sebastian." I rolled my eyes at Delia. He could be a drama queen sometimes.

"Look, Fern is part of this, umm, club, and I uh...I lost some money. Like, James covered most of it, but I still need seventy-five dollars. You have that, right? In your savings?"

"Sebastian, you idiot supreme burrito deluxe. I only have fifty."

"Okay, well, I'll pay you back, promise – Maybe uh, maybe ask Delia if she'll contribute?" – Delia shook her head at me – "and come to the alley behind the newspaper, next to the graveyard. Just stand on the corner. Make sure no one's following you, okay? Fern will meet you."

A drama queen, as ever. Or perhaps it was some sort of weird joke. "You want me to meet someone in an alleyway beside a cemetery?"

"It's not as crazy as it sounds, trust me. Fern will meet you."

He hung up. I grumbled and turned to Delia, who closed her eyes.

"Don't you dare," she said.

"Aren't you a little bit curious?"

"Fine, be curious, but don't give him money."

I opened the top drawer of my dresser, rummaged around until I felt that one particular fuzzy sock, and dragged fifty dollars from it. "He'll pay me back, with interest, or I'll feed him to the birds."

"I'll hold you to that," Delia said. She took out her map from her back pocket. "There's a pixie sighting around the museum, anyway."

<hr>

We stood on the corner by the alley, hands in our pockets.

"This is how we die," Delia muttered. She had changed from her typical church skirt and converses into wide-leg jeans with the occasional chain and a t-shirt that read THE NATIONAL FOUNDATION FOR THE PRESERVATION OF THE JACKALOPE encircling a very official-looking crest of a jackalope overlapping a crossed staff and stalk of wheat. "And don't worry, I left a note in my bed so they'll know why we were here, and who we met."

I didn't have anything to say to that. I wasn't particularly worried that Sebastian lured us there to die, and besides, I had walked down the alley and through the graveyard countless times, and the only sinister thing I'd spotted was a rancid chunk of meat that had missed the dumpster and fell to the ground. It was, at that time, being eaten by a mischief of rats. The rats were pretty cute, actually. It was the rancid meat that looked sinister.

"How long do we stand here?" Delia asked, crossing her arms. Her impatience only spurred me on to remind her that she did not have to come with me in the first place; she scowled. "Like I would leave you to meet some public schooler in a back alleyway, alone." She turned her back on me. "Really, Marion."

I gathered all the reasons why the situation was perfectly safe, and opened my mouth to list them in order of magnitude, when we heard –

"Ah, good." Fern ambled toward us, her face obscured by the tilt of her hoodie, zipped up to her throat. Under it, she wore a dress. We were so busy bickering neither of us had seen her coming. "You're here. You got the money?"

"Yeah." I pulled out my wad of cash. It looked impressive, but really it was only impressive because a wad of fifty ones achieves a level of volume that is somewhat misleading. Fern eyed it.

"That's a lot of ones."

"You can count it." I punched it into her hands.

"No need," she said, "I trust you." She placed it carefully into her crossbody bag, and my eyes, once again, were drawn to the small, trident pin on the outside pocket. I nodded to it.

"That pin, it's not a school club, is it?"

When her mouth wasn't busy spreading itself across her head, it hung on her face like a kind of sad upside-down hammock, too stretched out to bounce back. She looked at me like that for a moment, and then smiled again, so big that the edges of her lips passed her teeth, and I could see the inside of her cheeks. Those teeth were pearly white, and those gums a nice shade of pink, I'll give her that much.

"Maybe someday you'll know."

She retreated back down the alley, knocked on the back door to one of the shops, and disappeared inside. Delia nudged me.

"Let's go home." She looked around. "I feel like someone is watching us."

"It's just the graveyard," I assured her. "Those people get bored sometimes. You would too, if you were dead."

"Dead people don't watch the living, Marion." She took the lead with her back straight and incredulous, peering at the graveyard out of the corner of her eye.

"Whatever you say, Delia," I said, and followed her home.

Chapter Nineteen

We patrolled the waterfront that night. We mostly talked about Sebastian and the mysterious scrape he found himself in – although it wasn't all that mysterious. Obviously he lost a bet, but we still hadn't heard any details about whatever bet he placed and what exactly Fern had to do with the whole thing. The more we talked about it, the more Delia seemed particularly jumpy, so we gradually grew silent; plus, the lighthouse on Grackle Island kept flashing his light at us like we were fugitives. Delia pulled out her map (her cape had pockets) and waited until the next flash of light.

"There was a pixie sighting here." She tapped a dot on the map.

"Our mission awaits," I said, turning toward Market Street. We had no real plan for this patrol (we never do) so checking out pixie sightings was as good as anything, especially because we forgot to do it earlier, what with all the excitement of vaguely clandestine meetings in back alley-ways. We veered toward the museum and I stopped abruptly when I heard,

"You! Hoo! Hoo hoo!"

I spun around, my cape flaring. "Did you hear that?"

Delia faced me, her map close against her chest. "Hear what?" Her voice was taut, stretched thin like harp strings, and one wrong pluck from me would send her snapping.

"You! Hoo! Hoo hoo!"

"I've been summoned," I said, and Delia rolled her eyes. I lifted my head and twirled, scanning the dark shadows of the downtown rooftops and canopies of city sidewalk trees. Two large, dark eyes peered down at me.

"You! Hoo! Hoo hoo!"

I froze. "It's an owl." I pointed, and Delia followed my direction.

"Pretty," she said.

The owl stared at us, still as a statue, and the night air weighed on us like an enchantment.

"Did you summon me?" I asked, meeting his gaze. He sat in a Dogwood tree planted along Market Street. On the trunk was stapled a poster that said CHOOSE LIFE and under it, the number for the National Suicide Prevention Lifeline. Bird poop dripped down it in one long, white line. The streets were deserted, and it was so silent, I could hear the wind in the owl's feathers. He was a barred owl. And it was definitely a he, I could tell by the audacious clutch of his talons.

"Yes," he answered, his brown and white feathers a haze of gray in the night. His neck puffed slightly with each syllable. "I've heard of your magic from far and wide."

"My magic?" I cleared my throat. "Right. My magic."

"I didn't believe it," the owl said. "But I wanted to try for myself."

"All the wisest do the same."

The night wind rustled my hair, and the owl turned his head, his senses catching every movement around him (are owls real, or are they sprinkles of fairy dust with talons and beaks?).

"Few humans speak the tongue of the winged creatures. You are the only one, in fact, that I know."

I nodded. "Me too."

"How did you come by such magic? Is it your birth right?"

"Actually" – I held up my left hand – "I think it's this ring."

"A magic ring?" He blinked, slowly. His eyes were so dark, they rivaled the night sky. "How fascinating."

"It only works on my hand." I motioned to Delia, who watched me with her mouth open and eyes harsh with cynicism. A light breeze skittered past us and brushed her thoughts into mine; they were heavy and littered with questions, so I shook them out and they fell to the ground, absorbed by cobblestones and darkness. "It doesn't work for her."

"Doubly interesting," the owl agreed.

"The sea gave it to me."

"Ah, the sea." He dipped his head and hooted, swallowing me with his gaze. "The sea gives and takes, in equal measure."

"Does it though?" I paused to listen to the waves crash against the retaining wall. They were angry, desperate waves. Hungry waves. "It sure does take a lot."

"Perhaps you are not perceiving equally," the owl said.

"Perhaps."

He fluffed his feathers, reaching out with his long, elegant wings –

"What's your name?" I screeched, catching his attention before he could fly away. He stopped, wings out, and stared at me.

"My name is Moonlight," he answered. "Like my father before me."

I raised to my tippy toes, hoping a closer look would open up a world of intimacies and revelations, in the way I always hope for friendship when I am close to a bird. There's something special about a bird, something otherworldly. "Ah, well, Moonlight, may I ask you a question?"

He said not a word, only lowered his wings and stared at me with his cavernous, hungry eyes.

"Please?"

"You may ask, I may not answer."

I took a deep breath. He waited, shadows spinning around him, his eyes round and calm.

"Do you know who killed that woman? The woman who fell into the sea?"

"The woman the sea spat out?"

"Yes!" The excitement pulsed in my veins – he might know something! "The woman the sea spat out!"

"I might." Moonlight swiveled his head. "If I had a reason to talk."

"A reason?"

He hooted again, like it was my answer. I puffed my cheeks and let out my breath in one smooth stream, until Delia whispered into my ear,

"What's happening?"

I jumped. I'd forgotten she was there. "The owl's name is Moonlight," I whispered back, leaning into her. "He heard I could speak to birds and wanted to see for himself. I asked if he knows anything about Lily Anderson – "

"Yes, I know, I can understand *you*."

" – and he said 'if I had a reason to talk.'"

Delia furrowed her brow. "Like he wants you to pay him?"

"It would seem so." I turned back to Moonlight. "What would give you a reason, then?"

"Anything precious." The leaves of the Dogwood tree fluttered around him, but he was still, perfectly still, and perfectly serene. "Anything grand."

"Well..." My fingers wound around the items in my pocket. I pulled them out and examined each one in the darkness, praying for something shiny. "Would you take..."

and then I noticed a pottery bit in my palm, taken from the shore after the hurricane. "This precious piece of pottery?"

He swooshed, and in a rush of wind and feathers, grabbed the token with his talons and I fell back onto the sidewalk, out of breath. It had happened so fast, like a storm of wings and pointy things.

"It is sufficient," he said, settling back onto the branch. "What would you like to know?"

"Who killed her?" I struggled to get back on my feet; Delia had to grab my hand and hoist me up. "Can you describe him?"

"I do not know who he is, but I see him often, here, coming and going."

I glanced behind me. The windows of the Lady's Madness Maritime Museum looked back at me, black and full of secrets.

"His feathers are like flames. That's what I remember."

I turned to Delia. "At the museum a lot. 'His feathers are like flames.' Who do we know who has red skin?"

Her lips pressed together in a knowing, solemn kind of way. "Marv."

"Marv," I echoed, from the pit of my stomach. I turned back to Moonlight. "Do you know why? Do you know how?"

"I do not know the ways of the human," he answered. "I do not know why he killed. He did not eat her. She did not want to eat him. But he hit her, and threw her into the sea. And then the sea gave her back."

"And was he alone – "

But as the word *alone* left my lips, he spread his wings and glided past us into the darkness. I watched him fly away, one hand on the edge of Delia's cape. We stood in silence, the wake of his presence settling like sparkles on our skin. I shivered, and turning to Delia I breathed out slowly,

"So do you believe me now?"

She wouldn't look at me, her body rigid as she pulled out her map.

"The sighting was here," she said. "But there's nothing. Let's go home."

She stepped away, but something else moved in the shadows across the street – I couldn't see much in the dark, but the pink cotton and feathered mess told me it must have been a pair of pajamas and a feathered hat, and when those things are together, you can bet your bottom dollar my Grandma is there, too. I grabbed Delia's arm.

"Grandma."

"Really?" She scanned the street. "Where?"

"On the other side of that bench." I nodded toward it. "Near the waterfront."

We scampered across the street and came face to face with a hobbling Grandma (why didn't she ever take her walker on her escapades?) and, to my surprise, Max. Max was by her side, unimpressed, no life in his eyes.

"Grandma!" I took her arm and she smiled. "What are you doing out here?"

Grandma pressed down on the top of her hat as if to steady herself. "Why, I was taking pictures."

But she had no camera, and Max stood staring, his eyes glazed over like a zombie. "Max?" I said, gently, and Delia leaned close to his face, waving in front of his eyes.

"I think he's sleep walking, Marion," she said.

"Oh, right," I sighed, taking note of the spatula in his hands. "Then you take his arm and I'll take Grandma's – be careful not to wake him, he gets violent." I found that out the hard way, one night around Christmas, when I woke him up and he freaked out so hard I fell back into the Christmas tree. It took a solid twenty-four hours to pick all the Norway spruce needles out of my hair.

"Good thing you're here, Marion," Grandma said as she tottered beside me. "We were doomed."

"Doomed?" Grandma tripped over a cobblestone and I squeezed her closer to me to keep her from falling. "What do you mean?"

"What?" She inspected me through the gaps of her feathers, which were limp from the humidity and falling over her eyes. "Did I say something?"

"Never mind, Grandma." I grinned at Delia, who walked side by side with sleepy Max, unamused. She didn't smile, only narrowed her eyes, and set one gentle hand on Max's shoulder. I took the hint. "Let's go home."

We escorted Grandma home and then Delia went back to her house, tired of alleyways and secret meetings and ready for what she called "an evening spent exploring the world's truths" which meant she was going to watch a documentary on Bigfoot. Mom put both Grandma and Max to bed (after freaking out about not knowing they were gone) and I went to Posey, who sat at the kitchen table making her masquerade mask for Delia's party. I sat beside her to make mine too.

I sized up the tools: plain masks from the dollar store, sequins, glue, glitter, glitter glue, feathers, fake greenery, and ribbons (Mom's craft closet had been pillaged). Posey was gluing something pink to the edges of her mask. I grabbed a handful of sequins.

"These will do," I said to myself.

Posey sighed, and the ends of her bangs blew upward. "How goes the investigation?"

The sequins winked at me audaciously, and I rummaged through them, separating the pinks from the blues. "It was Marv," I said. "An owl told me."

"Right."

I looked up. "You don't believe me?"

"I don't believe owls. Notorious liars." She kept her eyes on her project, her fingers nimbly placing the trimming along a trail of hot glue.

I hmmm'd in my throat, going for the glue gun before she could pick it up again. Crafting is a quick, clever business, best suited for the heartless. I pointed it at her. "You would say something like that."

"That's because unlike you, I only say sensible things." She looked at me, her head down, her eyes searing my flesh behind thick, stocky eyelashes. "I don't talk to birds."

"Too bad for you," I said, gluing a sequin to my mask. "It's really quite exhilarating."

"Exhilarating, maybe. Crazy, definitely."

I stopped, mid-sequin. "You think I'm crazy?" My stomach sank, and my pulse quickened as she faced me, *duh* dripping off her lips.

"Just prove the birds are right." She leaned back, both hands in the air. "That's all you care about, anyway." She lifted her chin, her face tilted high, like the sharp, high tones of her words.

I didn't know why she was being snippy, but it didn't matter. Her words stabbed me in the heart, because I did care – I cared about finding Lily's murderer and proving my sanity. But that's not all I cared about. I cared about much, much more, like losing the house and Delia's party and even, sometimes, Posey. Whether I liked it or not, I cared about what she thought of me.

I left the table, snatching my wet-with-glue mask, and prepared my bed on the couch with a whirlwind of sheets and air and pillows. Her words shot through me like lightning, making the hair on my arms stand up, burning my heart. I crawled underneath the blanket and fell asleep, and in the night, I woke up to someone sitting on my chest.

My eyes opened wide and I tensed, ready to scream, but two small hands cupped my cheeks, and two small eyes looked into mine, and a voice that belonged to Max said,

"They've taken it to the sorrows."

Sleepwalking, yet again. Blinking a few times, I relaxed

my shoulders and sighed. I pried his fingers off my face and whispered, "Max, you're sleeping. Go to bed."

"But they've taken it to the sorrows."

"Taken what to the sorrows, Max?"

He blinked. "Marion?"

The pressure of his weight on my ribs stole my breath for one too many seconds and I pushed him to the side. He tumbled on the mattress and sat up, looking around.

"Why am I here?"

"You're sleepwalking," I said, rolling onto my side, my back toward him. "Go back to bed."

Quick footsteps pattered up the stairs, and a minute later, as I was drifting off to sleep, the blanket moved, and two feet snuggled next to mine.

"Max, why – " but I turned my head to see the wispy reeds of Posey's hair.

"Max is sleepwalking again," she whispered. "He's being weird this time." I couldn't see her eyes in the dark, but as I scanned her face, I saw something gentle there.

"As he does," I said, and turned back around. But Posey cleared her throat.

"I thought I saw a ghost on your bed. But it was just a blanket." She flipped onto her opposite side and brought my blanket with her. I shivered, but she didn't notice. "Did you do anything interesting on your patrol?" She spoke softly, like the words might break.

"Of course. I talked to an owl."

Outside, the night was soft and still, and it wrapped

around Finney and seeped inside. Everything stilled. Everything hushed. Everything smoothed around the edges, fading to gray. Then Posey sniffed, and in the silence it was loud and aggressive.

"Do the birds sound like humans when they talk, or different?"

I yanked the blanket back and closed my eyes, stifling a smile. "They sound like humans, but sometimes like a human with a cold."

"Oh," she said, her words filling the space around us. "I wondered."

CHAPTER TWENTY

Monday came with all the dull weariness of Mondays. I woke up in my couch bed, Posey hanging off the end, with a very clear direction in my head for how I wanted my day to go.

I wanted to go to WNYT News.

My mother, however, wanted me to do my schoolwork. This was a rather annoying and typical turn of events, but I trudged through my assignments nonetheless and came out the other side free, and I called Delia.

"I want to go to WNYT News," I said, leaning against the kitchen wall.

"I welcome the distraction. Mom can get us a meeting." She swallowed hard. "I had my first speech class today."

I straightened, switching the phone to the opposite ear to hear better. "How'd it go?"

"Half the class was improv training. Can you believe it?

I'm not so sure it's as academic as Mom thinks. But I'm not telling her. She might pull me out and put me in an etiquette class."

"A fate worse than death."

"Exactly."

Delia hung up and called James and Sebastian, and soon we were all in James' car, driving toward the address Ms. Gretchen gave us for WNYT News, and begging Sebastian to let us know what on earth went on yesterday afternoon.

"I can't tell anyone," he said. "And Dad can't know anything happened. Not even that I asked you for money. Got it?"

"Got it," Delia and I echoed.

"But you have to tell us something." I grabbed his wrist and batted my eyes. "I mean, you took my money."

He hesitated. "Well..." The tips of his ears burned red.

"Just, something."

He pulled his wrist away and fixed his eyes on the dashboard. "Okay, but only this: So, like, James was talking to Fern on instant messenger Saturday night, and he asked Fern about that pin again –"

"I was trying to help you out, Marion. Let it be noted."

"Right. So he asked her, and she said she'd show him, if he wanted. And I tagged along."

James huffed. "He invited himself."

"Stop interrupting me, dingbat. Yeah, so I went along. Anyway, I'm in now, see?" He held up his wallet, on which he had a trident pin. It shone in the sunlight. "You have to show it to get in." He grinned. "Man, if Dad knew…"

"Did you see that other guy? The one I chased through the graveyard?"

"I have my guesses." Sebastian looked out the window.

"And?"

"And, that's all I have to say."

"Obviously not, because you have not told me your guesses."

He shifted, impatience poking out of his every movement. "Look, Marion, he was probably feeling skittish about the secret order. It was a Sunday the first time you saw him, right? That's probably it. And he probably thought you knew something when you chased him the other day after the hurricane. It is a rather dramatic thing to do, you know."

"But you're not going to tell me what kind of secret order it is?"

"Nope."

Delia and I sighed in commiseration. Her shirt said DON'T BELIEVE THE LIES, GNOMES ARE AMONG US and I, too, believed that the world had too many secrets. It was ludicrous, maddening, that Sebastian would keep a secret from us.

He straightened. "Anyway, Jimmy here made some moves on his lady, so all in all the excursion was a success."

James sighed. "I did not make any moves."

"He bought her a scone." Sebastian giggled. "A scone."

James pulled into the small and underwhelming parking

lot of the news station, and we quickly forgot to keep talking. Delia looked at her map (there was a leprechaun sighting) and I studied the cars. One of the vehicles made me look twice – a beat up truck, with one headlight missing. Before the hurricane, when we were patrolling the streets, a car had passed us, with only one headlight. I filed the clue away, making a mental note to add it to my wall.

On the door of the news station was taped a suicide prevention poster, and another sat above the receptionist who told us where to find the owner's office, and yet another leered along the hallway to his door, which was also a carrier for a poster, this one particularly straight forward and to the point, with only the words SUICIDE PREVENTION LIFELINE and a phone number. We knocked. A man's voice told us to come in.

It was Doug.

Of all the things I expected to see in the owner's office, Doug was not one of them. We stepped through his door and I froze, disbelieving my eyes, as he threw his hands into the air.

"Marion! What a day!"

"Hello, Mr. Doug," I said, trying to remember if I knew he was the owner of WNYT News. I didn't know. He never mentioned it.

"Welcome! How nice! It's great to see you!" He stood up and shook each of our hands, guiding us to the chairs in front of his desk. He sat down and leaned back, one hand on the cell phone sitting on his belt. We sat down and my questions caught in my throat, my surprise suffocating me like a chemical gas. Always happy to talk, Doug jumped right in.

"What can I do ya for?" I cast a glance at the others while Doug stared at us, his mouth wide open, just waiting to gobble up our words. He asked another question before I could answer his first one. "Why aren't you kids in school?"

"We're homeschooled," James said, simply.

"Oh! How exciting. Homeschooled! Who'd have known! Kind of like the pioneer days, huh? I don't know any other homeschoolers myself, but I've heard of a few. I had a cousin whose neighbor homeschooled his kids. Twelve of them, he said. Twelve! And their names all started with the letter 'M.' Imagine the birthday parties! One every month! And you have friends, then?"

I sighed loudly and Sebastian answered, "Yes."

Doug nodded. We nodded. Doug coughed. James cleared his throat. Delia nudged me, I shifted in my seat. No one said anything (my questions still clung to the back of my throat), and so Doug tried again.

"And doesn't, uh, doesn't homeschooling – won't it limit your social skills?'

There are Five Main Questions Asked in Ignorance, and that question, by far, is the big kahuna. People are always concerned that homeschoolers are trapped in their homes, kept away from making friends or meeting strangers, and are therefore unfit for society. This is The Great Misunderstanding, in my opinion, as the rudest peers I have ever met are by far and without exception, public schoolers.

"I think we do okay," James answered.

"And you – I mean to say, are you – do you keep up with expectations, academically, I mean?"

"I've tested at college-level reading since I was eight," I said.

"Ah, well..."

"If you don't mind, I have a question."

He leaned forward, resting his elbows on his desk. "Well, spit it out."

Doug's homeschool queries allowed me to ponder the typical and mundane, and so banished all hesitation on my tongue. I was ready. I took a deep breath and pulled my question from the back of my throat.

"We heard a rumor...I mean to say, is it true that you censor your employees?" He cringed and shriveled, turning away like a bridge over a moat of questions, so I quickly mended my words. "I mean, we heard no one here can say anything about the death of Lily Anderson, except to say it was suicide. Is it true? Is there a hush clause?"

He shook his head so fast it almost flew off his neck. "No, no, no. Anyone here is free to say whatever they want to say. I just don't want them spreading wild theories. It's disrespectful. Hurts the family."

I frowned. "Well, the suicide claim hurt Lily's sister, her only remaining family, so mission failed."

His eyes grew two sizes, and he leaned back in his chair until his shoulders disappeared into the cushions. His voice was soft and fluttery. "I am sorry to hear that." A phone rang somewhere down the hall, and Doug rubbed his chin, staring into space.

His reaction was everything I'd hoped it would be – he was surprised and thoughtful, and therefore vulnerable. I leaned my elbows on the edge of his desk. I had a suspicion, a theory I wanted to test out, so I spoke with as much nonchalant conviction as I could muster.

"Can you make it up to her by sharing why you started the suicide prevention campaign?"

He shrugged. "It's an issue close to my heart."

Bang. There it was, he admitted it. He started the campaign. Surely that meant he murdered her, right? Surely that meant he was trying to control an entire town, to cover up his crimes.

"Is it, now?" The note of disbelief in Delia's voice bounced off the walls and bit him in the face. Doug ignored the bites.

"My mother killed herself. In front of me." Heavy silence sunk into us while Doug checked his watch, his confession as natural and casual to him as a remark on the weather. "She jumped off the pier, into the waterfront. It's the most traumatizing thing to ever happen to me." He looked up at us and smiled, and the flash of his teeth hurt my eyes. It was too fake, too ardent, like fluorescent lights. "Now, I feel it is my personal mission to keep everyone safe and happy!"

His eyes found their way to a picture of his wife on his desk. She was young and happy, holding a bouquet of sunflowers, with an orange lily behind her ear. The sea was behind her, and a sunset warmed the edges of the shot. Their honeymoon, probably. It was not a beach I recognized.

"My wife, I'm afraid, is quite sick. So much for my mission, eh?" We didn't answer, only studied the gentle curve of her face and the way she smiled into the camera, and he stood up, turning the picture face down. "What a thing, what a thing. Anyway, my wife has a doctor's appointment, and I'm afraid I have to go, so, I can see you out?" He walked to the door and waited, clicking together the heels of his tennis shoes. His white tube socks reached to his knees. We got up and shuffled out.

He was hiding something, filling his empty words with humbuggery, and I tucked the moment in my mind to examine later. We followed him out of the building, watched him climb into his truck (only one headlight), and then we headed home, windows down and radio blaring. When we pulled into my driveway a few minutes later, Posey ran out to meet us, her marsh hair flying in the wind.

"Violet!" she yelled.

I gave her a quizzical stare. "Marion," I replied, pointing to myself.

"No, Violet! That's the sister's name, right?"

"Yes."

Posey leaned into my open window, out of breath and wild-eyed. "Then it's over. Violet confessed to the murder. She killed Lily Anderson."

Chapter Twenty-One

It was hard to believe. Why would a woman who killed her own sister declare to the world it was murder and not suicide, then (presumedly) write an unconvincing and fake suicide note, only to turn herself in? But she had, Detective Mobley had called the house to let me know ("He wanted you to know you were right about the murder, Marion!" Posey said with a smile on her face) and now, it was over. The case was closed. Lily Anderson had been killed by her own sister and dumped into the water with motives as yet unknown. The birds were wrong, a woman killed Lily Anderson, and if they were right about the murder but wrong about the man, was this a good or bad sign for my sanity?

James and Sebastian went home, and Delia and I sat with Posey in the living room, eating popcorn and helping

Grandma take the personality quizzes we gathered from a few teenybopper magazines.

"Why do you think Violet killed her sister?" Posey asked while Delia rifled through a pile of old Trendy Girl monthlies, tossing the unwanted editions over her shoulder.

Detective Mobley told us that the autopsy report revealed Lily had been hit over the head, and *then* she drowned. I've wanted to hit Posey before, and I have once or twice, I'll admit – but boy, Violet must have been angry. At least I'd never sent Posey to her watery death.

"I have a few guesses," I answered, eyeing her. "Maybe she stole her sock money."

Posey did that once, and Mom made her pay me back with interest. Of course, I had no room to talk; I once stole Conrad's Halloween candy, the whole bucket full. Then I panicked, because I didn't know where to hide it – Conrad could always find my hiding places – so I ate it all in one sitting. I promptly threw up in his candy bucket. He was not pleased. Mom made me use my birthday money to buy him more candy, and while we were at the store a little boy made fun of my dress (pink with frills, even though I had nothing to celebrate) and Conrad punched him in the nose. It's one of my favorite memories, even though Mom claims that day produced her first white hair.

"Maybe Lily stole Violet's camera." Posey buried herself under a throw pillow.

"It's missing again?" I shot a glance at the old woman in

the recliner, blissfully turning through magazines and pulling at her purple hair.

"Yes," Posey mumbled, "and it's not...you know, where I thought it was." She gestured to Grandma with her eyebrows.

"I didn't take it." I elbowed Delia. "Did you take it?"

"Nope, definitely not." She pulled out a copy of Trendy Girl and opened to page thirty-two, ARE YOU A COMMITMENT PHOBE OR A COMMITMENT JUNKIE? "I have my own camera."

Of course, there was only one reasonable suspect, and that suspect had purple hair and a hundred wrinkles; the camera most certainly was in her room, Posey just didn't look hard enough. I watched Grandma for a moment before asking,

"Do you like taking pictures, Grandma?"

She smiled to herself, her lips small and thin. "Well, I suppose so."

"Do you know where the camera is?"

Her face opened, her eyes big and full of wonder. "I don't have a camera." She leaned toward us and dropped her voice to a whisper. "There are thieves in town, you know."

Posey sighed theatrically. "We know, Grandma."

"But what do these thieves look like?" I asked her.

She raised her hand, pointing toward the sky with one knobby finger. "The gnomes know. They know everything." She drew her romance novel from beneath her thigh and rocked her head slowly. "Your grandfather liked pictures, too. Have you seen his pictures?"

"They're in the attic," Posey droned.

"When I die, you can have them." Grandma opened her book in the middle and followed the words with her finger. "He loved pictures."

"What else did he love, Grandma?" I watched Delia tally out her own answers to a quiz, landing on *type lonely: you are an outlier, marching to the beat of your own drum. No man can bring you down.* She nodded her head soberly.

Grandma clicked her tongue, her answer coming out in a rhythm, like a child's song, while still reading her book. "He loved me." Her voice was bright and chipper. "And he loved flowers. And he loved you."

"I want to talk about something else," Posey said, but before I could ask her why, the phone rang. I ran into the kitchen to answer it.

"Want to know more?" Sebastian asked, rather cryptically.

I leaned against the kitchen doorframe. "More of what?"

"Don't play dumb. The secret order. I'll bring you in."

"When?"

Grandma sat in her chair, smiling to herself as she read. Posey pointed at something in Delia's magazine, and they both laughed.

"Now. We're leaving, be there in ten. Meet us at the waterfront." And then he hung up. I carefully set the receiver back on its base, locking eyes with Delia.

"Looks like we have another patrol."

We dropped the magazine pastime, told Posey she couldn't follow (she threw the throw pillow at me, which was appropriate, probably the only time the pillow was used as intended) and waited for James and Sebastian at the waterfront. Sebastian wore a big smile and James, I noted with amusement, wore his best outfit (the one with a blue tie, saved for weddings). He didn't look quite so happy; his eyes were open a little too wide, and he kept scratching the back of his head.

Young love is, I will always say, the worst. It takes a good time and ruins it with nerves.

"Ready?" Sebastian asked, rubbing his hands together.

"Ready," I answered, and behind me, Delia grunted.

Sebastian flashed his pearly whites, a glint in his eyes. "Follow me." He turned and led us into an alleyway and knocked on the back door of Lady's Madness Maritime Museum three times, followed by a kick. A man opened the door just a sliver, so only his left side could be seen, which was quite enough. He was massive.

"Password?"

"Leviathan," Sebastian answered, showing the pin on his wallet. "The girls are with us."

The man grunted, the stubble on his cheek brushing against the doorway trim, and he held up one hand. "Too young," he garbled. "Go home to mommy."

"Not too young." Sebastian thrust the trident-shaped pin

under his nose so that it was too close to see, and Massive Man pushed it back into Sebastian's chest.

"This place is too old for ya, kid."

"We've been here before," James said, stepping close. "Fern invited us tonight."

"That's right." Sebastian nodded. "Fern's expecting us."

"Good for you," Massive Man said, evenly.

"Like, *invited* us. Fern. So, you know...you know what that means." Sebastian leaned toward him, speaking low. "You'll want to let us in."

He hesitated, regarding Sebastian with curiosity, his tongue poking into the side of his cheek.

"Fern," Sebastian said, with emphasis.

"Fern, huh?" Massive Man repeated through chuckles, considering us while rubbing the dimple in his chin, as we shuffled awkwardly in the dim evening light. He leaned forward, craning his neck to see both ends of the alley. "You sure about that?"

"Sure as the sun rises in the east," Sebastian answered proudly, holding up the pin again. "And we know the magic word. Leviathan."

"Huh." He drummed his fingers on his bulging biceps, and my stomach dropped, slowly sinking through my hips and down to my knees. Part of me wanted him to roll out the red carpet and shoo us in, and the other part of me ached for him to once again tell us to get lost, to go back to our homes and our mommies. Something about the situation made me uneasy, made me think that maybe we weren't as safe and sound as I wanted to be. But I didn't want Sebastian to think me a coward, so I squared my shoulders and met the man's eyes, feigning maturity.

"I'll keep my eye on you," he said.

"Yes, sir," James and Sebastian chanted in unison, pocketing their pins and grinning like Grandma when she sees a gnome. "Thank you, sir."

The man opened the door and we scurried into a dark, dusty room. We'd been there before of course, when we asked Marv questions, but in the dark it was altogether different. It was sleepy and secretive, filled with shadows and locked boxes. It smelled of wood and saltwater, and nothing in sight even remotely resembled the meeting place of a secret order.

"Keep walkin,'" Massive Man said.

Sebastian led the way toward the back and pushed at a shelf lined with display boxes of bullets and cannon balls. The shelf swung open and a dark, empty hallway greeted us. We followed Sebastian's lead until we turned a corner, and bam – light, laughter, smoke.

On the other side of an open door, men sat around tables playing cards, and in the middle of the room, a craps table. Men and women stood around it, laughing, martini glasses in hand. Die clanked and clamored, ice cubes clinked, men whooped, and women clapped. Live music played from a tuxedoed man at a piano in the corner, the air smelled of mildew and cigars and perfume, and body heat slapped our faces and stuffed our lungs. Large men in tracksuits guarded every corner. Sleek men in ties whispered to each other and exchanged weighty handshakes. Secrets closed us in.

It was a gambling den.

Sebastian smiled at me. "So uh, well, they give newcomers this hundred-dollar credit, and uh, I got a little carried away. That's why I needed money."

"He lost three hundred dollars," James said drily.

"Wow." Delia brushed her fingers over her lips, mouth wide open.

"Yeah, well, let me tell you, three hundred bucks is nothing in this place." Sebastian spread his arms out wide just as the table in front of us erupted in cheers – someone beat the house. The shouts thundered, and James leaned down and yelled into my ear,

"You know who the leader of this operation is? Some guy they call Poseidon. See? I'm taking notes for you."

"Really?" I shared a glance with Delia. "That's interesting." Fancy titles and nicknames? Things were getting interesting.

James grimaced. "I have a bad feeling about him."

Delia grabbed my arm. "I don't like this," she roared into my ear, her eyes like saucers.

"Explains a lot, though," I yelled back, thinking of all the secrecy and back alley meetings. The cheers subsided, replaced by a spunky saloon tune played by the tuxedoed man at the piano; he smiled, bopping along on his bench. Sebastian leaned into us.

"Poseidon is a very level-headed criminal, apparently."

He played with the pin on his wallet, turning it around and around with the tip of his finger. "But also troubled. Something's very wrong, if you ask me."

"Like, how?"

"I'm not sure," he pocketed his wallet, tapping it for good measure. "But he's dangerous."

I bent toward his ear and asked, "What did you mean about Fern, back at the door?"

"Oh, that? Don't know. I overheard someone say that last time, figured I'd try it out, see if it got us in." He beamed. "Did the trick, didn't it?"

I snorted and raked my eyes around the room again, stopping at every face. A few faces were young and bright, with wide smiles and wild, empty eyes. They twisted through the people, saying this and that, occasionally meeting each other and whispering one or two words. I watched closely, waiting to see the teenage boy I chased through the graveyard, but I didn't see him among the juveniles – one boy about James' age bumped into a man with a pinstriped suit and wide rimmed glasses, and they exchanged a side glance and handshake before disappearing into the crowd.

My attention drifted to the bar at the opposite end of the room, where a young woman sat on a stool, fidgeting and wearing a dress far too old for her – Fern. She spotted James and waved, and we weaved our way through the crowd to see her.

"Club soda?" she asked. We all said no (disgusting).

"Glad you came. Did Lenny give you trouble?" We

shrugged, and her smile stretched across her face and her teeth sparkled in the smoky room. "I thought he might. I'll talk to him." She pointed at Delia and me, waving her finger between us. "If anyone asks, you're eighteen."

"No way I look eighteen," I said, my voice reaching over the clamor.

"I didn't say *look* eighteen. I said *say* you're eighteen." She winked at James, and my cheeks got hot. "It's all about semantics, sweetie."

James said something I couldn't hear, but she laughed and brushed his shoulder with the back of her hand, and I exchanged eyebrow raises with Delia. No one else was at the bar – all other gamblers were busy at their respective tables, but yet their eyes sat on us like the smoke in the air, heavy and flighty. Delia looked over her shoulder. Sebastian looked over his. We all felt the same thing: like we were prime entertainment, exposed and awaiting our doom. The music stopped between songs and for a moment all we could hear were voices and clattering glasses. And then –

"Fern."

I felt him behind me, towering. Fern's smile dropped from her face, so she swallowed (I think she almost swallowed her own mouth) and plastered it back in place.

"Yes?"

I turned. Marv held a glass of something brown, staring down at us and wearing fire in his eyes. There was no fake kindness in him this time. He was brutally honest, wearing his anger like a suit.

"I thought I told you to clear it with me before you brought newbies inside?"

Her smile almost dropped again. "They're friends."

"They're also kids. And they're Mobley's kids. And they're nosey."

Fern swatted at the smoke in front of her nose, crossing her legs with confidence even though her toes bounced up and down, up and down, in the air. "They're cool, trust me. And old enough. Right, guys?"

"We're eighteen," Delia said, clearing her throat.

Marv barked a laugh. "Yeah, and I'm a fairy princess." Spittle sprayed onto Delia's face and she cowered, wiping it off with her sleeve. Marv turned to Fern and raised his voice, the veins in his neck popping. "They're not welcome here, Fern, as I've told you before. This happened once already" – he leaned into a shout, stepping closer, his face red and cruel – "I'm tired of you – "

"Now just wait a minute." James stepped between Fern and Marv, his arms crossed, and his meaty, talkative shoulders saying *look at us, the barricade you weren't expecting and won't defy.* "You make us leave, we talk. You let us stay, well..." he shrugged. "Silent as the grave."

Marv took a drink, swishing it on his tongue as he looked down at me. The muscles in his jaw flexed and he swallowed, then opened his mouth to let out an *ah* over his large, pointy teeth. I shriveled. His face was sharp, gaunt, and yellow, somehow, his candy cane appearance replaced by something sinister, like a snake, or a poisoned dart.

"And you're eighteen, too, I suppose?" Sarcasm dripped from his lips.

"Yes," I squeaked. "I often buy cigarettes."

He laughed, and it came out like a snarl. But he turned away from me, his glass tipped at Fern. "You're still on probation, Fern. Don't give me other reasons to change my mind." His glass twinkled (visually and otherwise) and he pointed at each of us. "Tell no one."

"Yes, sir," we said in unison, shrinking into our shoes. His eyes narrowed, scanning every inch of me before he took a step toward James, bumping him in the chest with his glass.

"You tell, Fern here gets in trouble. Real bad trouble. Got it?"

James stood tall, meeting Marv's eyes straight on. "Got it."

"Good." And just as quickly as he came, Marv was gone.

"He can get under your skin real fast," Fern said, watching him. He disappeared behind a guarded door on the other side of the room, and it closed quickly, sharply. The guard moved to stand in front of it, his sunglasses reflecting the light fixture above him.

"What's behind that door?" I asked. "And is Marv Poseidon?"

Fern's face hardened, her lips draping down her chin like deflated pool noodles. "Don't ask questions." She set down her drink and nodded to the barman, who winked at us and placed two small things on the bar top, pointedly, so that each *plop* was a beat in the music. She motioned for us to take it. "Your pins," she said. "Wear them well. You'll need them to get in again."

I stared at mine, so small and innocent in my palm, and tucked it safely in my pocket. Something about pinning it to my clothes, right then and there, seemed like a statement I was not ready to make. I caught the eye of the bartender and he grinned at me, rolling up his sleeves before caressing his five o'clock shadow. I withered like a small child. I was not ready for a place like this.

Fern looped her arm through James' and jumped off the stool, shouting, "Let's check out the fun!" as she pranced away, James at her side. Sebastian followed, going another way with his eyes on a certain table, and Delia and I were left alone at the bar, fidgeting and swaying self-consciously. The sheen of Delia's eyes said that she wanted to leave, too.

But then I saw a familiar face: hair like straw, beady eyes; Francesca sat on the far side of the room, cards in her hands, a look of determination in her eyes.

"Bingo," I said, and we went to her, winding through people and tables.

"Ms. Lovely!" Delia called, as way of greeting. Francesca raised an eyebrow. The other players at her table quieted mid-conversation, pulling their cards close to their chests. They looked from her to us and waited.

"Marv let you in?" Francesca asked, taking in our jeans and sneakers (and tunic) amid a room filled with adults in beads and baubles and silk dresses. Eyes went from us, to the mystery door shut tight against the throng of people.

"Apparently we are unwanted," I said.

"But it's too late now," Delia added.

She laughed. "Our motto, if ever there was one." The man sitting next to her smiled and puffed his cigar, the cloud of smoke rolling proudly across the table. Francesca put down her cards. "I'm out." She nodded toward the bar. "Follow me."

The piano spat something frantic and bouncy. Francesca's dress glittered in front of us, black and covered in sequins, and I focused on it as we slithered through the mass of gamblers. We passed a table surrounded by people bent over, laughing, and Delia jumped aside to escape the arms of a man telling a story, his movements big and clumsy. I jumped aside to escape the arms of a man screaming, his voice rolling over the others in sharp waves.

"It's cheating! Cheating! He's counting cards –"

But the man next to him stepped forward and matched his volume as one of the large men from a corner pushed through the crowd, and I rushed away to the bar, not one bit curious to know who threw the first punch. With each step the crowd closed in, and the shouts muffled and mingled with laughter.

Francesca ordered a drink and sat on a stool, motioning us closer as she leaned in, aiming for our ears. "Don't come back here," she said, her voice like lead. "You'll get stuck."

"I think there's something to this place," I yelled, raising my voice above the clatter, leaning into the counter. I didn't like it, but a gambling den meant secrets, a million secrets that just might go beyond Lily and her murderous sister. "Violet confessed to the murder, but now that I know about this I think maybe – "

"If she confessed, what else is there to know?"

The room shrunk, the shouts and laughter faded into the background, and she sat before us, ice and fire, a challenge in her eyes. My mouth went dry. "I think we might find out something about Lily or Violet – "

Francesca held up a hand. "I had righteous intentions, too. I was going to bring this place down. But I got stuck. Now I'm a part of it." The bartender handed her something pink and cold and she tipped it to us before taking a sip. She smacked her lips. "Don't be like me."

I scanned the room for James and Sebastian, but they were lost in the crowd, one of the many huddled around tables, mingling in the in-betweens. "How'd you get stuck?"

"Same way everyone gets stuck, sweetheart." She took another long drink, head back, one finger pointed up. "First, I was drawn in by my good intentions. Next, I was kept here by my actions, by pretty promises. Then, I was stuck, both by my debts" – she looked away – "and by the promise of good things coming."

"What good things?" I asked.

"Doesn't matter." She swooshed her glass and Marv slipped back into the room, a smile on his face, baring his teeth. She watched him. "Marv always repays his debts," she said, then she turned back to us. "Go."

The room closed in around us, the people buzzed in our

ears, their eyes on the back of our necks. I searched for James and Sebastian among the teenagers zigzagging through the crowd, but all the faces blurred together until it was Marv, over and over again, everywhere. I turned to Francesca, my heart beating in my fingertips, and her dress glittered like a thousand stars in a room smothered in darkness.

CHAPTER TWENTY-TWO

Delia stayed over at my house that night. We left the museum after talking to Francesca, James and Sebastian trailing behind us, and made a pit stop at Delia's house before heading to my own. We waltzed through the kitchen and into the living room, where Mom sat on my couch bed, waiting for us. She smiled. It must not have been late – the gambling den only *felt* like an eternity, like each minute was an hour.

"Where have you been?" she asked, sipping hot tea from a mug that said *Finnegan's Galley, Our House is Your Home.* Her bedtime glasses fogged over from the steam.

"Just hanging out with James and Sebastian, downtown," I answered. A pang of guilt hit me.

I had told a half-truth.

Mom nodded. Her wild, graying locks flowed freely around her shoulders, over her pink and fluffy robe I once dubbed her "frumpy comfort." I wouldn't dare call it that again – it looked safe and warm, wise and innocent. She yawned and stood up.

"I'm going to bed." Turning off the lamp beside the couch, she motioned to the closed door by the foot of the stairs. "Don't disturb your dad, he's in his office. Does your mom know you're here, Delia?"

"Yes ma'am," Delia said.

"Good. Sweet dreams, girls."

Mom lumbered up the stairs to her bedroom without another word. We followed her, parting ways at my bedroom door. Delia rushed in and I closed and locked the door, leaning against it as I let the night fall off of me like a broken shackle. Delia tipped her chin and nodded to the handle.

"I don't know why I locked it," I answered. "I guess I just feel weird."

"I don't blame you," she quickly replied, adding a shrug. She turned around to face the mind map. "The whole night was unexpected."

I chuckled nervously, remembering Marv's face as he shouted at Fern, the veins in his neck popping, the spit flying out of his mouth. I pushed the vision away and stood beside Delia, where we stared at the mind map, arms crossed and mouths shut, as Posey watched us from her bed.

"It's over, you know. You don't have to look at it anymore," Posey said.

Delia and I cocked our heads to the side. We kept our backs to her. Posey tried again.

"At least now you can sleep in your own bed, right, Marion?"

"I have no such intention."

"Why not?"

I held out my hands, gesturing to the unmade bed in front of me. "It is a bed of death and sorcery."

"Right." Posey rolled her eyes and threw a pillow at Delia. "Are you staying the night, then?"

Delia stepped aside as the pillow landed on my bed. She picked it up and squeezed it to her chest, picking at the corners. "Indeed, it is so. Are we sleeping in the living room?"

"Yes." I took out an index card and wrote *gambling ring at museum* and *leader of gambling ring "Poseidon"* and pinned them underneath *Marv*. "It's all rather convenient, right?"

"What?" Posey asked, even though I wasn't talking to her.

"Marv. It all points to him. So suspicious. So criminal. He's the perfect suspect. And then Violet just...confesses?"

"Life is stranger than fiction." Delia tossed the pillow on my bed and collapsed on top of it, hands behind her head, and crossed her ankles. She pointed to my wall. "There is method in the madness."

"Maybe," I said, pinning Francesca Lovely's slanderous article about Finnegan's Galley to the side, unsure if and how it fit in.

"That's the way it goes sometimes."

"I still can't help but think of that guy I chased through the graveyard." I pointed to his index card and slapped it. "Something isn't right."

I wrote down the other clues, each on their own card, even though Violet was, at that very moment, in custody:

Doug is the owner of WNYT News

Doug started anti-suicide campaign

Doug drives a truck with one headlight

Doug is definitely hiding something

Francesca is a part of gambling ring

Violet confessed

"It's not like it really matters now." Posey stood up, threw back her covers, and landed in her bed with a sigh. "She confessed, the case is closed, it's done."

Delia nodded. "Now we can think about my party. It's tomorrow, remember. And Founder's Day."

"And the ruination of Finnegan's Galley," I said.

"Drama queen," Posey grumbled.

Be that as it may, my thoughts were nonetheless true. Everything was falling apart. Nothing made sense. Everyone seemed guilty. I was telling half-truths. And there were so many things to think about, I couldn't fall asleep until Channel 3 went to static.

Something still wasn't sitting right the next morning. Figuratively, that is; my stomach felt fine, as did my bowels. I woke up in the early hours, but not because I was emotionally and intellectually conflicted – though I was – but because Delia is one of those annoying mythical creatures who naturally wake up in the early morning and enthusiastically awaken everyone around them. I have told her many times not to be happy around me in the morning, and thankfully, after one incident involving an old eye mask and a bottle of hot sauce, she has obliged. So she woke me up, and I lay on that rickety couch bed, staring at the ceiling, acknowledging the feeling in my gut that something wasn't right (again, figuratively). Delia fiddled next to me, ready to be on with her day but reluctant to vex me, and so I said, rather more to the ceiling than to anyone else,

"I think we need to visit the old guys at the waterfront."

"Oh!" Delia sat up. "Alright. But I have to go home soon, you know, and do school."

"Then let's go now." I slowly raised myself to a sitting position. "I bet they're already there, anyway."

Delia bounced up and down and sang about sunshine and blood and daggers (oops, sorry, those last two were my thoughts) while I tried to remember how to put on shoes. I gave up and went barefoot.

We set out to talk to The Gatekeepers, creeping out the back door and following the waterfront, before cutting across Old Port Street, eyes peeled for three old men in the dark of the early morning. Only Buck sat on the bench, wearing his signature hat and coat, and smiling at nothing in particular while he waited for his friends.

"Ah!" His hands went up in the air as soon as he saw me (gnarled knuckles). "Marion! You're up with the sun!"

His memory was better in the morning. I waved at him.

"Good morning, Mr. Buck," I said as I peered up at the sky. It was still gray and hazy. "But the sun isn't up yet. It's still the devil's hour."

He chuckled. "I suppose you're right."

"Mr. Buck." I sat down beside him, and Delia sat on his other side. He tipped his U.S. ARMY VETERAN hat at us, still smiling, and the hair on the back of his head waved at us, too. Delia's hair, dried out from dye and flat irons, was sticking up and sticking out, and she tucked it behind her ears. I did the same. "I have a question for you."

"Well, I have some answers, let's see if they match."

I studied the sky again, mostly because I was falling asleep even as I talked and looking up took more concentration and helped me stay awake. "Tell me what you know about the gambling ring."

"Ah." Buck shifted uncomfortably on the bench. "Figured it out, did you? Well, we don't hold much store by it ourselves, but the pay is good."

"They pay you?'

"Just to sit here an' make sure people know to go to the back door. Make sure trouble stays away. Look out for suspicious types. Look out for...uniforms." He scratched his nose. "Frankly, it's mostly what we do every day anyway, minus the subterfuge."

"Do they do anything...else?"

"Sweetheart, I wouldn't know. I just sit here."

I dislike men who give me pet names. Goodness knows they don't give pet names to other men. At least when women give pet names it tends to apply to everyone, gender and age no matter. But Buck was such an old-fashioned gent, it felt more natural, and I didn't feel the need to remind him that my name is Marion (plus, it seemed like he remembered me this time, anyway).

"Did the murdered girl ever come here? Lily Anderson?"

"Not to my memory. Of course, it's my memory we're talking here, and I'm old." He laughed, and it exposed a row of straight, white dentures, gleaming in the morning light.

It was a lie. We had seen her talking to them before she was murdered. Why was every single person in Lady's Madness tied up in this? A wave crashed against the retaining wall, and I waited for it to recede before I said, "I could have sworn I saw her talking to you, the night she was murdered."

His mouth bounced up and down before he answered,

and he scratched his eyebrow (the hair dipped down into his eyes) with one bent pointer finger. "Why, I can't recall talking to her a single time."

Playing innocent. But how many times can a girl call an old man a liar?

I turned to give the museum door a good scrutinizing. It was an old wooden door, unassuming to the casual eye. But a new poster was taped to it:

IF YOU OR A LOVED ONE HAVE CONTEMPLATED SUICIDE –

I stopped reading. "So you sit here, and keep away trouble makers?"

"Yes, ma'am."

"Why you? Why not..." I almost said *someone younger* but caught myself. "Why not another big guy, like the guy at the alley door?"

"I suppose they do, sometimes. But less suspicious to outsiders this way, though, right?" I didn't answer, so he said, "You didn't suspect, did ya?"

I shook my head. "No, I never suspected."

"Well." He stroked his chin. "Guess it works, then."

"So." Delia leaned forward, elbows on her knees. "Who pays you?"

"Who else? Marv." Buck's eyes shot open wide. "Well, maybe I'm not supposed to tell you."

I held my gaze on the water, processing everything; I

didn't like that I lived in a small town rife with lies and secrets. I didn't like that it seemed so safe to me, up until last night. Even The Gatekeepers had seemed safe to me. But now they were criminals, aiding and abetting a gambling house – of course, I was a part of it now, too. I'd even told my mom a half-truth. My stomach twisted just thinking about it.

"You don't feel...weird? About helping a crime?" I asked.

"It goes to a good cause."

"What cause?"

He grinned and tapped the side of his nose. "I'm not allowed to tell you any secrets you don't already know. If they haven't told you yet, I won't, either."

I stifled a sigh. "Why do you bother keeping their secrets? You're a man of honor, I can tell. You served your country. You raised a family."

His chest expanded and he folded his hands, and words came out with a sigh, patient and practiced, as the waves beat against the retaining wall.

"Brotherhood is the truest form of honor, young lady. Doug's father was a Gatekeeper. He was one of us, 'till he up and died. Poor Doug, he was in Switzerland when it happened. Doug and Marv are thick as thieves, didn't you know? Doug saved Marv's life. Jumped in the water, saved him from drowning. Doug broke a shoulder. Lost a scholar- ship. It's these things that matter, in the end. Brotherhood. Loyalty." He raised his hat and wiped his balding head. "Keeping your word."

I leaned forward to lock eyes with Delia. Her face was

pale in the early morning haze, but her eyes were dark and filled with rushing thoughts. She tightened her lips. "Should have known."

We said goodbye to Buck (his friends showed up and the bench got too small) and meandered back toward our houses. I spotted a blue jay, hopping along the retaining wall at the waterfront, and got an idea.

"Excuse me!" I called, making my way to it. "Do you have a moment?"

It looked at me and said, "Ah, the human that can speak bird. How delightful to meet you." The range of his voice was low, so he was definitely a boy, and the blue on his back and face was brilliant and dark. The black band around his eyes and neck trailed down to his chest, which faded from a soft gray to white. He hopped to me, hopping in quick, easy steps, then stood still to watch me.

My chest burst with happiness – my fame preceded me! I squared my shoulders and Delia sighed, eyeing her fingernails.

"Yes, delightful." I curtseyed because that felt like the right thing to do. "If you don't mind, I have a few questions."

"Well, do go on," he said. "If I can answer, I will. I am Stewart, and you are?" His voice was happy and clear, like a clean, spring day.

I cleared my throat and leaned into Delia to whisper, "His name is Stewart, and he has heard of me." Turning back to Stewart I said, "I am Marion of Finnegan's Galley, and this is Delia, but she can't understand you."

"Very nice to make your acquaintance, Marion of Finnegan's Galley. What questions do you have for me, whatwhat?" He puffed his little chest and danced a little hop-dance, and I sat down in front of him, legs crossed.

"Well, I was just wondering if you knew anything about the girl that died. Who killed her, or anything like that."

"I have heard – do forgive me if this is awkward, but I have heard that you provide...incentives for those with whom you converse?"

Only after I sighed and straightened my shirt did I reply, "Ah, right." I felt in the little pocket of my pajamas and pulled out the penny I'd found the day I searched for Grandma at the waterfront. "One shiny thing, then, for your information?" I placed it in front of his feet.

"Very good," Stewart said. "We have a deal." He stepped on it in one quick hop, and stood very still as he said, "I did not witness the poor woman's demise, but rumor has it, she would feed the birds every day while the sun shone straight above us."

"Her lunch break, probably." I nodded. "Do you know anything else? How many people were present the night she was killed?"

"I'm afraid I do not know, so terribly sorry, very sorry, indeed." He fluffed his wings and pecked violently at his under-feathers, his tone high and pained.

"It's alright, Stewart – now, was she always alone, when she fed the birds? Did she ever meet a friend?"

A breeze spiraled around us and he spread his wings into

it, closing his eyes. His wings were dark, and his feathers stretched out like fingers.

"I assume not, or it would have been noted, along with the gossip." The air stilled and he shook out his wings, rapidly and repeatedly like a hummingbird, and shook his head. "I'm afraid I must go, it is time for me to defecate."

He bowed his head, snatched the penny, and flew away.

I shrugged at Delia. "He needs to poop. He was extremely polite, really." I paused. "She'd feed the birds on her lunch break."

"Typical newbie," Delia said. "Locals would never do such a thing."

CHAPTER TWENTY-THREE

We trudged back to our houses to do school and nap (or maybe just I napped) and pretend that life was normal. Delia also had to prepare for her party in the evening. There wasn't a whole lot to do, because her mom already cleaned the living room and hung up streamers, but there was enough to keep her busy while I did school and pondered Doug. I kept thinking about him, sitting behind his desk, avoiding my eyes, mumbling excuses. Then my mind would wander to Marv, all tall and menacing, standing behind me at the museum, threatening Fern. The two of them were friends. That had to mean something.

But then again, Violet had confessed. The case was closed. I massaged my temples and focused on the workbook before me, willing my imagination to cooperate. Algebra is the most acute form of torture known to man, and I had to face my trial with every resource I could muster. I could think about Doug and Marv and Violet another time.

I worked for a while until I grew hungry. I left my room and passed the open door of the office, where Dad was face down on the desk, his arms sprawled out on each side, perfectly still. I stopped, backed up, and held my breath, waiting to see him move, but he just sat there, like a dying houseplant, withered and brown (his shirt). I knocked softly on the doorframe and he lifted his head. Slowly he sat up and put on his glasses, rubbing the bridge of his nose. "Yes?"

"You looked dead," I said.

He snorted. "Yeah."

"House stuff?"

He rubbed the top of his head, and a few strays hairs stood up straight. Papers were scattered on his desk and he turned to gather them, collecting them into one pile. "You don't need to worry about it, kiddo."

I tapped the doorframe, leaning onto it as I examined my feet. "Okay."

"You finish your schoolwork?"

"No." He held the papers so carefully, his hopes and dreams in the palms of his hands. I looked away, staring at the wall instead, where there hung an old family photo, taken when Max was a baby and Posey was going through her "difficult" phase. Her face was red and blotchy, and Mom's smile was perfectly square (like a growl). Dad smiled at the camera, his hair slicked back, not a gray hair in sight. I was beside him, standing in front of Conrad, blissfully ignorant of the gum he had lodged in my hair. "No, I'm not finished. I'm getting a snack."

"Ah," Dad said, and I slipped away, shutting the door behind me. The last thing we needed was for Max to see Dad comatose, swallowed by his own paperwork. I shuddered at the thought, at the worry that would cloud Max's innocent (but still impish) child eyes.

"I'm trying, Finney," I whispered, and she hugged me.

<hr>

I had a snack and finished my schoolwork, and the phone rang just as Delia strolled through the door. I answered the phone, watching Delia flop on the couch, one arm over the back.

"Hi, Marion." It was Ms. Caroline. "Look, I hate to pester you about this, but did you ever find those curtains? I didn't get a chance to ask you about it on Sunday and we're getting a little too close to the big day for my liking..."

"Ah, yes, the curtains!" I caught Delia's eye and gave her my best look that said *I completely forgot and the world is on fire.* "I uh, I have not retrieved them yet, but I'll do so right now."

"Oh! Thank you, sweetie. Just bring it by as soon as you can, okay? Send it with Sebastian after the party tonight."

"Right. Will do." I hung up and marched across the kitchen, stomping my embarrassment into the tiles. I didn't like that Ms. Caroline had to call about the curtains when I'd been so confident in offering them. Offering something and forgetting about it is, after all, a half-truth. Telling Mom I spent the evening hanging out downtown with James and Sebastian was a half-truth, too. And since when did I deal in half-truths?

"Come hither, servant!" I called to Delia (I was feeling feisty), who responded with some choice British words.

The attic was accessible from the top floor (obviously) which was accessible by climbing the servant stairs from the kitchen. We hurried up the winding, narrow staircase and when we reached the top floor storage room, I pulled down the little wooden ladder of the attic hatch, armed with a broom and poised to destroy any spider webs that deigned to get in my way. Delia followed.

The attic was dull and dusty, lit by one single round window that looked out to the open sea. The brick common room chimney shot up through the middle. I liked it, except for the fact that I felt it was hiding something from me, much like Violet's A-frame yellow house.

The curtains were probably somewhere in a pile of boxes and old furniture, and eventually I found them, tied up in trash bags and looking very much like something a criminal would hide underneath freshly poured concrete.

"Found them," I said to Delia. She did not answer. "Delia?"

She stood poised in front of a great and disgusting fur rug draped over an old desk, grazing it with her fingertips.

"Delia, what are you doing?"

"It's him, Marion." Her eyes were fixed on the rug, on the subtle way the colors changed when she stroked it.

"What?"

"What kind of animal is this?"

"I don't know."

"Where'd you get it?"

"Haven't the faintest."

She inhaled sharply. "It's him."

"Who?" I couldn't imagine any man being so hairy; the very thought made me want to join a convent right then and there in my parent's attic.

"It's Bigfoot."

Oh, him. I rolled my eyes. "It's not Bigfoot."

"How do you know?"

"Because I think if we had Bigfoot's pelt in my attic I would have heard a rumor to that effect."

She picked it up, which took considerably more strength than she had anticipated, and so she grunted and stumbled. "But look at it, Marion. What else could it be?"

"A bear."

She glared at me. "It doesn't feel like a bear."

"How many bears have you felt?"

"Including you, one." She backed up to throw the pelt at me, but the heaviness made her lean back, and then her balance shifted and she leaned back more, and when she tried to correct herself she slipped on the bottom end of the pelt, which was dragging against the floor – and she went down hard against the chimney. The clunk of her head against the bricks echoed through the room.

"Ow!" she yelped, the pelt falling over her. She rubbed the back of her head.

"Did you die?" I asked, stepping closer.

"Almost." She checked her fingers for blood. "Except..." with great effort she pried the pelt off her body and turned around, eyeing the chimney. "Except that the brick went back with my head, and so it wasn't quite so...quite so..." Her voice trailed off as she felt the bricks, and I began to wonder if maybe she had brain damage. "Quite so impactful."

"What are you doing?"

She found the brick she was looking for and wiggled it. "Marion, this brick is loose. Did you know this brick was loose?"

"Why yes, Delia, I did know, because I personally inspect every brick in this house on an annual basis."

She glowered at me with a side-eyed stare and I knew, if she had the weapon, she would have stabbed me on the spot. "I'm serious." A small clump if mortar fell from the joint where she fiddled and bobbled, and it dropped on the edge of Bigfoot's fur.

"No, I didn't know the brick was loose."

Delia carefully gripped the edges and wiggled the brick out of its place, revealing a small cavern in the chimney that held dust and cobwebs and every banished-after-being-almost-killed-and-now-has-a-thirst-for-revenge spider. And then she did the one thing that most screamed haughty foolishness – she stuck her hand in it.

"Cordelia!"

She ignored me. "There's something in it." She dragged out a letter that looked as if it had been chilling in the chimney for generations.

Probably because it had.

It was brown, stiff, and curled up at the edges. The ink was fading, and spots of discoloration blurred the letters.

"Marion, this is like, really old." Delia gingerly opened it and scanned the first page, then held it out for me to take. It was dated September 22nd, 1725.

"Whoa," I breathed, eloquently. Delia spread the pelt on the floor and sat on it, legs crisscross style, and gazed up at me with a smile.

"Read it to me. My vision's weird."

I ignored her alarming confession and cleared my throat.

My Dearest Colleen,
Our troubles began with Uncle Claudius.
You know this as well as I do. And you know me best in all the world, which is why you are reading this letter, because you knew where to look for my last goodbye. Remember when we overheard Uncle say he buried his secrets? It makes me smile, to remember how we found his little hiding place, the grave of his indiscretions, and we took our stolen monies back from him. Now it is our little hiding spot, our secret we share, christened by this letter.

I have much to tell you, much to explain, but I do not have the words; so, I will start at the beginning, and hope I have the words come the end.

I cannot fathom that he was our dear father's only brother. How different they were! After Father died and Uncle Claudius married dear Mama, he proved himself to be a cold and vile man who thinks of no one but himself. But you know this better than I do, so I digress.

Delia was still smiling. "You okay?" I asked, and she nodded. I smoothed the deep creases of the letter. "This is interesting."

She fluttered her fingers at me, leaning back against the chimney. "Keep reading. Do you realize who this is? Colleen? Uncle Claudius? Both mentioned in a letter found in this house? This is Lady Madness. This is the true story!" She clapped her hands and bounced, motioning for me to go on with a tilt of her chin.

So I did.

He drank too much. His tirades were loud and violent; sometimes I felt a quaking in my boots at the mere sound of his footsteps. His outbursts were cruel; his fist a hammer; and our poor mother began to waste away, her mind poisoned by his lies, her frame becoming as nothing, until I thought a gentle breeze might carry her away to a distant shore – and oh, how I wished it would!

He claimed Finnegan's Inn, but he did not lift a finger to keep it running. Instead, he used the profits gained from our own sweat and tears to line his pockets, and the pockets of those who made the spirits that filled his stomach. I was sick of him. One day, Uncle screamed in my ears, telling me I pocketed the missing coins, even though I explained that if I stole the money, why would I come to him with concern? But he listened not to a word I said. Instead, he locked himself in his room until he was so roaringly drunk that he slept on the floor in a pool of his own sick. I had hoped he would choke on it; the world would be better for it.

Then Phillip begged to marry me. I must confess I was tempted, but how could I leave you and Mama under the clutch of that terrible man? Philip could not support us all. And as for me, it is all or nothing.

A great storm hit our shores. The windows screamed like they would break. Uncle screamed like he would kill us. We both cried without ceasing, but Mama had ceased to cry for many months.

I longed desperately for Phillip. I feared if I needed him, the storm would make sure he could not come to me. But that is our story, isn't it? No one can help us.

It has come to this: I have no fear of madness, and if it has found me, no matter.

The storm left us. Uncle did not kill us. And I, feeling worn and relieved, took a walk along the shore, where the ocean lapped up my tears and they were no more. Upon the sand I found two curious items: a shining ring with a black gemstone, and a gilded mirror. The ring fit my finger perfectly, *as if it had been made for me especially. I put it on and instantly could understand the words around me.*

Let me emphasize that I was surrounded by sea birds, and loud and complaining things they were, too. And I understood them, and they understood me.

And then I peered into the mirror that lay beside the ring. Large and clear, it was not a bit scratched or cracked, and it was set in a golden frame. When I peered into it, I gave a start, for in it I saw Uncle, dead upon his bed. And my heart, dark and bitter as it is, felt joy.

But my joy would not last long. In my hubris I talked to the nearest bird, and told of my joys and my hopes and, must exuberantly of all, my loves. And the bird told me the one thing I could not believe, and the one thing that shattered my heart into a thousand pieces until my whole self was nothing but an aching, pulsing mess kept captive within my skin. The bird told me my dearest, kindest Phillip was not true to me, and had been telling half-truths. For he did offer to marry me; but he never offered to be true. And for that, he was clever and conniving.

I ran to Phillip, and I am afraid I must have looked a state, disheveled and in tears. And I begged him to tell me it was not true, that he had not been so false and insincere. But then he asked how I knew, and I told him a bird told me. Now the whole town knows I talk to birds, and they laugh at me. They call me Mad Máire, and I cannot say I am angry. For I would gladly welcome madness over this constant ache of the truth.

I am ridiculed in the streets. I pass by shops and errand boys jeer at me. Mothers call home their children at the sight of me. I kept the ring and the mirror. These two things have not betrayed me. And you have not betrayed me, either; you kept by my side as the town reviled me.

I spied Uncle keeping a ledger in his own little notebook. He must have planned to steal our money and leave us; well, the better if he had! "Good riddance," I said! "Better come desertion, poverty, and shame; come quickly, and deliver us from the sharp clutches of our deranged uncle!"

And then Uncle beat you. He drank his poison until he was stumbling, slobbering drunk, and waited for you to cross his path so he might lunge at you with all the spite in his heart and fire in his fists. He beat you until he fell to the floor and slept.

I found you and carried you to bed myself. I feared for your life all through the night, but your breathing is steady, and I have hope for you, my love.

I decided that his reign of terror must end.

I went to Phillip, for while he was untrue to me, he does owe me a favor most assuredly. He did not deny it. He agreed to help.

I need to be quick. I have written you this letter so that when you are healed, you know the truth, and how to proceed, and how to find me. When you have read this, burn it.

Tonight, Uncle came home drunk. He fell upon his bed and made himself sick, and when his breathing became steady and his limbs heavy, I took his breath from him. And I wondered:

will they believe it was the drink? Will others accuse me, or worse – blame Mama? As for Mama, that man poisoned her mind, weakened her body, and I cannot know what she will do, what she will think of me.

So I have come up with a plan.

Phillip has agreed to wait for me on Grackle Island. I gave him a few precious belongings and told him to make sure he was unseen. I will run to the pier and wail, until I know I am seen, and then I will jump in – and the town will see that I jumped to my death. They will see and believe my crimes died with me. I will swim to Phillip, who will take me to Bath, where I can start again, a free and venerable woman. But, oh, Colleen! How I wish you will come, too! Please, if you can – come.

With all my shattered heart, your devoted sister,
Máire

I lowered the letter, locking eyes with Delia. "This explains everything."

She caressed Bigfoot's fur, her arms swinging back and forth. "What do you think happened to her?"

"They found her body later, right? After a storm?"

"It must have been the riptide." Delia's eyes grew wide. "It can't be trusted."

"Or maybe the ex-boyfriend killed her."

She sighed, leaning back against the chimney. "We'll never know." Then her face dropped, and she said softly, "Her sister never woke up, right?"

I studied the handwriting; so pretty, full of hope. "Posey told me something like that." I folded the letter and felt the old, worn corners, and let the words slip from my mouth like honey. "Do you know what this means? It means I'm not crazy."

"Well..." Delia held up one hand. "It means you both had similar experiences, yes." She smiled (oddly – her eyes looked weird).

I threw one bag of curtains at her face. She ducked behind her upraised arms, and it landed on her legs with a *thump*. "If I wanted that kind of nonsense, I'd have brought Posey up here."

Delia tossed the bag aside and rubbed the back of her head. "Fine, fine. But keep that safe." She pointed at the letter. "I'm going to see if Dad's home. I think I might have a concussion."

I did as I was told and buried the letter in my sock drawer, a secret treasure to examine later, like the hope I buried in my heart.

Chapter Twenty-Four

Delia did not have a concussion, at least not one to write home about, and seeing as she was home already anyway, it really wasn't anything to bother with in any capacity. So at seven that evening, as planned, her party began.

I wore blue because I was excited (the other face of severity), and seeing as it was a masquerade party, and I was wearing blue, I came as a blue poison dart frog. Delia wore black and red and went as a dragon (I expected her to be a mythical creature. Dragons are very real and not mythical creatures, but when I told her this, she said no mythical creatures are mythical creatures, and fair enough, I can't argue with that). She curled her hair in tight ringlets and trimmed her mask in gold. Something in her dazzled, and it burst from her skin and danced on her cheeks, like the fire-breath of a dragon. I approved.

James arrived early, because Delia had convinced him to

be the herald. I believe he set a price for himself, much like Judas, though the two men are admittedly hard to compare (James would make a terrible treasurer). Delia cleared out her entire living room and shoved the furniture in the den and lined the kitchen with snacks. As the first guests arrived, I left to greet the high tide (as I do), and then I joined the party to James bellowing,

"ALL HAIL MARION MORRISSEY OF OLD PORT STREET, LADY'S MADNESS!"

His voice echoed through the living room, arresting everyone's attention as he stood, one arm behind his back and heels together. I curtseyed. He wore black (the color of mystery), complete with a bow tie, a plain black mask, and pungent cologne.

"What are you going as?" I asked.

"Darkness himself," he answered, and winked at me (I don't trust a wink). My fingers twitched to slap him – but Fern stood at his side, and as much as he deserved it, I didn't want Fern to think we were a dramatic, physical bunch, so I glared at him instead.

Fern wore green (the color of trials, which is appropriate, seeing as she was at the party with James) and I think was going as, surprise surprise, a fern. It was almost as brilliant as Posey, who wore pink (appropriate – remember, pink is the color of celebration. I would be lying if I said I hadn't coached Posey on this choice) and attended the party as a posy.

Sebastian stepped in front of me, clad head to toe in gray (the color of whimsy, very fitting).

"Greetings," he said, waving a stuffed bunny in front of my eyes.

"Evening." I patted the bunny on the head. "Are you a rabbit?"

He guffawed, pulling up the rabbit's head to reveal a strip of red paint along its neck. "I am a wolf, thank you very much. This is my prey, obviously."

He wore a gray mask, but it was too big and fell over his mouth. He pushed it up and stuffed the rabbit under his belt, smiling proudly. I nodded.

"Ah, right. My bad."

"Good, right? James is lame and decided to go as something stupid. But I put effort into my garb, so clearly I'm the better brother." He spread out his arms. "Approve of the color?"

"Gray is a suitable choice," I answered. "Whimsy, and whatnot."

He smiled the kind of light-up, generous smile that only happens once in a full moon, and I patted him on the shoulder. It was true – gray was a suitable color; most others at the party wore arbitrary colors based on their shallow preferences and felt happy with themselves. Good for them. Their decisions lay on their own shoulders. I can only control my own choices.

One by one the guests arrived, waited for their name to be announced at the threshold, and bowed or curtseyed while we cheered. Then we gave a presentation on the "Fourteen Things We Love About Cordelia Ann Fortescue," and danced with unfortunate abandon until all collapsed on the floor, red faced and out of breath.

That's when we got hungry, so we took a snack break. I led the parade into the kitchen where Ms. Gretchen was deep in conversation with Francesca Lovely.

"Oh," I said when I saw her, nursing her cup of punch at the kitchen island. I had stopped so quickly that Delia bumped into me and grumbled,

"Watch your bloody step, Marion."

Ms. Gretchen scowled above her raised cup. "Language, Delia."

She stood across from Francesca, bent over the island counter, like they had been talking of secret things the walls couldn't hear. Briefly I smelled the gambling den, the smoke and the spirits, and I saw Francesca's face, her drink, her fingers as she laid down her cards and said, "I'm out," her eyes as she said, "I'm stuck," and "go." Was she confiding in Ms. Gretchen, telling her the things we longed to know? Did Ms. Gretchen know about the gambling den – about our escapades within it?

"Sorry, Mom."

I still had not moved, so Delia poked me in the ribs.

"Francesca Lovely," I said, more to myself than anyone else.

"Hi, girls." She smiled, squinting her dark, beady eyes. "I waved hello earlier, but you didn't see me come in, I think."

Ms. Gretchen stood up straight. "Oh! You know each other? Delia, this is the woman who told me about the hush-hush at the news station." She held out her hand to showcase Francesca's unruly mane, and Francesca placed one finger to her lips.

"Oh now, you didn't hear it from me, remember?" Her words were tangled in giggles. "You heard that somewhere else."

"Of course," Ms. Gretchen said. "You're right, it was someone else." She winked at Delia (ugh), eyebrows arched like a stretching cat, but Delia frowned. The last thing we expected to see was those two women, chatting and scheming, and Delia was lost in silence. No wink could bring her out.

"You work for the news station?" I asked, snatching at my thoughts, desperate to catch one, to know what to say, but my mind raced a million miles a minute. Worlds were colliding, and I was caught in the middle. NEWS STATION hit me in the face, and it was all I could think to say.

"I'm a freelancer," Francesca answered. "I do a bit of everything."

"My mom always told me..." Ms. Gretchen moved to sit beside Francesca, pulling out a stool and crossing her legs. Even on a stool her posture was perfect. But then again, of course it was. That was her career for years, good posture on stools, correct pronunciation, excellent enunciation. "'A woman should be classy, with a career to back her up.'" Ms. Gretchen patted her on the back. "You do well, Francesca."

"Your mom sounds like she had high standards," I offered, finally, after staring silently for so long that Delia handed me a cup of punch.

"And look where it got me." Ms. Gretchen slapped the granite countertops.

"Anyway, your mom's been giving me advice –" Francesca began, and Delia's ears perked.

"Oh, right. Ms. Francesca?"

"Yes, sweetie?"

"Are Mr. Doug and Marv working together?" She sipped on her punch innocently, giving me a knowing side glance.

"Oh." She leaned back, her lips tightening to a thin line. "That's an interesting question." She tossed her hair behind her shoulder –

Hair piled like straw, a woman dressed in orange, walking out of Waffle Madness that Sunday morning when Grandma ran away –

It was her.

The memory flashed before my eyes and my knees almost buckled. A memorable hair toss, with all its straw and curl. She caught my eye and forced a smile. How had I forgotten? Francesca Lovely was a recurring character in my life, and I hadn't even noticed. First I saw her at Waffle Madness, and then at Finnegan's Galley, just before she wrote that malicious article.

Ms. Gretchen studied her daughter, confused. "Marv?" she asked. "The museum owner?"

"They're friends," Francesca answered. "Everyone

knows that." She propped her elbow onto the kitchen island, head resting on her knuckles. "So what do you do all day, being homeschooled?"

Ah yes, question number five of the Five Main Questions Asked in Ignorance. Number one is, of course, *How will a homeschooler develop social skills?* Which leads to others such as, *Will a homeschooler be too sheltered? Will a homeschooler develop necessary life skills like sitting in a class and showing up on time?* And the old faithful, *Will a homeschooler be prepared academically?* (cue eye roll). But number five is an old friend, really, so I had a ready answer.

"Well, we do our schoolwork, and when we're done with that, we try to solve murders. Or one, really, in particular." I paused. "I suppose that's over now. We also put on plays."

"And look for fairies," Delia added, cookie in her mouth.

"Is that right?" Francesca tapped her lips, her long, fake fingernails (lies) brushing the edge of her nose. "Tell me – "

Sebastian exploded into the kitchen. He entered with the bang of his shoes on the tile floor and the shout of his voice and the outward spread of his arms. He was a bomb, with a better mortality rate.

"Delia!" His fingers wiggled in the air, mischief in his smile. "Time to bring this party outside!"

"I'm still snacking," she said.

"And this shindig's getting boring. Let's go to the waterfront." He backed out of the kitchen, waving for her to follow. "Please."

"I'm snacking," she repeated.

"Did I say I cared? Eat outside."

The dancers in the living room laughed, clapping at something happening in the dance circle; Sebastian bobbed the head of his rabbit, like it was nodding encouragement.

"No."

"Yes."

Delia swallowed the last bite of cookie, her patience wearing thin. "Can you be any more annoying, Sebastian Mobley?"

"Is that a dare?"

"It's question." She crossed her arms. "I'm genuinely curious."

"Then, yes. Bigfoot is a myth." His eyes shot wide open, and he broke into a broad smile, poised to run.

"You gobshite!" She yelled (she was dabbling in Irish curse words now), and he stepped out of sight, chuckling. Ms. Gretchen slammed her drink on the counter and it spilled over, the punch splashing into the air and onto the counter like blood.

"Cordelia! Really. Please watch your language."

"No one here cares." Delia adjusted the bodice of her dress, speaking from the back of her throat.

Francesca handed Ms. Gretchen a napkin and stood up. "I hate to leave before this shindig gets exciting, but I have an early morning." She tossed her straw hair again and patted Delia on the shoulder with her long, sparkly blue nails. "Happy birthday, honey." And she left, a trail of perfume and suspicion lingering behind her.

"She's our best contact," Ms. Gretchen said, wiping the counter. "Choose your questions carefully. Don't scare her off."

Delia stuffed my mouth with a chocolate chip cookie, leading me into the living room before I could object. "Believe me, we're trying," she called over her shoulder. "We can't help it if all the questions are interesting questions." Then she whispered in my ear, "No, Mom doesn't know, I guarantee it. Don't say a word." And she pushed me into the swarm of dancers.

We tossed our masks and moved to the pier for party number two (chatter and salt breezes). The water was restless again, and as I looked down into it, the waves clutched at me, one after the other after the other, trying to grab me, drag me down into its hungry depths. I gripped the railing tighter and focused on the lighthouse, whose light spun with a beat, flooding us in light, a visual song. Birds shouted in the distance; I knew it was the birds, because the only words carried on the wind were "shiny," and "sparkles," and "food." I blocked them out of my mind as Sebastian stood beside me, his wiry, wiggly limbs wrapped around the pier's wooden railings. He turned to me and said in scrunchy tones,

"Why didn't you come as a peacock? Why a frog?"

I wrinkled my nose. The answer was obvious, if only he'd think about it. "Only boy peacocks are pretty. I am, in fact, female, so if I dressed as a fancy peacock it would be a half-truth."

"Ah." Sebastian nodded. "Half-truths."

"You're not opposed to half-truths?"

"Oh, no." He placed one hand over his heart and cleared his throat, his voice coming out strangely high and squeaky. "I don't like them. Half-truths are bad, for sure. Best to avoid them, all in all."

"Right."

"They're worse than lies, really." He leaned close and spoke softly, barely audible over the waves. "You know, there's a lot – "

But footsteps thundered behind us, and James grabbed Sebastian's shoulders, feigning to push him over the ledge – Sebastian emitted a high-pitched squeal and Fern, at James' side, laughed. James laughed too (too hard), taking a sidelong glance at Fern, and Sebastian glared, adjusting his shirt and securing the stuffed rabbit at his belt.

"Very funny."

"It was," James agreed, reaching out to fist bump him, but Sebastian side stepped it and grumbled under his breath. Fern fist bumped James instead. She wore James' sport jacket over her shoulders like a real damsel in distress, but she only stayed on the pier for a few minutes before she declared it was time for her to go home. She left quickly, James at her side to walk her to her car. By the time he got back, Sebastian was in what the British (and therefore Delia) would call a "proper mood." He pointed to us without any sort of introduction or ceremony.

"This gets me thinking, I'm still twenty-five dollars short. I need it soon, too, Delia, if you're feeling charitable."

"No."

"I'll pay you back – "

The light of a thousand fires flashed in Delia's eyes, and the lighthouse was put to shame. "I'm not supporting your addiction, Sebastian Mobley. Not. One. Cent." She propped her hip against the railing, back to Posey, and crossed her arms. That was that, until James spoke.

"You agreed to pay me thirty bucks, Delia. Just spot Sebastian the twenty-five and we'll call it even."

She eyed him, surveying the truthfulness in his gait before turning her attention to her own fingernails, recently painted a fresh coat of black. "Fine," she said, an easiness flowing in the word. She had tossed her resolve to the water at the prospect of five bucks saved, and I detected a certain smugness coming from the lighthouse the next time the light came around.

"That was uncharacteristically thoughtful of you, James," I said. James only shrugged, so Sebastian answered,

"It's not just my debt."

"Dude, shut up."

I turned to James, leaning back against the railing. "You owe money too?"

"No," he said, definitively, without looking at me.

"Fern owes money too." Sebastian rolled his eyes. "She

started crying and whimpering about how many hours it would take her to pay it off and James said we'd take care of it. Like an idiot."

"Very chivalrous of you," Posey added in a small voice, staring at her feet. Her shoulders melted, drifting down her body, like a great weight sat on them.

"Not chivalrous," I said. "Blind and stupid. But with honorable intentions, I assume."

"He doesn't even know his own intentions." Sebastian spit over the side of the pier. "She's pretty deep in the group. She'll be losing money again. And then what, James? Will you take care of all her debts?"

"Shut up."

"You know I'm right."

"I know you like a bet a little too much." James stepped forward, pushing Sebastian into the railing. "And I know Fern didn't make you play that last round."

Sebastian did nothing but stare at the sky for a full minute, while James backed away, shoulders twitching, like he was holding in words that crawled through him, biting at the corners.

Maybe it was a mixture of boredom and jealousy, or maybe of hurt pride and stupidity, but whatever it was, while we were watching the sparkles in the sky, Sebastian found it an appropriate time to say,

"She's an idiot, and so are you." He whispered it, teeth clenched, but James heard him.

"At least I don't have a gambling problem."

Sebastian straightened up, and a numbness raced up my spine. I focused on the horizon, counting the flashes of the lighthouse.

Sebastian growled. "I don't have a gambling problem."

"Right."

"Speak for yourself, dingbat." Sebastian took a step forward.

(Three flashes).

James sneered. "I don't have a gambling problem. I'm also not infatuated with a crazy woman who thinks she can talk to birds."

Sebastian threw back his arm and hurled it forward, but Posey dove in front of James, and Sebastian punched her straight in the face. She crumpled to the deck as James yelled, "WHAT'D YOU DO, IDIOT?" and Sebastian stammered apology after apology. I knelt before her and brushed her hair out of her eyes; even in the darkness I could see the pink bloom around her left eye.

Posey propped up on her elbow and hissed into my ear, "Is James okay? Did he see me jump in front of him?" She grabbed my wrist and squeezed. I suppressed the need to roll my eyes and said,

"He's fine, dummy. He saw everything. Next time let him take the hit."

"Did he – "

But James screamed at Sebastian, and Sebastian cowered over us, taking it insult by insult – we watched, speechless. "WHY'D YOU PUNCH A GIRL, STUPID?"

Sebastian's breaths turned into a low sort of whine. "I didn't mean to punch her, I was trying to punch *you*. She jumped in front of *you*."

James leaned into his face, arms outstretched, the ends of his hair whirling in the wind. "What were you planning to do? I'm like three times your size!"

"PUNCH YOU IN THE FACE, THAT'S WHAT!" Spit flew from his mouth, and he turned away to kneel beside me as Posey groaned, holding her eye, the pain settling in. He looked up at James and set his jaw so hard the veins in his temples throbbed. "Marion is here, you know."

"So?"

"So? You said those things and you don't care she heard them?"

"Oh." James' face fell, his eyes meeting mine in a haze of fear and pity. I tried to melt into the pier, to slide between the cracks of the wooden planks. I really, really wished I wasn't there. He held both his hands behind his head, his face contorted, his gaze pulling at me for attention. "Sorry, Marion...I didn't mean – I mean – well..."

"Don't worry about it." But I worried about it. The others knelt over Posey too, and soon the air was loud with everyone asking her how she was (she was fine, a little punch wasn't going to kill her) but the voice in my head was even louder: they were starting to think I was crazy, which was fair enough, because I had come to the same conclusion once or twice, too.

We brought Posey into the kitchen and treated her like a

hero (You jumped in front of him? Really? Does it hurt? Is it bleeding?) while James and Sebastian reluctantly decided it was time for them to leave. Posey iced her face for a while and then Delia, Posey, and I went back to the water; the night was still young, and we intended to make good use of it. We followed the waterfront and ambled all the way to the end of the pier, where the world stretched out, and all the lines between sky and water, land and see, were smoothed into darkness.

"I wonder if it will scar?" Posey leaned over the railing, face open to the ocean, and gently touched the bone above her eye where the skin had broken. A tiny red stroke sat there, barely visible in the night.

"Be cool if it did," I said. "Face scars are the best. Prestige and intimidation by scar: it will get you far in life. It's more than Fern has to brag about, that's for sure."

"Oh." Posey smiled and leaned even farther over the ledge. She bit her lip and giggled. I didn't want to say anything else, mainly because I found her repulsive in that moment, but also because I wanted to think about what James said. I counted the ways in which he was right (I did think I could talk to birds. Perhaps it *was* crazy. But was there a pattern of madness? The water troll, maybe. But that's mere imagination. Is imagination a crazy trait?) and the ways in which he was wrong (Sebastian definitely didn't have the eye twinkles for me) and decided in the end it didn't matter. What's done is done, and the truth will out.

Sebastian called out to us.

"I didn't want to leave until I said sorry again." He trotted toward us, the rabbit on his belt bouncing, and James followed him, head down. "I'm really sorry Posey, I really didn't want to hit you, when Dad finds out he'll kill me."

"Yeah," James said. "That's the real problem here."

"Shut up."

"It's fine," Posey rushed to answer, smiling broadly. "Really." Then she smiled at James, only this smile was different, weighed down by giggles and bashful twitches. Sebastian cleared his throat.

"Well, thanks, I guess. So," Sebastian turned to me, "I might not be able to leave the house for a while after this, so I won't be able to help out..."

"No worries. Violet confessed, anyway."

He hesitated, intent to say something else, but I froze, my eyes catching a figure in the shadows along the retaining wall, walking our way – the boy I chased through the graveyard.

The boy with the trident pin.

My white whale.

Chapter Twenty-Five

"YOU!"

I ran so hard that my feet hit the wooden planks like great cannon balls. The boy's head popped up and he saw me coming (heard me, more like it) and ran the opposite way, at full speed.

He really was quite fast.

James was faster.

I chased him first, running as fast as I could in my taffeta dress, tossing my fancy shoes to the wind (good riddance), but the whole outfit was cumbersome and my insides were filled with junk food and I really wasn't at my best, so James quickly surpassed me, and the others fell into line beside me.

"Why are we running?" Posey wheezed.

"That," I answered between labored breaths, "is a question with many answers."

We chased him through Market Street and past the graveyard and into an old residential area where all the houses were grand and held plaques on their walls that read "such and such house, circa such and such year." James grabbed the strap of his backpack and swung him around, pinning him to the trunk of a large live oak tree in front of a house that, I saw with a start, was Francesca Lovely's family home. My heart pounded in my ears. This was it – this was the moment I'd get an answer, at least one answer to the million questions swirling around in my brain. We were all out of breath, but James had something to say right away.

"Why did you run?"

Fear danced in the ruffian's eyes. Real, visceral fear. I would be lying if I said I did not enjoy it; it meant we had the upper hand, and he knew it. I also would be lying if I said I did not want to explain to him right then and there that we had no intention of killing him, eating his flesh, and dropping his bones into the sea (this intent could be the only reason for the exact kind of fear in his eyes). I told him as much, and his brow crumpled and James grinned at me, eyeing me from over his shoulder.

"Nice, Marion."

"That's specific," the lout whimpered.

"I just wanted you to rest assured," I said. "Although we retain the right to cause some physical pain, should you refuse to answer our questions."

He swallowed and his whole face followed with it. The

flesh on his face was disturbingly movable. I didn't trust it. It was a metaphor for his character, stitched into his skin. Always moving and malleable, changing and adapting for each new circumstance. Even his arms were unnerving – he had arms like oars that propelled his canoe body, too long and too crafty.

"Why did you run?" James repeated.

"Because she came at me!"

"Come off it!" Delia yelled, over my shoulder. Her words, though helpful, blasted in my ear and I had to stop myself from pushing her away. "Do you think anyone is scared of Little Marion?"

"You would be, if she kept running at you while you were innocently taking a walk, minding your own business –"

I held up my hands to silence him. He would, at least once, answer one stupid question. "Enough with your drivel. Why don't you want to be seen by me?"

"Because – " He glanced at James, almost pleadingly. "Because you live in that house, right?"

"What house?" My stomach sank, dread filling it like lead and seeping into my veins. What did any of this have to do with my home, my sanctuary, my anchor in the maddening sea?

He bit his lip.

"I live in *A* house, yes, but what house do you mean?" Irritation fluttered in my chest. He only stared at me, so I stepped closer and said slowly, "It would behoove you to answer my questions, for I am impatient, and not to be trifled with. Now, what house?"

He gulped. "The one I've been digging holes around."

James turned to me again and Sebastian let out a low, "Well hot dog," and Delia cried out, "I'll be jiggered!" but I, feeling the realization make its way into my brain like thick molasses, did not say a word. Finally, James spoke.

"Why are you digging holes around her house?"

"Beats me." James tightened his grip and the oaf held up his hands. "Someone paid me to do it. I don't know why, I was told not to ask."

James leaned into him, unconvinced. "Really."

He cleared his throat. "The pay is good."

"At least tell us who paid you," I said.

"Oh, no. No, no, no, no. No. No, if I did that, they'd kill me."

"Kill you, you say? Like they killed Lily Anderson?"

He groaned. "No, it has nothing to do with that woman's death. I don't know anything about her. Honestly." He held his palms out to us, to show he had no secrets written on his skin, and literally nothing up his sleeves.

"Look, Todd – " Sebastian laid a hand on his shoulder and squeezed. He must have met Todd the first time he visited the gambling den, back when he lost all that money. Todd – it was not the kind of name I expected, although it was kind of bland and comical when said with disgust, as Sebastian managed to do, so upon further thought it was quite fitting. "Our dad's a detective, and we'll make sure he gets to the bottom of this, so it's better if you just tell us what you know now – "

"Your dad's a DETECTIVE? Oh, man, that's rough – "

"FOCUS!" James yelled, rocking him back and forth.

"I'm focusing, I'm focusing!" He held up his hands again. "I'm just saying, it's rough he's a detective, because in order for you to tell him whatever it is you think you know, you'd have to admit you went to our little shindig on Sunday, and my guess is Dad won't be so happy about that."

"We don't have to tell him," Sebastian said, too quickly.

"Well, maybe you don't, but I do." Todd smirked and James gave Sebastian a look filled with thunder and shadows. Our little investigation was falling deeper and deeper into darkness, and I had a sudden itch to go back home and hide under my covers.

"You won't tell him because it would land you and yours in hot water, too." James' voice was a command. Todd hesitated.

"Well…"

"WHO WANTED YOU TO DIG HOLES?" James picked him up off the ground (it was a little impressive, I must admit) and Todd's feet raced back and forth like a cartoon mouse trying to start a run. Posey giggled.

"FINE! Okay, okay. It was the curly haired lady, okay? The leader's girl." He nodded to the Lovely House. "She lives there. Rewarded me handsomely. Met me at that waffle place and told me to name my price. But I don't know why, honest, and I never asked. That's all I know. I'm just in it for the cash. I've got my eye on this clunker – ”

James set him back on the ground and said to me, “Francesca.”

Delia's eyes covered half the expanse of her face, growing so quickly that I thought the stress of it might make her eyeballs explode. My thoughts raced and I froze, replaying every conversation I shared with Francesca, every glance she ever gave me, every word that left her lips. The article, the holes, her help, her warning the night we discovered the gambling den; it all fit together somehow, but it sat like spaghetti in my head, all greasy and twisted together. The dread in my stomach climbed up my throat and I swallowed it down. Other questions tickled my lips, pushing at the corners of my thoughts.

“If that's all you know about Francesca, then tell us about Lily Anderson. Did she go to the Sunday shindig? Did she have gambling debts?”

“Not a clue.”

“Prepare for a purple nurple,” James said.

“It's the truth!” Todd squealed, his voice squeakier with every syllable, wiggling desperately to get out of James' grip and cover his nipples. “Honest truth! I never saw her before. Not even once. It's possible she had debt, I don't know, but it would have been before my time. Honest!”

“I believe him,” I said. The desperate honesty in his voice spoke to my gut, and I knew his ignorance was, unfortunately, deep within his soul. James loosened his grip and Todd relaxed.

"Look, bottom line, it's a rough place. If that lady owed something, then yeah, I could see her getting a bad end. But I've never seen her there, 'k? And I don't know why that other lady asked me to dig holes. It's a mystery to me. A lucrative mystery, but a mystery nonetheless." His face twitched (too movable) and I crossed my arms.

"Well then, here's another mystery for you: Francesca told me she didn't want to write that cruel and unusual article about Finnegan's Galley, but she wrote it anyway. Why'd she write it? Who forced her, and how? And why?"

Todd struggled against James for a moment, then huffed. "I don't know anything. I don't know anything about her life, or her articles, or why she does the things she does. She pays me, and that's it. Capiche?"

I stepped closer. "I heard the gambling den supports a good cause. What's that good cause?"

Todd's eyes grew wide and he stuffed his laugh back into his throat. "Good cause? You mean charity? No, can't say I know anything about that." He chuckled. "That place, a charity..."

James nodded to me. "You have any other questions?"

"No," I replied. "I'm tapped out."

He released Todd, and Todd brushed the front of his shirt like it was dirtied by James' touch, ran his fingers through his hair, and rearranged the straps of his backpack. "I'll be off, then."

"It was a pleasure," I said, bowing a little.

"Right." Todd eyed me, eyebrows pushed together, then turned and disappeared in between two large houses.

I looked at Delia. She grimaced, but then sighed and nodded. I looked at Sebastian. He nodded, too.

And, like sheep to the slaughter, we followed him.

We kept to the shadows, forming one strange, crouched conga line. Todd slipped through yards, cut between houses, and kept to the shadows, and we did the same, following at a distance, using our ears as much as our eyes. Posey's skirts swished behind me, and I spun around, my hand catching her elbow.

"You should go home."

Posey wrinkled her nose. "No."

I stood up straight, preparing my back to be a wall, fluffing my skirt to be the moat. "Mom would kill me if she knew where I'm about to take you – "

"Then my guess is she'd kill you for going, too."

I shook my head. "It's not a classy place."

"I don't care." Her marsh face froze over and the wisps of her hair floated above her head like the crown of a poltergeist. She was ice and poison. There would be no fighting her.

I gathered my skirt around my knees, my resolve melting. "Fine," I muttered. "But don't say I didn't warn you."

"It's not your decision," Posey insisted, but she smiled, and her footsteps were light and breezy as we hurried to the back of the line, following Todd through the shadows. We kept far behind him, so when he looked both ways before knocking on the museum door, he didn't see us. The door opened, and Todd disappeared.

A cry of despair rang in the night. Sebastian stood beside me, his chest heaving, mouth open as he stared at the alley door and howled, "There was a thing tonight?" His shoulders sank, like a kid on a playground who wasn't picked for a single game of tag. I placed one hand on his arm.

"Let's go."

Sebastian stepped forward but James grabbed his collar, pulling him back so quickly he stumbled and fell into me. His bloody (literally, not the swear word) rabbit fell out of his belt and onto the cobblestone street.

"We don't have the password," James said, ever the voice of reason.

I pushed Sebastian back onto his feet and glared at the door, easily seen by the bright SUICIDE PREVENTION LIFELINE notice taped to it. The password changed every session, and so we didn't have the password for the night. James was right. There was no way we were getting in if we weren't invited – Sebastian grabbed his stuffed rabbit and wiggled it back under his belt, doing a little hip dance to aid, and I got an idea. I faced Delia.

"It's your moment."

"What?"

"You're taking a speech class. You know the arts of persuasion. And you are a woman, so you can use your wiles."

"What? No, I – "

"Cordelia Rose!" I raised my arms to awaken her wisdom, and a gust of wind roared past, as if on command. The hair on my arms stood on end. "Perhaps you were made for such a time as this! Perhaps your destiny is but one block away! What have you to lose? Nothing! What have you to gain? Everything! Beyond that door lies the answer to this puzzle, the culmination of your future! Say it with me: serendipity!" A burst of wind blew through the alley, and it took with it the words of my peers. I tried again. "Say it: serendipity!"

"Serendipity," James and Sebastian repeated, but slowly and out of sync.

Posey crossed her arms and sized up the alley before us – ignoring me, no doubt, while she gathered her thoughts about the world beyond the door. The breeze stirred her bangs, like the wind stirs the marsh grasses.

"Don't listen to your doubts! Don't listen to your fears! Listen to your friends! You can do this. I believe in you, Cordelia Rose Fortescue. You are the protagonist in the spy thriller that is our life. You are the cornerstone of this operation. The world is your circus if you but don the top hat! You have the skills – you've been studying the art of persuasion, of eloquence, of improv! You are a student of destiny! Be strong, my sweet! Choose courage, and you shall be rewarded! GET US INTO THAT MUSEUM!"

She didn't bat an eye. "I don't do wiles."

"How do you know? You've never tried."

"Exactly."

I cupped her face and lowered my voice until it was raspy and masculine, like the voice of an ailing monk on an isolated mountainside speaking to a lonely shepherd in the rain – our favorite childhood game. "Be persuasive, then. Make your mother proud." I pushed her forward again and again (Delia griped, "I've only had one class!" but I didn't care) until she reached the door, where the same massive man poked out his head and said,

"Password."

Delia glared at me, but I prodded her with my elbow, and she squared her shoulders. The others gathered behind us.

"Ummm." She tossed her hair; it would have been a nice trick, except it was plastered with hair spray, and therefore made a loud *crunch*. "We've been here before, and ummm, were invited, but we forgot the password."

"No password, no entry."

"Wait!" Delia folded her fingers around the edges of the door and smiled. Really, really smiled, until the dimple on her chin was center stage and her eyes shone and crinkled around the edges. It was comical, but the massive man, for all his muscles and rules, almost smiled in return. He didn't, but something softened around his mouth. "What's your name again?"

He flicked the chain of the diamond cross on his chest. It snagged a tuft of hair that poked out from his V-neck shirt; he rubbed at it. "Lenny."

"Well, Lenny." Delia leaned against the door frame, never losing eye contact. "What do you have to lose? We're welcome. We're not the ones you're supposed to keep out. Just ask Fern. We were invited, we're just forgetful. We all have pins. And you know what else?" She tapped her fingers on the door. "It's my birthday. I'm eighteen now. All of us are, actually."

He sighed. The cross on his chest glinted; it said LENNY on the spine, inscribed in flowy cursive. "Truth and consequences."

"What?" Delia asked.

"Truth and consequences. That's the password. Say it to me."

"Truth and consequences," we repeated, in unison, like hypnotized zombies.

Lenny help up one finger and slowly pointed it at Posey. "Except for you, sweetheart." He tipped his head to the side, one eyebrow raised, a warning.

Posey crossed her arms and shot daggers out of her eyes. The swamp creatures emerged from her face, crawling the space between them, but Lenny didn't budge.

"I've seen these other lowlifes here before, but not you. And what are you, seven?"

"Actually I'm – "

He stopped her with an upheld palm. "I don't wanna hear it. You'll stay out here. Get some fresh air. It's good for growing kids."

"But – "

"It's that or you all go." Lenny kicked the door hard, purely for the shock of it. The *thud* reverberated through the alley and down Main Street, and a pair of crows flew from the roof and out of sight in a tumult of flapping and shrieks. He leaned against the door frame, a satisfied gleam in his eyes. "I have half a mind to insist you all skedaddle, anyway."

We shifted nervously in our taffeta and polyester blends, the movement of the fabric loud in the moment of careful silence. We exchanged defeated glances.

Posey would have to bow out.

"You'll stay here," I said, clasping the back of her neck. "Take the hit, for the good of the team."

"But it's not fair!" she cried, her voice fluttering. "I'm *always* the one left behind – "

"We have no choice." I forced her to face me and placed my hands over her ears, my palms resting on her jawline. She stuck out her bottom lip like a baby, so I pinched her cheeks. "I'll tell you everything. And we won't be long." I turned back to Lenny and took a deep breath. "Truth and consequences, Mr. Lenny."

Posey slid down the opposite wall of the alley until she sat, knees up, with her arms wrapped around her shins. Her skirt spread out around her and she stared at the cobblestones, brow furrowed, and mouth drooped down in a solid frown.

Delia whispered, "Sorry, Posey. We'll be back," but Posey ignored her, wiping her nose and looking away as Delia smiled sympathetically.

The others repeated the password again, and Lenny nodded and backed up, pushing the door open. "Them's the right words. Good thing you got 'em from the right people." He pointed at each of us and we scampered through the door, pins high for him to see, but as James passed, he grabbed his upper arm and squeezed. "You cause one ounce of trouble, you're outta here in a hurry, got it?"

"Got it."

"You tell anyone, especially that dad o' yours – I know who you are, don't look surprised – you won't have no one to tell next time. Got it?"

"Got it," James croaked.

Lenny surveyed him at arm's length, one hand still grasping his arm, starting at his shiny black shoes and ending at his bowtie. "You got guns on you?"

"No, sir."

"Knives?"

"No, sir."

"How 'bout you kids?" He glowered at us and we shook our heads. "Good." He pushed James forward and we scurried toward the back room, happy to get away from Lenny's rough hands and voluminous chest hair. This time we could hear shouting and laughter from a distance – and something else. Something brash. Something feral. Something angry.

Barking.

People crammed into the room, pressing against something that was in the middle, their voices shrill and restless against the cacophony of their peers. I tried to see over the heads, but it was no use. I was too short.

James' eyes fixed straight ahead, and like an ocean storm his gaze was gray and angry. Something disgusted him. The barking turned to snarling, and I knew.

It was a dog fight.

Chapter Twenty-Six

My stomach lurched. Nothing was interesting anymore; the world wasn't intriguing and secretive. It was disgusting. It was cruel. It was savage. Why was I even there? What was I trying to prove? I needed to leave. Half the crowd cheered, and something wet and bloody bolted past to cower in a corner. My stomach climbed to my throat and my jaw steeled itself, so I turned to Delia to say I was leaving, but instead I came face to face with an angry (very different from scared) Todd.

"What are you doing here?" The movable softness of his face had changed to iron, like the wave of anger washed away his fickleness and left resolve in its wake. I didn't like it any better. I swallowed. James answered.

"We followed you. This is disgusting."

Todd grabbed my arm and pulled me through the hall and back into the museum. The others followed, but when we crossed the threshold, Sebastian snatched Todd's wrists and tugged his hands away, standing between the two of us like a bulwark, like he wasn't made of grease and wire.

"What do you think you're doing?"

"Saving you," Todd answered, pointing to the door. "That way's out."

"Are you the one stealing the dogs, then?" James towered over him, his meaty shoulders threatening him with every breath. He pushed Sebastian out of the way and stepped closer. "What are they for, practice?"

"No." Todd looked less than convinced of his own answer. "Look, I don't like this place. I'd leave if I could. But you guys? You got no skin in the game. Keep it that way. I know Fern recruited you, but –"

"Recruited?" James backed up a little, his head tipped to the side. Calculations whirred in his brain, logic and revelations winning out, his emotions squeezing out of him drop by drop.

Lenny watched us from the door, silence weighty on his shoulders. One wrong move and he'd throw us out once and for all.

"It's her job." Todd looked him up and down. "You don't think we're here for fun? Look, I'm not an idiot. I see why all this is appealing, interesting to the innocent eye – or the corrupted eye, for that matter. But I'm not here for wiggles and giggles. I got goals, right? I want a car. I want to go places. Literally. And I wasn't getting there very fast mowing lawns. This pays real well. And I – " He hesitated.

"I'm in too deep. Forget what you saw, for your own good —
"

"James!" Fern glided in, fresh from the back room, beaming at James. She still wore her green dress, but her lips were fiery red and jewels glittered around her neck. The depravity of the night had no hold on her; her skin glowed, and her eyes sparkled in the dim light. Lenny smiled (I didn't know he could smile) and she held out her arms. "I didn't know you'd be here. I, uh, didn't think you'd like it."

"They're just leaving," Todd said.

"Nonsense. Let's go down." She took James' arm, but he resisted, looking down at her with a cool disinterest that (to the trained eye) revealed he was on the verge of rage. The revelations were waning, and his anger was inching back, finding a home behind his eyes.

"Am I your recruit?"

Fern glowered at Todd and her lips shriveled. For the first time, her mouth looked small. "What? No. You're my friend!" She chuckled and swatted his arm. "I'm supposed to recruit guys with *money*, Jimmy."

"But you recruited me."

Fern took his hand. "No, I — "

James turned his back to her, one hand on the back of his neck as he headed for the door. "I'm risking a lot, being here. If Dad knew — "

"If you figure things out, he'll be so proud, he won't care."

He stopped and stared at her, a paleness choking his face

like she had just announced his deepest secret – and then Fern winked. She actually winked. She had sought his most vulnerable spot, his flesh beneath his scales, and found it. She shot her arrow, and her aim was true, *and then she winked.* A protective fire bubbled up from my stomach, urging me to pull James away from her, but I stayed put. He needed to do it, to sever that tie himself. I tucked my hands under my armpits to keep from grabbing him.

"That may be true," he said, his words careful and steady. "But I think we're being stupid. You're stupid too, for letting us in. We even lost money..." James eyed Sebastian, then swung his head around to Fern. "Unless that was your plan all along? Sniff us out, see if our dad can be bought? Buy his silence? Spare him the shame of exposing his children and their criminal activity? Line his pockets?"

Fern's face turned gray like a summer storm. Her lips almost dropped from her face. "How dare you. Don't you think I'm risking things too? You saw Marv. He didn't want me to bring you. We have no secret plan; I just like you. And you're not the only one with a disapproving dad." She bustled toward him and pulled on his arm. "Let's go. It's fun."

James looked down at her with contempt in his eyes, but then she smiled, and he softened.

He traded his integrity for a pretty face.

Drat it all, her charms won again.

I opened my mouth to accuse him of being an idiot, but Fern spoke over me.

"After all, there's a lot you don't know, right?"

James paused, letting her words sink in before he brushed off her hand and took a deep breath, shaking his head. "We're going home."

I breathed a sigh of relief and we made for the exit, Delia and I locking arms, when Lenny opened the door and a gruff voice resounded through the room.

"Hi, Lenny. Truth and consequences."

"Long time no see, Henry." Lenny stood back for the man to pass, but something shot past him, knocking Henry into Lenny. Lenny roared and pushed him away, screaming, "Now, hold on – " as Posey blurred through the room and we watched, dumbfounded, as she ran past us. Lenny stumbled after her. His fingers brushed the hem of her dress and so she kept running, desperate not to be caught, darting through the open door behind Fern and down the hall, into the crowded den.

"CATCH HER!" Lenny yelled, his every hair standing on end, the cross on his chest flinging over his shoulder as he tumbled to the floor, his balance challenged by the solid heaviness of his limbs and the agility of Posey's escape. "SOMEONE GO AFTER HER!"

And without a thought James and I began the chase, Fern and Todd behind us.

The crowd jeered and swayed – another fight was about to begin, and Posey was nowhere to be seen. I stopped abruptly, partly because the crowd was so dense I couldn't run, and partly because I needed to pause and stand on my tippy toes to look for her. James and Fern froze beside me, calling for Posey, their voices lost in the noise.

The floor shone red with blood, and an excited murmur buzzed through the air. The collective greed was pliable and sharp, bouncing off the walls and cutting throats. I shrank underneath the weight of it, the way it shone in the eyes around me, in the smiles exchanged and the obscenities uttered.

One man dragged something away and I couldn't look, so I turned my face just in time to see a man nod and wink at Fern. She didn't acknowledge him, but turned and smiled at James, leaning into him like he was a warm blanket and she was cold – but it was boiling hot, and stuffy, and smelly, and why on earth would she want to get closer to another body? James let her cling to him as they traced the edges of the crowd, looking for Posey. Soon they were swallowed into the madness. My eyes held onto the strange man, mulling him over; he had a strangely familiar face, slimy and freckled –

It was Leo, the man who loaned my parents money and called it in at his whim. A recruit of Fern's, probably, that took the arrangement to mean more than an opportunity to place a few bets. He saw James and his eyes spit fire.

"Ten thousand dollars and one year in prison."

I turned toward the voice and saw Todd. "What?"

He leaned in closer. "That's the spectator fine, if you're caught."

"Really?" My stomach dropped, filling my gut like lead.

"Yeah." He tilted his head. "But we're minors."

"Oh, right." I closed my eyes and counted to ten before observing each corner of the room, turning slowly in place, looking for my little sister. Men placed bets one after the other (and they mostly *were* men, except a few women in sparkly dresses floating from arm to arm, massaging shoulders as they passed) and taunting each other to "shut up and pay up." A few men stood close to the ring, talking secretly. One turned around to place a bet with a man holding a notebook (small and cute).

"The handlers," Todd said, when he saw my eyes settle on them. "They train their dogs, bring them here to fight. If they're confident, they'll place a bet. Tonight they're betting ten grand."

The air left my lungs. The more I learned about this place, the more money seemed like an idea, an imaginary concept, a magical word, where possibilities were endless and grand and destructive.

"That's a lot of money," I said.

"They sell their soul." He wrinkled his nose, disgust trickling off his lips. "Dog fighters are worthless brutes."

Two men exchanged smiles, their eyes landing on their dog in the pen, who clung to the side like she'd rather be chasing squirrels. Something would have to agitate her to get her going; I cringed and looked away.

Leo spotted us, and it sent a shiver up my spine. Something in his eyes was jagged and detached, and something in his smile was hungry, open and ready for prey. As I watched, Marv ambled up to him, a tall, brawny man at his side. They said something, and Leo shook his head, arms out, pointing at someone else. Marv pointed toward the door and the burly man grabbed Leo's arm; I turned away, my heart racing. James and Fern appeared at my side again, no Posey, and I slowly began to inch my way into the multitude of bodies as they followed. Fern leaned closer to James and yelled into his ear,

"That man." She nodded to Leo. "He freaks me out."

"Oh really," James said, his voice flat.

"I'm serious. Look at him."

I didn't hear James' answer. The crowd cheered and a snarl rose above the din, and I couldn't take it. My heart beat fast. My stomach, once again, climbed up my throat. My fingers shook, and I spotted Posey. She cowered beside a brawny man with a beard and three gold rings, standing a few people in front of us. She was almost hidden among the shoulders and outstretched arms of the men around her. Her lips were pale, and she looked so small, so vulnerable, that a beast arose within me and I dove into the crowd, weaving my way under arm pits and double chins. She saw me and reached out to grab my hand.

I had to find a way out; the exit was blocked by a throng of people, and the walls were caving in – my lungs heaved – the chants, the barks beat against my ears – I spotted the door, the mystery door Marv used last time, unguarded – I dragged Posey with me as I turned the knob, ducked in, and slammed it shut. I leaned my forehead against it and panted, hard, against the cool metal. I could barely hear Posey's small voice over my wheezing.

"Marion?"

"I need a minute."

"*Marion.*"

I turned around. It was a small room, lit by a single light-bulb dangling from the ceiling. Below it was a metal folding table, loaded with bags of a fine white powder, and around it stood three men made of slime and gunpowder. One of them was Marv. He looked from Posey to me and moved to stand in front of us, hands on a gun shoved down the back of his pants, his lips dragging open like he kept something back, something lodged in his throat, begging to be said.

"What are you doing?" he snarled, teeth out.

My heart thrashed into my rib cage and a cold sweat trickled down my neck.

"We didn't see anything," I said, and I dragged Posey out with me before he could say another word. We had to get out. He would kill us, now.

I bulldozed through a wall of people, grabbed James and stuck out my elbows to stab my way through the mob. I cleared a path to the hall, rushing toward the open space of the museum, as I heaved all the way, unsure if I needed to breathe or vomit.

"Wait!"

A voice snatched at us, clutching at my back like I stole away with the evening's stash. It was Francesca, following us with reddened cheeks and wild eyes.

"Wait!" She reached for me and grabbed my shoulders. "What'd you see?"

Delia and Sebastian gathered around us, concerned by the desperation and urgency weaved into my every gasp. Lenny watched from a distance, relieved to see Posey in my grip and the door in my path.

Sebastian laughed one of his sharp, cruel laughs laced with edges. "What do you think? Bloody dogs."

But Francesca searched my eyes. I didn't answer, but she saw the truth anyway.

"It's not what you think," she said. I wrenched my shoulders from her grip and turned away. She seized a fold of my skirt. "It really isn't."

"Then what is it?"

"It's a charity."

I laughed.

"It goes to pay Penelope's medical bills." Her voice was open, to the point, hasty. It sounded like the truth. I paused, giving her a flicker of hope that sparked in her beady eyes.

"What?"

"The profits. The profits go to a medical fund Marv created for Doug's wife." Her breath was quick and shallow. "To pay for all her special treatments, Switzerland...I didn't like it, either. But then I found out..." She shifted nervously. "Marv really is a good man, Marion." Her eyes were pleading, overwhelmed, and completely – what was that? Oh yeah. Smitten.

"You *like* him."

She bit her lip.

"You actually like him."

"That's not – "

"Is he – are you two...?"

She backed away, squaring her shoulders. "Not anymore. He moves onto brighter things, you know. Better ideas, bigger goals. Prettier women." She crossed her arms as footsteps echoed from the hall.

"We have to go." I pulled at Posey's wrist and flew out the open door (God bless Lenny), the others following behind as I panted my story about the secret room, and why we needed to book it out and away as soon as possible.

We ran into the night, my bare feet slapping the cobblestones, keeping watch over our shoulders (the birds were still up, talking about food, but I ignored them) until we arrived at James' car, where he got behind the wheel without a word of goodbye. I stopped to catch my breath, and Sebastian stopped next to me. We stood underneath a streetlight, so I could see his face was somewhat pale, and his eyes had that squishy, glassy look I wasn't used to seeing in Sebastian.

"Hey, umm, look, Marion...about what James said – "

"We're cool." I nodded and bumped his shoulder with my fist, an action I couldn't help but take after a different kind of panic rose in my chest. Sebastian wilted.

"Oh. Okay – "

James stuck his head out of the driver's window and slapped the outside of his door. "Hurry up dingbat, if we get home after curfew the same night you punched a girl you'll be grounded 'till you're thirty."

Sebastian pursed his lips and coughed, the squishiness in his eyes glimmering. He leaned at me with his shoulder. "I think you would have made a cool peacock." His Adam's apple bounced up and down.

I didn't say anything, I didn't know what to say, so he turned and slowly got in the car, tossing his rabbit in first, through the open window. I followed him, the night's revelations bubbling up before my eyes.

"Will you tell your dad?" I asked, shuffling closer to lean into Sebastian's window. James shook his head.

"Not yet. Not 'till we figure this all out. Not if we want to live." He pointed two fingers at my face, like a gun. "And don't you tell anyone either. Dad will kill us and Marv will kill Fern, and nothing good will happen, okay? Now hurry up and get inside, you're making me nervous."

But he drove off without waiting for us to obey, leaving three girls on the sidewalk, huddled together like a herd of gazelles.

Chapter Twenty-Seven

I tried to tell my parents everything (well mostly – everything minus the drugs and the dog fighting, some things are best kept under wraps, so I mostly just talked about Todd and his job as a covert hole digger), and Delia tried to tell her mom too. But after a few phone calls and some rather condescending remarks by Detective Mobley, everyone decided Todd really wasn't worth looking into, and it sounded like the whole thing was some kid's prank and if we caught him in the act, give the police a call.

I was not so convinced, but my thoughts on the matter did not matter, as was evidenced by my mother's strong recommendation that I go to bed. She was more interested in hearing about how Posey got punched in the face, and when we told her that she jumped in front of James, her eyebrow raised in a way that told me her motherly instincts were elsewhere that evening, and so I made my couch bed and tried to sleep.

"At the end of the day," Mom said, in a rather lecture-y tone, "all it means is that some kid is digging holes in our yard, and if you don't know his last name or where he goes to school, and we haven't caught him in the act, well, what are we going to do about it? It's not like your dad and I are going to press charges on a child." She flicked her wrist in the air, a thing she often did to denote moving on, and then she left the room.

In the morning, I opened my eyes to see the front door wide open. I stepped out and greeted my mom, who was on the porch again, contemplating the freshly dug holes along the driveway.

"Todd," I said, dramatically. The name was quite fitting.

Mom sighed. "Todd."

The little snollygoster had urged us to go home, then slipped out of the den of sin, only to go digging up my yard. Oh well. We would just have to create some sort of lookout method, or security camera. I was just about to suggest it, when Mom stuck out her arm to guide me gently back into the house.

"Have you talked to Conrad lately?" she asked, trying to sound casual, but there was a strain in the back of her throat that gave her away.

I sighed. "That depends on your definition of 'lately.'"

"Maybe you should call him." She shut the door, prodding me forward with her cup of coffee. "It goes both ways."

The living room was messy, mostly because of my couch bed, but the morning sun streamed in through the windows and it cast a soft light everywhere. The room glittered, like a smile, and it was hard to believe such a nice morning could come after such a sinister night. I shivered, the sight of Marv's gun and the snarling dogs climbing up my eyeballs. I wasn't in the right frame of mind for a phone call with The Big Brother.

"I don't know why you think Conrad is a good listener," I said. "He mostly just repeats my words."

"It's good to talk about things." She passed me to stand in the kitchen doorway, one hand on the frame, her opposite hip flung out and her elbow resting on it. Her wrist turned her coffee mug back and forth with every word. "And sometimes it's easier to talk with someone you don't see every day."

"I'm not one to ever shy away from talking. You know this. If I want to say something, I do." I flopped on the couch bed, hands behind my head. "It doesn't always work out in my favor, but I can't help it. I'm not sure more talking is the solution for whatever it is you're worried about." But I knew what she was worried about. I just didn't want to put it into words, because that would give it a kind of heaviness, or realness, that I still wasn't ready to face.

Mom closed her eyes and finished her coffee in one gulp, turning to the kitchen with a sharp exhale. "Go do your schoolwork, sweetie. You're behind." Her steps on the tile were heavy slaps, slow yet harsh.

"I'm behind in everything," I groaned, then I puffed my cheeks to fill my mouth with air instead of the words I so desperately wanted to speak, words like *I'm not crazy* and *then again, maybe I am.*

I spent a painfully long part of my day under the throes of education. It was hard to concentrate. Not only did the thoughts of my own mind dance before my eyes (really, if no one else is going to look at them, who will?) but the gnawing, jeering knowledge of the holes and Todd's silly little job kept jumping out at me, and the dogs, and the drugs, and how on earth am I supposed to work out algebraic equations when that kind of nonsense is going on?

I finished the bare minimum of my responsibilities and stood in front of my mind map, pen and index cards in hand. Too many words swirled in my mind, I had to get them on paper.

The Gatekeepers are lying

Máire Finnegan could talk to birds and see the future in my mirror

Máire Finnegan didn't kill herself, but was trying to escape

Dog fights at the museum – explains missing dogs

Drug ring at the museum

Leo is part of gambling ring

Francesca paid Todd to dig holes

Francesca is in love with Marv

Drug ring pays for Doug's wife's cancer treatments

And then I stood back, my eyes grazing over everything. Did Violet really do it? Was I missing something? Surely Lily Anderson's murder had something to do with the drugs and illegal games. Why else would The Gatekeepers lie about seeing her? And that letter – I still hadn't shown Máire Finnegan's letter to Mom, because part of me knew she wouldn't believe it. I couldn't handle that. The letter was too precious. It was a fragile symbol of hope to me, and one skeptical word from her would break it. So I kept it in my sock drawer, to hide until I could prove that Lily was murdered, that I wasn't crazy.

Finally, mid-afternoon, the phone rang. Not that the ringing was anything special, but it rang for me, and after Posey handed me the receiver I heard Conrad's voice on the other line.

"Marion."

"Conrad," I spat, in imitation.

"How's the investigation?"

I sat on my bed, turning my back to the mind map. I considered telling him about the gambling den of dog fights and drug dealing, but I decided against it. His reaction could span across too wide a range of possibilities. The letter, though – perhaps he would believe Máire Finnegan. Mom might not, but Conrad liked to know things, especially old, specific things found in first person accounts.

"We found a letter," I told him, "from Máire Finnegan. In the attic. She talked about a magic ring." Then I told him everything written in it, but he snorted dismissively.

"I've never heard of this letter."

"Obviously not, it's been hidden in the attic." It's like he believed that anything he didn't know about, wasn't real. Well, there are plenty of things that are real that he doesn't know about. My mind map, for one. I could line the house with mind maps filled with the things Conrad doesn't know, but I don't have the time.

He paused. "She said her uncle was stealing?"

"Yup."

"Interesting." His voice was hushed and far away, like he was actually thinking hard about something I said. But the silence stretched on, so I coughed.

"So, then, Conrad, I shall be going."

"Fine. I'll see what I can find out about – " but I had already hung up the phone. It rang again. I answered.

"Yes, Conrad?"

Violet's voice (low and husky, hard to forget) garbled on the other line. "No, sorry, Marion, it's Violet. So glad you're home. Look, I'm sitting here, going through my sister's things, and it's just kind of overwhelming. Do you guys want to come help? You can look for clues in her stuff. I need help, but I don't know anyone, and I can't stand the thought of any of those suicide-spammers being in this house and touching her things." She paused, but it was a breathless pause, like she was holding back tears. "I guess you heard I confessed."

Finally, we got to the heart of the matter. "I did. Did you do it?"

"No, I...I had a breakdown. I wasn't in town, you know, when it happened, and...it wasn't me, and they knew it. So they let me go."

I ran through my files on Violet in my head. The breakdown checked out; she did have a curious mental situation, but alibi? She didn't mention an alibi before. She didn't mention she'd been out of town – that's why she didn't report Lily missing. She had left out the truth. She was a liar.

"I see."

The phone buzzed softly in the silence, and when she spoke, her voice was soft. "So you'll come?"

I leaned against my wall and picked at the paint, studying my fingers. She needed help. I needed clues. "Yes, I'll come."

Violet thanked me and hung up, and I called the others. Delia would come with me right away; Sebastian was grounded and couldn't even come to the phone, and James was "busy," which probably just meant he had some sort of plan with Fern (ugh). Posey begged to come, but Mom said she had too much schoolwork to do (I had finished) and anyway I didn't want another repeat of the excursion before – Posey had stayed with me on the couch bed, but not out novelty; I think she was too afraid to sleep alone.

Posey went to our room to sulk, her eye all black and blue and crying tears of bitterness, and the world fell off my shoulders. It was better to be solely responsible for myself. Things were easier that way; the risks were halved. I walked to Delia's alone, but as I got in the car, the echo of a slamming door bounced down the street and over the water.

"Is there a spotting near the house?" Ms. Gretchen asked, pulling out of the driveway. Delia consulted her map.

"Kind of. In a park, two streets away."

My attention snapped back from slams, midnight deals, guns, and the holes in my front yard, to Delia's quest for mythical creatures. I leaned forward, gripping the driver's seat head rest.

"So you're hunting the fabled and fabulous too, Ms. Gretchen?"

She ruffled Delia's hair and Delia slapped at her fingers. "That's the deal, right?"

"Right." I said. That night in Delia's bedroom seemed like another lifetime ago. "I forgot, for a moment."

"It's actually kind of fun." Ms. Gretchen's voice was sunny and soft. She turned carefully onto a busy road and cleared her throat, taking time to choose her words. "Cordelia's been showing me all the hotspots. It's very...colorful."

"Leave it to a sasquatch to change a woman's life." Delia adjusted her belt buckle, the corners of her mouth upturned, *I am chuffed* written on her face. Dark half-moons sat under her eyes. She, like me, had found it hard to sleep.

Violet's house sat on the edge of town, close to Dead Man's Swamp, and we had time to kill. I leaned forward, forcing my voice to be casual. "How do you know Francesca Lovely, Ms. Gretchen?"

I counted the seconds until she answered: five.

"We worked together, back when I worked in media." She met my eyes through the rearview mirror. "And kept in touch."

"Makes sense." I played an awkward beat on my knees, gearing up to ask, "Does she seem...normal to you? Any, umm, secrets, or anything?"

Ms. Gretchen grimaced at me empathetically. I didn't like it. It was too assuming, too gentle, and it always made my stomach hurt when people assumed they knew my thoughts and intentions, especially when they were dead wrong. And they are always dead wrong.

"I know she wrote that article, honey. It's such a bummer. It's her job, though. Sometimes you have to write what your boss tells you to write, if you want to pay the bills."

"I wasn't thinking about the article. Not exclusively, anyway."

"Then what were you thinking about?"

I shrugged. "Just, generally."

Her hands squeezed the steering wheel, and she tossed her head to shoo the hair out of her eyes. I caught Delia's glance, and it said *I already tried and got nothing.*

"Francesca has had a lot of family hardships," Ms. Gretchen explained, slowly. "She recently had her heartbroken. She's overwhelmed."

"Would you say she's simply overwhelmed if you found out she was a criminal mastermind?" I asked. Her eyes darted back to me.

"What?"

"Never mind," I said, and I watched the trees pass by.

———

Ms. Gretchen dropped us off (we didn't *exactly* tell her the truth about who we were helping, but we did assure her we wanted to go in alone, and that we knew the woman and it was perfectly safe, and we'd only be an hour) and she left to check out the mythical creature sighting on her own. Delia and I knocked on the door and Violet answered, her hair in a lopsided ponytail and her eyes bloodshot. She smiled when she saw us, but it was only with her lips.

"Thanks for coming," she said, and her voice was lower than when she called, low and full of scratches. "It was too overwhelming, all by myself."

"We wanted to come." I smiled, and Violet backed up to let us pass.

The interior was floor-to-ceiling pine paneling, shiny in

the light, the ground floor one open room that was both the kitchen and the living area. The floor was carpeted with something thick, red, and out-of-date. Trash and untouched plates of food littered the house, and the walls were still covered in Lilies. Except, this time, her face was covered with scraps of paper taped over her head. Some pictures had black marker blocking out her eyes. Violet didn't mention it.

She led us up the stairs to Lily's bedroom, swaying slightly while she held onto the railing. I shot Delia an apprehensive glance and Violet sighed, climbing so slowly I grabbed her arm to help. An uneasiness climbed up my spine. The house was unsettled.

"I'm not feeling too well today," Violet explained. "Another reason why I'm glad you came."

"I'm sorry to hear that." Delia held her hands out in front of her, to catch Violet if she fell. I was glad I wasn't alone. If Delia hadn't come with me, I might have turned away and ran back home. Delia added, "Glad we could help."

But Violet only nodded, her ponytail slowly falling, until the band drooped below her ear.

"Maybe we can look, and you can lay down," I suggested.

"Too much to do," she said. "And there's no time."

Lily's room was clean and orderly, the walls bright and bed made – a yellow quilt. Yellow is the color of suffering; I took it as a clue.

"I've got these here." Violet pointed to some boxes, still not put together, leaning against the wall. "Go through everything, see what you think. There's got to be something, right?" She considered the room, hands limp by her side, wavering slightly. She took one box from the wall and began to put it together, slowly, while sitting on the bed. Delia and I did the same, and then we started with the closet.

Lily had a closetful of shoes. Violet handed us a large trash bag and we filled it up, and then we found piles and piles of papers, buried deep in her closet. They were only old college papers and study guides, and with each document we grew more and more despondent. Nothing we found, it seemed, was relevant.

"I wonder why she kept all these, when she was so sparing with everything else?" Delia mused out loud. Lily's room was practically empty, just a bed and a dresser and one shelf of memories. Her closet was saved for shoes, papers, and old purses. One window let in light beside the foot of her bed.

"Lily loved her research," Violet answered, sniffing. We looked closely at the documents; it was true, they were all research papers, and they all, without fail, had received full marks. Violet got up from the bed and began to work on the other side of the room, dragging a pillow behind her.

"That's interesting," I said to myself. The moments crawled by, and I pulled out a question, forming the words gingerly, holding them between us like food for a wild animal. "Violet, do you know anything about that gambling ring in town?"

"Gambling ring?" Violet looked up from her station near the shelf, which held rows and rows of plaques and trophies. She wrapped each one in two layers of newspaper while sitting on the floor, pillow behind her back. "Not a thing."

"Really?" Delia stuck out her tongue as she thumbed through essays. Bright, happy A's shouted from the pages. "She doesn't seem to have any connection to the thing, yet it has to be related, right?"

I agreed, but Violet was silent, wrapping each trophy with shaking fingers. We boxed up the last of the college papers and came across a box deep in the corner, covered in spare blankets and old suitcases. Delia pulled it out and plopped it onto the bed, and we both leaned over the top as she opened it, eager to see whatever it was that Lily was trying her best to keep secret.

Inside the box, in piles and piles of printed articles and copied medical journals, was extensive research into alternative cancer treatments. Delia carefully picked up each individual page. We read headlines like SCORPION VENOM AND CANCER and EVIDENCE SHOWS DECREASE IN CANCER CELLS AFTER EATING THESE SEVEN FOODS. Delia and I looked at each other, my face saying *what's this mean, then?* and Delia's face saying *was someone dying?* I turned to Violet.

"Did Lily have cancer?"

Violet winced, stood up quickly (she stumbled), and rifled through what we found. "No. Of course she didn't." But her voice, deep and throaty, caught with the word *didn't*.

Delia dug farther into the pile of research and came up

with a thick, ratty stack of papers, held together by an old paperclip. We gasped, and Delia beamed.

"Jackpot!"

"You always find the good stuff," I groaned, trying to take it from her. She twisted away from me, clicking her tongue. The stack looked precious, like it had been combed through time after time, poured over every night. Delia examined it paper by paper.

There were newspaper clippings of drug overdoses, dognappings, and business foreclosures; research into the Penelope Medical Fund, and WNYT News company policy concerning job loss and insurance. There was also page after page of information concerning Coastal Breeze Rehabilitation Center, with prices and requirements highlighted, as well as *alcohol addiction* and *gambling* highlighted under *Addictions We Treat* and a little memo scrawled in the corner: *Doug, graveyard, 10pm. Don't be followed.*

Doug, the man who had clearly been hiding something.

Doug, who was friends with Poseidon.

Doug had arranged to meet Lily in the graveyard. We stared at her notes.

Slowly, I looked up. "Violet. Do you know something?"

Violet rested against the window, her fingers trembling. I held my breath, feeling the static in the air, the rushing current of Violet's thoughts. Something was happening. Violet's dam was crumbling. My heart beat faster.

"Violet. Did Lily know about the gambling ring?"

Her lips trembled, and her eyes fixated on the long leaf

pine outside the window, like it was holding her up. "I didn't tell you. You found out."

"What?"

She turned to us, all gray and full of cracks, her eyes dark, glassy, and bloodshot. "That's it, okay? I didn't tell you. You found out."

I swallowed and started again. "Alright. You didn't tell us. We found out. Did Lily know about the gambling ring?"

"She was too passionate. Too reckless in helping me, it seems."

"What?"

"I didn't know." Violet clutched at the windowsill and leaned into the glass. Her face was pained, scrunching up in all the corners. "I didn't know. I was mad. She brought up rehab, said it was the only way, that I had to go or she'd kick me out. She tried to come and see me, but I refused. Before that, I met Marv in our...in this little support group Lily made me join, right after moving here. He told me about the museum. I went, because I told myself I can say no to drinks, and – " her voice cracked. "I was rather in love with Marv, truth be told. But I – I found other things to – well, to spark an obsession. And Lily told me rehab, or the streets. I asked her for money...that's life at the museum. One minute I have thousands, the next I'm in the red. That thirty grand I promised you? Won it in a game of craps. Lost it in a game of blackjack.

"But I think she found out everything, tried to save me. Tried to shut it down. Tried to expose it, while I was safely tucked away. But the thing about Marv is he always pays his debts. It was his obsession. His identity. His self-worth. And he owed Doug. And I think she tried to expose it. And that wouldn't help Doug, or his wife. Not when she needs that money. Not while she's sick."

She wiped the hair out of her eyes. Sweat glued her hair to her temples. Delia and I were frozen, not daring to even breathe. One breath might make her shut down, forget that she was telling us the truth. She rambled on, her voice higher, faster, angrier with each word.

"So it was my fault, all of it, everything she went through, her death. She died because of me. She was murdered because she was trying to help me. I killed my sister! It was me! And I couldn't take it!" Her eyes were big, brown, and desperate. She beat her chest and I clutched at my own, backing away, my mouth going dry. She hung her head. "I couldn't take the guilt, the shame. I couldn't take it. I'm so sorry, Lily. I'm so sorry."

I inched to Delia until our shoulders touched. Violet formed the next words, heavy words, through sobs.

"So I told them. I said I did it because I did. I'm guilty of killing her. I needed help, and that's why she's dead. And I need to pay for it. It's my fault." The air in the room was tight, brittle, and Delia pulled at the collar of her t-shirt, shifting uncomfortably. Then Violet met my eyes for the first time and held her chin up high, the tears falling off one by one. "I went to the police, but they didn't keep me, not for long. They found out I was in rehab. They found out I was released as soon as the hurricane died down. That day, I came back and...and...and Lily wasn't home. And I heard..." Her voice broke. "Anyway, I knew my sister didn't kill herself. I just knew. I knew there was more to the story. So I made those flyers. But then I got that suicide note, addressed to me...and then, I found Lily's notes, and I was so mad, so mad at myself, and so I went to the police. Told them I did it, I killed her, I threw her in the ocean.

"But now, now I have to ask myself: Am I brave enough to blow the whistle? To expose everything?" She shook her head, shoulders heaving. "No, I'm not. I'm not brave. I'm – I'm scared. But do I want justice? Yes. I – I want justice for my sister. And those – the police – " Hair stuck to her face and she rubbed it away, swallowing a laugh. "I made a fool of myself. Don't think they'd believe a word out of my – and he might – I'm not – its – I'm scared, you know? And I'm – I can't – I can barely get out of bed these days, can't seem to leave my house...I...I can't think straight, I..." She took a deep breath. "I can't seem to...I can't. I can't. So I want you to know all my secrets. I want you to solve all this for me."

She trembled, one hand on the wall, the other over her heart. The sun shone around her, catching the dust in the air.

"And I'll get you that reward money, come hell or high water."

Chapter Twenty-Eight

Delia and I listed everything we'd learned as we walked from her house to mine, after Ms. Gretchen dropped us off:

- Violet's plants were dead because she was in rehab, and she wasn't there to take care of them
- Marv is up to no good
- Doug is up to no good
- Someone paid Violet's rehab bills (she told us this shortly before we left)
- Violet is a liar, but she's also scared, and broken, and she said a lot of things that answer a lot of questions

"It's like all of Lady's Madness in on the conspiracy," Delia said, just as we stepped into the kitchen and shut the door.

I didn't answer, because Posey greeted us like a swamp hag.

"You are the bane of my existence," she spat from the living room couch, her voice croaky and low. We ambled into the living room, confused, and she stood up, shaking with anger from head to toe. "First, you abandon me, and then, I am called upon to be your messenger boy." She marched to me and stopped an inch from my nose, her arms crossed and her hair a stringy bog around her head. "I AM NOT YOUR MESSENGER BOY."

"Of course not," I replied, poking one finger into her shoulder and easing her backward. "For you are, in fact, a girl."

The house shuddered. Posey geared up for a rampage.

"You leave to have all the fun, and suddenly I become your servant." The purple around her eye shone with indignation. "It's unfair, inhuman, and selfish."

"Blame Mom, not me."

"I AM NOT YOUR MESSENGER BOY."

"YES, BECAUSE YOU ARE A GIRL."

She dropped a packet at my feet and turned on her heels to march to the kitchen as Max entered, BB gun swung over his shoulder, ready to terrorize the neighborhood birds. I grabbed the packet and ripped it open without ceremony — only to drop it on the floor, my fingers tingling as the air left my lungs.

"What is it?" Delia asked, reaching for it. Posey turned and waited for my answer, and Max froze, watching our faces. The room plummeted into silence as Delia pulled out the pictures.

Pictures of me.

Pictures of me stumbling in the park, the day Ms. Caroline asked me to look for fabric.

Pictures of Delia and me talking to Buck after church.

Pictures of Delia and me meeting Fern by the alleyway, my hand outstretched, giving her fifty dollars in ones.

Pictures of me at the dog fight, sweat dripping down my temple, Delia beside me.

Pictures of Lily Anderson's dead body washed up on shore, her skin pale and mouth hanging open, dead and bloated on the waterfront. Next to her head, written in black marker, were the words, *you're next.*

Inside was a note that simply said,

We know everything.
You're one of us now.
One wrong move, we tell.
Breathe one word, we take your breath.
You'll wash up on shore, too.

I stared at the words in one terrified, silent moment of clarity: they will kill me. They will drop me in the ocean. Delia clasped her hands over her mouth, spilling the note and the pictures back onto the floor.

"Oh bollocks," she breathed, looking at me with wide eyes.

"What?" Posey asked, her face genuinely worried, all the marsh gone, replaced with a living, breathing heart. She ran back to us and scooped up the pictures and the note and the envelope and flipped through them furiously. "What is this?" she asked again, although I didn't know how on earth she expected me to form a coherent thought, much less answer.

Max came up from behind her and grabbed the images, going through them one by one. "But it's just pictures," he said, like we were being silly.

"What have we gotten into?" I asked Delia, but she, much to my surprise, stood tall, like she was giving a just-before-the-battle speech. She was impassive no more; the waters didn't churn in hidden places, underneath the surface. She was a rushing river, unstoppable, deadly.

"Well, you guys sure are in a pickle, aren't you?" Posey declared, scanning the note.

"More than a pickle, messenger boy," I snapped. "We're going to die."

"Now, hold up." Delia held up her hands to silence me, then whipped back her raven tresses with a wave of her fingers. "Let's not get *too* dramatic –"

I bristled. "Too dramatic? Delia. Those men had guns. They are *men*. With *guns*. And they sent us a *death threat*."

"Great. So you scared them. It means we have the upper hand."

"It most certainly does not."

"It means" – Posey forced the pictures back into my hands – "that you need to tell Mom. Or Detective Mobley."

I hesitated. "But James –"

"James is not in any of these pictures," Delia said. "Neither is Sebastian. They're not the ones being threatened. It's you and me. We're the ones with skin in the game, to quote Todd. So we decide if we tell anybody."

I looked into her eyes and pierced the part of her soul that spoke to me honestly and without words. *What do you want to do?* I asked her. *Though this be madness, yet there is method in it,* she replied.

I closed my eyes. "Be straightforward."

"Obviously we should tell someone." She shrugged. "But you needn't be all caught up in your head. This means we're onto something. It means someone is scared of what we know."

"Drug dealers tend to be that way," I said dryly. Then, Delia and I both turned to Posey, who stood watching us.

"Who gave you this packet?" Delia demanded.

"And how did they find you?" I added.

Posey twiddled her thumbs, backing up like she did something wrong. "I was rage walking downtown – "

"You were what?" Delia tipped her head, eyes crinkling.

"Expressing her anger whilst plodding the cobblestone streets," I explained. "It's a thing she does when she's mad at me."

"Mom told me to stop writing letters," Posey scratched her head. "They got to be a little too much. Anyway, this guy stopped me and asked if I was Marion's sister, and hey, that's the last thing I ever want to be known as, especially at that time, so I glared at him and said, 'unfortunately, yes,' and he said, 'give this to her,' and handed me the packet and left. I thought about throwing it into the ocean, but that's littering, and I had to write a paper on ocean pollution last week so I couldn't bring myself to do it."

"So it was a man?" I asked.

"Yes." She pointed one finger for emphasis.

"But you don't know who he was?"

"No. Not a clue."

"And you didn't ask him?"

"I cared not one little bit who he was," she answered. "I was busy rage walking. About you."

"Right." I turned to Delia. "So it's someone who knows me, at least a little bit."

Delia adjusted her belt buckle and tucked a bit of her t-shirt behind it. "Well, I'm off to tell my mom. So you better tell yours, before my mom calls and all hell breaks loose." She sauntered to the door, waving haphazardly behind her. "You can't let it bother you, Marion."

"It's a threat," I said.

She measured me, sizing me up from my toes to my widow's peak, one hand on the door handle. "Someone's scared. That means something." She paused, mouth open, and leaned into the door. "I've been thinking about what I've learned in this stupid speech class, and – and anyway, why spend time thinking about how you feel? Everything about this letter is trying to scare you. How true do you think it is? How close is it to reality? Is it a half truth? Are you going to let them scare you?" She waited for an answer, standing like a strong pillar in a crumbling house. But I was flesh and bone, liable to be crushed.

"Yes," I said. "I'm already scared. And if they're scared, well, scared people are the ones who do desperate things. I don't want to drown in the sea."

And then I trudged to my room and sat, gingerly, on my bed. And that's where I sat, staring into space, as the waves clutched at me from the shore, breaking against the retaining wall, and shouting for my corpse.

If we told Detective Mobley, we'd end up telling everything. And we were not exactly innocent bystanders.

And would it actually endanger Fern, like James feared?

But we were in danger, too. Maybe, if I could figure out how to prove everything, I could make all this go away. My chest heaved, stretching my seams, crashing against my bones, like my insides were at high tide. I gripped the edge of my bed, closing my eyes to let my roots grow deep. Finney anchored me.

Should I tell Detective Mobley everything, let it all out, and face the revenge of Poseidon?

Or should I keep it all locked inside, only to spill out when all is solved, and proven, and bulletproof?

Or should I drop it, pretend like it never happened?

I turned to study my mind map. It was the same.

Nothing had moved, nothing had come to life and written THIS IS WHAT'S HAPPENING AND THIS IS WHAT YOU SHOULD DO ABOUT IT on my wall. I wrote the names of every person associated with the gambling ring on their own index card and pinned them to the right, covering the quote NOTHING FEAR BASED IS TRUTH BASED:

Francesca Lovely

Fern

Violet Anderson

Then I wrote down everything we found in Lily's room:

Cancer articles

Gambling research

Appointment with Doug

Then, as the grand finale, I added the addendum:

I received death note

and put it under everything, willing the culprit to reach down and point at it, so that my little map would confess and

I'd know who was behind it all without a doubt, and everyone would believe me, and I wasn't crazy, and I wasn't about to die.

It had to be Marv, right? But how would I prove it?

I fell into a dark hole of thinking and staring and didn't climb out until Posey stuck her head through the door and said softly, "I told Mom about the threat."

I nodded.

"Delia went home. She's right, you know. You should tell someone. But she's also right that it means you're onto something, so there's that."

"There's that," I repeated, quietly.

Posey stepped in and shut the door, walking softly until she stood before me and then, with no ceremony, wrapped me in a stiff hug. I sucked in my breath – the smell of azaleas filled the room.

"I'm sorry you're scared," she whispered. I barely had time to rest one hand on her back before the door burst open and hit the wall with a *thud*. Mom waved the pictures in the air like she was fanning the ceiling fairies, and Dad followed, his brow furrowed, face gaunt, glasses dirty. The hair on the top of his head stood up, and he wore a dirty apron, one grease stain in the middle still fresh.

"Marion! What are these?"

She threw my name at me like a dagger. I placed one hand over my heart, to guard it from sharp edges.

"A threat," I said.

"What have you been doing?"

A flash of anger shot through me, bursting out of my lips, and I waved to the research pinned to my wall. What on earth did they think I was doing? "I've been looking into the murder of Lily Anderson!"

Mom sniffed and lifted her face to the ceiling. She was trying not to cry. Her head scarf slipped back, and the gray hairs of her hair line waved at me from across the room. "Are you sure this isn't some joke? A bet Sebastian lost?" She searched me, her eyes hungry for comfort, and I sank, my shoulders drooping, my heart sliding into my stomach.

"Of course it's not a joke. And you should call Detective Mobley," I said, gently. "There's a lot to tell."

She let out one long, labored sigh. "I already did." She looked at Dad, nudging him to speak.

"Don't leave your room," he advised, for good measure. He took off his glasses and rubbed them plaintively on a clean corner of his t-shirt. "I'm sure this will all work itself out. We have people waiting, Helena." He put on his glasses and smiled at me, then led Mom downstairs and back to the galley, where they were still serving customers.

"At least you know you're onto something," Posey said, but it was no comfort. She touched me lightly on the elbow. "Are you okay?"

I shook my head, biting my lip to hold back sobs. "I feel like I'm sitting on edges."

"Like pins and needles?"

"No," I answered. "Pins and needles just hurt. When I'm

sitting on edges, there are a hundred different ways I could fall off."

I crawled on my bed and curled up like a baby, and Posey covered me with her blanket.

I would have to tell Detective Mobley everything. No half-truths for me, even under threat of death.

CHAPTER TWENTY-NINE

Detective Mobley sat on the couch, the threat in his hands. Dad sat next to him, Mom stood behind him, hands clutched over her heart, and Posey stood behind me at the edge of the room, like a bodyguard. Grandma sat in her little chair beside the couch, reading, and Max strolled through the room, his rubber band gun under his arm. He threw back his shoulders and declared,

"I'll guard the house!"

No one stopped him; he shut the front door with a slam.

Detective Mobley sighed, elbows on his knees. "I hope I'm not about to learn you've been chasing outlandish theories."

"It doesn't matter what she's been chasing," Mom chided. "She's been threatened. That's what matters."

Detective Mobley grunted and fanned out the pictures on the coffee table, taking time to examine each one. He held up the note and read each word a dozen times. "Looks like someone's been stalking you," he said, finally. "Stalking a minor is very serious."

There was a knock on the front door and Delia and Ms. Gretchen walked in, Ms. Gretchen wearing a worried face and freshly styled hair, and Delia wearing a t-shirt that said BE THE CHANGE, VOTE UNICORN over a picture of a unicorn parading the American flag. She stood next to me and cleared her throat.

"Thank you for coming, Mr. Mobley."

"Well, you're welcome, Delia." He leaned back, one picture in each hand. "So who do you think sent you these pictures?"

I took a deep breath. "Lily Anderson was about to expose —"

"Ah." Detective Mobley set down the pictures. "So you've been doing your own detective work."

"Well, yes. James and Sebastian have been helping me."

His eyebrows climbed up his forehead, quickly, like they had one hundred little legs. "I didn't know that." He sighed and bowed his head, running his fingers through his thinning hair. "First, he hit a girl. Now this."

"They haven't done anything wrong," I said. "They just wanted to help me."

No one said anything. After a minute of staring at the pictures, Detective Mobley responded with, "Well either way, stop doing whatever you're doing. Someone's trying to scare you, is what I'd say. I'll look into it. Just lay low and they'll lose interest." I opened my mouth to protest but he continued, "And believe you me, I studied that handwriting, and it's not the handwriting of either of my sons, so it's not one of their pranks."

"I don't think it's a prank," I said.

"Then my advice still stands, don't do anything stupid."

"What about Founder's Day?"

"What about it?"

"Is it safe? Can I still go?"

He slapped his knees, a reassuring smile on his face. "I'll be there. I'll keep an eye on you." Then he twirled his fedora and stepped toward the door – but I couldn't let him leave. He wasn't listening, and I needed him to listen, to let all the secrets surface, death threat or not, because it was eating me alive, and if anyone was going to think me crazy or kill me, I might as well give them good reason.

I called him back in, and the words spilled out of me. I flooded my living room with everything – the gambling ring, the drugs, the birds, Lily Anderson's research – and Detective Mobley listened, eyes steely gray, and Mom gasped with every word. I swear Dad's hair turned white before my eyes.

With every word panic swelled within me, and I raised my arms, my warning bursting out of me like a waterfall.

" – and there's so much more going on in this town! So much! So much that we don't know, I'm sure of it!" All the things I'd seen – the gambling den, the drugs, the fighting – danced before me, swirling together, a muddled vignette into a sinister world, and I raised my voice. "Tear down the retaining walls, let the sea eat it all! Let it devour us in one final gulp!" I gasped for air, my cheeks burning, my throat a desert. I pointed to the threat, still in his hands. "Still think it's a prank?"

"No." He sat back down on the couch. "I don't think it is."

"No, of course not, because it is a threat, a serious threat born of greed, and selfishness, and murder. We've done a lot of stupid things lately. But we've also learned a lot. And one of the things we've learned is that humans are capable of a lot of things, they're capable of embracing things that are...that are...unthinkable, really. Especially novel, shiny, exciting, unthinkable things. Men love newfangledness, to quote Chaucer." I crossed my arms. "Which I do often."

"I see." He twirled his fedora over his knees. "And James drove you everywhere."

"He lost a bet," Delia said. "The stakes were if he lost, he had to drive Sebastian anywhere Sebastian wanted. And James lost."

Detective Mobley slowly spread out the photos once again. "All those overdoses..." he murmured, rubbing his face in an aggressive way, all frantic and mad, and I flinched.

"This is my daughter we're talking about, Kyle," Dad cautioned as Mom threw daggers from her eyes. She was Angry Mom, ready to throw down and break a few bones. Dad stood up and pulled her into his arms. "Our number one priority is her safety."

Detective Mobley nodded. "Here's what we're going to

do. I'll ask for a uniform to sit outside your house tonight, and any night, until we know what's going on. Your house too, Delia. We'll get someone to keep an eye on you on Founder's Day. But I want you to live your life. Don't let any of this control you. That's when they've won. Leave the rest to me."

"She has rehearsal tonight," Dad stated over Mom's shoulder.

"I'll arrange something. Don't worry, George. We'll catch the guy." And with that, he donned his fedora and left. Mom and Ms. Gretchen exchanged worried looks.

"You think it's enough?" Mom asked, to no one in particular.

"Kyle knows what he's doing," Dad assured her.

She exhaled slowly, her eyes focused on the worries playing in her mind. "There's more to be done than assign a few uniforms."

There was indeed more to be done, more to think about, more to rearrange, and it all sat pinned to my bedroom wall.

"I'm going to my room," I announced. I was dizzy and lightheaded, and I wanted to stare at my mind map, one last farewell gaze, after handing over my investigation to the professionals.

I left for my room, ready to stare at my clues, but I didn't see the clues. I didn't see the names or the articles or the dates, because when I opened my door I saw my own dead body, stretched out and lifeless on my bed, dripping water onto the hardwood floor.

Chapter Thirty

I looked into my own dead eyes. It was me, all drowned and saturated, my mouth open and hair a tangled mess.

I was dead, eaten by the sea.

The world went dark, except for my own face – it stared back at me, cruelly, and I stumbled and fell back into the door frame. My head *thumped* and I closed my eyes and screamed, but when I opened them, my dead body was gone.

Someone bumped into me and I looked up to see Delia, her cheeks red and blotchy.

"Why are you screaming?"

"I die." I pointed to the mirror, my speech desperate and rushed. "I saw my own dead body, just like Lily."

Delia marched to the mirror, grabbed it on both sides, and shook it. She looked it up and down, turned to the bed, and punched the covers. "There's nothing here."

Mom rushed in behind her, followed by Dad, Ms. Gretchen, and Posey. They stared at me as I told them I saw my own dead body, and Mom grabbed my face in both her hands.

"I was dead," I whispered. "In the mirror. Just like Lily Anderson."

"You're not going to die," Mom answered, with conviction, like she too could see the future. I pried her hands off my face.

"No. I am going to die. The sea is going to eat me."
"Marion –"
I help up a hand. "I need to think."
"Listen." Mom sat in front of me, her tone unyielding, even though her fingers shook. "It will all be okay. We'll make sure you're okay."

I got up, grabbed the blanket off my bed (it should have been wet; I was dead and soaking wet on it just moments before) and threw it over the mirror.

"I never want to look in that again."

I reached for my mind map and tore it down, each index card and each note, and threw them in the trash. The words BY NATURE, MEN LOVE NEWFANGLEDNESS stared back at me.

"Marion!" Delia cried. "What on earth are you doing?"

"I'm over it." I ripped the last index card from the wall. "I'm pretending it never happened. Nothing is real. Everything is made up. Otherwise, I'm going to die." My voice caught in my throat, and I clenched my fists. "I'm going to die in the water. The ocean is going to eat me. I always knew it."

"You might not want to give up just yet," Posey warned from behind me. "It's not over."

"Well, it's too late," I said. "Everything stops. This stupid investigation, my stupid theories, my stupid plan to save this stupid, stupid house. It's all over. I'm done. Tell Detective Mobley it was a lie. Tell him to stop. Tell him I made it all up. Tell him I'm crazy." Finney shivered and stilled, and something snapped in my gut, like a rope had been severed.

"You can't stop now." Posey stepped in front of me, her gait easy, almost happy. I bristled.

"Why not?

All heads turned to her, and her face opened like a rushing, muddy river. "Because you're obviously on the right track. Things are just now getting interesting." She grabbed the bedspread draped over the mirror and yanked it free. "Face it, Marion!"

I leapt forward, ready to snatch the blanket and cover the mirror again, when Delia jumped in my way, arms out. "The water is not going to eat you." She grabbed my shoulders and leaned in close. "We'll make sure."

"And how on earth can you promise me that?" The panic in my stomach expanded into all my pores, and I forgot about the people in the doorway watching us, and Mom on the floor, her scarf falling off her head. "The mirror was right last time. I saw her dead, and she died. What's different this time? I'll tell you: nothing. Nothing at all. My fate is sealed. I'm going to die."

"Not if we stop them first." She squeezed my arms. "We're one step ahead of them, right?"

I stared at her, awestruck at her confidence, even though it made me furious, made me see red. "Why aren't you scared?"

"Don't you get it, Marion?" Her voice matched mine, high pitched and angry. The waters churned underneath her skin. The current was pulling, the tide rushing in. "I believe you! I think you can talk to birds. I think you see the future in that mirror. And I think Lily Anderson was murdered, and I think he'll murder you, too, if we don't stop him. But I think we can stop him, because I believe in you." I stopped breathing. She smiled, tears pooling in her eyes. "I'm sorry I didn't before. I'm sorry I didn't tell you I believe you sooner, but I do. I think you're onto something. I think, somehow, you're – " She laughed out loud. "I think you talk to birds! And I think you see the future in that mirror! But I – I also think you can change that future, if you fight for it. And I think someone else believes you're on the right track, and they're trying to scare you." Delia pointed to my wall where the words THOUGH THIS BE MADNESS, YET THERE IS METHOD IN IT stared back at us. "We can't stop now, not when things are starting to make sense!"

She believed me – after days of me begging her to believe I could talk to birds, after days of raising her eyebrow and looking for fairies instead of simply saying, *yes Marion, I believe you* – after all that time, she deigned to believe me. Hot anger simmered under my skin.

"Great." I pushed her hands away. "The girl who believes in Bigfoot believes in me. That's a big help."

My heart shriveled so small that it left an aching, hot mess behind it. My fingers twitched, ready to reach into the air to take back my words, but it was useless. I'd said them, and they landed in Delia's gut, like a poisoned arrow. She stepped back, wrapping her arms around her belly, something in her bearing stunned and tender.

"Yes, Marion," she said, her voice strained. "The girl who believes in Bigfoot believes in the girl who can talk to birds and see the future. Which do you think is worse?" She stared at me blankly, her thoughts and feelings trapped down deep in her chest.

Posey snorted. "If she's delusional, Marion, you're nothing but chaotic madness."

I whirled around to face her, arms out, ready to hit. "Shut up, marsh face!"

"MARION, ENOUGH!" Mom snapped, jumping to her feet. Posey gaped at me, eyes glowing like swamp gas.

Delia didn't say a word, but Ms. Gretchen said calmly, "It's time to go, Delia," and Delia turned to follow her out as Ms. Gretchen nodded to Posey. "We'll see you at rehearsal."

The door shut behind them and Mom turned to me, reproach in her eyes. "I know you're scared, but –"

I shook my head. "I want to be alone."

Her face fell. She took a deep breath, burying all the

things she wanted to say, and ushered Dad out of the room, Posey behind her. I sat on the floor and stared at my wall, now so barren, but covered in quotes.

THESE ARE BUT WILD AND WHIRLING WORDS

"It all ends," I said to myself.

It was fitting, really, to have every aspect of my world fall apart. It was clear that my worldview shattered with the threat – if I wanted to live, I had to reject everything I'd been chasing, pretend that Lily Anderson's murder did not interest me, and live forever in a half-truth. Soon my house would be gone, too, and with it my sense of the world, my anchor in reality, and all would be lost – but it was that, or die.

And it's not so crazy a thing, to choose a lie to live, is it?

I sat on the floor, surrounded by my destruction. I didn't want to move. I didn't want to leave the house. I didn't want to do another single thing that would come back to kill me.

Like, literally.

I placed my feet flat on the floor and closed my eyes, ready for the roots to grow, to dig deep through the house and into the earth, but the roots did not come. I hugged my sides and squared my shoulders, ready for Finney to hug me back, to comfort me, to be my anchor in the sea of chaos and despair, but she did not. It was just me, sitting on the floor of a house made of wood and stone.

It was just me, alone.

And it paralyzed me.

I was paralyzed until Grandma shuffled in and sat on Posey's bed. The warm golden beams of the afternoon sun shone through the windows, splitting the floor between us.

"Good morning, dear," she said.

"It's afternoon, Grandma."

"Oh!" Her hands covered her mouth, and all I could see were her twinkly, mischievous eyes. "It goes by so fast." She wore my dress-up bonnet on her head with pride, tied under her chin in a bow.

"Lovely hat," I said.

"Oh, thank you." She fiddled with the buttons of her pajama top, pointing her feet, clad in her Sunday morning shoes. "They talked to me. Did they talk to you?"

Her face lit up in that strange, sparkly way that only old faces light up. I wiped the tears off my cheeks and turned to her. "Who?"

"The gnomes." Her smile stretched across her face. "They told me to take a picture. I like taking pictures."

Unlikely. Posey hadn't seen her camera for ages. "Oh. No. The gnomes never talk to me."

"That's too bad, but don't worry." She eased off the bed, coming close to hold me by the chin. She spoke sweetly, and I leaned into her, into the comfort of her touch. "They will soon."

And she smiled her one hundred smiles.

CHAPTER THIRTY-ONE

I wore white to rehearsal, the color of mourning, to mourn my own death. Dad walked me to the park, silent except for the deep, guttural sighs that accompanied his every turn of thought. His button-up shirt was buttoned to the top, his fingers twitched, and the veins on his temples strained against his skin. He watched the rehearsal while I stared at my feet.

Delia leaned against a pine tree, ripping off sections of bark layer by layer.

"Nark," James mumbled, approaching me with Sebastian behind him. I sat against the usual shrubbery, chin on my knees. "We're grounded for the foreseeable future, so, you know, thanks."

Sebastian stepped out from behind his brother, face serious. "James —"

"She saw herself dead in her mirror," Delia interrupted. My stomach churned. She wouldn't look at me, just tore off a layer of bark and tossed it behind her shoulder. I wanted her to look at me so badly that I wouldn't look at her, either.

"Oh." James shifted uncomfortably, eyeing me. "For real?"

Delia shrugged, and I only nodded, pulling up blades of crabgrass. I piled them on my feet. My drowned, dead face wouldn't leave my eyes, and the poisoned words I'd shot at my best friend weighed on me, pushing me down into the sand. It was too hard to speak with the weight of my words pushing at my shoulders.

James' eyes sat on me, searing and relentless, like a laser beam. "Are you sure it wasn't – "

"I saw it with my own eyes," I said, ripping up grass and tearing it to pieces.

"Right. Of course." He buried his hands in his pockets.

Sebastian whistled under his breath. "We'll make sure you don't die, Marion," he assured me, sitting next to me with a smile. He bumped me with his shoulder. "Don't worry about it too much, okay?"

But how could I not worry about it? His promise was sweet, but Sebastian couldn't defy fate. No one could help me, not Detective Mobley, not the Mobley brothers, not the police officer by the stage, stationed there to keep me safe. Not even my dad, who wanted the best, but couldn't control my destiny.

"Anyway, they threatened her, James," Sebastian said,

leaning back on his hands. "Did you really expect her not to say something?"

James sighed. "No, I guess not." He rubbed his forehead, staring at his feet as I wiped away a tear. "I'd have done the same thing."

And Delia turned her back on us, kicking at the sand.

Rehearsal ended well after dark, and Dad walked Posey and me home. Lights flashed as crowds of uniformed men gathered around the museum's front door, and we bumped into Doug, wearing tube socks and cargo shorts, with his cell phone locked on his belt. Penelope clung to his arm, her golden hair shining underneath the streetlight. The museum sat across the street, and they watched the officers come and go.

Doug turned his head at the sound of our footsteps.

"George! Marion!" He smiled broadly, to cover the glimmer of surprise in the corner of his mouth. "How are you this fine evening?"

Dad squeezed my elbow and moved to skirt around him, but I stood my ground. Penelope caught my eye, giving me a gentle smile, full of comfort and sealed secrets. She was still sunshine, still golden from her hair to her shoes to the light-yellow pallor of her skin. Maybe she knew something that could help, something that would help me sleep.

"Hello." I nodded to Penelope. She wore thick, velvety

socks that billowed out of her shoes, and the bags under her eyes were deeply blue, like bruises. "This is my sister, Posey." Posey, of all things, curtsied. "Seeing as you're here and I'm here and everything, I'd like to ask you a few questions, if that's possible?"

"What questions?" Dad sputtered, surprise coloring his face. I ignored him.

Doug fiddled with the phone at his hip and sniffed. He looked from me to Dad to Posey, and when I cast a wary glance at him, he stuttered, thrusting out his gut as he rubbed it.

"Always full of questions, this one!" he chuckled, and Dad didn't answer, only stared at Doug steadily, lips tight and pale.

"What kind of questions?" Penelope asked. She had the most vibrant blue eyes I'd ever seen; they sat on her face like headlights.

"Someone's going to kill me. Is it Doug?"

Doug laughed, his shoulders shooting back – he stammered a few consonants, but his wife touched him softly on the stomach and he shut his mouth. Her smile was bright and swift. "No. I should think not. He won't even kill spiders."

"Marv?"

She hesitated. "Why would Marv kill you?"

"So you think he's capable."

"I think he's a rather extreme type of person, but not

unreasonable." She tap, tap, tapped her chin, lifting it higher with every word. "Why would he kill you?"

"Do you know how he gets money for your medical fund?" I nodded to the museum, but Penelope held my gaze, biting her lip. Her voice dropped to a low whisper, turning thin and dry like tissue paper.

"No. Why?"

"Because I know. And I think someone is going to kill me for it."

She didn't say anything for five long breaths. Her eyes bored into mine, searching for something, and then she pondered Posey, examining her body, starting at her feet and ending at the crown of her head.

"Are you afraid of dying?" she asked us, her eyes all glisten-y, her chin trembling.

"I guess." I shifted my feet. "I'm afraid of drowning."

"Then we can't have that, can we?" With one finger she motioned me closer, keeping one eye on Dad. He gripped my elbow as I leaned forward, ear to her lips. Her voice was like broken glass, weak and breathy, sharp at the edges. "Stay away from the pier."

Doug coughed, his forehead pushing down into his eyeballs, but then he smiled. "She's tired." Wrapping his arms around her, he rubbed her back like she was cold. "It's the way things go these days, you know. Never know what she'll say if she's ready for a nap."

Penelope buried her head in Doug's chest, and Dad said

gruffly, "Let's go." He dragged me across the street, Posey behind me, and we barreled into Marv, who stood on the sidewalk talking to Detective Mobley.

"Nothing," Detective Mobley told us. "Clean as a whistle."

And Marv sneered.

As soon as I got home Mom handed me the phone. Conrad didn't even wait for me to answer – I put the phone to my ear and heard his voice.

"Marion, Mom called. You're being threatened?"

"I saw myself. Dead. In the mirror." I leaned my head against the kitchen wall. "The sea ate me."

"Well, that sounds like stress – "

"It's not stress, I saw it."

He paused. "I've been doing some research about the Finnegans."

"And I've been staring death in the face." I traced the frown of my sad face, made of thumb tacks on the cork board. I added one tack to its cheek, like a tear.

He sighed, again. "I'm coming home for Founder's Day."

"Why?"

"Because I am."

He hung up first, and I was left to my thoughts, left to suffer them on my own. They were demanding things, those thoughts, because they needed to be seen, to be known, and if I didn't greet them, who would? So I welcomed them with open arms, ready to make them treasures, even if they were as worthless and broken as the pottery bits at the bottom of the sea.

Chapter Thirty-Two

Founder's Day came bright and early the next morning. I woke up with the sun, my stomach aching and my knees shaking, staring at the familiar lines of Chaucer and Shakespeare. The ring was cold and tight on my finger.

THOUGH THIS BE MADNESS, YET THERE IS METHOD IN IT

I had to fix things. I had to talk to Delia.

I pulled my knees up to my chin and closed my eyes, breathing in the silence. I was unmoored, drifting here and there without my best friend, without her support, without Finney's anchor. In the silence all I heard were my own cruel words, sent like arrows to those I loved, and I had to make it right.

I crept out of bed and raced to the park, where I found

myself adjusting my homemade villager costume (handed to me by Ms. Caroline with the instructions to get ready, pronto) and looking for Delia. I spotted her crouched behind the shrubbery, and when she saw me coming, she put a finger to her lips.

What's going on? I mouthed.

James, she replied.

James' head rose above the shrubs, and the top of another head poked above the leaves. James' eyes were a storm, and his eyebrows crunched together so hard I thought his face might collapse. Delia and I shut our mouths and inched closer.

"Absolutely not," he said. "Stop asking."

A woman's voice answered, rushed and irritated. "But you don't understand the implications – "

"I don't care. Go away."

I couldn't take it any longer. The memory of my words weighed on me, and I turned to Delia, my voice low and raspy. "I was scared. Stuff just slipped out. I don't think you're weird or anything – "

She shushed me. The woman on the other side of the bush spoke, and I closed my eyes to hear better.

"You can find out all the things, all the secrets this way, and then maybe – "

"I've learned enough from you, I think," James answered.

I opened my eyes.

"James!" Her fingers shot in the air, the long, slender fingers of Fern. "I'm trying to help you!"

"Doubtful." His thumb and forefinger pinched the bridge of his nose – he must have learned that move from my dad.

Delia leaned close and whispered, "If you didn't mean to say it, that's even worse. That just means you really do think it, you just usually have the decency not to say it."

I cringed. "No, honest, I don't really think it. Honest. No half-truths. I promise."

It was the truth. I didn't think she was strange or delusional. But I did know which words would cut the deepest, and I had used them, swung them at her like weapons. Music blasted from a few streets down – the parade was about to start. As soon as it was over we'd begin. My stomach fluttered and I shivered, looking her in the eyes. She had vulnerable eyes this time, all glassy and full of hope. I dragged a leaf out of my hair.

"Listen, Delia, I'm really sorry – "

She swatted my shoulder. "Don't worry, I'm just giving you a hard time. I'm over it." The dimple in her chin winked at me. Her villager dress was a soft pink, and it brought out the color in her cheeks. "I'll insult you when you're not expecting it, then we'll be even."

"Fair enough," I said. We shook on it, spat on the ground, and stomped our feet. The voices on the other side of the bushes twisted into shouts.

"Why on earth do you care?" Fern screamed, her voice slicing the air, spitting fire and double-edged blades.

"Why wouldn't I care?" James replied, looking peaky, as

Delia's imaginary British Grandma would say. He was pale and drawn out around the mouth. "She's my friend."

"It's no big deal!" Fingertips poked up from the tops of the shrubs; she was throwing her hands in the air. "Take the job. We can find out more."

"No."

"We'll see each other every day."

"I'm not too keen on that, either."

Fern made her voice harsh and solid. "You were never a project, James."

I peeked through the bushes, pushing away twigs and leaves, but all I could see was a pair of lips, and before my eyes they shriveled up like a salted slug. "I choose you."

"Nah, you don't." James dug in his back pocket and slapped something in her hands. "There. Our debt is settled. We're done."

There was a moment of silence, punctuated by a clap and a swoosh. Fern was brushing off her hands, washing them of James' decisions. "Fine. Do what you want. I don't care."

He frowned at her in his classic James way, with his eyes all stony and his jaw set to crush diamonds. "I will," and then he looked straight at us, like he knew we were staring all along, and Delia and I observed the sky.

There really were quite a few fluffy clouds; one looked like a gnome trying on lipstick. I said as much to Delia, but she nudged me quiet as James came to stand beside us, his presence all heavy and filled with needles.

"You two are about as subtle as the mating call of a white bellbird."

"You okay, James?" Delia asked.

"I've been better."

I crossed my arms and eased into a wide stance, to mirror his posture. My skirt swayed back and forth; Ms. Caroline had put me in a raggedy brown number, tied simply at the waist. It looked awful but it provided optimal movement, so I didn't complain. "There was this one day, Dad made chocolate chip pancakes for breakfast, and I found ten bucks in my coat, and then I went to see an impromptu movie at the theater east of town."

James stared at me silently and Delia closed her eyes like a wearied mother. "What does that have to do with anything, Marion?"

"I was better that day," I answered.

James almost smiled. Then, "I found something out."

"What'd you find out?"

"You're not gonna like it."

"Try me."

He took a deep breath. "Fern knows who took those pictures. She knew all along. But she didn't tell us."

"Who?" I turned at him, the swing of my feet accusing him of all Fern's crimes.

"Francesca Lovely." But he didn't look relieved. He looked like he was about to tell me something even worse. "Fern thinks you're in danger, that it's not a bluff."

"Did Francesca write the threat?"

His presence became even more heavy and filled with needles, but I stared him down.

"Fern doesn't know who wrote it."

"She doesn't know?"

He stared at his feet and kicked at a clump of dirt. "She wanted me to get more involved. Said something about an open spot. Like, on Marv's payroll. Bet you a million dollars she gets a percentage of it if I accept. So I'm done."

Delia's eyes were spacey, trying to take it all in. "She tried to bribe you? With information?"

"It seems so." He shoved his hands in his pockets. "I don't want to go back, Marion. Sorry. Plus, I don't think my dad will let me out of his sight until I'm thirty."

"Sorry, James," Delia said.

"Yeah, sorry James," I repeated.

He shrugged. "It's cool."

I sighed, letting out every frustrated breath kept between my bones. "Well, we all know someone might kill me. That's no grand revelation. If we can't prove who it is exactly, it's all the same to me whether it's Francesca or Marv or Doug." I paused. "But you got mad at her? For me?"

"She was trouble."

Trouble she was, and more trouble was coming our way: a young woman approached us, frantic and weathered, her hair wild and her dress askew. She was in full costume, her curly red hair bouncing off her bodice as she held up her skirts – but it wasn't a woman, she was too boney, too angled, too flat –

It was Sebastian.

He scuttled toward us in full village woman garb, corset and all, a dollar store wig clinging to his head. His feet plunked at the ground in a distinctly unwomanly way, so that every punch of his knees made the skirt go flying. James breathed out a "What the..." and Delia and I watched as he lumbered to us, our words lodged in our throats, too big, too numerous to get through.

"I have news," he said. His dress was deep red with golden trimmings, and honestly, it did not go well with his ginger ringlets.

I looked him up and down. "Apparently so."

He tossed my comment aside with a shake of his head and declared, "I lost a bet," then, "I saw that one guy lurking around. The one that bothers Fern. And it was not a pleasant experience."

"Really?" James put a hand to his chin and examined every detail of Sebastian's costume, his eyes alight with delight, his frown drenched in false sincerity. "I thought men like that were always nice to pretty girls."

"Hardy har-har." Sebastian tossed the curls of his wig over his shoulder. "Anyway, he's up to no good, I'm sure of it."

"What makes you think that?" I asked.

"He may have made me a proposition."

James' eyes stretched wide, and his teeth glimmered in the sunlight. "He hit on you?"

"He *harassed* me." Sebastian set his fists on his waist and narrowed his eyes. "He catcalled me from behind, but when he realized it was me, he got all butthurt and threatened me. He's off his rocker, Marion. Totally hammered. So, yes, James, he did hit on me." He scowled. "He hit on the woman he thought I was, in his head."

"Well, who wouldn't?" James shrugged, his voice (deceptively) somber.

"*It's not funny*," Sebastian insisted, crossing his arms. "It's *violating*."

"He's got a point," Delia said. "It *is* violating."

James held up one hand. "Violating or not, I want to know why you're in a dress."

Sebastian drooped. "Fine. I bet Posey that it would rain today. I had a feeling. I was wrong. I may have a problem, but that's not the issue I'm here to discuss."

"Thursdays *are* detestable," I said.

"I also saw Todd," Sebastian continued, adjusting his sleeves. "He said he quit his job."

"Really?"

Sebastian nodded. "He looked nervous."

Ms. Caroline, a force of nerves and adrenaline, sprinted by us. "It's time, darlings! To the stage! Is everyone dressed? Please tell me everyone is dressed." She almost lost her footing when she noticed Sebastian, standing before her in a wig and a dress. "What – oh, never mind. I won't ask. I don't want to know." She adjusted his bodice so that it sat, as best it could, correctly on his chest. Then she leaned close to him and whispered, "Please be modest, dear, you're in public," before she patted him on the cheek and hurried off to the stage (to the sound of James cackling. Sebastian turned red like a lobster and muttered something about not having anything to show). "Come along," she added, calling over her shoulder. "It's time."

The backdrops were finished (using our curtains), and the stage was set. It was nothing fancy, just a black background with a cutout town, and two sets of stairs on either side to come and go. Behind it was the majority of the park, just grass and plants, and in front a few rows of fold up chairs and room for blankets. Everything was ready. A crowd had gathered around the stage, and Ms. Caroline weaved through it, calling, "Gird your loins!" and, "Onward and upward!" as she disappeared behind a mass of costumed homeschoolers.

We followed her, but a seagull screeched at me from a nearby bush.

"Human. I heard you speak bird."

I stopped and let the others continue without me, my heart skipping a beat at the sight of him. "Yes, I do."

He was a handsome seagull, with a wide girth and smooth, shiny feathers. The tilt of his head suggested an easy confidence, matched by the pull of his gaze. He considered me, his beak open and feet restless. I smiled.

"Do you have something to tell me?"

He nodded and shook out his plumage. A few patches on his belly and back were thin and showing skin. "I heard you've been asking for witnesses. For birds who saw that lady die."

"Yes, I've been looking for a bird that was there." I inched closer, my heart thumping against my ribs. It wasn't too late – I could still prove everything, solve the murder, change my future, if I learned the right clue, the clue that would help me find the method in the madness. I could live, maybe, if the bird helped. "Did you see it?"

He stretched his wings and let his feathers catch the wind – the feathers were sparse and ragged, and he scoffed. "The crazy bird attacked me, you know. She and her friend. Dive-bombed me and pulled out half my feathers. Then she told me a human was talking to all the birds, asking about that other human's death. In fact, every bird this side of the Atlantic has been bothering me, telling me I need to talk to you, that you have questions, and it's annoying. I have a life, alright? I have things to do. Fish to eat. Women to woo. Did my ex-lover tell you about the night that woman died?"

I stiffened. "A little."

"He hit her. Then threw her into the sea."

"Yes, she said so. Do you know who he was?" I couldn't accuse Marv based on a seagull's testimony, but I was curious if he could give me something to go on, something that would lead to proof. With a sigh, he flew to the ground and walked in circles in front of me, his neck outstretched.

"No, and I haven't seen him since. That was a terrible night. So much screaming. And it made my eyes hurt. The light was too bright."

"Ah, the lighthouse. Well – "

"Not the flashy night light. The magic light. From the box."

I thought hard. "From a camera?"

"Whatever it was, it was bright. It hurt my eyes. But he was...he was a mean human. Feathers like fire. The smile of a fox."

The smile of a fox. I backed up. "Say that again."

He stopped and faced me. "He was a mean human, the smile of a fox. You're a little hard of hearing, huh?"

That was it. The seagull had identified him. I had no voice, my heart was in my throat, and the bird stepped away, saying,

"Well, if you're out of questions, I'm leaving..."

I had no more questions. I knew who had the smile of a fox, and yet it was useless.

I could know all I wanted, but I still didn't know how to prove it.

I spun the ring around my finger, again and again and again and again, without saying a word, and the seagull flew away.

Chapter Thirty-Three

The play began, as all good plays do, with the beginning. There were enough chairs for the old and sick and selfish to inhabit, and the rest stood around, faces blank, ready to watch Máire Finnegan die. Detective Mobley watched us (per Mom's request) with crossed arms and a loaded gun at his hip. The whole situation was distracting, especially while we were chanting, "Vile wench!" at Máire Finnegan, because the birds were chanting, "MURDERER! MURDERER!" until I, too, was chanting, "MURDERER!" but I didn't discover it until my costars looked at me funny and a few people in the audience began to snicker. I searched for the birds to ask them to keep it quiet when I saw a flock flying in a circle, led by a large seagull with tattered, missing feathers. They flew frantically around one particular person:

Leo.

The smile of a fox, the redhead with feathers like flames.

Then it hit me: if I knew the truth and didn't speak all of it, it would make me a half-truth. I would have to tell everyone, right then and there. And they would call me crazy.

If the bird was right, and I knew he was, then I had to do something, and drat it all, I knew what I had to do.

"Thank you, birds!" I screamed, and I ran off the stage dragging Posey with me, but Max followed and grabbed my arm.

"Why were you screaming 'murderer'?" he asked, out of breath. We snuck behind the stage, the confused spectators painfully silent as the cast picked up the pieces of my improv.

Ms. Caroline ran to us, hoarsely whispering, "What are you doing?"

I placed one hand over my heart for sincerity. "It's important, I promise. I'm solving the murder, I think."

She sagged. "Oh, Marion." The unsettled rustling of the audience reached us, and she buried her face in her hands. "What will I do with you?" Then, after a sigh, "Just keep quiet, alright?" And she left, hands up. Max tried again.

"Marion, why did you scream 'murderer'?" He was dressed from head to toe as a poor urchin, his cheeks black with dirt, his under eyes gray like a sickly ghost.

"Not now, Max," I said, wrenching my arm from his grasp to address Posey. "A resolution of genius potential is permeating in my brain."

He frowned at me. "Doubtful."

"What's this about, Marion?" Posey demanded, inching away from me. She was in brown too, like the dying grasses in a marsh, wearing the muted tones of Sebastian's villager trousers and linen shirt.

I paced in front of her, hands on my hips, skirt rustling against the tops of my feet. "Does the sea remember? Of course it does. But how?"

Max sighed the sigh of a thousand sickly urchins. "You sound like one of those gravestones. 'The sea is full of sorrows'..."

I stared at him. His round face stared back at me, unimpressed. "What?"

"Did you say 'sorrows'?"

He glared. "Did I stutter?"

"They took it to the sorrows. The gnomes, they took it to the grave."

"What?"

"You sleep talk, Max!" I cupped his cheeks in my hands. "And what a beautiful, wonderful habit."

He pulled my hands away. "You're weirding me out."

He was there, asleep but aware, when someone stole the camera – someone stole it because Grandma had taken a picture of the murder.

She knew Lily. They hunted gnomes together. And she was there, a witness, when Lily was murdered.

Maybe Grandma wasn't quite as crazy as everyone thought.

"Max, Grandma took a picture, that night at the docks. That's what the seagull said. Someone took the camera, and I think I know where it is."

"Someone took the camera?" He raised an eyebrow. "Why didn't they destroy it?"

"Because it wasn't a bad guy." I nodded to myself, checking off every possibility in my mind to conclude that maybe, just maybe, we weren't alone. "I think the gnomes are helping us. I think it was a message. I think it's in the geocache box by Colleen Finnegan's grave." I pointed a finger in Max's face. "Don't go anywhere."

I grabbed Posey's arm and dragged her even farther from the stage, ignoring her pleas for reason and sanity.

"This is no time for half-truths," I urged in her ear. "Listen. I know where your camera is. Detective Mobley and the killer are both in the audience. We need to prove things while they're both here, in front of everyone, so I don't die, mainly." I bobbed my head. "And also there's a slight chance I'm wrong, but I'll know for sure when I see his face."

"There's a chance you might be wrong?" Posey backed up, her voice low and unsteady, the picture-perfect skeptic. "Really?"

"Marion!" Ms. Caroline whispered sharply. "What are you doing? We need Posey!" She poked her head around a group of actors waiting for their cue to go on stage, clipboard in her hand. I couldn't see the crowd on the other side, but I could hear them, and I could sense them by the way Ms. Caroline spoke, all wild and desperate.

"It's a matter of life and death," I called back, "I promise."

"Posey!" Ms. Caroline hissed, waving her over.

"Just have Sebastian say my line," Posey answered. "He's in my dress and everything." She turned back to me. "You might be wrong?"

Ms. Caroline growled and disappeared behind the crowd of teenagers.

"Yes, I might be wrong. My main sources are birds and sleep-talking boys. But I don't think I am. Please. This is your chance to help us – the camera is by Colleen Finnegan's grave. In the geocache box. Go get it."

Posey sighed out of her bottom lip and her bangs blew upward, like an evil stepsister. Then she nodded, the swamp creatures behind her eyes retreating.

"Alright. I'll be right back."

She jogged toward the graveyard, holding up her trousers in two fistfuls. My heart warmed in my chest to see her bear the mantle so easily. I had expected a much harder fight.

My attention spun back to Delia, who came much more readily, her fist mid-air as she shouted, "Death to the madwoman!" I shook her until she came back to reality.

"I know everything."

"I know you know everything."

"No, I mean, I know where the camera is. Grandma took a picture of the murder. I think we can prove it, if we get the film. But we need to explain the theory here, in front of everyone, while Detective Mobley is watching. And Leo.

Leo was with Marv that day we met Fern at Waffle Madness, Delia. Leo does the dirty work." I stole a glance at the stage, where the play droned on, the audience silent and captivated, oblivious to the criminals in their midst. "Detective Mobley will have to listen, and no one can kill us if we're in front of everyone. The whole town of Lady's Madness is watching!" I looked her in the eyes, to beseech the churning underneath the surface, where her thoughts and actions began.

"Fine." Delia put her hands on her hips and swayed, and the circumference of her skirt made a nice swooshing noise. "How do you propose we do this?"

I clasped her shoulders. "I want you to reenact the murder."

"What?"

"I'll push Máire aside and announce the takeover. Then you reenact the murder. We'll help, but you'll lead us. Max!" He stood near the backdrop, waiting, as I had instructed (Such a good little urchin). "I know what happened. Max, this is your moment." I pointed at him, and he smiled.

"Aren't we going to get the guys?" Delia asked, inching their direction.

"Of course not. Ms. Caroline would have a heart attack, and they're in enough trouble as it is. Delia, it's improv time. You're going to act it out, now, while Leo is watching, to see how he reacts, and to make sure Detective Mobley listens. The whole case depends on you." She backed up, head tilted to the side, the wind blowing in her hair, but I grabbed her wrist. "You can do it. Max will help you. Listen closely, here's how it went..."

And I briefed them on my theory, and we made a quick plan – then I set my sights on the play.

I ran to the stage (Ms. Caroline clutched at me, hissing my name, but I ran past her) –

Máire Finnegan stood center stage, giving her big monologue, but it was not important. I pushed her aside and screamed to my captive audience –

"I KNOW WHO KILLED LILY ANDERSON!"

The crowd shifted; of course they would be wary, as far as they knew Lily had killed herself. I waved my hands to clear their thoughts. It was not a time for half-truths – I would have to tell them whole ones.

"Trust me, the birds told me everything."

Silence. Then, clapping – Grandma sat first row center, smiling and clapping wildly, her purple hair blowing in the wind, a table runner draped over her shoulders like a shawl. Mom sat next to her, face pale alongside her bright red scarf. I cleared my throat. Dad winked at me, but Mom elbowed him, and he gradually got to his feet.

Slowly a murmur rippled through the crowd, and I waved them silent again. "The truest of true things," I said to my audience, their eyes on me with rapt attention, "is that there is a dark underworld in this town, and though it seems overwhelming and unknowable, there is method in the madness. Watch and see."

I waved Delia on stage, and she came hesitantly, hands folded in front of her.

"I'm Violet," she said, voicing from deep in her abdomen.

I followed suit, saying, "And I'm Lily!" (complete with jazz hands).

The silence was deafening. Spectators shifted in their seats and those standing on the outskirts of the crowd stepped closer, closing in the space between my words and their curious minds. Dad turned into the multitude, snaking through the people, heading toward the stage.

Delia took the lead. "We're sisters, and we're new in town!"

Max ran to center stage, arms out, yelling: "And I'm Marv!"

The Founder's Day actors moved out of his way, baffled, and the crowd laughed. Max smiled wide, holding out a hand to Delia. "It's nice to meet you. Would you like to join my illegal gambling club?"

"Why, yes I would," Delia answered, her shoulders relaxing. One man in the back of the audience barked two deep laughs.

"How delightful!" Max (playing Marv) declared.

Ms. Caroline rushed on stage, clipboard held high above her head, and grabbed the microphone. "This is not the Founder's Day play," she said in one quick breath. "I don't know what this is, actually – "

I snatched the microphone. "This is an explanation of

how and why Lily Anderson was murdered." Ms. Caroline froze, her dark, wiry hair fluttering around her, and I smiled apologetically. "Please, Ms. Caroline, it will take, like, five minutes."

She bared her teeth, speaking quietly from the back of her throat. "Perhaps you can share with us your theories after the play."

That would not be ideal. The audience had waited patiently, Detective Mobley and Leo among them, and I would not have them wait any longer. I covered the microphone and whispered, "It's imperative that certain parties present in the audience hear what I have to say. I can't afford to wait." Then, when she lifted her chin to fire back, I added softly, "Please?"

Dad stood at the side stage, gesturing for me to leave; Ms. Caroline noticed him and bit her lip, then leaned into the microphone.

"It seems we will take a break from our planned production to present another matter of local importance. Please be patient, it won't take long." She nodded to me. "Be good, Marion. I'm watching."

I waited until she took her place next to Dad, watching from the sidelines. Dad asked her something and she shook her head, motioning vaguely to me with her clipboard. He rubbed his belly and winked at me, but Ms. Caroline watched with one hand over her mouth, her eyes following my every move.

And thus, our little play began.

I backed away from center stage as the other Founder's Day actors filed away in a cloud of confused whispers and shrugs. They formed a group behind Ms. Caroline to watch us, James and Sebastian among them – Sebastian tripped on the hem of his skirt and fell into James. James pushed him away without ceremony, only to flinch and cower when Ms. Caroline smacked him over the head with her clipboard. Sebastian fell into Dad, who helped him back to his feet, shaking his head as he observed the wig and dress with golden trimmings.

Max repeated, "Would you like to join my illegal gambling club?"

He trotted to the opposite side and Delia followed, pantomiming her surprise at an underground casino. Max led her to a corner, and she threw dice, digging money from her pockets. After groaning a good three times, she raised her hands and declared,

"I'm destitute! I've squandered all my money!"

The crowd shifted uncomfortably, unsure if she was joking or serious; I called, "Violet!" and ran to her, grabbing her wrist. "It's me, your sister, Lily. You have a gambling addiction, and it's time for you to get better! Go to rehab!"

Delia crossed her arms, sitting on the floor like Posey in the alley, lips pouting and chin on her chest.

"Don't come visit me!" she called out as I walked away.

I circled the gambling den ("Marv" was still gambling), holding a pretend pad and paper and scribbling my discoveries. "There appears to be an illegal gambling den in Lady's Madness," I told the crowd.

One unknown voice carried over the silence. "Not again!"

A trickle of laughter bobbed through the park.

Max got up, and looking both ways, surreptitiously picked up something from the floor. "I hope no one sees me," he said, filling his shirt with air. "I'm picking up my drugs to pay for Penelope's doctor!" Then he brought it all back to the gambling den and began to distribute it, pocketing money every few seconds. I took notes.

Grandma watched, hands clasped to her chest, completely enraptured; Mom watched with one hand over her mouth. Detective Mobley stood to the side, hands on his hips, observing everything – I did a double take. He really *was* watching. He was paying attention. Maybe – maybe it would work.

I turned my back to the audience, knees knocking together, when Max grabbed my attention. He stared blankly ahead, arms frozen at his sides.

"Be Doug," I whispered. *'I'd like to talk to you. Meet me at the waterfront.'*

He nodded, the light switching on behind his eyes, and jumped to center stage.

"I'm Doug!" he exclaimed. He turned me to face the audience. "I'd like to talk to you. Meet me at the waterfront."

"Sure thing," I said, giving a thumbs up.

An unsettled murmur fluttered through the crowd. They

knew where it was going, what would happen to Lily after she met Doug at the waterfront. The truth unraveled at our feet, flowing down into the onlookers, hitting them row by row, and my heart skipped a beat.

Max moved to the side and stretched his arms above his head, yelling, "I'm Marv again!"

I backed away to keep the attention on him, holding my breath. The murder was eminent, and the "why" was the key to it all. It was Max's big spiel.

Delia stepped forward and announced, "I'm Leo." She flexed her biceps, and Dad laughed from offstage.

And Max forgot his lines. He stared at the audience, wide-eyed, fear dripping off him; Delia leaned down to whisper in his ear. He nodded.

"I'm Marv again." He waved a finger at Delia. "Leo, you owe us a lot of money from gambling..."

His face went blank – so Delia fed him his lines, word for word, while Max shouted them back at her with all his might.

"We'll forgive it if you do something for me. I don't want Lily to expose our secret. If she does, Doug won't have the money for Penelope's doctor. If Doug can't get Lily to be quiet, kill her."

Sebastian clapped, and Max smiled so hard that all his teeth showed.

"Will do!" Delia agreed, flexing again.

Ms. Caroline rushed onto the stage, taking the microphone once again. "Time's up, guys. Thank you for that...presentation."

I felt one hand gently grasp my shoulder and pull me toward the side; Dad looked down at me, his glasses near the tip of his nose, a slight twinkle in his eye.

"That's some heavy stuff, kiddo."

"I'm not done," I said, grabbing the ends of my skirt in one hand for mobility, planning my exit.

"Yes, you are." He guided me to the edge, but I ducked and ran, screaming the last of my lines –

"Doug," I yelled to Max, dodging Dad, "I know everything! I'm going to expose it all. You can't convince me otherwise! You will not keep me quiet!"

"Please don't tell anyone," Max pleaded (as Doug), "I'll do anything!"

"Nothing's good enough," I shouted. Dad caught me around the waist and threw me over his shoulder. "Bye!" I cried, waving at Max as I floated over the stage.

"Bye," he replied, and scrambled away to stand on the opposite side.

The Real Leo searched the crowd, planning his exit out of the audience. I raised my head above Dad's to see clearly, and my heart quickened. He was shifty, eyes restless, body on high alert. We had him: the guilt was showing. Grandma sat in front of him, hands clasped to her chest.

Delia ran to us, pointing at Dad and screaming to the audience: "He's Leo!" and in a lower, hoarser tone, "Mr.

George, drop her! drop her!" And, out of curiosity, he did. He let go of me at the last moment and I slid off, exaggerating my landing, screaming as I pretended to fall to my watery death.

Max ran to me, screaming, "I'm Grandma!"

He held out his hands like a camera. He took a picture, capturing everything. Grandma cheered and I snuck a peek at the crowd, searching for The Real Leo.

He was gone.

And where was Posey?

I climbed to my feet, brushing myself off, scanning the area for Posey and Leo. Ms. Caroline stomped by me, muttering, "This is so weird," but I put one hand on her arm.

"We're done," I said, out of breath and surveying the crowd. "Can we wrap it up? Give a call to action?"

She bowed her head, rubbing her forehead and sighing one deep sigh. "Fine. At this point, who cares? You've got one minute."

I ran to center stage. The three of us stood in a line and bowed. Grandma clapped. Someone coughed.

"And that's how Lily Anderson was killed," I said into the microphone.

The audience was silent.

"And we have proof!" Delia turned to me. "Don't we?"

Posey still had not returned with the camera, and Penelope, sitting beside Leo's empty seat, caught my eyes like fire. Her eyes were two flames, boring into mine, her jaw set like iron.

Penelope didn't want to die.

Realization seeped into me like water in a boat, leaching in as the cracks slowly opened.

"I'll go find Posey," I said. "Stall a while."

And I ran off the stage (cutting my way through Dad and the angry villagers) as Delia announced, "There are five core reasons why we know Bigfoot is alive and well in the pacific northwest..."

I watched my feet as I ran along the waterfront, looking for colored glass and old pottery bits out of habit, willing my legs to move faster with the force of my eyeballs. That's why I didn't see anything ahead of me, but I heard the birds, those blessed, lovely birds, screaming,

"MURDERER!"

I looked up. Posey stood at the end of the pier, her face a wide-open expanse of fear and dread and desperation, as Leo's hands squeezed her neck.

Leo was choking my little sister.

And there was no one to help her. The waterfront was empty – everyone was at the play.

I screamed so loud that my brain went to static, and I yelled and pounded and thrashed my way to them, the marshy face of Posey falling, in my mind, to the marshy floor of the waterway, all browns and greens and filled with secrets. Leo didn't want to hear me. His eyes were wide with crazy, his fingers gripping Posey's neck, Posey's hands trying in vain to separate them. The camera sat at their feet, forgotten.

I jumped on his back, threw my arms around his neck

and squeezed – but Leo thrashed backwards, and my head hit the railing and I saw thunder and lightning under my eyelids, and then, all strength and instinct gone from my body, I was thrown over the edge, one hand reaching out, begging the lighthouse to save me.

I was devoured in one gulp, and my last glimpse of the world was the hungry water before it all went dark.

CHAPTER THIRTY-FOUR

Kind of.

One single bubble floated from my mouth to the surface. My arms stretched out before me, my lungs filled with water, and the sun shone through the surface ripples. The skirt of my dress billowed around me.

So this was what it was like, to be devoured by the sea.

I had no strength to fight back. I let the water flow past my fingers, let my back touch the bottom. It had finally happened; we had our meeting, the sea and I, and I was lunch.

And then, strong arms folded around me, pulling me up, and I was in the cold salty air, coughing, sputtering, spraying brackish water.

"Keep coughing," he said, wading through the waves. "You're going to be okay."

My eyes stung, the cellphone strapped to his belt stabbed

my hipbone, and his polo shirt's audacious shade of blue pushed into me as one giant blur. The birds screamed. Some screamed, "MURDERER!" and others screamed, "HERO!" but the fact of the matter was they all knew something big and exciting was happening, and it helped ground me in the knowledge that I was not making it all up.

Doug shuddered, his breathing desperate and masking tears. He placed me gently on the sand and I winced, feeling the welt on the back of my head. I looked at my fingers. There was a little blood, too. Thursdays really were detestable.

I coughed and rubbed my eyes, looking over at him sitting on the sand next to me, shoulders slumped and head down.

"I wasn't a part of it," he said, frantically, as the town gathered around the pier, my parents leading the pack. Posey ran crying to Mom and buried her head in her arms. Dad hugged them both, engulfing Posey between them.

Apparently my noisy arrival had summoned everyone, including Detective Mobley, who was at that moment running toward the pier while James sat at the end – what was he doing? I squinted. He sat on top of Leo, punching him in the face.

Sebastian punched Doug.

Straight in the nose, he clocked him with all the force of his body, so hard that his wig turned sideways, and his skirts flew up and I saw the pasty white flesh if his left thigh. Doug's head snapped back and he grunted. Sebastian lifted his arm for a second blow, and I lurched myself over Doug, screaming –

"He saved my life, dagnabit!" And I stretched out my arm, holding him back with my open palm and the brutal honesty of my eyes.

Sebastian's face fell. "Oh." He shook out his hand and wiped his knuckles on his dress. "Guess that was for nothing. My bad, sir. I assumed..."

But his voice faded as the birds screamed, and the wind blew so hard it was like thunder in my ears. I shivered as I sat on the shore, dripping, my wet, salty hair whipping and tangling. My dress clung to me. Sebastian's knuckles were tinged red, and the back of my head was bleeding, too.

Bleeding. Just like Lily Anderson, the birds said, before she was tossed in the water. I turned to Doug, who wiped the blood from his nose, gingerly touching where the cartilage bent.

"I didn't know she wanted to kill her," he said, softly. "Honest I didn't. Then she told me, after they found her body..." He shook his head. "What's done is done, I thought. I didn't want anyone else hurt. I just wanted to take care of my wife. She is dying anyway. I thought I could just let nature take its course." His voice wavered. He took one deep breath, calming his shivers. He was wet too, from his penny loafers to his collar, and the wind was cold. And he was an open book, if I knew the right pages to read.

"Penelope is Poseidon," I said, hoarsely, through coughs.

Doug nodded, just a slight movement of his chin. I wet

my lips and tried to swallow. My hair and my clothes were dripping wet, but my mouth was bone dry.

"But why'd you meet Lily at the graveyard?"

"I'm sorry you are wrapped up in this." His eyes glistened, and he fiddled with the wet ends of his shirt, squeezing out the water. "I didn't want you wrapped up in this. I was just trying to help, you see. Trying to keep my wife safe. I'd lose my job if Lily exposed everything. Lose my insurance, and I can't have that, you know? We can't even afford the basic treatments without that insurance. And we can't afford – we've been going to clinics all over the world, Germany, Switzerland, Finland. We couldn't do that, without the money from Marv's fund. Lily had ideas about alternative treatments, said Penelope could still try some, had this list in this little folder of hers – it was kind, really. I offered her money, she refused. I offered to pay for her sister's rehab, she refused. I begged her, she refused. Then I left, and...after the hurricane, when they found her body, Leo came to me, all shaken up, and I knew I had to help him. That's what I do, I help. I try to keep people safe."

"Great job," Sebastian said. "Real good work. A murderer almost got away with his crimes, and Marion got death threats. Spectacular."

"I never wanted her to get caught up in this." Doug's voice punched at our ears. He watched Detective Mobley tear James off Leo to handcuff him, slowly shaking his head. "Marv said he'd help me. He got the old men to lie. Pulled a few strings, reminded a few people of their debts, got everyone to participate in that narrative...he thinks he owes me. He was trying to settle our score, trying to fix a problem in my life. I just wanted everything to go back to normal, for everyone to be happy."

"You paid for Violet Anderson's rehab anyway," I said. He nodded, and out of the corner of my eye I saw Todd at the end of the street, watching. "But why was Todd digging holes?"

The question dropped between us when I heard my name.

"MARION." I knew that voice. My own name, stabbed at me like a weapon.

"Hello, Conrad," I said, without looking. When he didn't answer I tipped my face up toward the sun; he stared down at me, his floppy frame and dark blond hair familiar but unexpected as I shivered and twirled the ring on my finger. His face, like always, had the distinct aura of midnight firepits and undone cornbread. He held a stack of papers in his hand, his hair was unwashed and sticking up, and, like always, he was annoyed.

"You had to go and get yourself almost killed before I could get here."

"It's not like I planned it."

Sparks flew out of his eyes. He sighed. "Well, seeing as you're alive, it's as good a time as any to tell you that you have the worst phone etiquette known to man. It's a problem. I found our conversations deeply offensive. I got tired of trying to talk to you, so here I am. You owe me gas money."

"It's nice to see you, too."

He rolled his eyes. "I looked into the Finnegan family. The school's library has copies of the uncle's letters in its archives. I think I was the first person to check it out." He dumped the papers on my lap. "Photocopies. He hid some precious elixir stuff, claimed it could heal anything. Left a clue. I looked at his family tree. You know who's related to him?"

I shook my head.

"The Lovely family. The woman who wrote that article."

The whole world fell away and I heard Sebastian breathe out, "Ohhh..."

Conrad smiled. "Told you I know everything."

I stood up and started to pace, holding the uncle's letters close to my chest. "Bet you a million dollars Francesca Lovely knows about the elixir. Bet you two million she believes it would work. So she must have told Penelope."

"What?" Conrad and Sebastian asked in unison.

"And they hatched a plan, with Doug, to buy the house. Drive us out. Dig up the yard looking for it in the meantime. All to save her."

"It was the dying woman?" Sebastian summed up, one hand on his hip.

I raised an arm above my head, shoulders shrugging. "What else do you have to lose, when you're dying?" The wind blew through my dress and I shivered, and the salt on my skin and in my nose and down my throat was sharp, and it raced through my body until my mind was clear and fast.

"She pulled strings with Marv. Got Leo involved. Somehow, she knew he loaned us money. She knew he owed even more. That's what he was talking to Marv about, in Waffle Madness, the day we met Fern. We got caught in the middle." I stopped. "Of course, now that they're caught, we won't be losing our house, after all. At least not soon. Not now that Leo is in jail."

Doug didn't wait to be asked. "Francesca thought the elixir would heal my wife. I thought it better to just buy the property..." His voice cracked. "Leo was in debt up to his eyeballs. Marv told him to pay up or die; then my wife decided if he helped get that house in my name, well, she'd convince Marv to forgive the difference. I'm sorry, Marion." He wiped his eyes. "Leo called in the loan. No matter what, I was getting that house."

I could only take in one thing at a time – I sat down and blindly flipped through the letters, trying to understand even just one word, but I heard my name again.

"Well, Marion." Detective Mobley walked toward us, his fedora in his hands. "It seems you've uncovered a whole host of information." The ocean raged behind him, and his hair whipped and waved. He squinted at me, like he was trying to look apologetic.

"Oh really?" I carefully touched the welt on the back of my head, where the pain hit like a battering ram.

"I'm fairly certain the photos developed from the camera will come up with solid proof. Leonard seemed desperate enough about it."

James jogged up beside him, his knuckles bandaged, his face bright and self-satisfied. He stood beside his dad, throwing his shoulders back to stand straight and tall.

"Did it really happen that way?" Detective Mobley asked. "Like in the play?"

I nodded, doing a half shrug in between nods. "More or less. With a few newly acquired exceptions."

"Then I owe you an apology. Somehow, you were right all along. I don't know how, honestly I'm flabbergasted, but you were right." He held out his hand and I took it, making sure to squeeze and hold, like my dad taught me.

"It was the birds."

His eyebrows climbed up his forehead. They were active, those eyebrows. Almost as active as his shoulders were talkative. "Of course. Anyway, we're taking the film to be developed. I have no doubt we have a case, whether or not the picture turns out. The man tried to choke Posey. He threw you in the water. And he seems...well, he isn't going anywhere anytime soon."

"Thank you, Detective Mobley."

"Of course. I'll have to ask you a few questions, officially, but that can wait a minute." He motioned to Doug. "You'll come with me."

Doug nodded. "Penelope didn't threaten you, Marion, for what it's worth," he said, getting to his feet. "I need you to know that."

Detective Mobley flashed him a look of scrutiny, his eyes peering through Doug's skull to piece together the truth behind his words. Slowly he motioned for Doug to move, following him closely, his fingers turning, turning, turning, his fedora. They ambled toward the flashing lights of the police cars, and I watched them go while turning, turning, turning, my ring. One single wave swelled above the others and slapped against the rocks. Low tide permeated the air, sour and rotten.

Penelope stood in the distance, waiting. She caught me staring and lifted her chin – she held everything in her chin. The weight of her body, the weight of her thoughts, the weight of her judgments. It made her face heavy and swollen, and her body thin and frail. Francesca Lovely stood beside her, and when she met my gaze, she lowered her eyes.

Conrad followed after Detective Mobley and Sebastian sat beside me, shifting nervously. I set the pile of Conrad's photocopied letters at my feet and placed a large rock on top to keep them from blowing away. We didn't say anything for a moment. I had no idea what Sebastian was contemplating; he was being a tad bit mysterious, honestly, seeing as he usually says what he's thinking, but he was just quiet.

"I can't tell what you're thinking," he said. He was still dressed as a woman, complete with the wig, and he tossed the ends of it over his shoulder. I challenged him with my *don't test me* eyes and he smiled painfully. "Glad you're okay."

I had always thought Sebastian bore the same ocean colors as James. But he was warmer, his eyes darker, his smile kinder, his face the depths. James was the surface, changed by the weather, stormy or icy or sunny. Sebastian was the steady unknown, the constant and the dark, the deep sea, where secrets lie. It was like I was seeing him for the first time.

Of course, it could have been the dress.

"I'm alive, much to the sea's regret."

"I doubt it." He pulled up his corset. "You did its bidding, after all."

"She's a fickle woman, the sea."

"Right. The sea's a half-truth, probably."

He eyed me knowingly, and we both laughed, and a nearby seagull laughed too, until all the birds were laughing, laughing, laughing, along the shoreline.

Chapter Thirty-Five

Sebastian joined his dad, and I sat on a wide, barnacle-covered rock, watching the sea. The swells were methodical and soothing, and the trickle ends of a wave reached for me. I let it wash over my ankles, cold and gentle, and I smiled.

Posey loomed over me, arms crossed and face pale. She was outlined by the sun, a shadowy mass glowing at the edges.

"I want to go home," she said, holding out her hand to help me up. "Conrad is here. He wants to get something to eat but I told him I'm not hungry and he's callous and unfeeling for having an appetite so soon after his sisters faced their untimely deaths. He said he doesn't care and left with Dad to get food. Mom's ready to go home, too."

"Alright." I let her help me to my feet. "But Detective Mobley beckons me." I gestured to Detective Mobley, who walked our way, pen in hand.

I gave my statement as clearly as I could manage, making sure to emphasize that Doug had saved my life. He jotted that down, nodding.

"Seems like everyone is guilty of something," I said, when I was done. "Even the ones who helped me."

He scanned his notes, the muscles in his jaw flexing. "The trick is to remember we don't know everything." A gust of wind blew his fedora off his head, and he caught it midair, eyes still on his notes. He held it to his side. "Never know what we'll find out when the whole story unravels."

"Right," I agreed. "No point in dissecting half-truths."

He grinned (barely) and left to talk with someone else, and I waved at Delia, who stood next to a uniformed officer, giving her statement as he scribbled away in his (cute) little notebook.

"Meet us at our house?" I called to her, and Delia gave a thumbs up.

I walked home with Mom and Posey (she had fingerprint bruises around her neck, they matched her eye). I changed and made popcorn and we sat on the couch under a blanket and recounted our adventures, starting with a sleep talking Max and ending with my fight with a deranged man on the pier. Delia joined us on the couch and Mom did whatever moms do when their daughters face death and taste victory (I think she was in the kitchen).

Thursdays were improving rapidly.

"Why was he choking you, anyway?" I asked Posey,

before stuffing my mouth in a decidedly unladylike manner. My head still hurt, and my hair was sticky and damp.

"I had a weird feeling while I was walking back," she answered. "Like something bad was about to happen. Then I saw him walking toward me, and he was the guy who gave me that death threat for you, so I said, 'It's you,' and apparently it was the wrong thing to say."

"What a creep," I muttered.

"I think something else was wrong." Posey shivered. "I can't place it."

"Well it's over now," Delia said, throwing one kernel of popcorn and catching it in her mouth.

Posey's face scrunched, the marshy green of her eyes shining through the stringy slats of her bangs, and she wrinkled her nose. "I watched you topple over the edge – "

"I'm fine," I interjected. I was barely concussed, after all.

"Yeah," she said. "And you're fine." Then she giggled. "James threw him off me and punched him so many times."

I sized her up out of the corner of my eye. "Of course he did. Anyone worth their snuff would do the same."

But Posey buried her face under the blanket until nothing but her eyes showed. I threw my head against the couch cushion, staring at the ceiling as Finney giggled in her corners. James must have run pretty fast once he heard me scream. And he overcame deranged, desperate Leo pretty easily, too. What a life it must be, to be that athletic. I tried to tackle Leo and it got me thrown in the ocean.

"I guess it was impressive," I relented. James deserved his moment of glory; Posey had plenty of time to be morbidly disappointed in him later. She stopped giggling.

"How did you know? How were you so sure about – about the birds, and stuff?"

I didn't have to think about it – the answer was in my blood, really. I'd been preparing for it my whole life. I was well versed in the practice of being crazy. So well versed, in fact, that the truth was obvious, for the most part.

"Most things that sound sane are half-truths. They are not whole truths. Whole truths are wild and whirling, explosive and mesmerizing, infuriating and devouring. But often, quite simple." I smiled. "Like, if it looks like a talking bird and sounds like a talking bird, it's probably a talking bird."

"Oh," she said. And I didn't have anything else to add, so we sat eating popcorn, not speaking a word, as we crunched and swallowed and crunched again – until Conrad threw open the front door and stood expectantly before us, slurping a drink, looking pleased with himself.

"Did you look for it yet?" he asked.

"Look for what?"

He pulled the straw out of his mouth and sighed. "The elixir. There's a clue in the pages I copied. Haven't you read it yet?" He stuck his dirty hand into (my) popcorn and stuffed his mouth. "I came all the way here, and you don't even look at it – "

"The waterfront!"

I sat up straight, hands on my head – papers! I left the papers by the water, they were definitely wet, maybe even drifting out to sea – I jumped up, but Delia seized my wrist and pointed to the coffee table, where a pile of photocopies sat politely waiting their turn.

"I saw you left them. Thought they might be important." She wiped her buttery fingers on her t-shirt, a dark gray number that read STOP THE SLANDER and in smaller letters: Werewolves Are Our Friends. She had changed at the first chance, too.

"Delia, you are a gem." I sighed with relief and sat down, giving her a grateful high five.

"I'm a sea fairy," she corrected, "not a fancy rock."

If I had lost those papers, Conrad would have been mad enough to throw me back into the sea. I lost one of his comic books once and he tied me to a tree in Old Towne Cemetery. It took Mom a full hour to find me, once she knew I was gone. I looked up at his face and planted my feet on the ground, in case I needed to run.

Conrad flushed and pointed his drink at me, his mouth wide open. "I brought those copies ALL THE WAY HERE and you left them at the waterfront?"

I grabbed the stack of letters, knitting my brow like he was being silly. "I didn't leave them, they're right here. Where's the clue?" I flipped through the pile, scanning the opening lines and dates. Conrad slapped my hands away and turned to a certain dog-eared page.

"Here," he said, and he pointed to a passage that, lo and behold, he had highlighted.

I BURIED IT WHERE I BURY MY TREASURE WHERE IT WON'T SHINE AND GLITTER, WHERE THE EDGES WON'T BITE

It was in the attic.

I dropped the papers and ran toward the servant's stairs, Delia, Conrad, Max, and Posey behind me, flying up the narrow passage to the attic hatch, where we climbed the ladder and stepped inside. I moved Bigfoot's pelt and ordered Conrad to stick his arm into the abyss (I wasn't going to do it, not without a flashlight) and he pulled out a bottle, foggy and scratched, with an inch worth of golden-brown liquid. It had been at the back of the chimney, farther than my arms could reach.

"The elixir of life," he said, holding it up. "Looks like whiskey to me."

"But that can't be it." Posey held up the highlighted clue she had snatched before following us. "See the clue? See? Liquid has no edges."

"Liquor bites," Conrad offered.

"No, I think Posey's right." I shushed Conrad with an upheld finger, and he glared at me. "There's something else. Is there another loose brick? Or maybe a floorboard this time?"

I spun in circles, looking for another clue, and the others searched too. Delia felt every crack in the chimney. Posey and Max got on their hands and knees to inspect the floor. Conrad moved junk around to search for hidden doors or compartments. And I, feeling whimsical (I was wearing gray), gazed out the single, circular window at the sunlight.

"Thanks for helping, Marion," Conrad grumbled.

I ignored him, keeping my eyes on the waves. Ever hungry, the water tossed and turned, all gray and secretive. I closed my eyes, let my roots grow from my feet into the floorboards, down the walls, and into the foundation. Finney hugged me, the gesture warm and inviting. I opened my eyes and saw the sea, still and glittering, and knew where to find the healing elixir.

"It's in the walls."

Conrad stared at me. "What?"

"Trust me." I tapped the wall below the window. "It's in the wall."

Without a word, he grabbed a forgotten table leg from a pile of old furniture, and with a *whack* cracked open the wall on his first try. Again and again he hit it, until he dropped his weapon and pulled at the crumbled bits to make a wide hole, and then he reached in and pulled out a sword, forgotten in the space, waiting to be found. He brandished it. It reflected the sunlight streaming from the window, like a wink. The blade was double-edged, half the length of Conrad, and the hilt was bedighted with black sapphires.

"How'd you know?" he asked.

"Finney showed me," I said. "Do you think it works?"

"No." Conrad swiped the sword to and fro, so that Delia and Posey cowered in a corner and I warned him not to kill Max, who was too enamored of the thing to back up. Conrad ignored me (typical). "Relax. It heals, remember?"

"You just said you don't think it works." He smirked and my limbs grew heavy, weariness pervading my flesh. "*And* it has yet to be tested." I grabbed Max by the collar and pulled him back. "However, if you would like to volunteer – "

Another head popped through the attic hatch. "Marion," it said – it was Sebastian. He hopped in and James followed, both boys disheveled and fidgety. Delia pressed her lips together until they shrank like accordions.

"Must we have more troubles?" she said to me, eyeing the cloud of anxiety that followed the Mobley brothers.

"Well, it *is* Thursday," I answered.

"We've been with Dad." Sebastian was so excited he fought for breath.

"Congratulations," I said.

"No, no. Listen. There's been a development. Something washed up on shore on Grackle Island. Marion – " He handed me a picture, printed on copy paper, of something dark and massive, lying on sand. "It's a water troll."

I stared at it. "What?"

"It's a water troll. At least, that's a good descriptor. Dad got the call like thirty minutes ago. It's huge, it's ugly, no one knows what it is – "

"I've got to call Mom," Delia interrupted, pulling her map out of her back pocket.

I focused on the picture and ignored the throbbing in my head, mumbling, "I can't believe it," as I traced its shape with my fingertip.

"Try," James said. A bandage covered the knuckles of his right hand and Posey eyed it from her corner, a smile pulling at her lips. "You coming with us?"

The blob in the picture looked to be the size of a whale, but with hands, or hooves, maybe – I looked closer, forming the word *yes* on my lips, when Mom's voice screeched into the attic.

"Code red!"

Finney stiffened.

"Huh?" I kept my eyes on the troll. "You mean code orange?"

"Children!" Mom slapped the floor, over and over again, until we faced her. She stood on the ladder, her upper half in the attic, a crown of stray hairs reaching out from beneath her head scarf. "Listen! Grandma ran away. I don't know how long she's been gone, I haven't seen her since Posey and the pier, and she left a note about finding a monster – " The attic stole her words, so she punched the floor and waved her hands – I locked eyes with Delia.

"The water troll!" we cried, and Mom disappeared. I rushed down the ladder and raced to my room to grab a few dollars from my sock drawer.

"I bet she stopped for waffles first!" I called out, because she probably had stopped for waffles. But when I opened my door I saw Todd, stretched out on my bed, a dagger stabbed through his heart.

"Drat," I said. "Not again."

Acknowledgments

I am grateful to you, dear reader, because as soon as you're done reading this you're going to leave a review. Right?

My beta readers, Angela, Mikaela, and Sarah, I appreciate the time and effort you took to read a manuscript that was not your own. Thank you.

Hats off to the guy dressed up as Spider-Man at the 2004 LIFE conference who told me to eat my vegetables. It's solid advice I've tried to follow these many years.

Leslie Sossong, thank you for writing about the Loch Ness Monster in Mr. Mill's ENG 101 class. It was the paper the world needed, and you rose to the occasion.

Many thanks to Geoffrey Chaucer and William Shakespeare, for obvious reasons.

Thank you, Mimi, for everything, especially that one thing we don't talk about for legal reasons.

Paisley and Tricki Woo, I am forever grateful for the time we spend cuddling, even when you pretend you don't like it.

Big thanks to Daniel Chaffin, for this beautiful cover.

And finally, shoutout to the potato, for being practically perfect in every way.

About the Author

E.M. Chaffin lives in Stillwater, Oklahoma with her dog friends, Paisley and Tricki Woo. She enjoys eating mashed potatoes, petting fat animals, and taking vitamins. There was this one time she floated down the Yellow River in a raft made of inflated sheepskin, but that doesn't have anything to do with this book. Visit her online at emchaffin.com and find her on Facebook and Instagram @emchaffinwrites.

www.emchaffin.com

ALSO BY E.M. CHAFFIN

Dead Man's Swamp

The woods hold a secret. She holds the clues. But will uncovering the truth behind her father's murder unleash hell?

"I didn't even have to read this masterpiece to know it will change the way I look at an entire genre. Get ready for a thrilling journey that you won't be able to resist!" Myriam Conley, Literature Enthusiast

Made in the USA
Columbia, SC
06 November 2022